"I am your wife," Blythe answered. She closed the short distance between them, entwined her arms around his neck, and pressed her body against his.

"I want you," she breathed against the base of his throat. "As much as you want me."

Before he could embrace her, Blythe stepped back a pace. For one awful moment Roger thought she was going to desert him.

And then she moved.

Reaching up, Blythe slipped the straps of her nightshift off her shoulders. The gown fluttered to the floor to form a pool of silk. She stood naked before him, a proud beauty who belonged only to him.

Roger worshiped her with his eyes. Holding her gaze captive to his, Roger pulled his shirt over his head and tossed it on the floor, where it mingled with her silken nightshift even as they were about to mingle with their bodies. . . .

Also by Patricia Grasso:

Patricia Grasso

My Heart's Desire

A Dell Book

Published by
Dell Publishing
a division of
Bantam Doubleday Dell Publishing Group, Inc.
1540 Broadway
New York, New York 10036

Copyright © 1996 by Patricia Grasso

The trademark Dell® is registered in the U.S. Patent and Trademark Office.

ISBN: 0-440-22086-6

Printed in the United States of America

Published simultaneously in Canada

January 1997

10 9 8 7 6 5 4 3 2 1

OPM

For the woman who convinced me that pasta, pizza, and pastry were low-calorie. I salute you, Aunt Rose, and "your sister's tonsils."

A special thank you to Gary Dascoli, Everett High School's "Mr. Humanities," for sharing his knowledge of the ancient Greeks.

Prologue

London, 1589

He had loved her forever.

And she was smiling at him. Even from this distance the sunshine in her welcoming smile warmed his heart. It always did.

Since her entrance into this world thirteen years earlier, Roger had considered her the sister he'd never had and harbored intensely protective feelings for her. Returning his affection, she showered him with childish adoration.

Twenty-five-year-old Roger Debrett stood in the Earl of Basildon's summer-lush garden and stared across the green expanse of lawn at the girl who sat on a stone bench in the shade of a weeping-willow tree. A gentle breeze teased the sweeping tips of the willow, and Roger paused a long moment to admire the girl's feminine serenity. She always reminded him of a delicate, elusive butterfly. His *psyche*, as the Greeks had so aptly named both the butterfly and the soul.

Thirteen years old today and no longer a child, Roger thought. Soon she would step across another of life's thresholds into womanhood, and eager young swains would flock to Devereux House to court her.

Roger Debrett, the Earl of Eden and the second richest man in England, could purchase whatever pleased him. Since their very first meeting the girl sitting beneath the willow had pleased him more than anything else. And what had always pleased him most was the unconditional acceptance mirrored in her sunny smile.

Reluctant to end the moment by starting across the lawns toward her, Roger admired the earl's garden, a paradise on earth. Low clipped hedges of thyme, myrtle, and germander had been fashioned into intricate patterns, while lavender and rue provided contrast. Perfectly manicured lawns carpeted the grounds between lines of yew, clipped to form high hedges. Red roses, purple love-in-a-mist, white sweet alyssum, and blue forget-me-nots bloomed in a wanton blending of vibrant color. Yet nature's beauty paled when compared with the girl.

Watching her, Roger saw through her cloak of innocence to the budding beauty beneath. This moment would forever linger in his mind as one of the best days of his life. He would present his little butterfly with her very first adult birthday gift and then share his own happy news that he'd become betrothed. Oh, he could hardly wait to see her reaction to that.

Roger saw her tilt her head to one side as if puzzled by his failure to approach. Surrendering to her magnetic smile, he started across the lawns toward her.

"I knew you'd come," she said, gazing at him through the most disarming violet eyes he'd ever seen.

"Lady Blythe, the sweetest blossom within this earthly paradise withers beside your uncommon beauty." Roger bowed formally over her offered hand.

His compliment seemed to please her. *Immensely.* Roger refused to ruin the moment by scolding her, but made a mental note to warn her to beware of men's flattery.

"How fares Elizabeth's 'soaring eagle'?" she asked, using the pet name the queen had bestowed upon him.

"Seeing your sunny smile has brightened my day," Roger replied. Then he teased, "How did you know I'd visit? Are you a fortune-telling Gypsy?"

"Past precedence, my lord." She tilted her head back to gaze up the long length of him, for at six feet and two inches he stood more than a foot taller than her petite height. "You never miss my birthday."

" 'Tis your birthday?" Roger feigned embarrassed dismay, his blue eyes widening with counterfeit surprise. "God's bread, how could I have forgotten such a momentous occasion?"

Blythe laughed, a sweetly melodious sound that reminded him of a songbird. "Sit beside me," she invited, casting him a flirtatious look from beneath the thick fringe of her ebony lashes.

Roger grinned. He knew she was practicing her wiles on him, but didn't mind in the least.

Sitting beside her, Roger stretched his long legs out and glanced at her perfect profile. Her mane of ebony hair and her disarming violet eyes conspired with generous lips and a small straight nose to attract any man who saw her. Her faint scent of roses teased his senses.

Blythe was a beauty all right. He'd kill any cocky swain who dared to trifle with her heart.

"Are you planning to make me wait all day for my gift?" Blythe asked, giving him a look obviously meant to seduce.

Roger felt like laughing. Instead, he fixed a suitably disapproving look on his face and chided her, saying, "Sweet psyche, greed is exceedingly unbecoming in a lady."

"Psyche?"

"*Psyche* is Greek for *butterfly*, which is what you have always seemed to me. A pretty, elusive butterfly."

"Psyche also means *soul*," she added with an ambiguous smile.

Her words surprised him, though he knew he should have expected them. Richard Devereux, the Earl of Basildon, had insisted his daughters receive a man's education.

"Are you knowledgeable in Greek as well as mathematics?" he teased.

"I'm as fluent as Archimedes," she answered. "I knew him once. In another life, that is."

Roger chuckled. "At times you give voice to the most delightfully bizarre thoughts."

With both hands Blythe reached out and grasped his forearm. "Guess what Papa gave me for my birthday," she said, her voice animated, her violet eyes gleaming with unmistakable excitement.

Her uninhibited joy enchanted him. " 'Tis jewelry?"

Blythe shook her head.

"A new horse?"

She shook her head again.

"I give up," Roger said, smiling. "What did your father give you?"

"A beautiful ship," Blythe answered, closing her eyes as if in sublime ecstasy.

"A ship?" Roger couldn't credit what he'd heard. What would a girl do with a ship?

"Papa gave me a ship and control of my own wool and corn export business on the condition that I confer with him each week," Blythe told him. "I've named my ship *Paralda* in honor of the elemental god of the east. Papa says if I turn a profit he'll give me another ship and business when my birthday comes around again."

Roger frowned at her. Turning a profit was a man's domain and a decidedly unfeminine pursuit. What could Devereux be thinking? How many families would starve when the chit mismanaged their commodities?

"Is aught wrong?"

Hearing the tentative note in her voice, Roger patted her hand and assured her, " 'Tis merely that your father's gift surprises me."

"Indeed, 'tis a wondrous gift." Blythe cast him a flirtatious smile and said, "I'm certain I'll love your gift even more. That is, whenever you give it to me."

Roger winked at her and produced a rectangular box from inside his doublet. "Happy birthday, little butterfly," he said, handing her the box as he leaned close and planted a chaste kiss on her cheek.

"Thank you, my lord." A becoming blush rose upon her cheeks. Blythe traced a finger across the top of the box as if savoring the anticipation.

"Open it," Roger said, watching for her reaction, knowing he'd outdone himself this year.

Blythe lifted the lid. "Sacred Saint Swithin," she gasped, surprised by the sight of the exquisite necklace.

The jeweled cross of Wotan, a cross inside a circle, winked at her from its bed of black velvet. Attached to a heavy chain of gold, the cross itself had been created in diamonds with a single ruby in the center. Amethysts formed the circle around the diamond cross.

" 'Tis a necklace fit for the queen," Blythe said, gazing at him through eyes the exact shade of the amethysts.

"Allow me," Roger said. He lifted the necklace out of the box and set it over her head. Its jeweled pendant rested against the center of her chest.

Blythe reached up and touched it with her right hand. "Will you speak to me of a marriage now?" she asked, surprising him.

"How did you know about that?"

"Woman's intuition."

"Thirteen years old and already a great lady?" Roger teased.

Blythe gave him an ambiguous smile and dropped her gaze shyly. With a high blush coloring her cheeks, she informed him, "I've begun my menses. That means I am a woman."

Roger suffered the almost overpowering urge to laugh out loud, but he managed to control himself. Rising from the bench, he walked a few paces away and gazed in the direction of Devereux House. "Lady Darnel has accepted my proposal of marriage," he told her. "She's inside visiting your parents."

"Darnel Howard?" Blythe echoed in a voice no louder than a whisper.

Hearing the surprise in her voice, Roger whirled around and noted the sudden change in her demeanor. One moment she'd been as happy as a butterfly flitting around the Garden of Eden, and the next moment she appeared perilously close to tears. Good Christ, what would he do if she started to weep?

"You cannot mean to marry Darnel Howard," she cried. *"I love you."*

Shocked speechless, Roger stared at the unspeakable hurt etched across her lovely face. He'd known her since the day of her birth but had never seen her like this. Why had he failed to recognize the signs of her infatuation?

Blythe stood and stepped toward him. "I have always loved you," she announced, unshed tears glistening in her eyes.

Roger swallowed the lump of raw emotion that had risen in his throat. "I am a full-grown man of twenty-five," he said gently. "You are still a child."

Blythe stepped back a pace as if he'd struck her. Anger and anguish warred on her finely etched features.

"On my fifth birthday you promised to wait for me to grow into womanhood," she reminded him. "You promised to marry me."

" 'Twas a jest," Roger said with an inward groan. "Empty words meant to appease a pretty child."

Blythe stiffened visibly at his honest explanation. "I will never forgive you for betraying my trust," she said in a scathing voice. With that she turned her back on him.

"Blythe, I do love you, as a brother loves his favorite sister, as an uncle loves—" Roger broke off, realizing it was the wrong thing to say.

Searching for words more comforting, Roger glanced at the sky. Clouds had gathered together, blocking the sun's warming rays, and a sudden gust of wind sent the willow's sweeping branches slashing against his ankles.

"Little one, I would never purposely hurt you," Roger said by way of an apology.

Blythe whirled around and pleaded as only a thirteen-year-old would. "Then send *that woman* away and marry me."

"I love her," Roger insisted, running a hand through his hair in utter frustration. How could he make her understand?

"Darnel Howard is unworthy of you," Blythe cried, her voice rising with her obvious agitation.

Roger realized he'd let their conversation get out of hand, and he refused to argue the point any longer. Fixing a suitably stern look on his face, he said, "I love Darnel Howard. Come October I will marry her."

"And you will live to regret the day you did." Blythe lifted the empty gift box she still held and threw it at him, catching his left cheekbone dead center. Turning her back on him, she hurried in the direction of her father's quay.

Roger felt a painful constriction around his heart that hurt more than his bruised face. Aching loss assailed him as he watched her walk away.

She would never forgive him for rejecting her; nor would she cast that sunny smile at him again. Roger knew that as surely as he knew she'd drawn blood with the damned gift box.

Yanking his handkerchief out of his doublet, Roger pressed it against his bleeding cheek. Unexpectedly, a branch of the willow slapped the uninjured side of his face as the wind off the Thames River grew in strength. He looked up and noted the ominous darkness of the afternoon sky. Slowly and wearily, Roger walked across the garden toward the mansion.

Struggling against her tears, Blythe paused where the quay met the River Thames. She closed her eyes and took a deep, calming breath.

The only man she'd ever loved was marrying another woman.

How could she live without him? How could she bear to see him, knowing that he belonged to another? And yet how could she survive if she never gazed upon his beloved face again?

Blythe turned around and watched Roger walking back to the house. She knew with her blossoming Druid's instinct that they were meant for each other. Oh, why was he unable to see that? Having loved each other through many lifetimes, the Great Mother Goddess had brought them together again.

Blythe reached out in silent supplication as Roger disappeared inside the mansion, and hot tears welled up in her eyes. The clouds above her head darkened, and the wind gathered strength.

The man she'd loved since the beginning of time loved another woman.

A sob caught in her throat. And then another. Surrendering to her heartache, Blythe bowed her head and wept for what she'd lost.

"Don't cry, sister," said a familiar voice. "You'll make it rain."

Blythe looked up and gazed through tear-blurred vision at eleven-year-old Bliss. Her sister touched her arm, which brought a reluctant smile to her lips.

"Is your touch making me smile?" Blythe asked.

Bliss nodded.

"Weeping is sometimes necessary to cleanse the soul," Blythe told her, removing her sister's healing hand from her arm.

Bliss glanced at the threatening clouds and suggested, "In that case let's sit in the willow. Her branches will protect us from the elements."

Hand in hand Blythe and Bliss hurried back to the willow tree. Using the stone bench as a lift, Blythe climbed the willow first and then helped her sister up. Ensconced on a thick branch, the two sisters peered through the willow's sweeping branches in the direction of the mansion. In the distance Lord Roger assisted Lady Darnel onto her horse, while Earl Richard and Lady Keely stood nearby.

With her right index finger Blythe touched her heart and then her lips, whispering, "O ancient willow of this ancient earth, older than I can tell, loan me your power to charge this natural spell." Then she pointed her finger outward at the brunette beauty sitting on top of the horse.

A sudden whirlwind swept through the gardens. The dark clouds yawned, and pelting rain lashed the earth and the four adults in the distance.

Lady Darnel uttered a cry of dismay and yanked the hood of her summer cloak up as Lord Roger swung into his saddle. The Earl and the Countess of Basildon hastily retreated inside Devereux House.

"Did you do that?"

Blythe cast her sister a sidelong smile and nodded.

Bliss giggled and clapped her hands with delight. "Lady Darnel looked like a drowned rat. 'Tis certain the petty use of your talent will displease Mother, though."

Blythe closed her eyes for a moment and whispered, "Thank you, O wondrous willow, for sending your power through me."

Ten minutes later the rain abruptly ceased, and five minutes after that the sisters spied their mother advancing like a general on the willow tree.

"Here she comes," Bliss said needlessly, casting Blythe an "I-told-you-so" look.

Blythe swallowed nervously. Her mother appeared none too happy.

"Get down!" Lady Keely turned on the eleven-year-old when the girls dropped to the ground in front of her and ordered, "I desire private words with your sister. Return to the house."

"You always make me leave at the most interesting part," Bliss complained, but started toward the house without being told a second time.

"Using your special gift in such a cavalier fashion will certainly anger the Goddess," Lady Keely said, giving her oldest daughter her attention.

"I'm sincerely sorry," Blythe apologized. "But Roger—" She broke off with a sob, unable to control her raw emotions any longer.

Lady Keely sat on the stone bench beneath the willow and said, "Come here, dearest."

Blythe sat down and rested her head against her mother's shoulder. "You said that Roger would be mine," she sobbed. "You said that our fate had been written in the holy stones. Didn't you know what would really happen?"

"Being Druid means knowing," Lady Keely said, tilting her daughter's chin up. "At the moment of your conception the wind whispered your destiny to me, and Roger Debrett is that destiny. Trust me, dearest, for I have seen it."

Blythe managed a wobbly smile. She trusted her mother without question. Only she hadn't expected Darnel Howard to capture Roger's heart before she did.

"Please tell me the story again," Blythe said.

"Once upon a long ago time, the winged creatures of the air held a great assembly," Lady Keely said with a smile. "They decided that kingship of all those with wings, whether bird or insect, would go to the one who flew highest. Naturally, the majestic eagle became the immediate favorite and began his flight toward the sun. Soaring high above the others, he proclaimed his lordship over all. A clever butterfly, who had hidden herself beneath the eagle's feathers, popped out unexpectedly from under his wings. She flew one inch higher than the eagle and squeaked, 'Winged creatures, look up and behold your queen.'

"Unused to flying so high in the sky, the butterfly began to fall. The eagle, amused by the butterfly's womanly wiles, stretched his wing out and caught her before she fell to her death."

"Together, the eagle and the butterfly ruled the heavens," Blythe added, knowing the story by heart. "The majestic eagle and his clever butterfly—*his soul*—could be seen gliding across the horizon forever after."

"Roger is the queen's soaring eagle, and you are his clever butterfly," Lady Keely finished the tale.

Blythe smiled at that.

"I have a birthday gift for you," Lady Keely said, reaching inside her pocket.

"'Tis lovely," Blythe said, inspecting the gold emblem ring that her mother slipped onto her right index finger. Engraved on the ring's flat surface was a butterfly perched on top of an eagle's wing.

"Together, Roger and you will soar to paradise and beyond," Lady Keely told her. "Never concern yourself again with Darnel Howard."

"I love you," Blythe said, hugging her mother.

"And I love you, dearest."

Lady Keely inspected the jeweled cross of Wotan that her daughter wore. Turning it over, she looked at the back of the pendant and smiled at what she saw.

"Here lies the proof of my words," the countess said.

Blythe peered down at the necklace's inscription: *And thee I chuse.* Puzzled by the sentiment, she asked, "Why would Roger inscribe these words on my necklace when he planned to wed Darnel Howard?"

"The Goddess moves in mysterious ways," Lady Keely said with a shrug. "Always place your trust in her, and never doubt that Lord Roger will be yours one day. With these words he has chosen his path in life."

Blythe smiled, happy once more. The man she'd loved forever would be hers. The Goddess had decided their fates.

"Unless 'tis an emergency, manipulating the wind for your own satisfaction is an abuse of power," Lady Keely reminded her in a stern voice. "Do I make myself clear?"

Blythe nodded.

"And throwing a gift box into the giver's face is unpardonable," the countess went on. "Violence against another is sinful."

"I'll write Roger a note of apology," Blythe promised.

"Give it to me when 'tis written, and I'll send it to Debrett House," Lady Keely said, rising from the stone bench. She paused and added, "You will not see Roger again until the moment has arrived for the butterfly to perch on the eagle's wing."

Watching her mother walk back to the mansion, Blythe placed the palm of her right hand on the jeweled cross of Wotan, and renewed hope swelled within her breast. Roger would belong to her. She sensed it with her blossoming Druid's instinct.

And thee I chuse.

Those four words of eternal love echoed within her heart, her mind, her soul.

Blythe smiled. Aye, the queen's eagle and his butterfly—his soul—would soar to paradise and beyond. Her mother had seen it, and whatever her mother saw came to pass. Always.

The wind in her father's garden calmed to a caressing breeze, and the afternoon sun peeked out from behind the clouds.

Blythe was happy again.

Chapter 1

April, 1594

Dusty and tired, Roger Debrett opened the door to his chamber and stepped inside. The journey from Eden Court, his ancestral home, had been long and grueling, but he'd managed to reach Whitehall Palace in time for Queen Elizabeth's Saint George's Day gala. First he needed a strong drink and a hot bath, and then he'd be ready to face the world.

"You're back already?" said the brunette beauty, admiring her own reflection in the mirror.

Doffing his hat, Roger flicked a sidelong glance at his wife but made no reply. Instead, he crossed the chamber to the table where he poured himself a dram of whiskey. Raising the glass to his lips, Roger downed the amber liquid in one gulp. Then he refilled the glass and turned around to look at her. She preened in front of the mirror as if she were unable to bear parting with her own flawless image.

"I warrant 'twas the fastest trip from Winchester on record," Darnel said, without bothering to spare him a glance. "Perhaps Elizabeth should give you a medal."

"Sorry to disappoint you," Roger replied, raising his glass of whiskey in a silent but mocking salute to her. "Find other accommodations for your nightly rendezvous with your lover of the moment."

Darnel Debrett smirked at him in the mirror and gave her attention to her tirewoman, who held a tray of jewels for her perusal. She lifted an emerald necklace up, held it against her throat, and then tossed it carelessly down on the tray. Darnel concentrated on the jewels as if the realm's security depended upon which necklace she wore. Finally, she decided on the diamond choker.

"I wish to bathe and change my clothing," Roger said. "Send the girl away."

"Leave us," Darnel dismissed her maid.

"Shall I wait up for you, my lady?"

Darnel cast Roger a sidelong, measuring look before answering, "No, I'll be quite late tonight."

The tirewoman bobbed a curtsy and left the chamber. The door clicked shut behind her.

Roger removed his doublet and tossed it aside, but then paused to watch his wife putting the final touches on her appearance.

Once upon a long ago time he'd loved her more than life itself, Roger thought bitterly. How incredibly naive he'd been. After getting herself pregnant with his child, Darnel had married him for his fortune and trapped him into this fiasco posing as a marriage. Even worse, her amorous adventures now threatened to bring disgrace on the honorable Debrett name.

"That gown is particularly low-cut, even by court standards," Roger remarked. "Are you planning on wet-nursing a few courtiers this evening?"

"Don't be crude," Darnel snapped. "Besides, do you really care what I choose to wear?"

"I cared once," Roger said softly, capturing her dark gaze in the mirror.

"Humph! You cared so much that you ordered the goldsmith to engrave my betrothal ring with the oh-so-romantic sentiment *My special friend*," Darnel shot back, apparently unmoved by the regret in his voice.

Roger smiled without humor. "I've told you at least a thousand times, the goldsmith confused your ring with Blythe Devereux's birthday pendant. Besides, my gold has purchased you a hundred new rings since then."

"Your explanation doesn't matter anymore."

"No, I suppose it doesn't."

Abruptly turning away from her reflection, Darnel crossed the chamber to stand in front of him. "Why, you haven't even reached for me in years," she said, a note of accusation in her voice.

"I've always preferred the road less traveled," Roger told her, his voice purposefully cold as he stared at her lush cleavage.

Darnel raised her hand to slap him. With lightning-quick reflexes Roger grabbed her wrist and yanked her against his hard, unyielding body.

"Don't force me into rash action," he warned.

"Spare me your empty threats," Darnel said in a scathing voice, meeting his gaze unwaveringly. "Everyone at court believes you are the queen's dangerous, soaring eagle, ready to pounce on the unwary, but I know better. Hurting a mosquito is beyond your capability."

"Given the correct dose of provocation, each of us is capable of violence," Roger countered, but then released her wrist and folded his arms across his chest lest he strike her.

Darnel smirked and cast him an "I-told-you-so" look. She retreated across the chamber.

"Miranda and Mrs. Hartwell are safely ensconced at Eden Court," Roger said conversationally. "Miranda is looking forward to the three of us summering together in Winchester like a real family."

Darnel stared at him blankly.

"You do remember our daughter, Miranda?" he asked.

"I shan't be in Winchester this summer," she informed him. "I've decided to accompany the queen on her progress."

"You've scarcely glanced at Miranda since the day of her birth," Roger said. "You will be passing the summer with her at Eden Court."

"I think not," Darnel replied. "Next year perhaps."

"And who is the lucky gentleman of the moment?" Roger

asked. "Edward deVere? Dudley Margolin? One of my own brothers?"

"Each would be preferable to you," Darnel answered. "A lady never kisses and tells, you know."

"You are no lady," Roger said.

Darnel smiled at his impotent insult. "Are you implying you don't take lovers?"

"I'm hardly celibate," Roger conceded. "Nevertheless, resign yourself to summering with Miranda and me in Winchester. I also attend this court and still manage to visit our daughter five times each week. You've disappointed her for the last time. The only acceptable excuse for your absence is your untimely demise."

"I just told you I'm attending the queen's summer progress," Darnel said. "*My* daughter will understand."

The snide, almost secretive tone in her voice jerked Roger into instant alertness. He crossed the chamber, grasped her arm, and whirled her around. "What do you mean by 'my' daughter?" he demanded.

Darnel smiled, apparently pleased that she'd managed to crack the wall protecting his feelings. "Miranda is mine because she slipped from my body. As for her paternity"—she shrugged—"I was already pregnant when we wed. Miranda could have been sired by another."

"Liar," Roger said in a clipped voice.

"Am I?"

In a flash of movement Roger grasped her throat. How easy it would be to squeeze the life's breath from her adulterous body.

"Your death isn't worth the trip to the gallows," Roger said, dropping his hand. "Miranda resembles me. Admit it, you want to cast a shadow across my love for her. You hate me so much, you can't bear that my own daughter loves me. She would love you, too, if you gave her more of your attention."

"You're correct about one thing. I do hate you." With those parting words Darnel started for the door. "Don't bother to wait up for me, dear husband. I may dance all night."

"Is *dance* now a euphemism for *fuck*?" Roger asked baldly.

Darnel cast him a withering glance. The door slammed shut behind her.

Roger poured himself another whiskey. He raised his glass in salute to the empty chamber and murmured, "Would that the bitch was permanently gone from my life."

An hour later Roger stood in the entrance to Queen Elizabeth's Presence Chamber. England's finest musicians stood on one side of the enormous rectangular chamber and played their various instruments. Along the wall opposite the entrance, Queen Elizabeth sat in a chair upon a raised dais surrounded by imported carpets. The middle of the chamber had been saved for dancing.

Doublets, hose, and accessories created in golden brocade, crane-colored silk, or murrey velvet harmonized on each nobleman. Earrings fashioned with gold and precious gems dangled from their ears, and rouge colored many a masculine cheek. The noblewomen wore scandalously low-cut gowns and bedecked themselves with every priceless jewel they owned.

Dressed completely in black, Roger appeared like a bird of prey invading a land filled with gaudy peacocks. He stared into that noble throng and spied the only other black-clad person in attendance: Richard Devereux, his illustrious mentor, with his countess, Lady Keely.

Intending to speak with them, Roger raised his hand in a silent greeting and started forward. He hadn't taken more than five steps when a hand on his arm stopped him.

Roger glanced at the woman's hand and then lifted his blue-eyed gaze to the voluptuous redhead, his mistress. He cast her a devastating smile, meant to make her heartbeat quicken.

"Welcome back to court, my lord," twenty-five-year-old Lady Rhoda Bellows greeted him.

"Thank you, my lady." Roger bowed over her hand and then asked in a teasing voice, "And how fares your husband?"

Lady Rhoda gave him a feline smile. "Poor Reggie wearied

from today's activities and retired for the evening." She lowered her voice to a whisper and added, "I could meet you later."

"I rode straight through from Winchester in order to gaze upon your lovely face," Roger said smoothly. "Unfortunately, I have depleted my energy. Could we possibly meet tomorrow instead?"

"Yes, but you'll never know how disappointed I am," Lady Rhoda replied.

"I'm certain I'm more disappointed," Roger assured her. "However, I fear my fatigue would embarrass me." He flicked a glance across the chamber and added, "I'd like to consult with Devereux before I retire. Will you excuse me?"

"Until tomorrow." Lady Rhoda drifted away.

Again Roger started forward in the direction of his friends, but stopped short when he heard someone calling his name. Turning toward the voice, he spied Lady Sarah Sitwell, his *other* mistress, advancing on him. Blond-haired and blue-eyed, Lady Sarah at thirty-seven was a spectacularly beautiful woman and *so* appreciative of attracting a younger man's attention.

"How lovely you appear this evening," Roger complimented her, bowing formally over her hand. He dropped his gaze to her exposed cleavage, smiled lazily, and added, "The cut of your gown enhances the perfection of your exquisite breasts, my lady."

"Will you have time this evening for a private supper in my chamber?" Lady Sarah asked, obviously pleased by his words.

"You do tempt me," Roger answered silkily. "Unfortunately, I've ridden straight through from Winchester. The only feasting I'll be doing this evening is with my eyes. Could we sup together tomorrow?"

"Of course. You'd be no good company if you fell asleep," Lady Sarah answered.

"My lady, your understanding is surpassed only by your beauty," Roger replied.

"Would you care to dance?"

"Tomorrow, sweetheart." He flicked a glance in the direction of the Earl of Basildon. "At the moment I do desire conversation with Devereux."

Lady Sarah inclined her head in a gesture of dismissal. "Then, my lord, do not let me keep you from your intent."

Roger kissed her hand again and walked away. Hoping that no other woman crossed his path, he headed in the direction of the Earl and the Countess of Basildon.

"You've become quite a lady's man," Lady Keely teased when he reached them. "I can remember when you were a twelve-year-old page purchasing aphrodisiacs."

"I'd hardly refer to these jades as ladies," Roger replied, bowing over her hand. He shook the earl's hand and asked, "How is our Levant Trading Company doing?"

"Prospering beyond our calculations," Richard Devereux answered. "Will you keep Keely company while I dance with the queen?"

" 'Twould be my pleasure." Roger watched the earl walk away and then remarked, "Seeing you here is a surprise."

"I always attend the queen's Saint George's Day gala," Lady Keely replied. " 'Tis poor substitution for my absences on her annual summer progress."

"Since Miranda's birth I summer with her in Winchester each year," he said. "Why is it that Richard and you never attend the queen's progress?"

"For the same reason," she answered. "We visit my brother in Wales because I couldn't bear to be separated from my children for the length of the progress."

Roger nodded in understanding. How different this mother's love for her children was from his own wife's attitude.

"Would you care to dance?" he asked, turning his head to watch his fellow courtiers.

"I'd prefer conversation," she answered. "At the moment you're in need of a sympathetic friend."

Roger snapped his head around to stare at her. How could she possibly know the misery that dwelled in his heart?

"You do appear troubled," Lady Keely explained, as if privy to his thoughts.

Roger gazed at the passing dancers. His wife, he noted, had changed partners. Now she was flirting with Edward deVere, the Earl of Oxford, his bitterest rival for the queen's regard.

"Spill it, Roger," Lady Keely ordered in a quiet voice. "What troubles you?"

"I never should have married her," he admitted, gesturing in the general direction of his wife. "She's a brazen harlot and intent on disgracing the Debrett name. Nothing good and fine has come from this union."

"What about Miranda?"

"Aye, my daughter makes up for a great many things," Roger agreed. "Too bad my wife cares nothing for her."

"I'm positive Darnel loves her only child," Lady Keely disagreed. "Appearances can be deceiving, you know."

Roger nodded and glanced toward the dance floor. A sudden bolt of anger shot through him when he saw Edward deVere lean close to Darnel and plant a kiss on the side of her throat.

"Excuse me—" Roger started forward.

"Do *not* create a public spectacle in the queen's presence," Lady Keely warned, snaking her hand out to stop him.

"I'm *ending* the spectacle," he said, shrugging her hand off.

With grim determination etched across his features, Roger stepped onto the dance floor. He pushed his way through the myriad couples who stopped dancing and watched his unprecedented behavior.

Ignoring Oxford, Roger whirled his wife around to face him. "The party is over," he said. "Return to our chamber at once."

"I will not," Darnel cried, clearly appalled by his behavior. "I refuse to go anywhere with you."

"Leave this gathering now," Roger ordered as if she hadn't spoken.

"I said no." Without warning, Darnel slapped him.

Pushed beyond endurance, Roger grabbed her throat and yanked her toward him, saying, "I would that you were married to your grave instead of me." At that he sent her crashing into the Earl of Oxford, who kept her from falling.

" 'Til death us do part," Darnel said, obviously relishing the angry misery etched across his face. "Do not forget that, dear husband."

"In that case, dear wife, a just and merciful God will part us sooner than you think." Roger turned on his heels and marched out of the Presence Chamber, leaving a titillated audience in his wake.

Roger retraced his steps down the torchlit corridors of Whitehall Palace. He would be rid of his adulterous wife one way or another. Passing the next thirty years married to a harlot was simply out of the question.

He'd believed in the power of love. Too late, he'd learned that gentle emotion was actually the product of an idle brain.

Edward deVere . . . Dudley Margolin . . . God's bread, even his own brothers had made love to his wife.

Reaching the sanctuary of his chamber, Roger poured himself a fortifying glass of whiskey. Unreasoning anger numbed him to the amber fire burning a path to his stomach.

Roger sighed in growing despair. What terrible flaw did he possess that prevented others from loving him? Since his mother's death when he was five, he'd tried unsuccessfully to win his father's regard. For years he'd tormented himself about his father's lack of love for him; and then he'd met Darnel Howard, whose dark eyes had held the sweet promise of love. Her sweet promise had been nothing but the bitterest of lies.

Let the slut find another place to sleep, Roger decided, deliberately throwing the bolt on the door. Wearily, he sat down on the edge of the bed and removed his boots. Then he stood and disrobed. Naked, he lay on the bed and flung one arm across his eyes.

Divorce leaped into his mind. Come morning he would request an audience with Queen Elizabeth and broach the subject of his divorcing Darnel. Surely, Elizabeth would not refuse his request to be free of an adulterous wife. And then . . . he'd keep his distance from designing jades. Never again would he marry. All he needed was his daughter's love.

The burgeoning hope of freeing himself from his wife calmed him. Roger dropped into a deep, dreamless sleep.

Bang! Bang! Bang!

Roger swam up slowly from the depths of unconsciousness.

"Open the door, Debrett," a voice ordered. "I charge you, in the name of Her Majesty the Queen, to open this door."

Roger bolted up. Bloody Christ, what was happening? He leaped out of the bed, staggered sleepily across the chamber, and yanked the door open.

"Are you alone?" Edward deVere asked, apparently startled by the sight of his rival's nakedness.

Roger nodded and focused on the group in the corridor. Behind deVere stood a contingent of five armed guards. Richard Devereux and William Cecil stood directly behind the guard.

"What do you want?" Roger demanded, rubbing the sleep from his eyes.

"By order of Her Majesty, Queen Elizabeth, I am placing you under arrest," deVere announced, brushing past him into the chamber. "Pack your belongings."

The Earl of Oxford's declaration startled Roger into full alertness. "Arrested for what?"

Oxford smiled without humor. "For suspicion of murder."

"Murder?"

"The murder of your wife, Darnel Howard," deVere explained.

Roger cast a confused look at his rival. "Darnel is dead?"

"Get dressed, and be quick about it," the Earl of Oxford snapped. "Or I'll drag you naked to the Tower."

Ignoring the command, Roger looked helplessly at his friends, who now stood directly behind deVere. "What happened?" he asked, his gaze on the Earl of Basildon.

"I'm sorry," Richard Devereux said. "Someone strangled Darnel."

Roger felt his whole world crumbling around him. Only a few

hours ago he'd grabbed his wife's throat and threatened her life in the presence of the whole damned court.

"We believe in your innocence," William Cecil spoke up, drawing his attention. "Richard and I will investigate this fully and discover the guilty."

"We'll soon have you out of the Tower," Devereux added, handing him the clothing he'd worn the previous evening. He flicked a contemptuous glance at deVere and added, "I'm accompanying you downriver to verify that Roger arrives safely."

Wishing his wife dead did not make it so, Roger thought as he pulled his breeches on. That left him with one unanswerable question: Who else wanted to rid the world of Darnel?

The sun on the fifteenth day of July reached its highest point in the sky and slowly began its westward descent.

Two young women sat inside the Earl of Basildon's garden in the shade of a willow, its sweeping branches shielding them from the sun's relentless rays. Their younger siblings sat together beneath an enormous oak on the other side of the garden and ate their afternoon picnic snack.

" 'Tis the feast of Saint Swithin," Blythe Devereux informed her younger sister. "Whatever weather the Lord of the Winds sends this day will remain with us the whole year through."

"Then I suppose we'll be having a warm winter," Bliss replied. " 'Tis hotter than the bowels of hell today."

"Bowels of hell?" Blythe echoed, suppressing a smile. "Mama would scold you for your vocabulary. Ladies never use profanity, you know."

"She also insists we should never trust a man whose eyes are set too close together," Bliss reminded her. "Heaven help us if we should trust a man with a pretty dimple in his chin."

"Eat your vegetables or you'll grow warts," Blythe warned, imitating their mother. The two sisters dissolved into giggles.

"The mountains of Wales would have been refreshingly cool

this summer," Bliss said, a wistful tone in her voice. "I don't understand why we couldn't go this year."

"Papa attended the queen's progress in order to investigate Lady Darnel's death," Blythe said. "Poor Roger has been wilting in the Tower for three months."

"Well, Papa returned two days ago," Bliss replied. "We could have gone then."

"By the time we reached Wales 'twould have been time to return to England," Blythe said, gazing in the direction of the house. Feeling her sister's touch on her arm, she turned and saw the solemn expression on her face.

"I'm glad you never married Roger," Bliss told her. "You could have been the one who lies in an early grave."

"I'm positive Roger had nothing to do with his wife's death," Blythe insisted, placing her hand on top of her sister's. "Though I do appreciate your concern."

"Perhaps you're correct." Bliss cast her a sidelong glance and remarked, "September is nearly upon us. Are you eager to leave us and assume your duties as one of the queen's maids of honor?"

"I'm not eager to leave you, but 'twill afford me the opportunity to help Roger," Blythe answered, touching the jeweled cross of Wotan she'd worn each day for the past five years.

"Becoming involved could prove dangerous," Bliss warned. "If Roger is truly innocent, then a murderer stalks the corridors at court."

"I promise to be very careful."

Wild whoops drew their attention to their younger siblings. Ranging in age from two to fourteen, the six youngest Devereux children raced across the lawns toward them.

"We want to play *rhibo*," fourteen-year-old Aurora said, referring to the traditional harvest game they played each summer when they visited their mother's family in Wales.

" 'Tis entirely too early for *rhibo*," Bliss said.

"Aye, we play *rhibo* to celebrate Lammas on the first day of August," Blythe agreed.

Four-year-old Adam Devereux, the sole male in a tribe of females, leaned close to his oldest sister. Nose to nose with her, he demanded, "Tell us the story."

"Please?" chimed Summer and Autumn, the eleven-year-old twins.

"Pretty please with sugar on it," eight-year-old Hope pleaded.

"Everyone must sit down," Blythe said, lifting two-year-old Blaze onto her lap.

With no thought for soiling their garments, the children plopped down on the grass and looked expectantly at their oldest sister. Blythe smiled as she gazed at their violet eyes and shining ebony hair, so much like her own. Only Blaze, the youngest, had managed to inherit their father's copper hair and emerald eyes.

"Lady Blythe! Lady Bliss!" interrupted Jennings, the Devereux majordomo, as he hurried across the garden toward them. "The earl and the countess require your presence in the study."

"Both of us?" Blythe asked.

Jennings nodded. "All the other children accompany me to Mrs. Ashemole," the majordomo ordered. " 'Tis time for napping."

When they reached the mansion Blythe led the way into the study. She paused inside the door and stared in surprise at the five people gathered there.

Her father sat in the chair behind his desk. The elderly Lord Burghley, Queen Elizabeth's most trusted adviser, claimed one of the chairs in front of the desk while Grandpapa Robert Talbot, the Duke of Ludlow, her mother's father, sprawled in the other chair. Her mother and Grandmama Chessy, her grandfather's second wife, stood near the window that overlooked the garden.

"Oh, my sweet darlings, 'tis a momentous day for both of you," Grandmama Chessy cried, rushing across the chamber to kiss them. "How I wish I were your age again."

"Chessy, please," Duke Robert said. "Allow their parents to broach this subject."

"I'm just so excited," the duchess gushed.

Though puzzled by this exchange between her grandparents, Blythe maintained her poise. She curtsied first to Lord Burghley and then greeted her grandfather with a kiss on his cheek. Bliss followed her sister's lead.

"Shall I begin, dearest?" Earl Richard asked, glancing at his wife.

Lady Keely nodded and cast her oldest daughter an ambiguous smile.

"As you know, Roger Debrett has been imprisoned in the Tower for three months," Earl Richard said, giving Blythe his attention. "Meager circumstantial evidence prevents his being brought to trial. On the other hand, Elizabeth cannot release him, because of the public protests that action might incite."

"I have an idea that will allow the queen to free Roger," Lord Burghley spoke up. "However, we need your cooperation to implement this plan."

"I'd do anything to help Roger," Blythe said without hesitation.

Earl Richard flicked a sidelong glance at his wife, who took her cue and crossed the chamber to her daughter. "If you harbor any reservations about this plan, then I urge you to refuse," Lady Keely said. "We will understand your reticence."

Blythe felt confused, but nodded in agreement.

"Are you willing to marry Lord Roger?" her mother asked.

"You want me to wed with Roger?" Blythe echoed, surprised by the request.

"Roger requires a bride whose father is both powerful at court and popular with London's commoners," Lord Burghley explained. " 'Twould be enough of a show of faith from your father to enable the queen to release Roger and to prevent the commoners from grumbling publicly about such an action."

Blythe touched her pendant and stared off into space as if pondering what they'd said, but the hint of a smile flirted with her lips. Her mother's prophecy was coming true! The eagle and the butterfly would unite and soar together across the horizon.

Blythe slid her gaze to her mother. Lady Keely nodded as if she knew her daughter's thoughts.

"I still think Roger Debrett is too old for her," the Duke of

Ludlow remarked before Blythe could answer. "Twelve years do separate them."

"The older the fiddle, the better the tune," the duchess replied. "Take us, Tally, darling. You are sixty-two and I'm only a shade above forty."

Blythe and Bliss looked at each other and giggled. Their grandmother had been a shade above forty for as long as they could remember. Only God and she knew her real age.

"Love acknowledges no boundaries like age," Blythe said, and then blushed when the others shifted their gazes to her. "I will gladly wed with Roger," she announced, trying to keep her eagerness out of her voice. "But what about my position with the queen's maids of honor?"

"I cannot like this part of the plan," the earl said, glancing at his wife. "At sixteen Bliss is entirely too young to attend court."

"Tally and I will protect her," Lady Chessy argued. "Besides, Bliss is a virtuous maiden. Aren't you, darling?"

"If any man tries to kiss me, I'll say 'yuck-yuck-yuck,' " Bliss promised, reciting the words her father had taught each of his daughters. "And if any man does kiss me, I'll slap his face."

Blythe smiled when she saw her father roll his eyes and then look at his wife. Lady Keely shrugged and nodded.

"Very well, but 'tis against my better judgment," the earl agreed finally.

" 'Tis settled. Blythe will marry Roger, and Bliss will assume her position as a maid of honor," Lord Burghley said, rising from his chair. He turned to the countess and added, "The wedding ceremony must be as public as possible. London's populace must see that Richard believes in Roger's innocence enough to give him his daughter in marriage."

"Will Saint Paul's Cathedral suit?" Lady Keely asked.

Lord Burghley nodded and started for the door, saying, "Are you coming, Richard? We'll go downriver together to tell Roger."

"I'll meet you at the quay in five minutes," Earl Richard said, escorting the queen's minister to the door. "I'd like a private word with my daughter before we leave."

"Come, darling," Grandmama Chessy said, drawing Bliss toward the door with her. "Planning your wardrobe is our first order of business. I have impeccable taste, so you can trust me with this."

The Duke of Ludlow stood to follow his wife and his granddaughter out.

"And what will you do, Papa?" Lady Keely asked.

"My sixty-two-year-old bones need enough rest to keep up with my shade-over-forty wife," the duke said with a grin. "I believe 'tis time for my afternoon nap."

Alone with his wife and his oldest daughter, Earl Richard asked, "Are you absolutely certain this is what you want?"

"Yes, but—" Blythe broke off.

"But what, poppet?"

"Will I retain control of my ships and businesses?" Blythe asked. "A woman should have her own fortune, you know."

"Poppet, you are indeed my daughter," her father said, planting a kiss on her cheek. "The betrothal agreement will stipulate anything you want. Roger Debrett is in no position to negotiate." At that he headed for the door.

"And thee I chuse," Blythe murmured, echoing the inscription on the pendant Roger had given her. "The choice Roger made five years ago is coming true."

"Yes, but listen carefully to the warning that came to me in a dream," Lady Keely said, looping her arm through her daughter's. "Find happiness with the soaring eagle in the Place of the Winds. Beware the dark sun."

"Roger is the soaring eagle, and Winchester is the Place of the Winds," Blythe said. A chill of apprehension rippled down her spine. "What is the dark sun?"

"You must discover what or who that is," her mother told her. "You will sign the betrothal agreement on Lammas, the most auspicious day for unions in the year's cycle."

Yes, Blythe thought. She would find happiness in the Place of the Winds, Winchester, where Saint Swithin's shrine was located.

Blythe knew with the confidence of youth that she possessed sunlight in abundance to vanquish clouds, shadows, and even dark suns. Roger, the queen's eagle, would soar majestically across the horizon, and perching on the eagle's outstretched wing would be his psyche, his butterfly, his soul.

Chapter 2

"Your deal."

Roger slid the deck of cards across the table toward the Tower of London's chaplain royal, who was gathering the betting chips he'd won. Glancing at William Kingston, the Tower's constable, Roger said dryly, "I never realized how talented a gambler a holy man could be."

" 'Tis God's will," the chaplain told him.

"Amen," Kingston added.

"I've fallen in with a couple of thieves," Roger complained, but smiled as he poured himself another whiskey. "If the queen keeps me imprisoned much longer, the two of you will pauper me."

"Do not begrudge us a piece of that mountain of gold you built," the chaplain said.

Though far from luxurious, Roger's chamber in the Beauchamp Tower was well-lit, airy, and clean. The hearth had been built into one wall, and in the center of the room stood a table with three chairs. A spiral staircase in the far corner led to his sleeping quarters one floor above.

"Any news from Basildon yet?" Kingston asked, offering him the platter of roasted chicken.

Roger shook his head and stared at the cards in his hand. Like an old friend, an oppressively morose feeling settled upon him.

Darnel was dead, murdered by one of her many anonymous lovers and here he sat wasting away in the Tower of London.

The worst part was that he hadn't seen his daughter in three months. Darnel had never spent any time with Miranda, and Roger worried that his daughter might fear that her father had also abandoned her. He missed her, especially their ritual of a bedtime story and a good-night kiss.

"I wonder what is happening at court," Roger said without looking up.

"Her Majesty is on progress, not at court," the chaplain remarked.

"Court is wherever the queen perches," Roger corrected him, managing a faint smile.

"I suppose so," the chaplain agreed.

Silence descended upon the three gamblers as they studied their cards. Suddenly, the sound of footsteps on the stairs reached their ears. The three of them shifted their gazes toward the other side of the chamber.

The door swung open slowly. Lord Burghley, followed by the Earl of Basildon, walked into the chamber.

"My lords," Roger said, bolting out of his chair, as did his companions. A wave of relief surged through him at the thought that they'd discovered information concerning his wife's murder.

"Gentlemen," Lord Burghley greeted them with a nod and his usual somber expression.

"I see these two Tower thieves are stealing your hard-earned coins," Earl Richard remarked. Ever the polished courtier and infinitely more affable than his illustrious companion, the earl smiled and extended his hand to the Tower constable and then the chaplain.

"Gentlemen, Her Majesty's business requires we speak privately with Debrett," Burghley said.

Kingston and the chaplain royal nodded in understanding and left. The door clicked shut behind them.

"My lords, please sit down," Roger said, clearing the table of their gambling paraphernalia.

The aging Lord Burghley sat down and cast him a look of

supreme disgust. "And how much gold have you lost?" he asked.

"A man can read only so much," Roger hedged, feeling like an errant schoolboy.

"Too much, I glean from your words of evasion," Burghley replied.

Richard Devereux chuckled. "Those two old foxes have been swindling gold from unfortunate nobles since time immemorial. As I recall, they won a small fortune from me eighteen years ago."

"Have you discovered anything at court?" Roger asked, unable to hide his eagerness.

"No, the murderer is being exceptionally cautious," Earl Richard replied.

"Damn," Roger swore, banging his fist on the table. "How can I clear my name if I'm locked away?"

"Control yourself, Debrett," Lord Burghley ordered. "A wise man never shows his thoughts or his emotions."

"Unless he's among friends."

"Oh, really?" Burghley countered, cocking his brow at the younger man. "Tell me how you can be certain if a man's friendship is genuine or feigned."

Roger stared at him. Burghley was correct. One never knew for certain who was a true friend.

"I see you agree with the veracity of my words," Burghley said.

Roger nodded and then glanced at the earl, who was smiling at him. "Well, have you traveled to the Tower to tell me no news?" he demanded. "Or is my execution imminent?"

"No execution," Richard assured him. " 'Tis merely a long-overdue visit from two old friends."

A friendly visit, my arse, Roger thought as he stared at the earl. These two old foxes had something in mind, else they never would have journeyed downriver.

"Your brother insists he's helping with the investigation," Richard said. "Though your sister-in-law and he seem indifferent to your imprisonment. Perhaps they're just embarrassed by it. At any rate, I cannot like them."

"Cedric and Sybilla?" Roger echoed, surprised. "I'd trust my brother with my life. Why, he and his wife are more prim and proper than any ten men in England." He grinned. "With the exception of Lord Burghley, of course."

"Behaving properly is a virtue," Burghley replied. "However, caution is never wasted. Perhaps you should consider Devereux's opinion."

" 'Tis my brother Geoffrey who is untrustworthy," Roger said, turning to the earl. "He's always been a womanizer."

"As my wife is fond of saying, appearances can be deceptive," Earl Richard replied.

"Your lady-wife is wise," Burghley agreed. "For a woman, that is."

"And my daughters are almost as wise as their mother," Earl Richard replied. He smiled at Roger and added conversationally, "Cedric looks nothing like you."

"Cedric resembles our father," Roger told him. "Geoffrey and I look like our mother."

"Oh, I never met her."

"I barely knew her myself. I was very young when she died birthing Geoffrey."

The earl glanced at Burghley and changed the subject. "Was deVere upset when he learned why you were traveling to London?"

"Do you think deVere could have murdered Darnel?" Roger asked.

"Edward deVere has more piss in his body than brains," Burghley said baldly. "He's also short on courage, which eliminates him as the murderer. I know this for a fact because he fostered in my household."

Confused by the seemingly casual and aimless conversation, Roger looked from one lord to the other. He positively itched to shake both illustrious lords until they divulged all they knew.

Roger was smarter than that, though. The Earl of Basildon had tutored him well in the art of dealing with men. If he exhibited any impatience, these two favorite sons of England would only toy with him like a couple of cats tormenting a captive mouse. Then they would chide him for forgetting the lessons they'd taught him.

"Well, I'm glad for your unexpected company," Roger said, pouring whiskey into three glasses. He offered one to Burghley and then slid the other in front of Devereux.

"To my two best friends in the world," Roger said, raising his glass in salute. He sipped his whiskey and then added, "Cook is always available. Would you care for refreshment, my lords?"

Both Burghley and Devereux smiled at him, apparently pleased by his nonchalance.

"He's adopted an appropriate attitude," Burghley observed. "Perhaps he's not a complete loss."

"Aye, he's behaving remarkably well for a man who never fostered with you," Richard replied.

Burghley nodded at the compliment and then asked, "Will you do the honors or shall I?"

"After you, my lord." The earl inclined his head in deference to the older man.

"We have formulated a plan that will secure your release," Burghley began. "Her Majesty has already approved it."

That piqued Roger's interest. "Tell me more."

"The queen and I agree that you need an exaggerated show of faith in your innocence from a man who is beloved by both courtier and commoner," Burghley told him. "This man's gift of his daughter in marriage will dispel any lingering suspicion of your involvement in Darnel's untimely death."

"No brides," Roger said in a clipped voice, staring the aged lord straight in the eye.

"Now, Roger—"

"I said no brides," Roger snapped at the earl. He shot to his feet and crossed the chamber to stare out the window overlooking Tower Green and its scaffold. In thirty short years he'd lived with his father's cold disdain and his wife's adulterous contempt. He needed no more poisonous entanglements tainting his life. The scaffold on yonder green held more appeal than a second marriage.

"My oldest daughter will soon be married at Saint Paul's Cathedral," Richard said.

"To whom?" Roger asked without turning around.

"You."

Roger stiffened. "Blythe is a child."

"She's eighteen."

"I said no."

"But why?"

Roger whirled around. When he spoke, he was unable to mask his bitterness. "First comes the betrothal ring, next comes the wedding ring, and last comes the torture ring. 'Twould be highly unseemly for me to marry again so soon after Darnel's death, no matter that I toyed with the idea of divorcing her."

"Marrying Blythe is the only way out of the Tower for you," Richard argued. "Besides, my daughter is nothing like Darnel."

"Yes, she's a sweet child," Roger agreed, unaccountably making his visitors smile. "Still, my answer is no. I plan never to marry again."

"Do you also plan to pass the next forty years in Beauchamp Tower?" Richard asked him.

"What do you mean?"

"The evidence is too strong to release you," Burghley said, drawing his attention. "Do you recall threatening Darnel's life in front of the entire court, in the presence of Elizabeth herself?"

"Then let Elizabeth bring me to trial and have done with it," Roger said, becoming angry.

"We believe in your innocence and have convinced Her Majesty that the evidence is too circumstantial for trial," Burghley replied, his voice low and calm. "Elizabeth fears scandal, and we have reached an impasse. Marrying Devereux's daughter is the only way we can secure your release."

"You do wish for the freedom to investigate this crime yourself?" Richard asked. " 'Tis the best Burghley and I can do. Take it or leave it."

Frustrated beyond measure, Roger ran a hand through his hair. He shifted his piercing blue-eyed gaze to the earl and asked, "Have you mentioned this to Blythe? Or will you force her down the aisle?"

"Blythe has always held you in the highest regard," Richard answered. "She believes in your innocence and is willing to assist you."

Roger sighed. He had two choices: Marry the chit or rot in the Tower. His choice was actually no choice at all.

"When is this sacred ceremony to take place, dear father-in-law?" Roger asked, his voice bitter.

Richard grinned, rose from the chair, and crossed the chamber to shake his hand. "Blythe and I will return in two weeks to sign the betrothal agreement," the earl told him. "Come the nineteenth day of September, you will be released from the Tower to travel to Saint Paul's Cathedral for your bride. After the ceremony you will be free to go your own way."

"However, you may not return to court until Elizabeth invites you," Burghley said, rising from his chair. "The queen wants to judge the public's reaction to this development. I can guarantee that you will be back at Hampton Court in time for the Yule festivities."

"I do appreciate your unwavering support," Roger said, shaking hands with Burghley. He turned to the earl and said, "I meant to cast no aspersions on Blythe. After five years with Darnel—"

"I understand," Earl Richard interrupted. "I swear that all will be well."

Roger nodded, but doubted the earl was correct. "I've a question for you," he said as the two lords started to leave.

Devereux turned around. "Yes?"

"I've been auditing the accounts for my wool and corn trading companies," Roger said. "Recently, my companies have lost substantial profits, and my agent tells me this loss is due to an Elemental Trading Company. The anonymous owner of this company has been undercutting my prices."

Richard smiled. "I'll do my best to discover this merchant's identity."

"Thank you, my lord." Then Roger added, "I get no furloughs here. Purchase Blythe a suitable betrothal ring, and I'll reimburse you."

"Very good." Richard opened the door for Lord Burghley, and the two of them disappeared down the stairs.

Roger wandered across the chamber to the window. He watched Burghley and Devereux crossing the Tower Green in the direction of the Lieutenant's Lodging.

Closing his eyes, Roger sighed with a mixture of hope and defeat. As much as he loathed the thought of taking a bride, their plan did have merit. He needed to return to court and discover the real murderer in order to clear his name.

And what of Blythe Devereux? How did she profit from this union? Or, contrary to what the earl had said, was she being forced down the aisle?

Roger tried to conjure the image of her as she would now appear. All he saw in his mind's eye was a pretty thirteen-year-old professing her love for him. That was the last thing he needed. Getting around the marriage part of the bargain would require all of his powers of concentration. Well, he had two weeks to formulate a plan that would enable him to escape a second marriage.

Roger gazed in the direction of the Lieutenant's Lodging. Burghley and Devereux had disappeared inside, but a movement near the Lodging caught his attention. Strangely, a scarlet-and-black-clad woman paced back and forth in front of the windows. The woman turned in the direction of Beauchamp Tower and lifted her gaze to his second-story window.

A ripple of unease danced down his spine, yet Roger was unable to tear his gaze from hers. He recognized the woman whose portrait he'd passed many times in the Long Gallery at Richmond Palace: Anne Boleyn, the queen's long-dead mother.

And then Roger heard her warning as clearly as if she'd been standing beside him in the chamber: *"Beware the dark sun."*

And thee I chuse....

Blythe placed the jeweled cross of Wotan over her head and then stepped in front of the mirror to study her image. The gown she wore for her betrothal featured a high neckline and a long-waisted bodice and had been created in maiden blush silk. The soft neutrality of its color accentuated her violet eyes and the jeweled pendant resting against her breast.

A troubled frown marred her usually serene expression as she searched for flaws in her appearance. What would Roger think when he saw her for the first time in five years? Would he compare her with the beautiful wife he had loved and lost? Did he remember that humiliating scene on her thirteenth birthday when she'd professed her love for him? Would he be pleased that she'd agreed to become his wife, or would he reject her love again?

The Druidic festival of Lammas marked the beginning of the season when the sun consummated its union with the earth. Supposedly, the first day of August was an especially auspicious time in the year's cycle for weddings and betrothals, and Blythe fervently hoped that belief would prove true. Winning Roger's love wouldn't be easy, and she needed all the divine help she could get.

Blythe crossed the chamber to look out the window. The sun had not yet reached its highest point in the sky. Her father and she would leave for the Tower after dinner, which allowed her time to sneak outside and seek the Great Mother Goddess's help in bolstering her courage. The deserted garden suited her needs perfectly.

Blythe fastened a belt of golden links around her waist. Attached to the belt was a black leather sheath containing a small, jewel-hilted stiletto. Then she grabbed her pouch of magic stones and headed for the door.

Reaching the garden without being seen, Blythe hurried across the lawns and hid beneath the sweeping branches of her old friend, the willow tree. She glanced over her shoulder to verify that she couldn't be seen, then placed the palm of her right hand against the willow's trunk and whispered, "Good Lammas Day to you, my friend."

The tips of the willow's branches twitched in the gentle breeze and then stilled.

Blythe backed away from the tree but remained hidden within the curtain of its sweeping branches. She faced north and emptied the contents of her pouch into her left hand. There were six stones: an emerald, an aventurine, a ruby, an amethyst, an amber, and a black obsidian.

Using these stones, Blythe formed a makeshift circle. She placed the emerald in the north, the aventurine in the east, and the ruby in the south.

"All disturbing thoughts remain outside," she said, and closed the circle in the west with the amethyst.

Blythe walked to the center of the circle and set both the amber and the black obsidian down. Then she drew her stiletto. Beginning in the east at the aventurine, she traced the circle's invisible periphery shut until she faced the east again.

"Welcome, Paralda, Lord of the East," Blythe called in a loud whisper. "And welcome to Eurus, the east wind."

Walking sunwise around the circle, Blythe stopped at each stone and called to the Elemental who ruled that particular quadrant. "Welcome Dijin, Lord of the South, and Auster, the south wind. . . . Welcome Niksa, Lord of the West, and Zephyrus, the west wind. . . . Welcome Ghom, Lord of the North, and Boreas, the north wind."

Finally, she approached the center of the circle and called, "Welcome Ngu, Lord of the Four Directions and Winds."

Blythe touched the jeweled cross of Wotan and said, "Hail Sacred Swithin, my patron saint. Aid my cause, I do implore thee. Bless my union with Roger Debrett, and bind us together with the winds of love."

Blythe paused a long moment, conjuring in her mind what came next, gathering the proper emotion much as nature gathers its forces. She turned around three times sunwise and opened her arms.

"Spirit of my journey, guide me to hear what the trees say." Blythe closed her eyes. "Spirit of my ancestors, guide me to hear what the wind whispers. Spirit of my tribe, guide me to understand what the clouds foretell. Great Mother Goddess, open my heart that I may see beyond the horizon."

Long moments passed. And then it happened. Images floated across her mind's eye. . . .

A solitary eagle flew overhead. Suddenly, a butterfly lurched upward from the earth. The majestic eagle dipped one of its powerful wings and scooped the struggling butterfly up to perch safely on his wing. The eagle and the butterfly glided across the vast blue sky toward the western horizon and vanished together into eternity.

And then the image faded into the reality of the garden.

Blythe knew without a doubt that all would be well. The Great Mother Goddess smiled with favor upon her impending union with Roger. Their future was secure.

"I thank the Great Mother Goddess for passing her wisdom through me," Blythe whispered. She lifted the amber and the black obsidian off the ground, saying, "I dismiss you, Ngu, Lord of the Four Directions and Winds."

Starting with the emerald in the north, Blythe dismissed each of the Elementals and retrieved her magic stones. Then she touched the willow's trunk once again and whispered, "Thank you for shrouding me within the curtain of your arms."

Without another word Blythe turned on her heels and started back to the house. She felt considerably more lighthearted than she had a few minutes earlier. Anticipation swelled within her breast, and she wondered idly if Roger would be pleased with the physical changes five years had brought to her.

"I've been searching for you," Lady Keely said, meeting her in the foyer. "Your father wants to leave now."

"I've been worshiping," Blythe told her.

"Give me the dagger and the pouch," her mother said with a smile. "Neither Roger nor your father would approve of calling down the elements."

Blythe handed her mother the pouch of stones and the golden belt with its sheathed stiletto. The earl walked into the foyer just as her mother passed her the lightweight summer cloak that matched her gown.

"Are you ready, poppet?" her father asked.

Blythe nodded. Today marked the beginning of her life with the man she'd loved forever, and she could hardly wait to affix her name to the document that would bind them together.

Richard shifted his gaze to his wife and then to the dagger and the pouch in her hands. "What do you have there, dearest?"

"Nothing."

The earl cocked a brow at her and said, " 'Tis precisely what I've been telling you for nineteen years."

"Skeptic," Lady Keely muttered, rolling her eyes.

"Are you certain you won't accompany us?" the earl asked.

"I cannot abide that place," the countess refused.

Late summer blessed the world of men with clear blue skies, radiant sunshine, and gentle breezes.

Looping her arm through her father's, Blythe crossed the lawns toward the quay where their barge awaited them. She successfully squelched the urge to forget her newly acquired sophistication and kick her slippers off. Joy tempted her to run barefoot across the lawns and let each blade of grass tickle her feet.

At the quay the earl hopped onto the barge and then helped her to board. Father and daughter sat together as the barge glided downriver.

"You are my firstborn, the child of my heart, and I would

never even consider forcing you to the altar," Richard told her. "Are you certain this marriage is what you desire?"

Blythe cast him a sunny smile. "Yes, Papa."

The earl nodded. "Then we do have a matter of importance to discuss."

"Yes?"

"Life jostles every man, but Roger Debrett has been jostled more than most," he said. "I fear the man you once knew does not exist any longer."

Blythe lost her smile. "Are you trying to dissuade me?"

"No, but harboring high expectations could prove painful to you," the earl answered.

"With my love to heal him, Roger will be as he always was," she told him, her youth lending her confidence. "Trust me, for I have seen it."

"And *I* see that your mother has infected you with her strange beliefs," Richard replied with a fond smile. "Never reveal those beliefs to Roger. I doubt he would understand. Eventually, your husband will return to court. Be circumspect in all of your words and your actions."

"Papa, I am always circumspect," Blythe assured him, patting his hand. "Do I keep sole control of my businesses?"

"Ah, Blythe. I do see that I have had some good influence upon your thinking," Richard said. "To answer your question, I hid those clauses in the midst of the more mundane articles of the contract."

Their journey downriver lasted an eternity. The traffic upon that great street of water called the Thames proved horrendously congested. Though inconvenienced by the crush of barges, the boatmen seemed in high spirits and called greetings to friend and stranger alike. The earl's barge slipped beneath London Bridge and passed enclosed ship basins, from which the mingling scents of spices, grain, and lumber wafted through the air.

Soon Blythe recognized the pepper-pot turrets and forbidding gray walls of the Tower of London. Trying to bolster her waning confidence, she touched the jeweled cross of Wotan. The sentiment it carried heartened her.

Their barge docked at the water gate of St. Thomas Tower, also known as Traitor's Gate, the most dreaded portal in all of England. Such notoriously dangerous criminals as Anne Boleyn had passed through it, as had her daughter, Queen Elizabeth. Some had come out; others had never been seen again.

"Now I understand why mother dislikes this place," Blythe said, staring at the hideous mouthlike gate that had swallowed her beloved. "Tormented souls have passed through this gate."

"Aye, but thinking about them is futile," her father replied.

He helped her disembark and led her in the direction of the Lieutenant's Lodging. They passed through the Lodging to the grassy inner courtyard on the other side of the building and then advanced on the Beauchamp Tower, which loomed above Tower Green and the menacing scaffold.

The atmosphere inside the courtyard was eerily hushed, as if the stone walls trapped unearthly silence within. A cool stillness pervaded the air.

The chaplain royal awaited them at the entrance to the Beauchamp Tower. He shook the earl's hand and nodded at Blythe.

"I suppose we'll soon be losing Roger's company," the chaplain said, his disappointment obvious.

"Kingston and you will find another unfortunate nobleman to swindle," Richard assured him.

"You wound me, Basildon," the chaplain said with a smile, and led the way up the stairs to the second floor.

Blythe wet her lips, gone dry from nervous apprehension. She'd longed for this day forever, but now insecurity swept through her and slowed her step. What if Roger wasn't happy to see her? How would she survive the remainder of her days with a man who could not love her?

And then Blythe reached the top of the stairs. Almost reluctantly, she walked into the chamber and then looked around in confusion. The room was deserted except for an unknown man.

"Kingston, you old thief," her father greeted the man.

The Tower constable grinned. "Basildon, Roger is still upstairs and will be down— Ah, here he comes now."

The click of boots on the spiral staircase drew their attention. Blythe whirled around and fixed her gaze on Roger as he descended the stairs.

Roger appeared exactly as Blythe had remembered him. Tall and well-built, her beloved moved with grace. He seemed slightly sinister in black, yet his shaggy light-brown hair and handsomely chiseled features were the same.

Five years, however, had altered his expression. Tight-lipped grimness had replaced smiling affability.

And then Roger shifted his piercing sky-blue gaze to her. For one brief moment his expression mirrored his surprise as he looked at her with the critical eye of a connoisseur of women. In an instant Roger shuttered his feelings.

Blythe understood his ploy. She'd seen her father do the same thing thousands of times with visiting courtiers and merchants. Only among family did her father allow his emotions and his thoughts to show.

Blythe watched Roger cross the chamber toward her. She felt the heated blush upon her cheeks when he halted only inches from her.

"You have grown up rather nicely," he said, bowing formally over her hand.

Blythe nodded, unable to find her voice through her shyness. Sacred Saint Swithin, the man would think she was a blinking idiot. How could she ever compete with the sophisticated court ladies to whom he was accustomed?

Gazing into his eyes, Blythe forgot her own fears. She recognized his heart-wrenching misery. It was as tangible as the stones beneath her feet.

Abruptly, Roger turned away. "I trust you carry the betrothal contract," he said, shaking hands with her father.

Richard nodded. "Shall we get down to business?"

"I desire private conversation with Blythe before I sign," Roger said.

"We can step outside," the chaplain offered.

"Do not bother. Blythe and I will go upstairs," Roger replied. He flicked a glance at the earl and added, "The door will remain open."

Richard inclined his head.

Blythe hesitated when Roger turned to her and offered his hand. She flicked a nervous glance at her father, who gave her an encouraging smile.

"Child, you will be perfectly safe," Roger said in a clipped voice.

Blythe snapped her gaze to his and tried to explain. "My lord, you misunderstand."

Roger cocked a brow at her. "Do I?"

Blythe nodded once and, feeling his presence close behind her, crossed the chamber to the spiral staircase. Troubling thoughts bade her climb the stairs slowly. This reunion wasn't exactly what she'd envisioned in her daydreams. Roger's displeasure was all too obvious.

Blythe walked into the bedchamber and scanned it quickly. Against one wall stood a four-poster bed, complete with draperies and fur coverlet. A summer-darkened hearth had been built into another wall. Two windows allowed the afternoon sunlight into the room.

" 'Tis a pleasant chamber," Blythe said conversationally.

"Losing one's freedom is the height of pleasantness," Roger replied, close behind her, so close she could smell his bay scent.

"I'm sorry," she apologized, whirling around to stare at his chest. "I didn't mean—"

"Please sit down," he interrupted.

The only place to sit was the bed.

Blythe crossed the chamber as slowly as a woman going to the gallows and perched on the edge of the bed. Five years of separation had made Roger a stranger. He was still a desirable man, but she was no longer a child. They would become man and wife in a few short weeks. And then? Oh, Lord, they would share a bed like this one. Intimately . . .

That impure thought kept her gaze downcast and flushed her cheeks. The heated blush deepened to a dark rose when she spied his black boots planted on the floor in front of her.

"Is aught wrong?" Roger asked, his voice gentle.

Blythe lifted her gaze from her white-knuckled hands to meet his questioning look and gave him an uncertain smile.

"You do not have to marry me," Roger said.

"I am content."

"Haven't you wondered if your husband-to-be is a murderer?" he asked.

"You are innocent of any wrongdoing," she answered emphatically.

Roger knelt on one bended knee in front of her, but refrained from touching her hand. "Are you certain you wish to do this?" he persisted. "Is the earl forcing you to the altar?"

"My father would never do that," Blythe answered. Without warning she reached out and brushed a fingertip across his left cheekbone, asking, "Did they beat you?"

Her question seemed to surprise him. "No. Why do you ask?"

"I see the faint traces of a scar," she answered.

" 'Tis *your* mark upon me," he said, amusement lighting his eyes. "Do you recall a certain gift box used as a weapon?"

"I'm sorry about that," Blythe apologized in a choked voice.

"I forgave you long ago," Roger assured her. He stood then and added, "As a matter of fact, you were correct."

"About what?"

"You predicted I'd regret marrying Darnel," he answered, then turned away, discouraging further conversation. "Shall we go below?"

Downstairs, Earl Richard had the betrothal contract spread across the table. The ink and the quill sat beside it.

"Signing a contract without reading it first is bad business," Richard said as Roger reached for the quill.

Roger flicked an unamused glance at him and, without bothering to reply, affixed his name to the document. Blythe signed next, then Richard, followed by their two witnesses, the Tower chaplain and the constable.

"Do you have the ring?" Roger asked.

Richard nodded. He produced a small gift box from inside his doublet and passed it to the younger man.

Roger opened its lid and smiled. "My lady, you have always reminded me of this," he said, slipping the ring onto her finger.

Dropping her gaze from his handsome face to her left hand, Blythe knew their marriage would be blessed. Her betrothal ring was a delicate butterfly perched on top of a gold band. The butterfly's golden wings and body had been set with rubies, emeralds, sapphires, and diamonds.

His message was clear. She was still his butterfly, his psyche, his soul.

" 'Tis exquisitely lovely," Blythe said, casting him a shy smile. "I shall cherish it always."

"Cherishing gold and jewels is what you ladies do best," Roger replied, unable to mask his bitterness. " 'Tis nothing personal, child. I have vast experience with the ladies and no real wish for a second marriage."

His stinging remarks wiped the smile off Blythe's face, and her proud Devereux nature surfaced to vanquish her maiden's shyness. How dare he humiliate her in such a manner. Even an unwanted bride deserved pleasant memories of her betrothal and wedding. Embarrassment mingled with anger to color her cheeks, but pride made her strike back.

"My lord, you do demonstrate your appreciation for my charity in the oddest manner," Blythe countered, cocking an ebony brow at him.

"Charity, my lady?" Roger asked, rounding on her.

She lifted her chin a notch and informed him, "I am not the one in need of a spouse."

Blythe regretted her words as soon as she heard her father's chuckle. Sacred Saint Swithin, how dare she publicly insult the man she loved. She should have met his rudeness with kindness.

"Touché, my lady," Roger said, and inclined his head.

Blythe tried to make amends, saying, "Shall I visit you between now and the—"

"No." The curtness in his voice precluded argument.

" 'Tis time we return to Devereux House," Richard announced, breaking the strained silence that followed.

Roger shook her father's hand and then turned to her. "Until September, my lady."

Smarting from his rejection, Blythe managed a nod and then turned to her father. Relief at leaving her betrothed's presence swept through her.

"By the way, did you investigate that merchant?" Roger called, stopping them at the door. "I tallied the latest figures, and I'm still losing profits. As soon as I'm free, I plan to pauper that odious knave."

Richard hesitated and glanced at Blythe. Then he looked at Roger and shrugged.

"What merchant?" Blythe asked.

" 'Tis a man's business," Roger told her.

Ignoring his comment, Blythe rounded on her father and asked, "To whom does he refer?"

"The anonymous owner of the Elemental Trading Company," her father answered with a smile.

"The bastard," Roger muttered.

Blythe retraced her steps across the chamber until she stood in front of him. "*I* own the Elemental Trading Company."

"You?" Roger echoed, staring at her as if she'd suddenly grown another head.

"Is there a problem?" Blythe asked, casting him a sunny smile.

"You're undercutting my prices," he snapped.

" 'Tis nothing personal," Blythe replied, leveling a cool gaze on him. " 'Tis merely business."

Roger's complexion mottled with suppressed anger, and his expression told her he'd like to box her ears. And then he threw her off balance by smiling.

"Come the nineteenth day of September my problem will be solved," Roger told her.

Now Blythe suffered the urge to box *his* ears. Instead, she returned his smile and said, "I doubt that, my lord."

"As your husband, I—"

"You misunderstand," the earl spoke up from where he stood at the doorway. "Blythe retains sole control of her businesses. The betrothal contract stipulates that."

" 'Tis of no importance," Roger replied, and then slid his gaze to hers. "You will take a vow of obedience on our wedding day, and then I will order you to cease undercutting my prices."

"Thank you for the warning," Blythe replied, managing to keep her face expressionless. Turning on her heels, she crossed the chamber to her father and, without a backward glance, started down the stairs.

Marriage was one thing, Blythe fumed, allowing herself the pleasure of an irritated grimace, but business had nothing to do with love, honor, and obey. Forewarned was forearmed, and Blythe had an idea that would prevent Roger from ruining her successful businesses.

"What do you think?" her father asked as they crossed the Tower Green to the Lieutenant's Lodging.

"Roger is in pain," Blythe answered. "Will he recover, do you think?"

"With your patience and love, Roger can be made whole again," the earl said, putting his arm around her as they walked.

"I love you, Papa."

"And I love you, poppet. Now, tell me how you plan to subvert Roger's intended control of your businesses."

"I do have an idea," Blythe admitted, "but you must persuade Bishop Grindal to cooperate. Will you do that?"

"A generous gift to the church always works miracles." Richard grinned. "I can almost hear the sounds of the crockery crashing in the Debrett household."

"You are mistaken, Papa." Blythe cast him a mischievous smile. "What you hear are the battle cries of a price war."

Chapter 3

"How do you think Roger will react?"

"Only God knows for certain," Earl Richard answered. "I suspect Roger will gracefully accept your out-smarting him. What other choice does he have?"

Blythe stood with her father inside the tiny candlelit chamber off the nave of Saint Paul's Cathedral. The bridal party had arrived early in order to avoid the crush of commoners who would undoubtedly crowd the streets surrounding the church in the hope of glimpsing two of England's favorite sons, namely Richard Devereux and Roger Debrett.

Blythe was subdued as they awaited Roger's arrival. In a very few minutes her father would escort her down the aisle and give her to a man who didn't want her. Would he ever love her?

Blythe wondered if she should have allowed him control of her businesses but knew she could never do that. Wasting her days planning entertainments for the shallow noblewomen who peopled the Tudor Court was something she could never bring herself to do.

Blythe doubted those court ladies would even accept her. Her own mother shunned most court festivities and was sublimely happy. Besides, the more social intercourse she had at court, the greater the chance that her pagan beliefs would be discovered.

Roger savored his reputation as a polished courtier, an

insider, and one of the queen's personal favorites. If she became an embarrassment, her husband would despise her.

In spite of her troubled thoughts Blythe appeared serene and regal. She looked like a princess in her mother's wedding gown, which had been created in cream-colored satin and adorned with hundreds of seed pearls. Its formfitting bodice had a square and daringly low-cut neckline, displaying an ample amount of cleavage. Narrow, tight-fitting sleeves puffed at the shoulders.

Any resemblance to a proper English earl's daughter ended there, and her pagan spirit reigned over her appearance. With her mother's approval, Blythe let her thick ebony mane cascade to her waist in pagan fashion. Like her mother before her, she'd left her head uncovered and her face unveiled in defiance of English tradition. The glittering cross of Wotan nestled provocatively above the valley between her breasts. The only other splash of color—her butterfly betrothal ring—had been moved to her right hand.

Blythe carried a bouquet of orange blossoms. The fragrant white flowers represented her virginity and were thought to be a fertility charm because both the blossom and the fruit appear simultaneously on the orange tree.

Suddenly, a thunderous cheering arose from the crowds outside the cathedral. Blythe turned in alarm to her father and asked, "What is happening?"

"Apparently, Roger has arrived," Richard said with a smile.

"So the populace believes him innocent of—" Blythe broke off, unwilling to bring bad luck down upon her marriage by mentioning murder on her wedding day.

"The Devereux and the Debrett men do mingle with the commoners in order to sway them to benevolence," her father told her. Then he warned, "Do not be surprised by the tossing of coins into the crowds when we leave."

The door swung open slowly, admitting the Duke of Ludlow. He smiled, planted a kiss on his granddaughter's cheek, and said, "Yea, Blythe. Your beauty does remind me of the day I walked your mother down the aisle to your father."

"Thank you, Grandpapa."

"Debrett awaits you at the altar," the duke said, and then left the chamber.

Blythe turned to her father and said, "Papa, I love you and always will."

"And I love you," the earl replied, putting his arm around her. "The years since your birth have passed faster than an eye can blink. Watching you grow from infant to woman is something I wish I could do ten thousand times."

"I shall miss you," Blythe said, unshed tears glistening in her eyes.

Her father smiled wryly. "Debrett House stands two doors down from Devereux House."

"Yes, but it won't be the same as living beneath the same roof," she replied.

"Devereux House will always be open to you and yours," the earl said, planting a kiss on her cheek.

"Oh, Papa. How will I ever win Roger's affection?" Blythe asked, her voice rising in near panic.

"Roger Debrett already loves you beyond measure, but he doesn't realize it yet." He winked at her. "Your mother has seen it, and whatever your mother sees comes to pass."

Blythe smiled. "Papa, I do believe you are beginning to see the truth."

He gestured toward the door, saying, "Let's not make Roger worry about what is keeping you from becoming his wife."

Blythe and her father left the tiny chamber and positioned themselves in the rear of the cathedral. He reached for her hand to escort her down the aisle. She stepped forward two paces and stopped short. The church was deserted except for a few people in the front two pews.

"Where are all the guests?" Blythe asked, turning in confusion to her father.

"I'm sorry, poppet, but Roger is out of favor at the moment," he explained. "Only those courtiers confident in their position at court would dare attend his wedding. Remember, this ceremony has been designed to appease London's commoners."

Blythe nodded in understanding. What really mattered was that the eagle and his soul would be joined together for all of eternity.

"Who sits there behind our family?" she asked.

"The Earl of Essex owed me several favors, and London's commoners adore him," her father answered. "Sir Francis Drake sits beside him."

"You've called in the hero of the Armada," Blythe remarked, casting him a sidelong smile. "Who sits there on Roger's side of the aisle?"

"Lord Burghley," he told her. "Roger's two brothers and his sister-in-law sit beside Lord Cecil."

Blythe stared down the long length of the empty cathedral. She'd always imagined that the firstborn daughter of England's favorite son would enjoy the grandest wedding ever celebrated. That wasn't to be. On the bright side, Roger wouldn't be too embarrassed when she outsmarted him at the altar. Still, her wedding wasn't the festive occasion she had envisioned.

Blythe started down the aisle with her father. Ignoring the rows and rows of empty pews, she pasted a serene smile onto her face and fixed her gaze on her betrothed.

Waiting with Bishop Grindal at the altar, Roger stared at her. His interested gaze dropped from her face to her display of cleavage, lingered there a long moment, and then traveled down her body. When his gaze returned to hers, the mask that shuttered all expression from his face fell into place.

Reaching the plainly decorated sanctuary where she would register her sacred vows before God and man, Blythe turned to her father and kissed him farewell. Then the earl stepped back a few paces.

"Where is your veil?" Roger demanded in a whisper as they turned to face the bishop. "Tradition requires you wear a veil."

Blythe couldn't credit what she was hearing. The man had

been cast into the Tower on suspicion of murdering his wife, but what he chose to gripe about was her lack of a veil?

" 'Tis the bride's prerogative to wear what she chooses," Blythe whispered. "I walk in my mother's path."

"What do you mean by that?"

Blythe opened her mouth to reply, but the bishop cleared his throat to gain their attention. She knew from the holy man's expression that he harbored no hope of happiness for them. They were arguing before they even exchanged vows.

"Children, are you ready to receive the holy sacrament of matrimony?" Bishop Grindal asked.

Roger nodded, and so did Blythe. Together they entered the inner sanctuary and stood in front of the bishop.

"I shan't be overruled in *this* marriage," Roger whispered in a harsh voice.

"And neither shall I," Blythe replied in a voice loud enough to reach the ears of family and guests.

"Dearly beloved," Bishop Grindal called loudly, interrupting whatever the irritated groom would have replied, "we are gathered here in the sight of God and in the face of this congregation to join together this man and this woman in holy matrimony . . ."

Blythe stopped listening. She disliked Christian services. In her personal philosophy, God did not dwell upon an altar inside a building. The Supreme Being, whom she firmly believed to be female, lived outside in nature. Why would God sit inside a cold, stone building when She could dwell outside amidst Her own creations?

"Who giveth this woman to be married to this man?" she heard the bishop ask.

"I do," Earl Richard said, stepping forward. The earl placed his daughter's right hand in Roger's right hand, and then joined his family in the front pew.

Bishop Grindal looked at Roger and instructed, "My lord, repeat after me. . . ."

Gazing at his bride, Roger vowed in a clear, strong voice, "I, Roger, take thee, Blythe, to be my wedded wife, to have and to hold from this day forward, for better or for worse, for richer, for poorer, in sickness and in health, to love and to cherish, till death us do part, according to God's ordinance; and thereto I plight thee my troth."

After casting her beloved an ambiguous smile, Blythe repeated her vows, "I, Blythe, take thee, Roger, to be my wedded husband, to have and to hold from this day forward, for better or for worse, for richer, for poorer, in sickness and in health, to love and to cherish, till death us—"

"Excuse me?" Roger interrupted.

Blythe stared in surprised dismay at him. So he'd caught her deliberate omission, had he? Well, it wouldn't do him any good.

"My lord, is aught wrong?" Bishop Grindal asked. "Are you ill?"

"With all due respect, you have deleted the most important vow of all," Roger said.

"What is that, my son?"

"Obey."

Blythe grimaced when she heard the chuckles emanating from the front pews. She flashed Roger a thunderous glare and shifted her attention to the obviously anxious bishop.

"I, Blythe, take thee, Roger, to be my wedded husband," she repeated in a disgruntled tone of voice. "To have and to hold from this day forward, for better or for worse, for richer, for poorer, in sickness and in health, to love, cherish, and to ob—"

Blythe stopped talking and searched her mind for a way out of this dilemma. She cursed silently when she heard someone laughing from one of the pews. Roger's side of the aisle, no doubt.

"My child," the bishop prodded her to continue. "To obey, till death—"

"To love, cherish, and to obey *in all matters except those concerning my ships and my businesses*." Blythe rounded on Roger, saying, "My lord, 'tis my last concession. Take it or leave it."

Blythe expected his fury. Instead, Roger stared at her for an excruciatingly long moment, and then he inclined his head in agreement.

Blythe gifted him with her sunniest smile and completed her vows in a rush, "Till death us do part, according to God's holy ordinance; and thereto I plight thee my troth."

"The ring, my lord," Bishop Grindal instructed.

Roger produced an exquisite three-banded wedding ring, the likes of which Blythe had never seen. Two yellow-gold bands surrounded a center band fashioned in rose-gold hearts.

"With this ring I thee wed," Roger said, slipping the ring onto the fourth finger of her left hand. "With my body I thee worship, and with all my worldly goods I thee endow."

Together Roger and Blythe knelt in front of the bishop.

"Let us pray," Bishop Grindal said. Without thinking, he wiped the nervous sweat from his brow with the sleeve of his vestments. "O eternal God—"

Shutting the bishop's words out, Blythe breathed a sigh of relief. She'd won the right to retain sole control of her businesses, and she'd done so without too much trouble. If only she could win Roger's love, the eagle and his butterfly could soar together across the horizon.

So intent was she on the myriad ways she could please her husband, Blythe never heard the end of the ceremony. She did, however, sense Roger's movement when he began to rise, and she stood too.

Blythe turned to him with a smile, expecting him to seal their sacred vows with a kiss. Instead, Roger ignored her and turned to face family and friends.

Lady Keely reached them first. With tears of joy glistening in her eyes, she kissed her daughter and then her new son-in-law.

"Seeing Blythe marry makes me feel old," Lady Keely said.

"To me, you will always be the beautiful Welsh girl whom Basildon married nineteen years ago," Roger told her.

"And you will always be that twelve-year-old page who boosted me over the wall into the queen's Privy Garden," the countess teased him.

By this time the other Devereux children had surrounded them. Blythe handed Bliss her bouquet of orange blossoms and whispered, "You'll be next."

"Come, children," Lady Keely ordered. "Wait over here while your sister greets her guests."

The charismatic Earl of Essex stepped in front of them. He bowed formally over Blythe's hand and then turned to Roger. "Congratulations, Eden. I hope this marriage fares better than your first."

With those parting words, the Earl of Essex turned on his heels and marched down the aisle. Wild cheering arose from the commoners outside as one of their favorites came into view.

Sir Francis Drake wished them the best on their nuptials and stepped aside for Lord Burghley. "I will soon be contacting you," Cecil told Roger, and then left the cathedral with Drake.

"Blythe, may I make known to you my family," Roger said. "This is Cedric and his wife, Sybilla. And this is Geoffrey."

Cedric Debrett sported dark hair and eyes and swarthy skin. Geoffrey, the youngest, resembled Roger. Blond-haired and blue-eyed, Sybilla Debrett could have been reasonable pretty except for the sour expression she wore.

Blythe smiled at her in-laws and then glanced at her husband. She'd heard the change in his tone of voice when he introduced his youngest brother.

" 'Tis a pleasure to meet my lord's family," Blythe said. "Of course, you will be returning to Devereux House for our wedding dinner."

" 'Tis impossible," Sybilla said.

"We must return immediately to Whitehall, because the court moves to Windsor in the morning," Cedric said by way of an explanation.

"You do make an exquisitely lovely Countess of Eden," Geoffrey complimented her. He winked at her and bowed formally over her hand.

Charmed by his gallant words and actions, Blythe gave the youngest Debrett brother a sunny smile.

"How refreshing for a bride to marry a man for other than his title or his money," Geoffrey remarked to his oldest brother.

Roger nodded once but made no reply. He stared straight ahead as his family walked down the aisle to leave.

Blythe peered at her husband's grim expression and wondered what had happened to cause Roger to dislike his own brother. And what sort of family preferred returning to court rather than celebrating their brother's marriage?

"I think 'tis best for appearances if I leave with Roger and Blythe," Earl Richard was saying to his father-in-law. "Escort Keely and the children to the coaches. We'll wait until you're away before we leave."

In silence, the earl watched his family depart. A smile touched his lips when he heard the cheers of London's populace as they spied the Duke of Ludlow escorting the Devereux children to their coach.

"Ready?" he asked when the noise outside subsided.

Roger and Blythe nodded.

The three of them walked down the aisle toward the cathedral's entrance. When they stepped outside into the bright sunlight, an earth-shattering cheer arose from the sea of people crowding the cathedral's grounds.

Stunned by the sight, Blythe hesitated for a moment. She feared the mass of humanity would refuse to part for them.

"Damn it, Blythe," Roger whispered, leaning close to her. "Smile, or they'll believe you fear me."

Blythe snapped her head around to look at him. His piercing blue eyes and incredibly handsome face were close to hers; his fresh bay scent incited her to impulsive action. She threw her arms around his neck and planted her closed lips on his.

In an instant Roger encircled her with his arms. He yanked her against the long length of his muscular body.

The crowd went wild, shouting and cheering and whistling and clapping.

Drawing back from her, Roger smiled and waved at the crowd. "I ought to box your ears for that stunt," he whispered.

"Good show, poppet," the earl complimented her, as he waved at the crowd too. "I could not have planned it any better."

Blythe looked at her father in time to see him nod at someone in the crowd. Instantly, a voice shouted, "God bless the Earl of Eden." Then others took up the chanting.

"God bless the Earl of Basildon!"

"Long life to the Earl of Eden!"

"Fruitfulness to Eden and his bride!"

Earl Richard appeared as if he were enjoying himself immensely. He laughed, tossed a handful of gold pieces into the throng, and called, "Long live Elizabeth, Queen of England."

The delighted crowd roared its approval. Only a few feet away their enclosed coach waited to deliver them to the quay. From there the Devereux barge would take them upriver.

Blythe began to panic, fearing they would never reach the coach. Several Devereux footmen hurried forward and made a path for them through the crowd to the coach.

Roger entered first and then helped Blythe inside. Her father gave the crowd a farewell wave, tossed another handful of coins, and joined them.

Blythe sat beside her husband. Earl Richard sat opposite them.

She reached to draw the window's curtain, but her father stayed her hand, saying, " 'Tis imperative that all of London see the three of us together."

The ride to the quay seemed to take forever. Throngs of Londoners, eager to glimpse England's favorite sons, lined the streets and the lanes.

Blythe knew from her father's expression that the morning's events had pleased him. She had no idea what her husband was thinking. He stared straight ahead without saying a word, and she feared speaking to him.

When their barge arrived at Devereux House, the others had already gone inside. Only Lady Keely waited for them at the quay.

Blythe smiled to herself. She knew her mother intended to trick Roger into solemnizing their sacred marriage vows in the

Druid manner. Since her husband was a skeptic, the utmost care needed to be taken to do this without his knowledge.

"All went according to plan," Lady Keely said, smiling at her husband as the trio disembarked. "Don't you think so, dearest?"

"Aye, but I'm relieved 'tis over and done."

"Dearest, would you go inside and play the gracious host?" the countess asked. "I desire a private word with Roger and Blythe."

The earl cocked his brow at her. "Why?"

"Blythe is my firstborn," Lady Keely answered, "and Roger was always my favorite page at court."

"That makes everything perfectly clear to me," Earl Richard teased. He planted a kiss on her cheek and left them.

Lady Keely watched her husband disappear inside the house. Looping one arm through Roger's and the other arm through Blythe's, the countess gently guided them toward the section of the garden where an oak, a birch, and a yew tree stood together like old friends.

"Gentle Roger, words can never express how happy I am that Blythe and you are one," Lady Keely said. She leaned back against the oak tree. "Join your hands please."

Blythe swallowed a smile when Roger opened his mouth to protest, but Lady Keely stopped him by saying, "Humor an old lady. Besides, if not for those ten gold pieces I loaned you when you were twelve, you'd be almost as poor as your brothers."

"Thirty-seven years is not old," Roger insisted, taking Blythe's hand in his.

"Thank you for that," Lady Keely said. "Now, as you know, marriage is a profound commitment that should never be taken lightly."

Blythe glanced at her husband, who appeared to be listening intently to her mother. Her hand in his felt so good. His skin was warm and his grasp firm. Oh, she could hardly wait for night, when her beloved and she would join their bodies into one.

"How long will your union last?" Lady Keely asked.

"I beg your pardon?" Roger asked, apparently surprised by the countess's question.

"Forever and a day," Blythe spoke up.

"Your bride says forever and a day," the countess told him. "Is that acceptable to you?"

Blythe held her breath. If he said yes, they would be married forever. The Great Mother Goddess would see to it.

His lips quirked in obvious amusement. "Forever and a day seems a goodly amount of time," Roger said dryly. "Aye, 'tis acceptable."

"Blythe, is there something you'd like to tell your husband?" her mother asked.

Knowing what was expected of her, Blythe faced Roger and lifted their entwined hands into the air. She raised her gaze to his and said, "May the skies fall down to crush me, may the seas rise up to drown me, may this ancient earth open wide to swallow me if I break faith with you."

"So be it," Lady Keely said, placing her hand on top of theirs.

Their wedding feast was a simple affair. Only the Devereux family and retainers were in attendance, including her mother's Welsh cousins Odo and Hew Lloyd with their Devereux wives, June and May. Daisy Lloyd, Odo's and June's daughter, was the only missing person. She had won the coveted position as Blythe's tirewoman and so had gone ahead to Debrett House with her mistress's belongings.

They dined on Colchester mussels and braised sides of beef, accompanied by a medley of seasonal vegetables. Cheshire cheeses, pine-nut candy, and a single-layer wedding cake were served for dessert.

Blythe felt decidedly uncomfortable sitting in the place of honor with her husband. Although she'd never before had trouble conversing with Roger, her mind remained humiliatingly blank, and he seemed determined to ignore her presence. How embarrassing that he should treat her this rudely on their wedding day.

She knew she was an unwanted bride, but he could at least smile occasionally in her direction.

Life jostles every man, but Roger Debrett has been jostled more than most, her father had warned her. *With your love and patience Roger can be made whole again.*

Determined to put a brave face on this less-than-ideal situation, Blythe summoned her inner reserves of patience and seized the opportunity to study her husband without being observed. Roger sat arrogantly erect, yet relaxed. His profile was pleasingly chiseled and his light-brown hair a mite too long on his neck.

Blythe dropped her gaze to his hands when he reached for his wine. With their long fingers his hands looked strong enough to handle a rapier with deadly ease and expertise, but his touch on the delicate stem of the crystal goblet appeared gentle. Although the thought was wickedly impure, Blythe could hardly wait to feel his hands caressing her.

""How is our Levant Trading Company faring?" Roger was asking her father.

" 'Tis prospering handsomely, probably because Blythe owns several shares and is not competing against us," the earl replied. "Shall we adjourn to my study and read the latest reports on it?"

"Conducting business on your wedding day is deplorable behavior," the Duchess of Ludlow spoke up.

Blythe defended her husband's actions. "Grandmama Chessy, Roger has been away."

Roger snapped his head around to look at her for the first time since sitting down at the table. "I haven't been away," he corrected her. "I've been rotting in the Tower."

The men stood and left the hall. As soon as the Devereux children drifted away with their nursemaid, the duchess rounded on her, saying, "Blythe, darling. I want to give you some practical advice."

"Yes, Grandmama?"

"Most important of all, do *not* refer to me as Grandmama when you go to court," she said. "Call me Aunty Dawn."

Blythe and Bliss looked at each other and giggled. Lady Keely hid her smile behind her hand.

"Always judge a man by what he does, not what he says," her grandmother instructed her. "Watch how Roger treats his daughter and his horses, because he'll treat you no better. Be sure to keep him guessing about your affections. Never be too available."

"And remember this truth above all else," Lady Keely added. "God created woman after man because He wanted to correct the mistakes He'd made on His first attempt."

The duchess chuckled throatily. "Keely, darling," she drawled. "After all these years you've begun to view the world as I do. My wisdom must be contagious."

Blythe smiled at their wit, but the day's events had taken their toll on her. She never realized how much of a battle the relationship between a man and a woman could be. Her head ached from extreme tension and nagging doubts, and she needed to clear the cobwebs from her mind before journeying down the Strand to her new home, Debrett House.

Standing abruptly, Blythe turned to her mother and said, "I-I'd like to walk alone in the garden for a few minutes."

"Of course, dearest," Lady Keely said with an understanding smile.

Leaving the house, Blythe stepped into the deserted garden. Autumn had begun painting its vivid colors within the earthly paradise of her father's garden. Chrysanthemums in a variety of hues adorned the manicured landscape, along with white baby's breath, purple flowering cabbage, pink sweet alyssum, marigold, and snapdragon.

Blythe sighed deeply at the glorious array and crossed the lawns in the direction of her favorite willow tree. The autumnal equinox would be upon them in less than two days, and that would be the first Druidic holiday she would observe in her new home.

And then on the thirty-first day of October came Samhuinn, the beginning of the Druid cycle of life, when the gates of the year opened upon the past and the future. The thin veil between this earthly world and the beyond lifted for exactly three days. This Samhuinn was especially important because she planned to commune with the spirit of her late-grandmother Megan and seek her advice about "the dark sun" that threatened her life with Roger.

Roger. How could she win his love without losing her business profits? Her husband should have been courting her today in order to allay her maidenly fears about their marriage bed. Instead, he'd closeted himself within her father's study, which boded ill for a harmonious union.

Blythe walked beneath the curtain of the willow's sweeping branches. She placed the palms of her hands against its thick trunk and felt its power.

"Thank you for being my friend," she said, and then planted a kiss on the willow's trunk. "I shall miss you as much as you miss me, but I promise to visit whenever I can. One day soon I'll be introducing you to my chil—"

"To whom are you speaking?" asked someone behind her.

Blythe recognized her husband's voice. With a smile of greeting lighting her face, she whirled around. In an instant her smile vanished.

Roger appeared none too happy. In fact, her husband looked damned suspicious. Sacred Saint Swithin, whatever could he be thinking? The expression in his piercing blue eyes boded ill for her tranquillity.

"I'm waiting for an answer," Roger said in a clipped voice.

Blythe leaned back against the willow's trunk and felt it lending her its strength. "I was speaking to this willow," she answered honestly. " 'Tis my favorite tree."

"Try again, my dear," Roger said, cocking a brow at her. "Your lies must have a semblance of truth if you want people to believe them."

"I swear 'tis the truth." Blythe pointed up at the willow's branches. "I passed many enjoyable summer afternoons sitting in its arms." She added, "I suppose I wanted to bid farewell to my childhood. After today my life will be different."

His gaze softened on her. "I have a willow tree in my garden."

"Oh, I must meet—I mean, *see* it," she said.

"My garden has a variety of trees, plants, and flowers," Roger told her. "Gardening relaxes me."

Blythe nodded sagely. " 'Tis good for a man to be well-planted."

Roger smiled at her words, and Blythe felt her legs go weak. Her husband was the most incredibly handsome man she'd ever seen.

"Perhaps you will allow me to help with the gardening," Blythe ventured, returning his smile.

His smile became a wry grin. "Of course. Just as soon as you allow me to help with your businesses."

Blythe frowned at him and then stared down at the ground.

Roger reached out to lift her chin a notch and waited until she lifted her gaze to his. "I'm jesting," he said. "Now we must return to Debrett House. I have hours of work ahead of me. My able competition in the wool and corn trades has placed me in an untenable position."

"Thank you for the praise." Blythe touched his arm and gazed deeply into his piercing blue eyes. "Though leaving my family does sadden me, I'm positive I'll be happy with you at Debrett House."

"Do not bet the company's profits on that," Roger advised.

"I know my purpose in life and will risk all to achieve it," Blythe said, giving him an ambiguous smile. "Only then can the soul enjoy true happiness."

"Would that I knew my purpose," he said in a quiet voice.

"Roger, you must see with your heart to understand that."

"Lady, I have no heart."

Blythe said nothing. Oh, her husband had a heart, all right.

"The coach awaits our pleasure," Roger said, gesturing toward the house.

Blythe nodded. Without permission she looped her arm through his and walked beside him toward the house.

Blythe glanced at the sky overhead and felt hope swelling within her breast. Nary a cloud marred the perfection of the blue horizon or her happiness.

Today Roger and she crossed the lawns together.

Tonight they would worship each other with their bodies to become one.

Tomorrow the eagle and his butterfly would soar across the western horizon toward paradise and beyond.

He abandoned her in the foyer.

When their coach halted in front of Debrett House, Roger climbed out first and then assisted Blythe. Turning toward the mansion, she gazed at her new home and noted its resemblance to Devereux House.

As the Countess of Eden, Blythe was now the lady of this palatial estate. More important, her beloved and she were joined as one in the sight of Goddess, as they had been in so many previous lifetimes.

Together, Roger and Blythe walked toward the mansion's main entrance. The door swung open slowly to reveal a middle-aged man, the Debrett majordomo.

Blythe paused in front of the open door and waited. Tradition required that her husband carry her across the threshold in order to secure good luck for their future.

Surprisingly, Roger walked past her into the foyer and then glanced over his shoulder, asking, "Are you coming inside, or were you considering living in the courtyard?"

Her husband was apparently unfamiliar with that tradition. " 'Tis customary for the groom to carry his bride across the threshold," Blythe informed him.

Roger leveled a cool gaze on her and remained where he stood.

Blythe cocked an ebony brow at him and remained where she stood.

Muttering to himself about the silliness of women, Roger retraced his steps outside. He scooped her into his arms, carried her across the threshold, and unceremoniously set her down inside the foyer.

Blythe suffered the awful feeling that her husband hadn't wanted to touch her.

You insisted before God and man that he keep his hands off your businesses, an inner voice reminded her.

"Welcome home, my lord," the majordomo greeted them.

"Blythe, I present Mr. Bottoms," Roger made the introductions. "Bottoms, this is the Countess of Eden."

Blythe smiled at the highest-ranking servant in Debrett House, but the man's attention had already turned to his master. Feeling like an outsider, she stood quietly and listened to her husband.

"Have my agents arrived?" Roger was asking.

"Yes, my lord. They are gathered in the hall."

"Good. Send them one by one to my study in the order in which they arrived today." Roger flicked a glance at Blythe and added, "Except for my corn and wool agents. I'll speak with them first. Everyone else must wait his turn."

Marching down the corridor to his study, Roger called over his shoulder as an afterthought, "See that the countess gets settled." Then he disappeared from sight.

Blushing hotly with embarrassment, Blythe looked at the majordomo. He seemed at a loss for words. She felt like a damned fool to be standing there in her wedding gown while her husband had obviously abandoned her.

Blythe caught the majordomo casting an anxious glance in the hall's direction. Apparently, the poor man had no idea what he should do first.

"Of course, his lordship's needs take precedence over mine," Blythe said, taking pity on the man.

The majordomo cast her a grateful smile.

"Where is my tirewoman?"

"Upstairs, my lady. I'd be honored to escort you there."

"Directions will suffice."

"Your chamber is the last door on the right upstairs," the majordomo told her.

"Thank you, Mr. Bottoms." She turned to climb the stairs, embarrassed that a servant should witness the extent of her husband's disregard for her.

Blythe started to walk down the second-floor corridor. A man's and a woman's voices raised in argument emanated from behind one of the closed doors. Blythe thought nothing of it, but the farther she walked down the corridor, the louder the voices got.

Entering the last door on the right, Blythe found herself in an enormous, ornately decorated chamber. Where was Daisy Lloyd? And then those angry voices reached her again. One sounded exactly like Daisy's.

Blythe spied an open door on the opposite side of the bedchamber and hurried in the direction of her kinswoman's voice. She paused in the doorway to listen to their argument.

"I already told you," the man said, clearly annoyed. "Her belongings should be settled in the other chamber."

"Isn't *this* the earl's bedchamber?" Daisy challenged him, her hands resting on her hips.

"The earl sent me specific instructions," the man explained. "She's to sleep in her own chamber."

"The Countess of Eden is not a *she*," Daisy snapped. "Show proper respect when you refer to my lady."

"*I* am the earl's personal servant and take precedence over you," the man replied. "If you don't care for the arrangements, take it up with his lord—"

"Kiss my feet, Hardwick!"

The man's face mottled with anger. " 'Tis *Mister* Hardwick to you."

"Mister Hardwick, is it?" Daisy shot back. "Ha! Looks to me like you have *no wick*, never mind a hard one."

"'Tis enough, Daisy," Blythe ordered, stepping into the chamber.

"And who are—" Hardwick's gaze dropped to her wedding gown.

"I am the Countess of Eden."

"My lady, I apologize for my tone of voice," Hardwick said.

"You'd better be sorry," Daisy piped up.

"I forgive you," Blythe said, and then threw him off balance by gifting him with her sunniest smile. "What is the problem, Mr. Hardwick?"

"His lordship instructed me to prepare the other chamber for you," he explained. "'Tis tradition in the Debrett family. His lordship's mother had that chamber and Lady Dar—"

"I wouldn't wish to break with tradition," Blythe interrupted him. "Daisy, settle my belongings in the other chamber."

"The earl has a lopsided view of marriage," Daisy grumbled, marching back to the other chamber.

Blythe slid her gaze from her tirewoman to her husband's servant. His expression on Daisy told her that he'd love to box the girl's ears. And then it changed suddenly, warming to something more intense than annoyance.

Blythe glanced from Hardwick to Daisy and then back again. The man appeared mesmerized by the angry sway of Daisy Lloyd's hips.

"My thanks for your assistance," Blythe said, suppressing a smile. She closed the connecting door, and pasting a suitably reproachful look on her face, turned to her tirewoman.

Daisy gave "the fig" to the closed door and then winked at her.

Blythe giggled, and then hugged her favorite third cousin. "Oh, I am ever so glad you agreed to accompany me to Debrett House."

"Well, I couldn't let Cousin Daffy take my place," Daisy said.

Though younger than her mistress by six months, Daisy Lloyd appeared several years older. Brown-haired and brown-eyed, she was buxomly built and blessed with a contagious smile.

"Mr. Hardwick is a very attractive man," Blythe remarked as her cousin carried several gowns into the tiny dressing closet off the bedchamber.

"That old f—"

"He appears of an age with my lord husband," Blythe interrupted whatever vulgarity her cousin would have uttered.

"Sorry," Daisy said, flashing her a repentant grin.

"Have you brought my business ledgers and ceremonial objects?"

"I put them in the desk."

Blythe scanned the chamber. On one side of the room stood an enormous four-poster curtained bed with heavy draperies. The hearth had been built into the opposite wall, and two chairs sat in front of it. Near one of the windows was an oak desk.

The chamber's accessories were entirely too ornate and the deep burgundy of the draperies too dark. Blythe wondered idly if the room reflected Darnel Howard or Roger's mother. She preferred much lighter colors and at first opportunity would ask her husband's permission to redecorate.

Blythe wandered across the chamber to the window and smiled at what she saw.

"Daisy, my chamber faces the east, so I'll be able to worship properly," she called to her cousin. "And below is the garden. I can even see the stableyard over yonder."

"Very nice, indeed," Daisy agreed, sounding unimpressed. "Let me help you out of that gown."

Daisy unfastened the row of tiny pearl buttons that ran the length of the wedding gown and then helped her mistress step out of it. She handed Blythe a silken wrapper and took the wedding gown into the dressing room.

"Supper is served at six o'clock," Daisy said, walking back into the chamber. "You should rest until then."

"I shan't need your services until the morning," Blythe told her. "See to your own needs."

"Whatever flips your skirt up," Daisy said with a smile. And then she disappeared out the door.

Too excited to rest, Blythe wandered around the chamber, but constantly returned to look out the window. She could hardly wait until the morning when she'd be able to explore the garden.

At precisely six o'clock Blythe left her chamber. She wore a violet silk gown with a low-cut neckline in keeping with her new status as a wife. She didn't think Roger would appreciate his bride wearing a virginal high neckline to their wedding supper.

Blythe stood uncertainly in the entrance to the nearly deserted great hall. Her husband was nowhere in sight and she wondered if she should return to her chamber until someone summoned her.

"Good evening, my lady," Mr. Bottoms called, rushing across the hall to her side.

Blythe smiled. "Where is my lord?"

"He's still working in his study," the majordomo told her, "but I'm certain he'll be along shortly. Let me escort you to the table."

Walking the long length of the torchlit hall, Blythe spied two portraits hanging on one of the walls and paused to inspect them. A dark-haired, swarthy man with a somber expression stared at her from one painting. The other portrait was of a fair-complexioned woman with lively blue eyes and a mysterious smile.

"Who are they?" Blythe asked.

"His lordship's parents," Mr. Bottoms answered.

"So Roger and Geoffrey resemble their mother," Blythe said softly. "Cedric has the look of his father."

Mr. Bottoms escorted Blythe to the high table. No sooner had she been seated than a footman appeared in the hall and whispered in the majordomo's ear.

"My lord sends his regrets," Mr. Bottoms said. "His lordship needs to sup while he works, but promises to see you directly when he's finished."

Blythe managed a faint smile and nodded. She wanted no one

to guess that her heart had just sunk to her stomach. Was her husband getting even for her undercutting his wool and corn prices?

Feeling conspicuous, Blythe sat alone at the high table during supper but ate very little. Her head ached from her husband's rejection, and what she wanted most was to escape this humiliating scene.

Blythe stood abruptly, and the majordomo rushed to assist her. "Sir, I commend your impeccable service," she said. "If you ever leave Lord Roger's employ, I'm positive you will find a position of honor at Devereux House."

Mr. Bottoms smiled at her compliment. "Shall I escort you upstairs, my lady?"

"I know the way." With her head held proudly high, Blythe left the hall. The last thing she wanted was a majordomo escorting her to bed on her wedding night.

Reaching her chamber, Blythe found her nightshift lying across the bed. She undressed and slipped it over her head, then stepped in front of the mirror to study her image.

The gauzy nightshift was virtually transparent. For all that it covered she might as well be wearing nothing.

And that fact made Blythe smile. Her husband wouldn't be able to ignore her once he saw her dressed in this nightshift.

Uncertain of what to do while she awaited his arrival, Blythe wandered across the chamber to the window and gazed at the night sky. A solitary star shone in the black velvet sky. For some reason that image of loneliness reminded her of her husband.

After a time Blythe heard muffled voices inside her husband's chamber. Too nervous to stand still, she padded on bare feet to the connecting door and listened. One voice belonged to Roger and the other to Mr. Hardwick. Abruptly, the talking ceased. She heard a door click shut and then her husband moving around his chamber.

Soon Roger will walk through this door and make me his in fact as well as name, Blythe thought. Anticipation made her heart pound faster, and her breathing came in shallow gasps. If only he'd passed the afternoon courting her, she wouldn't be this frightened.

Blythe stared at the door for what seemed like an eternity. And then the sounds of movement from the other chamber ceased. What was he doing?

Backing away from the door lest he surprise her, Blythe sat in the chair in front of the hearth. For one hour she fixed her gaze on the connecting door and waited. Was she expected to go to him? She couldn't endure this waiting any longer.

Summoning her courage, Blythe rose from the chair and crossed the chamber. With a badly shaking hand she reached out and opened the door.

Blythe spied her husband immediately. With his back turned to her, Roger sat in the chair in front of his hearth.

"My lord?" Blythe called in a loud whisper.

Roger bolted out of his chair and whirled around. "Why aren't you sleeping?" he demanded.

"I-I've been waiting for you."

Blythe watched his piercing blue gaze drop from her face to travel the length of her scantily clad body, lingering on the swell of her breasts and the curves of her hips. Lord, but she felt like a horse he was considering purchasing. Would he next cross the chamber and insist on examining her teeth? Or was he comparing her with Darnel Howard? If so, would he find her lacking?

When his gaze returned to hers, Blythe recognized the heated interest in it before he shuttered all emotion from his expression.

"Return to your chamber," Roger ordered, his voice mirroring weariness. "I have no intention of bedding you tonight."

Blythe flinched as if she'd been struck and, in an aching whisper, reminded him, "You vowed before God to worship me with your body."

"I lied," Roger said, his gaze on her colder than the north wind in winter.

"But—"

"Get out, damn it."

Blythe scurried back to the safety of her own chamber and

slammed the door behind her. Trying to put as much distance between them as possible, she raced across the chamber to the window.

Blythe bowed her head as tears streamed down her cheeks. Surrendering to her sobs, she cleansed her injured soul of the day's myriad disappointments.

When her tears subsided, Blythe became aware of an insistent tapping. She looked up and saw raindrops on the windowpane. That lonely star had vanished behind a shroud of clouds.

"Great Mother Goddess, pass your wisdom through me," Blythe prayed, placing the palm of her right hand against the window. "Help Saint Swithin send his winds of love to Roger and me."

Unfortunately, the Great Mother Goddess kept her wisdom to herself that night, and Saint Swithin's loving winds remained stilled. A familiar voice did echo within her mind, penetrating her misery to offer her hope.

With your patience and love Roger can be made whole, sounded the voice of her pragmatic father.

"Oh, Papa, 'tis easy for you to say," Blythe whispered to the empty chamber. "I am the one who must conquer the cherished memory of Darnel Howard."

Chapter 4

Blythe awakened during those hushed magical moments before dawn. She yawned, stretched, and then rose from her lonely bed.

Ignoring September's early-morning chill, Blythe padded on bare feet across the chamber to the window. Like her mother before her, she always greeted the dawn.

Blythe opened the shutters and saw the eastern horizon ablaze with orange light as dawn rapidly approached. Trying to get closer to the rising sun, she opened the window and leaned forward.

"Father Sun kisses Mother Earth," Blythe murmured the chant her mother had taught her. She closed her eyes for a brief moment and prayed, "Great Mother Goddess and Saint Swithin, let this be the day my husband and I become one."

Blythe opened her eyes and watched the bright streaks of orange light reaching over the horizon for the world of men. The rising sun, different each day of the year, seemed especially inspiring on this September morn.

And thee I chuse.

Blythe fingered the jeweled cross of Wotan nesting against the swell of her breasts. Roger had already decided his path five years earlier. Why did he fail to recognize that truth? Yes, his rejection hurt her feelings, but her eagle had somehow been injured and needed her sunshine in order to heal.

Blythe dropped her gaze from the sky's vast horizon to the

river. The mist shrouding the banks of the Thames was beginning to recede beneath the rays of the newly risen sun. Intending to return to bed, she started to turn away from the window, but a dark figure caught her attention.

Dressed completely in black, Roger sauntered up the path from the stables. He carried what appeared to be gardening tools.

Lest he spy her at the window, Blythe stepped back a pace to watch. He set the gardening tools down on the lawn and stole a moment to wander about, apparently greeting the plants and the flowers he hadn't seen since the previous April. His touch on them appeared gentle and as reverent as a Druid approaching a tree.

Ready to work, Roger removed his black leather jerkin and tossed it aside.

Grabbing his gardening tools, he advanced on the rosebush near the house and set about preparing it for winter. He touched it like a father stroking a favored child and, if she wasn't mistaken, moved his lips as if soothing the rosebush in a hushed whisper.

Blythe delighted in his gentility. Heaven reserved a special place for a well-planted man.

Dropping her gaze from his face, Blythe admired his broad shoulders and his back, which tapered to a narrow waist. His thighs, covered by tight-fitting breeches, appeared well-formed. Her husband was a perfect specimen of manhood as his sinuous muscles flexed with his movements. Pausing a moment, Roger stood statue-still to inspect his work.

And then Blythe noticed the pretty butterfly flitting through the air near the rosebush. She held her left hand palm outward toward her husband's willow tree and, using her right index finger, touched her heart and her lips.

"O ancient willow of this ancient earth, older than I can tell," she whispered. "Help me weave the magic of this natural spell."

Blythe pointed her index finger outward toward her husband's right side, and the butterfly landed upon his right shoulder. Roger looked at it and gently brushed it off.

Blythe smiled and pointed her finger toward his left side, and the butterfly alighted on his left shoulder. Roger looked to his left and again gently flicked it off his shoulder.

Blythe felt her merriment bubbling up as a naughty imp entered her soul. She pointed her finger at the top of her husband's head. Flitting above him, the butterfly landed on it.

"Good Christ!" she heard him exclaim.

Unable to control herself another moment, Blythe burst out laughing, and Roger whirled around in surprise, his gaze darting to her open window. Wearing her sunniest smile, Blythe leaned forward and gave her husband a spectacular view of her ivory breasts above the provocative neckline of her nightshift.

"Good morning, my lord," she called.

"Good morning, my lady," Roger called, inclining his head. He smiled at her, a sight she hadn't seen in more than five years.

Morning becomes her, Roger thought as he stared up at his bride. She appeared as happy as a butterfly flitting about the Garden of Eden. Apparently, she harbored no anger concerning his behavior the previous night. Perhaps his plan to win his freedom would work.

And then another thought popped into his mind. Hadn't his rejection angered her? Was there some other young man whom she would have preferred marrying? That she seemed almost relieved by his rejection was highly insulting.

She was smiling down at him, her special smile that had always made him feel loved and accepted. The sunshine in her expression warmed his heart.

"I thought I felt watching eyes," Roger said.

"My lord, you are up and about very early," Blythe remarked.

"And so are you."

"I always greet the dawn," she told him. " 'Tis my favorite moment of the day."

"I also enjoy the morning's stillness," Roger said. "Hope pervades the air."

Blythe gazed toward the landscaped grounds and returned her attention to him, saying, "Your garden is exquisitely beautiful."

"I thank you," Roger replied, surveying her with the same interest with which she had surveyed his garden.

The most incredible violet eyes he'd ever seen lit her whole expression. Her face was hauntingly lovely, and the color upon her cheeks was high. Her seductive nightgown displayed her breasts to best advantage, and her dusky nipples taunted him through the gauzy, almost transparent material.

Roger felt his manhood tingle and stretch. With an inward groan, he closed his eyes against the provocative sight. Knowing that she was his for the taking, how would he survive her presence in his house?

Oh, he desired her, all right.

"I can hardly wait to see this paradise in summer," Blythe was saying. "I do love roses."

Roger looked from her to the rosebush. His gaze fell on a ladder propped against the side of the house.

After gifting her with his devastating smile, Roger turned to the rosebush and plucked one of its last blossoms. Then he lifted the ladder upright against the house below her window and began to climb. When he stood on the upper rungs, he was eye-level with her breasts.

"For you, my lady," Roger said, offering her the rose.

"Thank you, my lord," Blythe said, accepting it, the brilliance in her smile nearly blinding him.

" 'Tis my pleasure."

For a long, long moment they stared into each other's eyes. Her faint rose scent wafted like an invisible cloud around him, beckoning him to kiss her. Roger suffered the almost overpowering urge to climb through the window and make passionate love to her.

"Would you care to come inside?" Blythe asked as if she'd read his thoughts.

Roger peeked past her into the bedchamber and spied the rumpled bed. His breath caught raggedly in his throat at the thought of embedding himself within the soft folds of her womanhood.

"Another time, perhaps," he said, refusing her invitation. "I would speak with you later in my study."

Blythe cast him a smile meant to seduce. "That can be arranged."

"Shall we say ten o'clock?"

She inclined her head in agreement.

Reluctant to climb down the ladder and leave her presence, Roger prolonged the moment by asking, "And how will you idle the hours away until ten, little butterfly?"

"Return to my bed and sleep."

"Then I'll leave you to your slumber and do wish you pleasant dreams."

Blythe leaned forward, her breasts so close he could have dropped a kiss on each. "If my dreams be pleasant," she said in a whisper, "your image will fill each and every one of them."

Escaping her and her oh-so-tempting breasts, Roger began to climb down the ladder. He stopped in his descent when she called to him.

"My lord?"

Roger paused and looked up. "Yes?"

Blythe stared at him blankly for a long moment. Finally, she blushed and giggled, saying, "I have forgotten why I called you back."

"I won't move until you remember," he said.

"Your nearness will keep me from remembering," Blythe told him.

"Then I'll still stay and await your memory's return," Roger said with a teasing smile. "Perhaps I'll pass the remainder of my days with my little butterfly here within my garden."

"Your rosebush does demand your attention," Blythe said, "and my comfortable bed does call to me. Farewell until the hour of ten, my lord."

Roger inclined his head. "Until ten, my lady."

Roger gave her a final smile and then forced himself to return to his gardening. For fifteen excruciatingly long minutes he worked on his rosebush, but his mind climbed the ladder to lie beside his bride in her bed. Unable to control the impulse, he peeked at her window, but she had disappeared inside.

Roger stared at the window. All he needed to do was climb that ladder and tell her he'd changed his mind. And then what? His life would undoubtedly be miserable again.

Determined to resist her siren's call, Roger depleted every ounce of strength he possessed. Finally, he tossed his gardening tools down on the ground and marched in the direction of the stables. A few moments of pleasure weren't worth surrendering his peace of mind.

He was going to apologize to her.

At precisely two minutes before ten o'clock Blythe touched the jeweled cross of Wotan and stole one final peek at herself in the mirror. She smoothed an imagined wrinkle from the skirt of her gown and decided to make this meeting as easy as possible for her husband. Poor Roger had lost his first wife and then passed five months in the Tower of London. Apologizing for his behavior the previous night would be difficult for him. She would be as gracious and pleasant as she could.

"Wish me luck," she said to her image, and then headed for the door.

Blythe hurried down the corridor to the stairs. She refused to be even one moment late; men loved punctuality. When she reached the foyer below, Blythe marched down the corridor to her husband's study, but paused in indecision outside the closed door.

Deciding not to knock, Blythe pasted a sunny smile onto her face and reached for the doorknob. "Good morning," she called, breezing into the chamber.

Seated behind his desk, Roger looked up in surprise when she entered. Out of habit, he bolted to his feet and cast her a smile.

Blythe noted that he'd shaved and changed his gardening attire into more formal garb. Renewed hope surged through her as his blue gaze perused her body from her face to the tips of her toes and then back again. Yes, her husband regretted his behavior of the previous night. First he would apologize to her, and surely then he would make love to her.

"Sit down, child," Roger invited her.

Child?

Blythe ignored his poor choice of words and sat in the chair in front of his desk. She took a moment to arrange her skirt and then gazed at hm.

Roger sat down. "And were your dreams pleasant?"

"Yes, and you appeared in each one of them," Blythe answered.

Her husband frowned as if displeased by his presence in her dreams. He opened his mouth to speak, but Blythe's nervous tongue was faster.

" 'Tis Alex's birthday today," she announced. "We should plan something special to commemorate it."

Roger narrowed his gaze on her. "Who is Alex?"

"Alexander the Great, of course. Don't you remember?" she asked. "The twentieth day of September marks his birth."

"Many a year has passed since I studied history," Roger replied, a smile flirting with his lips.

"We must never forget the lessons of history lest we repeat our mistakes." Blythe cast him a purposefully ambiguous smile. Allowing him time to summon his courage and apologize to her, she glanced at her surroundings.

Rows of books lined two walls from floor to ceiling, and a third wall sported a hearth. Perched in front of the darkened hearth were two comfortable-looking chairs. The fourth wall, behind her husband's desk, had two windows that allowed sunlight to filter inside.

"Oh, I shall definitely enjoy working in this room," Blythe said. "Your essence clings to everything."

Roger snapped his brows together. "What do you mean by 'work'?"

"I need a place to conduct my business dealings," she explained. " 'Twouldn't be proper for my agents to visit me in my bedchamber, and the great hall would be too distracting. Also—"

"Be quiet, child."

"I beg your pardon?"

"I haven't summoned you here for social conversation," Roger told her. "We must discuss a subject more serious than that."

Blythe inclined her head. Apologizing was no easy task for any man, never mind an eagle like her husband.

"Feel free to say whatever you wish," she said in an effort to help him. "After all, I am your wife."

"Wife!" Roger exclaimed. "That *wife* is the very topic I wish to discuss."

Blythe said nothing.

Roger cleared his throat. He rose from his chair and walked around his desk. Leaning against the edge of it, he folded his arms across his chest and stared at her.

"As you know, the purpose of our marriage was to gain my release from the Tower," he began. "I had no desire to marry again. One wife was more than enough."

Feeling the first stirrings of unease, Blythe dropped her gaze to her hands folded in her lap. This didn't sound like the preamble to an apology.

"The age difference between us is great," Roger went on.

Blythe looked up and dismissed his words with a gesture of her hand. "Twelve years hardly signifies," she said. "My grandfather is sixty-two and his wife is only a shade above forty."

Roger's lips quirked at her lie. "I'd already bedded my first woman before you were born," he countered. "I could have sired you."

Feeling her cheeks grow warm, Blythe groaned inwardly. Blushing was childish. She wanted to appear more womanly.

"Love does not exist," Roger continued. " 'Tis a figment of idle brains."

"My lord, what is it you wish to say?" Blythe asked, becoming irritated by his hedging.

"Simply this." Roger looked away and said, "Our marriage will remain unconsummated. Once I discover who murdered Darnel, you may annul me and marry one of the young swains who—I'm positive—pursued you before our betrothal."

"I have no desire to annul you," Blythe cried, leaping out of her chair.

Roger frowned. "Then I will annul you."

Blythe felt her heart sinking to her stomach. Now that she had him, she refused to let him go. Perhaps there was something wrong with her that needed improving.

"My lord, is . . . is aught wrong with me?" she asked in an aching whisper.

"No, you are a sweet child."

"I am *no* child."

"Compared to me, you are practically a newborn," Roger said.

"Oh, really?" Blythe arched an ebony brow at him. "Shall I disrobe and prove my womanhood? You certainly appeared interested in my breasts this morning."

Roger flushed. "You are dismissed," he said, his voice stern.

Dismissed?

How dare he! Her husband had many lessons to learn, and she was just the woman to teach him.

Squaring her shoulders, Blythe walked proudly to the door, but paused before leaving and turned around to face him. "My lord, there will be no annulment. Five lonely months in the Tower have apparently impaired your thinking," she said, unable to control her rising anger. "To cure your confusion, sit beneath that birch tree in your garden."

Roger stared at her blankly.

"When we lose our way in the forest, the shining white of the birch lights the way and leads us on our true path."

"You speak in riddles."

"Having reached the venerable age of thirty, you should understand my words," Blythe countered. "You know everything else, or think you do." And then she breezed out of the study, leaving her husband to wonder if he'd just been insulted.

Upstairs, Blythe marched into her chamber and slammed the door, startling Daisy, who was straightening her mistress's belongings. Ignoring her tirewoman, Blythe crossed the chamber to gaze out the window. The morning's brilliant sun had disappeared behind a shroud of clouds.

Sacred Saint Swithin, she'd married a man who refused to touch her. If only she could entice him into her bed, Roger would realize that she was a woman. And how was she to accomplish that? She'd never even kissed a man, never mind seduced one.

"What's wrong?" Daisy asked, standing beside her.

"My husband and I are in discord," Blythe answered.

"Already?"

Blythe nodded.

"About what?"

Blythe blushed but answered honestly, "My husband refuses to bed me."

Daisy dropped her mouth open in surprise. For once in her life she was speechless.

Blythe cast her a sidelong glance. "Any suggestions, cousin?"

"Gawd, no. I never heard of a man who refused to futter," Daisy answered, finding her voice through her shock. "I always heard the opposite about men. They never say no to futtering."

"How comforting to learn that my husband is unique among men," Blythe said glumly.

And then an outrageous idea popped into her mind. She had no knowledge of seduction, but she knew someone who had practically written the book on the art of love and flirtation.

"Tell Bottoms to send word to the stables that I want Achilles saddled and awaiting me in the courtyard in fifteen minutes," Blythe ordered, rounding on the other girl.

"You aren't running home, are you?"

"No, I'm going visiting for an hour or two."

Daisy left to do her bidding, and Blythe stared out the window again. Grandmama Chessy—"Aunty Dawn," as she wished to be called—had managed to entice four men into marriage, never mind her countless flirtations. Blythe would visit this fabled expert on men and beg her advice.

Fifteen minutes later Blythe hurried downstairs to the foyer. She reached for the doorknob, but a hand covered hers and prevented her escape.

Blythe gasped in surprise and whirled around.

"Where do you think you're going?" Roger demanded, a fierce scowl darkening his expression.

Blythe felt hopelessly confused. "I beg your pardon?"

"You heard me," Roger said, placing the palms of his hands against the door on either side of her head, trapping her there. "Never answer my questions with questions of your own."

"I'm going out," she told him.

"To rendezvous with an admirer and bring dishonor on the Debrett name?" he asked. "Tell me the truth, lady. I'll know if you are lying."

Blythe was stunned. "I-I don't understand."

"Come, lady. A lovely young woman like you must have had dozens of swains courting her favor," Roger went on. "I know your father forced you to the altar, else you would never have agreed to this match."

Blythe relaxed. Her husband was jealous of nonexistent rivals for her affection. Yet, what incited such terrible suspicions against women in him?

"Gentle Roger," Blythe said, touching his arm, "I am riding to Talbot House to bid farewell to my grandparents. They leave for court tomorrow."

Blythe felt her heart lurch as her husband closed his eyes against his obvious embarrassment. He sighed, dropped his hands, and stepped back a pace.

"I apologize," Roger said simply.

" 'Twas a misunderstanding and entirely my fault," she replied, giving him a sunny smile. "I should have told you my intent."

"Do you require an escort?"

Blythe shook her head. "Talbot House is merely three doors down the Strand. Unless an escort would make *you* feel better?"

"I have accounts that demand my attention," Roger said, shuttering all expression from his face. "Do what you will. You are not a prisoner in my home." Without another word he retreated down the corridor to his study.

Our home, Blythe corrected him. A smile kissed the corners of her lips as she watched him retrace his steps. With her grandmother's assistance she would soon be one with her eagle.

"Aunty Dawn?" Blythe called, entering the great hall at Talbot House.

"Darling, I'm here."

Blythe hurried toward the two enormous chairs set in front of the hearth on the far side of the hall. Walking around them, she managed a smile of greeting for the two older women who sat there.

The auburn-haired and brown-eyed Duchess of Ludlow, her stepgrandmother, was voluptuous of figure. When she smiled as she did now, two dimples decorated her cheeks and made her appear much younger than her fifty years. She wore a red and gold brocaded gown, more suitable for a court gala than an afternoon in front of the hearth. Diamonds and gold draped her neck, earlobes, and fingers.

Lady Tessie Pines occupied the second chair. Her grandmother's longtime crony was short, blond, and talkative.

"Why did she call you 'Aunty Dawn'?" Lady Tessie asked.

"She's practicing for court," the duchess answered. "I don't relish being called a grandmother in front of every courtier there."

"You look especially well considering the wild midnight ride you took last night," Lady Tessie remarked to Blythe, winking suggestively at her.

Uncertain of what she meant, Blythe stared at her blankly.

The two older women looked at each other and giggled like young girls.

"Darling, you seem a bit under the eaves," the duchess remarked. "Roger didn't keep you awake *all* night, did he?"

Reluctant to discuss her problem in front of anyone but family, Blythe hesitated in answering. She supposed there was no help for it without being rude to Lady Pines. Besides, Lady Tessie had always boasted about her victories in the gentle battles she'd fought with the opposite sex. Perhaps the lady would have a few suggestions that would help solve her problem.

"Lord Roger did keep me awake most of the night, but not in the manner you think," Blythe said.

"What do you mean?" her grandmother asked.

"My husband and I are in discord," Blythe admitted.

"Already?" the two women exclaimed.

"Dearie, men are like imported carpets," Lady Tessie said. "If you lay your husband correctly the first time, you can walk all over him."

" 'Tis precisely my problem," Blythe blurted out. "My husband refuses to lay me, and I need advice on how to seduce him."

"You've certainly come to the right woman for advice about that," the Duchess of Ludlow drawled.

"Women," Lady Tessie corrected her.

"Pour yourself a goblet of cider, my poor darling, while Tessie and I consider this astonishing situation," her grandmother said.

Blythe nodded and crossed the chamber to the high table. More impressive than her husband's hall, the Talbot great hall sported two massive hearths, one at each end. Overhead were heavy-beamed rafters, from which hung myriad Talbot banners. Brass sconces and vivid tapestries, most depicting the hunt, decorated the walls. One tapestry was different from the others, its motif being a maiden and a unicorn sitting together.

Forgetting her cider, Blythe walked toward the tapestry. That particular one always called out to her and invited her touch. Grandmother Megan, her maternal grandmother, a woman she'd never known in this life, had made it for her grandfather almost forty years earlier.

Blythe closed her eyes and placed the palm of her right hand against the tapestry. She felt her grandmother's essence dwelling within it, and a soft smile kissed her lips.

Find happiness with the soaring eagle in the Place of the Winds. Beware the dark sun.

Her mother's prophecy popped into her mind. Blythe knew her Grandmother Megan's spirit was near.

Come Samhuinn she would call down the elements and speak to her. Grandmother Megan would know what the dark sun was.

"Darling!"

Grandmama Chessy's voice intruded on her thoughts. Turning away from the tapestry, Blythe hurried across the hall toward the hearth. Oh, the Goddess had blessed her doubly by giving her two maternal grandmothers, one in this world and one in the unseen world. She felt better already.

"Tessie and I discussed several aphrodisiacs," Lady Dawn began.

"Such as?" Blythe asked.

"Cockle bread works quite effectively," the duchess said. "Knead a small piece of dough and press it to your privates. Then bake the mold and serve it to Roger. He will immediately fall under your spell."

Blythe crimsoned in horrified embarrassment. "I don't think—isn't there another way?"

"Albertus Magnus," Lady Tessie told her.

"What's that?"

"Brains of partridge calcinated into powder and swallowed in red wine."

Blythe gulped back her sudden nausea and shook her head.

"Alcohol does provoke desire," the duchess told her. "Unfortunately, it also impedes performance."

"There's always candied sea-holly roots or pansy juice rubbed on the eyelids of a sleeping person," Lady Tessie suggested.

"Perhaps we should save the aphrodisiacs as a last resort," the duchess said.

"Then how shall I get Roger to bed me?" Blythe cried.

"Darling, tell me exactly what happened," her grandmother ordered.

"You mean what *didn't* happen," Lady Tessie interjected.

"Shut those lips," the duchess ordered her friend. Then she turned to her granddaughter and waited for her to speak.

"Two times Roger did gaze at me through eyes mirroring his desire," Blythe told her. "Though I invited him into my bed, he emphatically refused and called me a child."

"Darling, you haven't been listening to my words of wisdom," her grandmother chided her. "Only yesterday I told you to watch what a man does, not what he says, didn't I?"

"Yes, you did."

"Roger cannot deny his desire forever," the duchess said. "Proud man that he is, your husband was forced by terrible circumstances into this marriage. He harbors an anger for feeling powerless, not for you."

"So what am I to do?" Blythe asked, her frustration getting the better of her. She could, in theory, be an old woman before her husband surrendered to his desire.

"Go home and be merry," the duchess instructed her. "Flirt with your husband. Visit him in his chamber each morning and each evening. Wear gowns as light as the air and more transparent than a gossamer butterfly's wings."

Blythe smiled at the image.

"Kindness could work a miracle with Debrett," Lady Tessie spoke up. "Your husband grew from childhood to manhood without a mother's love, and his first wife was certainly *not* the kindest of women."

"Lady Darnel was unkind to him?" Blythe echoed, pouncing on that bit of information. "What else do you know about her?"

"Nothing much," Lady Tessie answered with a shrug.

"Spreading gossip is a deplorable activity in which I never engage."

"What a liar you are." The duchess chuckled at her friend's innocent expression and then looked at her granddaughter, insisting, "Knowledge of his first marriage is unnecessary, darling. If Roger realizes you know about his unhappy past, he could harbor suspicions about your intent. Feeling pitied is the greatest shriveler of men, if you know what I mean."

"But I don't know what you mean," Blythe replied, unaccountably making the two older women dissolve into a fit of giggles.

"And may you never have occasion to understand those words," her grandmother said.

"Go home and taunt Roger with your gentle presence," Lady Tessie advised.

"Darling, court your husband," the duchess added. "But remember this: A fine line exists between being kind and being taken for granted."

Blythe felt heartened by their advice and their confidence in her. "I haven't given Roger his wedding gift yet," she remarked.

"No!" the two older women cried in obvious horror.

Surprised by their outcry, Blythe leaped back a pace. "What's wrong?" she asked.

"Never give a man a gift," the duchess ordered.

"Men are supposed to give gifts to you," Lady Tessie added.

"You always give Grandpapa a birthday and a New Year's gift," Blythe said.

"And you will give Roger gifts once he's professed his love and taken you into his bed," her grandmother replied. "On second thought, a gift could work a miracle with Roger. Since his mother's death, I doubt any woman has given him a gift. 'Tis certain Darnel Howard never gave him anything but his daughter."

"I strongly doubt any of his mistresses gave him gifts," Lady Tessie agreed.

"My husband keeps mistresses?" Blythe echoed, shocked.

The Duchess of Ludlow rounded on her friend and cast her a deadly look.

" 'Twas long before he married you," Lady Tessie amended. "All that is now in his past."

"Darling, trust your female instincts," the duchess said with a smile. "If kindness and tantalizing clothing don't work, we'll speak about aphrodisiacs."

"Perhaps I should seek my mother's counsel," Blythe said.

The Duchess of Ludlow burst out laughing. "Your mother never seduced a man in her life."

"What about Papa?"

"Your father seduced her," the duchess said with a soft smile of remembrance. "Of course, the poor man needed my expert strategic advice. My wisdom did not fail him then, nor will it fail you now."

"I'm so glad Grandpapa Talbot chose you for his wife," Blythe said.

"Darling, I chose him," the duchess corrected her.

Blythe smiled. She curtsied to Lady Tessie, kissed her grandmother's cheek, and hurried out of the hall. She was eager to try her new wisdom on her reluctant husband.

Encouraged by her visit to Talbot House, Blythe rode up the lane that led to Debrett House. The sun peeked out from behind its cloud cover as if agreeing with her lightened mood.

Blythe dismounted and waved the waiting groomsman away. In keeping with an ancient Welsh custom her mother had taught her, Blythe intended to bless her marriage by walking Achilles through her husband's home. Good luck would follow the horse and stay inside forever.

Ignoring the groom's astonished stare, Blythe grasped the reins and led her horse toward the door. The dinner hour had come and gone. She needn't worry about offending her husband's sensibilities by parading her horse through his hall while he ate.

"Come, Achilles," Blythe said. She opened the door, led the

horse into the foyer, and then looked in surprise toward the stairs.

"You mentioned your name was Dick," Daisy Lloyd was saying as she marched down the stairs behind the earl's personal servant.

"I never gave you permission to use it," the man insisted.

"Dick Hardwick is a fine name," Daisy replied, then dissolved into giggles.

"I said, call me Mister—"

At the same moment Daisy and Hardwick saw Blythe standing in the foyer with her horse. Daisy's mouth formed a perfect *O* of surprise. Mr. Hardwick wasn't quite as silent.

"Lord Roger! Mr. Bottoms!" the man shouted, running in the direction of the hall's entrance.

"Pipe down, Hardwick," Blythe ordered. "You'll make Achilles nervous."

With her horse in tow Blythe marched around the inside perimeter of the great hall. Just as she completed her tour and reached the entrance, her husband walked into the hall.

"Holy horseshit!" Roger swore.

Blythe stopped short. Dropping the reins, she paused a moment to look at the floor behind her horse and then flushed with embarrassment.

"Oh, I'm sorry," she apologized. "I never imagined Achilles would have an accident."

"Are you mad?" Roger shouted, grabbing the reins. "What do you think you're doing?"

" 'Tis an ancient Welsh custom," Blythe explained, giving him a bright smile. "I'm bringing good luck to our household."

" 'Tis *my* household," he shot back. "Not yours."

"I am your wife," she replied, her smile drooping. "What's yours is mine."

Roger ignored her statement. He flicked a glance at his man and ordered, "Hardwick, clean this mess."

"Me?" Hardwick exclaimed.

"I'll clean it," Blythe said.

" 'Tis unseemly for a countess to wipe shit off the floor," Roger snapped.

Blythe flinched at his words and dropped her gaze. She'd never seen her husband like this and felt uncertain of how to calm him.

"The hall is Bottoms's domain." Hardwick was arguing against his cleaning the mess.

"Stop barking at the moon, Dick," Daisy interjected. "His lordship told you to clean it, not eat it. Now fetch me a bucket and I'll clean it."

"Come with me," Roger ordered, rounding on Blythe. He grabbed her wrist and the horse's reins.

"I'll return the horse to the stables," he said, gaining the privacy of the foyer. "Go directly to your chamber and reflect upon your unseemly behavior. You may return to the hall for supper."

Go to her chamber? Only her father had ever ordered her to do that.

"I am no child to be sent to my chamber," Blythe challenged, raising her gaze to his.

Roger cocked a brow at her. "Only yesterday you promised before God and man to obey me in all matters except your business dealings," he reminded her.

"I lied," Blythe said, echoing his words of the previous night.

Roger suddenly developed a twitch in his right cheek, and his face reddened with anger.

Kindness could work a miracle with Debrett, she heard her grandmother's friend say.

Swallowing her pride, Blythe gave her husband a sweet smile and said, "Thank you for saving me the trip to the stables, my lord. I believe I'll nap before supper."

Blythe climbed the stairs slowly. She refused to look back but felt his piercing blue gaze upon her until she disappeared from sight.

At precisely six o'clock, Blythe breezed into the great hall for supper. Determined to seduce her husband, she wore a violet

silk gown with a daringly low-cut neckline. Her violet eyes
gleamed like amethysts, and her jeweled cross of Wotan glittered provocatively between her ivory breasts.

Blythe mentally prepared herself for her husband's absence,
but saw him standing in front of the hearth as if waiting for her
arrival. "Good evening, my lord," she greeted him.

Roger turned around at the sound of her voice. His gaze slid
from her face to her display of cleavage and lingered there for a
long moment before returning to her face.

"You look lovely tonight," Roger said.

Blythe smiled, pleased by his compliment. Perhaps the afternoon's unfortunate mistake was forgotten.

"Shall we sup?" Roger suggested, gesturing toward the high
table.

Blythe nodded and let him escort her across the hall.

Mr. Bottoms served them a variety of appetizing dishes.
There were thin slices of ham sprinkled with cinnamon and
served with a sharp mustard sauce, a side dish of peas mingling
with baby onions, and rissoles of dried fruits and nuts enclosed
in batter and fried in oil. Crystal goblets filled with red wine
stood beside their plates.

Sitting beside her husband at the high table, Blythe cast him a
nervous glance. What flirtatious remark could she utter that
would incite him to bed her? Contrary to what her grandmother
believed, flirting was easier said than done.

"And how was your visit to Talbot House?" Roger asked.

"Enlightening."

"In what way?"

"My lord, I guarantee you would find women's talk very
uninteresting," Blythe hedged.

"So Ludlow returns to court tomorrow," Roger said conversationally.

Blythe nodded. "My grandparents promised to supervise
Bliss, who'll be assuming my position as one of the queen's
maids of honor."

"I'm sorry you had to relinquish your position because of me," Roger apologized.

"There's no need to apologize," Blythe replied. "I chose my own path."

"I have something important to tell you," Roger said, relaxing in his chair.

"Yes?" Blythe turned to face him.

"Achilles is a female."

"Yes, I know."

"You named your mare after a man?"

"Well, Achilles was always a favorite of mine."

"You knew him personally?" Roger teased.

Blythe laughed, a sweetly melodious sound that drew smiling glances from Bottoms and the two footmen who assisted him.

"I have a gift for you," she said, sounding more confident than she actually felt.

"For me?" he echoed in obvious surprise.

Blythe nodded. She reached into her pocket, produced a ring, and then handed it to him. A scrolled band of gold, the ring had been set with a deep-blue lapis lazuli.

Seeming uncertain of what to do, Roger gave her a faint smile and accepted the ring. Instead of placing it on his finger, he stared at it in silence.

Blythe felt her heart wrench at his reaction to her gift. Had no one ever given him a gift? What kind of boyhood had her husband experienced?

"Lapis lazuli is associated with Venus," she said conversationally. "Some say the stone contains the soul of a deity who protects the wearer. Lapis lazuli promotes healing, love, and fidelity; but I purchased it because the deep blue reminded me of your eyes."

"What's the occasion?" Roger asked, looking from the ring to her face.

"Our wedding, remember?" Blythe answered. "I had a message engraved inside."

Holding the ring up, Roger looked inside the gold band and read aloud, *"Amor vincit omnia."*

"Love conquers all," Blythe said in a voice barely louder than a whisper.

Roger felt himself falling beneath the magical spell she'd woven about him. Her exquisite beauty, her warm smile of acceptance, and her precious gift had been designed to enslave him and to make him miserable. Women had no honor, no honesty. Roger knew he needed to guard against all gentle entanglements.

Steeling himself against her incredible sweetness, Roger slid his gaze to hers and chuckled without humor. He pressed the ring into the palm of her hand and folded her fingers around it.

"Very pretty, but I have no need for a ring inscribed with such a lie," he told her. "Save the ring for some other, less enlightened gentleman."

Blythe paled and rose slowly from her chair. The pain she felt etched itself across her hauntingly lovely face. She stared at him for a long moment and then set the ring on the table between them.

"Bastard," she swore.

Roger raised his brows at her. "I assure you that I am legitimate issue, child."

"I purchased the ring for you," Blythe said, her eyes glistening with unshed tears. "If you don't want it, throw it away."

"Discard such a costly ring?" Roger asked. " 'Twould be a shameful waste of money."

"I purchased it with the gold earned from besting you in the corn and wool trades." At that, Blythe showed him her back and stormed out of the hall.

With a grim expression on his face, Roger stared after her. He hadn't meant to hurt her feelings, only to protect himself. All he needed in this life was his daughter's love, and he wanted nothing more from any woman.

Roger lifted the ring off the table and stared at it. His bride had done something no other woman had ever done—given him a gift—and he'd repaid her kindness by hurting her feelings.

His father had been correct to despise him. Perhaps Darnel had seen the same flaw in him and so had sought the comforting arms of other men. Nothing noble or fine dwelled within his character.

"Congratulations, my lord," said a haughty voice beside him.

Roger glanced to his right and saw his majordomo. "For what?" he asked.

"For hurting that sweet young lady," the man answered.

Roger snapped his brows together. "You forget your place, Bottoms. I am the master and you are the servant."

"I have not forgotten my place," Bottoms insisted.

"And?" Roger prodded, expecting an apology.

"And I have seen you extend more courtesy to London's jades."

"Mister Bottoms, that sweet young lady is bent on paupering my corn and wool businesses," Roger said dryly.

His majordomo had the audacity to smile. " 'Twould serve you right if she did."

"You'll be out of work if she does," Roger warned.

"Lady Blythe has informed me that I'd be welcomed with a position of honor at Devereux House," Bottoms replied.

"Oh, really?" Roger drawled. "Basildon's own majordomo might have something to say about that."

"I doubt it," Bottoms replied, turning away. "Mister Jennings is my cousin."

Roger watched his majordomo walk away. The man had spoken truthfully. He *had* shown more courtesy to jades. However, he wasn't in danger of losing his heart to a whore. His survival demanded he shut his bride out of his life. He had a murderer to catch and hadn't the time or the inclination to court an innocent wife.

Roger lifted the lapis lazuli ring off the table and pocketed it. He left the hall and went directly to his study to work on his corn and wool accounts.

For hours Roger tried to concentrate on tallying columns of

numbers that refused to be tallied. He finally gave up and threw the quill down in disgust.

After pouring himself a glass of whiskey, Roger relaxed in his chair, but then heard the rumble of thunder. A summer storm this late in autumn was an unusual occurrence.

Roger rose from his chair and gazed out the window. A streak of lightning zigzagged across the black sky, followed by a loud roll and boom of thunder. The light drizzle suddenly intensified into sheets of windswept rain that slashed mercilessly against the window.

Deciding his accounts could wait until the morning, Roger left the study and went upstairs. He wondered if his bride feared the storm. Most women of his acquaintance needed comforting during such turbulent weather. After hurting her feelings, the least he could do was verify that she wasn't frightened.

Without knocking, Roger walked into her bedchamber. One night candle burned on the bedside table. No movement came from the bed where she lay sleeping through the worst of the storm.

Instead of leaving, Roger approached the bed and stared down at her lovely face. Remorse coiled itself around his heart when he spied the tears on her cheeks.

His gaze dipped lower, and his breath caught raggedly in his throat. Apparently, his bride's sleep was as turbulent as the elements outside. She'd thrown the coverlet off her body and lay exposed in that ridiculously sheer nightshift. Her tossing and turning had slid the shift up to her curvaceous hips, and one of its straps had slipped, exposing a plump ivory breast, perfectly formed with a pink-tipped nipple.

This is no child. That thought slammed into his mind.

Roger suffered the almost overpowering urge to kneel beside the bed and suckle upon that pink peak. Once she'd awakened beneath his gentle ministrations, he would spread her thighs and bury himself deep within her soft womanhood.

God's bread, Roger chided himself, if you do what you desire, you'll regret it for the rest of your life.

Unable to resist, Roger reached out and lightly cupped her breast in the palm of his hand. Her skin felt softer than the finest silk. He slid his thumb across her pink nipple, which hardened into arousal at his touch.

Blythe sighed in her sleep, breaking the spell.

Roger quickly yanked his hand back as if scorched by the contact with her flesh. Escaping to the safety of his own chamber, he leaned his back against the connecting door and tried to regain his composure.

He wanted her. *Desperately.*

Yet if he loved her even once, his hope for a placid future would be ruined, and misery would dog every step he took.

Thoughts of a peaceful existence brought him no ease while his body ached to possess his bride. Her silken skin and oh-so-pink nipple taunted him mercilessly. A long, long time passed before Roger found refuge from raging desire in a restless sleep.

Chapter 5

Paupering her husband and then forcing him to accept a meager allowance held an almost irresistible appeal at the moment.

Blythe closed her eyes, breathed deeply, and banished all negative impulses from her heart and her mind. She needed to vanquish the heartache of her husband's rejection of her gift and wanted to win his unwavering, undying love.

Knowing what she must do, Blythe opened her eyes and moved silently around her chamber, collecting the items necessary to achieve her goals. From her desk she took a tiny bell, a red ribbon, and fourteen gold pieces.

After placing the gold on the bed, Blythe grabbed a chair and carried it into her dressing closet, which faced the western horizon. She opened the shutters of the small window and smiled as a gentle breeze rushed into the tiny chamber.

Night's dark-lavender hue still painted the western horizon while the rising sun washed the eastern sky with dawn's first light. Oh, how she loved dawn and dusk, the day's two in-between moments, when nature's magical intensity was most powerful.

After inserting the red ribbon through the bell loop, Blythe climbed onto the chair and tied the ribbon to the window. The tiny bell caught the breeze and tinkled, a sound as delicate as fairies' laughter.

"Come Zephyrus, gentle wind of the west," Blythe prayed. "Make my bell of love whisper my need to the Goddess and her servants, the elements. O little bell, draw Roger and his heart of love to me."

Blythe hurried back to her bedchamber. She had no time to waste; she needed to ask her favors before the household awakened.

Leaving her ebony mane cascading wildly to her waist, Blythe donned the silken robe that matched her nightshift. She placed seven gold pieces in one pocket and seven in the other pocket, then left the room.

On bare feet Blythe walked noiselessly down the dark, deserted corridor to the stairs and descended to the foyer. Reluctant to leave the house via the most direct route to the garden because she might encounter early-rising servants, she sneaked out the front door and then glided like an apparition around the mansion.

A hushed, magical stillness pervaded the air within the garden. The sky above brightened rapidly as the moments rushed toward dawn. Heavy morning mist blanketed the Thames River and swirled with natural grace up its earthen banks.

Listening for danger, Blythe paused and cocked her head to one side. The only sound to reach her ears was the faint tinkling of her love bell.

Come, Roger, it seemed to whisper into the predawn silence. *Surrender your heart of love to Blythe.*

"Ngu, Lord of the Four Directions and Winds, I seek the aid of the elements to win the love of my eagle," Blythe prayed, touching her jeweled cross of Wotan. "O mighty Boreas, dazzling Eurus, fiery Auster, gentle Zephyrus ... Aid my love spell, I do thee implore. Fiery Auster and gentle Zephyrus, mingle together to melt the ice surrounding the eagle's heart and, in its place, ignite a fiery passion."

With those words Blythe advanced on the mist-shrouded river. She knelt on its bank and dipped her hand in the water, then sprinkled it on her forehead and her heart.

"My pain flows into the Thames and rushes down to the great sea," Blythe said. Then she pulled seven gold pieces from her pocket and tossed them into the river. Payment in one form or another was always required.

Blythe stood and hurried across the garden to her husband's willow tree, confident that its curtain of sweeping branches would shield her from prying eyes. She placed the palms of her hands against its thick trunk.

"O ancient willow of this ancient earth, brother of my childhood friend," she whispered. "Tree of healing, protection, enchantment, and wishing . . . Grant my heart's desire, the love of my husband."

Blythe leaned forward and planted a light kiss on the tree, then dropped to her knees. Using her hands, she dug a small hole in the dirt at the base of the willow, tossed the seven remaining gold pieces in it, and then replaced the dirt.

She stood and touched the willow a final time, saying, "Indeed, you are a handsome tree."

Intending to sneak back to her chamber, Blythe turned around and found herself face to chest with her husband. How long had he been there? How much had he seen and heard?

Blythe lifted her gaze and became mesmerized by the intensity in his blue eyes. Fascinated, she watched him leisurely peruse her body clad only in the ridiculously sheer nightgown and robe. Anger and desire warred across his handsome features. And then he spoke.

"Cease flaunting your nakedness in front of me or I'll—"

Roger reached out, grabbed her upper arms in his steely grip, and pulled her against the planes of his body. He captured her mouth in a demanding kiss that stole her breath and made her senses reel. His tongue persuaded her lips to part and then slipped between them to ravish the soft sweetness of her mouth.

Blythe, her body on fire with her first kiss, moaned low in her throat. Entwining her arms around his neck, she molded her young body to his and returned his kiss in kind.

Roger broke their smoldering kiss and stepped back a pace. He appeared none too happy about kissing her.

"Come with me," Roger ordered, grabbing her wrist and forcing her toward the house.

Was he going to bed her now? Blythe wondered. *Her first kiss.* She'd certainly made progress that morning. Was it her grandmother's advice or her own natural magic?

Roger led her into the mansion, past sleepy-eyed servants, and up the stairs. Opening the door to her bedchamber, he pulled her across the room and gently but firmly forced her down on the edge of the bed.

"God's bread!" Roger exploded with anger. "What possessed you to walk outside half-naked?"

Blythe looked down at herself and then raised her gaze to his, saying, "I'm fully clothed."

"Never mind," he snapped. "What were you doing outside at this early hour?"

Blythe smiled brightly, feeling herself on safe ground. "Insuring good luck to our household."

" 'Tis *my* household," Roger said, echoing his hurtful words of the previous day. "Besides, you already paraded your horse through my hall."

Our hall, Blythe thought, but said, "One can never have too much good luck."

"I don't give a fig about luck," he told her. "My daughter will soon be arriving from Winchester, and I refuse to have her exposed to your bad habits."

"What bad habits?" Blythe demanded, rising from her perch on the bed, ready for battle.

"Your behavior is too unseemly for a countess," Roger said in a cold voice. "Thankfully, you shan't be *my* countess for long. Now, get dressed." Turning on his heels, he marched toward the door connecting their chambers, but paused before leaving.

"Do you always tell trees how handsome they are?" he asked, his voice laced with sarcasm.

"Certainly not."

He opened the door to leave, but halted when he heard her speak.

"I compliment the females on their incredible beauty," she told his back. There could be no mistaking the laughter in her voice.

Without giving her a glance, Roger retreated into his own chamber. The door clicked shut behind him.

Watch what a man does, not what he says. . . . Her grandmother's words slammed into Blythe's consciousness.

And then she heard it—the faint tinkling of her love bell.

Blythe smiled, pleased with her progress. Her husband's lips said "no," but his piercing gaze and his traitorous body shouted "yes."

The eagle hungered for his butterfly, his psyche, his soul.

He wanted to bed his bride.

Seated at his desk inside his study, Roger fixed his gaze on the column of numbers in his ledger. The lush roundness of the number eight reminded him of breasts; and each time his gaze reached an eight, his thoughts drifted to his bride's lushness.

Roger doodled a sideways number eight and, in his mind's eye, saw his bride's curvaceous hips. When he intersected the eight's juncture with a pointed seven, the two numbers appeared to be fornicating.

Becoming aware of what he was doing, Roger tossed his quill on the desk in disgust and poured a dram of whiskey. He needed to exorcise his bride from his thoughts. Imagining the numbers on his corn and wool accounts making love was a sign of a disturbed mind. Fornicating numbers, indeed!

Closing his eyes, Roger leaned back in his chair. How could he bolster his inner strength in order to keep his hands off his oh-so-tempting bride? Pretending Blythe Devereux was still a child wasn't working; her body disproved that lie each time he glanced in her direction. He hadn't bedded a woman in more than five months. How much longer could he remain celibate when she flaunted her beauty in front of him?

A wry smile touched his lips. Now Roger knew how the first Earl of Eden—namely, Adam—felt when that temptress Eve twitched her naked hips and invited him to taste that infamous apple. The world's first man never had a fighting chance.

Banishing his desire for his bride was of utmost importance if he wanted to win an annulment. Unfortunately, neither Lady Sarah nor Lady Rhoda was available; both attended the Tudor court.

Roger had no intention of patronizing a brothel and catching the French pox. Since he was unable to satisfy his needs, he would take himself out of temptation's path for a few hours. It couldn't hurt.

"My lord, dinner is served," Bottoms announced from the doorway.

"I'll dine later," Roger told his majordomo. "Send Hardwick to me, and fetch me the latest playbills."

Bottoms nodded and left to do his master's bidding.

With his mind set on a defensive course of action, Roger reached for a piece of parchment and wrote a brief message on it. He let the ink dry and then folded and sealed the parchment. On the outside in a bold, flourishing script he wrote two words: *Madame Dunwich.*

"How may I serve you, my lord?" Mr. Hardwick asked, walking into the study.

Mr. Bottoms returned before Roger could reply and set a tray down on the desk. A platter filled with beef and turnips lay beside the playbill.

"The countess insisted that missing dinner would be too unhealthy," the majordomo informed him.

"Instruct a courier to deliver this and wait for an answer," Roger said, passing him the missive. He looked at his valet and ordered, "Lay out dress clothes."

"Going out, my lord?" Hardwick asked.

"The theater in Shoreditch," Roger answered, lifting the

playbill off the tray. "The Lord Chamberlain's Men have a new play in production. Listen to this, Hardwick. Its title is *The Taming of the Shrew*."

"Ah, yes. 'Tis the latest offering from William Shakespeare," Hardwick replied. "I heard Will Kemp gives an outstanding performance in the lead as Petruchio." The valet started to leave, but then paused to ask, "Shall I send word to her ladyship's tirewoman?"

"No, the countess will not be accompanying me."

After his man had gone, Roger picked his quill up and began to work on his ledgers. He felt considerably more lighthearted than he had only ten minutes earlier. Taking positive action always made him feel better.

The door swung open again, drawing his attention. Three people marched into his study. First came Mr. Bottoms, carrying a small table that he set down near the window; behind the majordomo was Daisy Lloyd, carrying a chair. With several ledgers in her arms, Blythe followed the two servants into the room.

"What do you think you're doing?" Roger demanded, though he already surmised what her answer would be.

Blythe set the ledgers on the table and then gifted him with a sunny smile. "Since you're engaged for the afternoon, I've decided to work on my accounts. Two of my agents will be arriving later for a conference."

Roger suffered the urge to order her out of his study, but thought better of it. He would be gone for the whole afternoon, and his study would be empty. Besides, he could "accidentally" leave Madame Dunwich's answer to him on top of his desk.

Females were as curious as cats. He'd wager his last gold piece that his bride would inspect the missive once he'd gone. Of course, Roger intended to reseal it before leaving. Fortunately for him, Madame Dunwich always sprinkled a few drops of her perfume on messages to men. His bride would mistakenly believe the worst of him. Perhaps then she would give him some breathing space.

Pleased with this plan, Roger smiled at Blythe and inclined

his head. He watched her sit down at the table, open one of the ledgers, and begin to work.

Forcing himself to give his attention to his own ledgers, Roger found his bride's presence in his study as distracting as hell. He peeked at her. She looked so damned beautiful with that intent expression on her face.

Finally, Roger began to work on his own accounts. He'd already lost enough profits to his bride. She seemed unaffected by his presence in the study, but he had difficulty totaling the column of numbers in front of him.

"God's bread," Roger muttered, tossing his quill on the desk. He'd just tallied the same column of numbers for the tenth time and reached his tenth different sum.

"Your total is 15,379," said a voice beside him.

Roger snapped his head around and found his gaze level with his bride's bosom as she leaned close to stare at his ledger. Shifting his gaze from her breasts to his ledger, he tallied the column of numbers again.

"How did you do that?" he asked, surprised that her sum was correct.

Blythe shrugged. "I suppose I've inherited my father's mathematical ability."

"Your father never tallied a column of numbers in his head," Roger told her.

"Perhaps 'tis a divine gift," she said with a smile, and then returned to her own ledgers.

How could she possibly tally the columns of numbers without using parchment and quill? Roger wondered, watching her work. No logical answer came to him.

A knock on the door drew his attention away from her. Hardwick walked into the room, handed him the missive, and said, "My lord, your clothing is ready."

"Thank you." Roger opened the parchment, read Madame Dunwich's reply, and then resealed the missive. Setting it down on the desk, he glanced sidelong at his bride, who watched him through those disarming violet eyes.

Roger stood then. "I bid you good day," he said with a pleasant smile.

"Have a profitable meeting," she called after him.

Blythe watched him disappear out the door. Her husband did not trust her. That was the reason he'd resealed his message. He believed she'd spy on his businesses and use that information to increase her own profits.

Blythe knew she should be insulted, but could only sympathize with her injured eagle. All would be well once she enticed him into her bed.

"Mr. Rodale and Mr. Hibbert request an audience," Bottoms announced, walking into the study an hour later.

"Escort them here," Blythe said. She rose from her chair and sat behind her husband's desk. Her gaze fell on the sealed parchment and she wondered with whom he was meeting.

"Sirs, please be seated," Blythe said when the two middle-aged agents entered the study. "What emergency has arisen that requires my immediate attention?"

Mr. Rodale flicked a glance at the other man and said, "The Eden Wool Company has lowered its prices."

"Aye, the same for the earl's corn company," Mr. Hibbert added.

"Undercut him by one guinea per bushel," Blythe ordered without hesitation. When both men opened their mouths to protest such a bold action, she gestured for silence and added, "Your commissions shall be based on the regular price rate, and I also want our suppliers to receive the regular price for their goods. Do I make myself clear?"

"With all due respect, my lady, you'll be the one who suffers a loss," Mr. Hibbert said.

"I shan't suffer alone," Blythe replied. "The Earl of Eden will also be suffering a loss."

"The earl is now your husband," Mr. Rodale said.

Blythe smiled brightly. "So he is."

"Your father would never condone such a risky game as a price war," Mr. Hibbert remarked.

"My father has complete confidence in my ability," Blythe replied, her tone of voice pleasant though the agent's comment irritated her. If she'd been born a man, her agents would never question her judgment.

"I do appreciate your advising me of this situation in such timely fashion," Blythe said, dismissing them. "If Eden lowers his prices again, do not fail to notify me."

Rodale and Hibbert took her hint. Looking none too happy, both men left the study. Blythe would consider herself lucky if they didn't go directly from Debrett House to Devereux House to complain to her father.

Instead of returning to her ledgers, Blythe sat in her beloved's chair and glided the palms of her hands across the top of his oak desk. She could feel his presence in the wood.

Blythe lifted the sealed paper off his desk. The seductive scent of gardenia tickled her nose and made it twitch. Granted, being well-planted was an excellent quality in a man, but no business agent would send his employer a perfumed missive.

I strongly doubt any of his mistresses gave him gifts. . . . Lady Tessie's disturbing remark slammed into her consciousness.

Blythe stared at the parchment. Her fingers positively itched to open it. Who would know? *She would.*

Good marriages needed a solid foundation of trust and love. Opening the sealed parchment meant she would never be worthy of her husband's love.

Blythe set the missive down on the desk. There could be an infinite variety of logical explanations concerning this perfumed message. Taking herself out of temptation's path, she gathered her belongings and finished her ledgers within the safety of her own bedchamber.

At precisely six o'clock, Blythe walked down the stairs to the great hall and told herself for the hundredth time that she wouldn't question her husband about that perfumed missive. Expecting to see him standing in front of the hearth, she was surprised when he wasn't there. In fact, Roger was nowhere to be seen. He'd probably returned from his appointment and gone directly to his study.

Blythe sat alone at the high table. When the majordomo approached to pour wine into her goblet, she said, "Please inform my husband that supper is served."

"His lordship hasn't returned," Bottoms announced.

"When is he expected?" Blythe asked, surprised.

"He didn't say."

"With whom was he meeting?"

The man hesitated for a fraction of a moment and then answered, "The earl had no meeting scheduled."

With only her violet gaze, Blythe kept the man rooted to the spot where he stood. "Well, where did he go?" she asked.

"Shoreditch."

"For what?"

"His lordship attended the theater," Bottoms answered, and then hurriedly escaped when she dropped her gaze.

Her feelings hurt by that bit of information, Blythe stared with unseeing eyes at the retreating majordomo. Her husband had gone to the theater and hadn't invited her to accompany him. What was so wrong with her that he publicly refuted their marriage vows by pursuing his own entertainments? And, more importantly, had that gardenia-scented missive accompanied him?

That wrenching possibility troubled her all night. After a night of tossing and turning, Blythe rose early and stood at her window to greet the dawn. The rising sun always filled her with hope, which was what she particularly needed at the moment.

Blythe fixed her gaze on the brightening eastern horizon. And then she heard the faint tinkling of her love bell. The sound of it heartened her and gave her the courage to face another frustrating day.

Blythe started to turn away from the window but saw Roger sauntering up the path from the stables. Elegantly attired in black, her husband didn't appear ready to work in his garden. Apparently, he'd passed the night sniffing gardenias.

Jealousy and anger surged through her body, casting a shadow across her usually sweet disposition. From nowhere, clouds materialized in the brightening sky and glided across the horizon from west to east, dimming the light of the newly risen sun.

Blythe stared at her husband. Roger paused, looked up at the suddenly darkening sky, and saw her standing there. He smiled and held his hand up in greeting.

Banishing all emotion from her expression, Blythe gave him a long look and closed the shutters. She intended to confront him at first opportunity and set him straight about his less-than-husbandly behavior. He would refrain from sniffing gardenias for as long as he was married to her, or he would regret it.

Blythe left her chamber thirty minutes before the noon meal and headed downstairs. Mentally prepared for battle, she marched like an invading general down the corridor to her husband's study. She paused for a moment outside the door in order to bolster her waning courage and then knocked.

"Enter," she heard him call.

Blythe opened the door and stepped inside. Then she advanced on the desk.

"Yes?" Roger asked, rising from his chair when he saw her.

"We have an important matter to discuss," she told him.

He flashed her a devastating smile. "Please sit down."

"I'll stand."

Roger lost his smile. He inclined his head, saying, "I'll sit if you don't mind. I'm a bit tired this morning."

"I'm amazed you're even conscious," Blythe replied, her sarcasm unmistakable.

"I beg your pardon?"

"Who is Lady Gardenia?"

Roger stared at her blankly.

Blythe shifted her gaze from his face to the perfumed missive still lying on top of his desk.

"Ah, I understand," Roger said. "However, her identity is none of your business."

"Sacred Saint Swithin! How dare you publicly humiliate me,"

Blythe exploded, his words igniting the fuse on her temper. "How disrespectful, how depraved—" She searched her mind for stronger words to hurl at him.

"I do apologize for my depravity," Roger said dryly. Sarcasm laced his voice when he added, " 'Tis exceedingly strange to hear that word *respect* slip from between a woman's lips."

"Why?" she asked, cocking an ebony brow at him.

"That's also none of your business," he told her.

"Let me make this perfectly clear," Blythe said, placing the palms of her hands on his desk and staring him straight in the eye. "Flaunting your whores is unacceptable. If you plan to annul me, then you can damned well practice celibacy until that day arrives."

"And if I don't?" Roger asked, his voice low, the corners of his lips quirking into an amused smile.

Furious that he wasn't taking her seriously, Blythe told him, "You shall undoubtedly become the most wretched man in England."

"Are you threatening me, my lady?"

Blythe smiled sweetly. "Take it as you like it, my lord."

"What will you do?" Roger asked with a sardonic smile. "Beat me with your superior strength?"

"Nothing so primitive as that," Blythe replied, standing up straight and lifting her chin a notch. "My superior intelligence will pauper you before New Year's."

"Daddy!"

At the sound of a child's voice, Roger and Blythe whirled toward the door. Five-year-old Miranda Debrett ran across the study to her father and leaped onto his lap before he could rise from his chair.

Blythe watched in surprise as joy replaced her husband's bitter expression. He closed his eyes and held his daughter tightly within his embrace.

That Roger valued Miranda above everything else was all too obvious. Blythe smiled to herself. With the little girl's love and her own magic, her injured eagle would surely begin to heal.

Brown-haired and blue-eyed, Miranda Debrett resembled her father. For that reason alone, Blythe cherished her already.

Roger kissed his daughter's cheek, and glancing at Blythe, said, "Poppet, this lady is my new wife."

"Meeting you is a distinct pleasure," Blythe said, a sunny smile lighting her expression.

Miranda smiled shyly, dropped her gaze, and whispered loudly to her father, "Daddy, where's the other one?"

"What other one, poppet?"

"You know, Lady Darnel."

Lady Darnel? Blythe was startled that a child would refer to her own mother in such a formal manner. Into what kind of an unnatural family had she married?

"Lady Darnel has gone far away," Roger was saying. "She won't be returning."

"What should I call this one?" the girl asked.

"Lady Blythe," Roger answered.

"Lady Blight," Miranda echoed.

"That's *Blythe*, not blight," Blythe corrected her.

" 'Tis what I said . . . Lady Blight."

"Poppet, I do believe you have the correct pronunciation," Roger said with a smile. "And where's Mrs. Hartwell?"

"Upstairs," Miranda answered, pointing to the ceiling. "Riding makes Hartwell's bones ache."

"I'd like private time with my daughter," Roger said, looking at Blythe. "We'll discuss that other matter later if you don't mind."

Blythe felt her heart wrench for the hundredth time since exchanging vows with her husband. He was shutting her out of his life again. What could she do but honor his request? Though her feelings were mightily bruised, she refused to let him see her pain.

"Welcome home, Miranda," Blythe said, pasting a sunny smile on her face. "Perhaps I'll see you later in the garden?"

The little girl's answering smile could have lit the whole mansion. She nodded eagerly, as if surprised by the attention.

Blythe felt an insistent tugging on her heartstrings. Miranda's smile was her father's before he'd met and married Darnel Howard.

Blythe turned to leave. Just as she reached the door, she heard the child whisper loudly to her father, "Lady Blight is pretty. And she even smiled at me."

"Aye, poppet, Lady Blythe is very pretty," Roger agreed, "but she's not quite as pretty as you."

Reaching the great hall, Blythe sat in one of the chairs near the hearth and pondered her husband's behavior. One moment he'd been wickedly sarcastic, and the next moment pure joy had lit his expression.

Watch how Roger treats his daughter and his horses, because he'll treat you no better.

Blythe recalled her grandmother's words of advice. Miranda loved her father unconditionally, and in return Roger considered her the most precious jewel in the realm. And so would her husband consider her once he realized that she would love him unconditionally for all of eternity.

Blythe let her thoughts drift to the motherless little girl who sat so happily upon her father's lap. The eagerness in Miranda's smile told Blythe the eagle's nestling desperately needed a mother's nurturing.

With seven younger siblings, Blythe had long experience dealing with children. Oh, she would enjoy seeing her husband's daughter bloom in the warmth of a mother's love. Soon the three of them would be a family. Miranda would surely want to live in a home that echoed with the laughter of younger sisters and brothers.

"My lady, dinner is served," announced a voice beside her chair.

Blythe looked up at her husband's majordomo. Then she shifted her gaze to the deserted high table.

"Where are my husband and his daughter?" she asked.

"Lady Miranda succumbed to sleep," Bottoms answered. "His lordship intends to dine while he works in his study."

Sacred Saint Swithin, Blythe thought as a gust of anger swept through her. She'd had enough of solitary meals and gardenia sniffing. No longer would she allow her husband to trample on her feelings. If he refused to share a meal with her, he'd never share her bed.

"Serve my husband and me dinner in his study," Blythe ordered, rising from her chair.

Mr. Bottoms smiled. "Yes, my lady."

With determination stamped across her fine features, Blythe nodded at the majordomo's obvious approval and marched out of the great hall. She paused outside the study to touch her jeweled cross of Wotan, hoping the sentiment expressed on the back of the precious pendant would bolster her flagging courage.

It did. Without bothering to knock, Blythe opened the door and stepped inside the study. She forced a sunny smile onto her face and advanced on her husband's desk.

"Yes?" Roger asked, standing when he saw her.

Blythe sat in one of the chairs in front of his desk, leveled a cool gaze on him, and announced, "I shan't be eating my meals alone again."

"I apologize for my inattention," Roger said, sitting in his chair again. "Pressing business requires my—"

"Do you fear me?" Blythe asked, leaning forward in her chair.

Amused surprise registered on her husband's face. "What ridiculous notion is this?"

"Your avoidance of my company—"

"I am *not* avoiding you," Roger insisted, but then slid his gaze away from hers. "My businesses demand every moment I can spare away from my daughter."

"I am relieved that you do not dislike my company." Blythe smiled. "Sharing meals will consume very little of your time. After all, I didn't agree to this marriage because I wanted to live alone."

The door swung open before her husband could reply. Mr. Bottoms directed a footman to place a tray on the desk between the earl and the countess. The footman left the study, but the majordomo remained to serve them.

"Patina for my lord," Bottoms said as he set their plates in front of them, "and boiled oysters for my lady."

Roger looked ar Blythe and inclined his head in silent surrender. Taking his cue from that gesture, the majordomo served them brown bread with creamy butter, a pasty of sweet peas, braised leeks, and raspberries with clotted cream.

"My lady is certain she wouldn't care for patina?" Bottoms asked solicitously before leaving.

"I have no liking for boiled brains," Blythe refused.

"Will there be anything else, my lord?" the majordomo asked.

Roger flicked a glance at Blythe and then ordered, "I want my desk cleared of this dinner in exactly thirty minutes."

"As you wish, my lord."

Thirty minutes, Blythe thought. She had thirty glorious minutes to savor her husband's undivided attention. Thirty short minutes in which to charm him into her bed. Her task seemed impossible.

"Are you absolutely certain you wouldn't care for a taste of brains?" Roger asked dryly. "I believe you could use some."

"I'm not the one whose corn and wool trades are losing profits," Blythe returned.

"Do not be too sure about that," Roger said with a smile.

Blythe returned his smile with one of her own. Apparently, her husband was unaware that she'd undercut his prices again. Sniffing gardenias had cost him a heavy price.

"Miranda is a lovely child," Blythe remarked, steering the conversation away from their business ventures.

Roger inclined his head to acknowledge her compliment. "I hope you'll be kind to her."

"Do you think I wouldn't be kind to a child?"

"Darnel never cared for her," he admitted.

That surprised Blythe. "You must be mistaken," she said. " 'Twould be highly unnatural for a mother not to love her own child."

"At times Darnel could be unnatural," Roger replied, and then changed the subject. "Tell me about your mathematical abilities."

"What would you like to know?"

"How did you total that column of numbers inside your head?"

"I've always possessed that talent," Blythe said with a shrug. "When I was younger, my father had me total his numbers, and then he would verify my answers. He saved himself hours of paperwork that way."

Roger nodded, accepting her explanation, and gave his full attention to his dinner. Silence reigned for several long minutes.

Blythe stared at her plate and searched her mind for something interesting to say. Her thirty minutes was rapidly running out.

Lifting her gaze to his face, Blythe caught him staring at her breasts. In an instant Roger dropped his gaze to his dinner.

"My lord, is aught wrong with my gown?" she asked, a smile lurking in her voice.

Roger lifted his blue gaze to hers as a ruddy flush colored his cheeks. He shook his head in answer to her question and said, "I was admiring your pendant."

Blythe knew he was lying. She nodded, accepting his words as truth, and then said, " 'Twas your thirteenth-birthday gift to me, and I've worn it each day since."

Her admission made him frown.

"May I redecorate my bedchamber?" she asked, hastily changing the subject.

He fixed his gaze on hers. "Why?"

"The colors are too dark to suit my taste."

"Do whatever you wish."

A strained silence fell like an ax between them, and once again Blythe searched her mind for a suitable topic for discussion. Roger wasn't making this dinner easy for her.

"What is a 'dark sun'?" Blythe asked abruptly.

Roger snapped his piercing blue gaze to hers. Blythe knew from his surprised expression that he'd heard those words before.

"Where did you hear that?" Roger demanded.

"Do you know what it is?"

"I'll ask the questions," he said. "Now, tell me about the dark sun."

"I know nothing," she answered. " 'Tis the reason I asked you."

"Where did you hear that phrase?"

"I-I dreamed it," Blythe hedged. From the doubtful expression that appeared on his face, she realized he knew she was lying.

"Tell me about this dream," Roger said.

A smidgen of truth would wipe the suspicion from his mind. "I have no memory except a voice warning me to beware of a dark sun," Blythe replied.

"Was it a woman's voice?"

"Yes, it was. Have you also heard it?"

Roger nodded and looked past her. "A woman's voice gave me the same warning when I was locked in the Tower."

Blythe sensed that he wasn't telling her the whole truth. "You heard this voice in a dream?"

"I dreamed the queen's long-dead mother spoke those words to me," Roger told her.

"How provoking that we should share a dream," Blythe remarked. *But not a bed* was left unspoken.

"Why did you agree to this marriage?" Roger asked, leaning forward, his piercing gaze holding hers captive.

Blythe stared at him, unable to tear her gaze from his. She refused to allow him to lure her into professing her love as she'd done five years earlier. Let him doubt her feelings. Uncertainty was sometimes good for the soul.

"I agreed to this marriage in order to gain your release from the Tower," Blythe answered.

"How do you profit by it?" Roger persisted.

"Oh, poor my lord," Blythe said, shaking her head, "Personal profiting is *not* the most important thing in life."

"Do my ears deceive me?" Roger asked with a sardonic smile. "Altruistic advice from the lady who undercut my prices?"

"I believe thirty minutes has expired," Blythe announced, rising from her chair. "I thank you for your company. I'll see you at supper, then?"

Roger nodded.

Blythe realized she'd won the battle over their sharing of meals. Joy made her feel like jumping up and kicking her heels together; instead, she walked with graceful dignity to the door.

"Blythe?"

She halted and glanced over her shoulder. "Yes, my lord?"

"I mean no offense, but befriending Miranda could be a bad idea," Roger said. "Her feelings will be injured when you leave Debrett House."

"I have no intention of leaving Debrett House."

"I meant after our annulment."

"There will be no annulment," Blythe told him.

Roger stared at her. "How can you be so certain when I've already said otherwise?"

"You agreed that our marriage would last forever and a day," she reminded him. "And love *does* conquer all."

With those parting words, Blythe escaped the study before he could question or contradict her.

Chapter 6

"Once more around the garden, Daddy!"

Blythe heard the little girl's excited exclamation from somewhere outside in the garden. Rising from the desk where she was working on her ledgers, she looked out her bed-chamber window and watched Roger with his daughter.

Amused fascination appeared on Blythe's face at the unexpected sight that greeted her. With his daughter clinging to his back, her husband galloped in the most undignified manner up and down the garden's walkways.

Finally, Roger set Miranda down on a stone bench where a graying middle-aged woman sat. He knelt on one bended knee in front of his daughter and said something that incited the little girl to clap her hands in obvious excitement. Then he stood and returned to the mansion.

"Daisy," Blythe called, whirling away from the window.

"Yes?" Her kinswoman's voice sounded from within the dressing chamber, and then the woman herself appeared in the doorway.

"Forget about my gowns," Blythe ordered. "Come with me to the garden to meet Roger's daughter and her nursemaid. After I introduce you, escort the nursemaid inside and warm her a mug of spiced cider."

"Why?"

"I wish to become acquainted with Miranda in private,"

Blythe answered. " 'Twill be more comfortable for me that way."

The two women left the bedchamber and hurried downstairs. Within minutes they stepped outside into the garden and, assuming a casual demeanor, strolled at a leisurely pace toward the stone bench where the older woman sat alone.

"You must be Mrs. Hartwell," Blythe said with a sunny smile.

"Yes, my lady." The woman began to rise from the bench.

Recognizing the cool formality in her expression and her tone of voice, Blythe gestured for her to remain where she sat. "Please do not stand for me," she said.

"Why, thank you, my lady." The woman appeared surprised by the kindness shown her.

"I am Lady Blythe, and this is Daisy Lloyd, my tirewoman."

"Pleased to meet you, Hartwell." Daisy gave the woman her infectious smile.

"I'm pleased to meet both of you," Mrs. Hartwell replied, blushing as if flustered by their friendliness.

"Where is Miranda?" Blythe asked.

Mrs. Hartwell pointed across the garden. The little girl stood beneath a gigantic oak tree and watched something in the branches high above her head.

"Miranda," Blythe called, cupping her mouth with her hands.

The little girl whirled around. Her expression shone with joyful surprise.

"You came," Miranda cried, racing across the garden toward her. "I didn't think you would, but you did."

"Didn't I promise to meet you in the garden?" Blythe asked.

Miranda nodded. "Aye, you did."

"I never break my promises." Blythe turned to the watching women and said, "Dear Mrs. Hartwell, you appear travel-weary. Let Daisy escort you inside and warm you a mug of cider."

"Why, I can't think of anything I would rather do," Daisy said, taking her cue from her mistress. "Becoming acquainted over a mug of cider sounds delightful."

"I cannot leave Miranda unattended," Mrs. Hartwell said, refusing.

"I shall be with her," Blythe assured the nursemaid.

"Well, I really shouldn't leave her," the woman said, her expression mirroring her doubt.

"I commend your sense of responsibility," Blythe replied. "However, I am the oldest of eight and have long experience caring for children. His lordship has complete confidence in me."

"In that case, I do feel a bit parched," Mrs. Hartwell admitted, rising from her perch on the bench.

Daisy looped the woman's arm through hers and led her toward the mansion. "I love cinnamon sticks with my cider," Daisy's voice drifted back. "How do you like your cider, Hartwell?"

Blythe smiled at Miranda, sat down on the bench, and patted the spot beside her. "Sit here," she invited the little girl.

When Miranda sat down, Blythe sighed and inhaled deeply of the mild autumn air. The afternoon sun felt warm, and a blanket of blue colored the sky overhead. Vibrant autumnal colors, destined to dominate the garden in a few weeks, tinged the trees.

Blythe heard the call of wild geese and looked up to see a squadron flying above the tops of the trees. "See those geese?" she asked. "They are practicing for their long journey south."

"Where do they go?" Miranda asked.

"The geese fly to a warmer climate when the days turn cold," Blythe answered. "They are building their endurance for the trip. What were you watching in the oak tree?"

"Two squirrels were playing together and leaping from branch to branch," Miranda answered. "I was wishing I also had a friend."

"And your wish came true."

Miranda smiled. "Yes, my wish did come true."

"Come with me." Blythe stood and held her hand out. "I want to introduce you to a special friend of mine."

Miranda accepted the outstretched hand. Together, they strolled across the garden toward the weeping-willow tree.

"Where's your friend?" Miranda whispered loudly. "I don't see anyone."

"You don't see anyone?" Blythe echoed, feigning surprise. "Your father's garden is absolutely crowded with fairies, spirits, and elementals who adore playing with children. But you must see them with your heart."

Stopping beside the willow, Blythe said formally, "O ancient willow, this is my dear friend, Miranda." She turned to the little girl, saying, "This is He, the willow tree."

" 'Tis a boy?"

Blythe nodded.

"I am pleased to make your acquaintance, He," Miranda said to the willow.

"Would you care to sit beneath He?" Blythe asked.

"There's no bench."

"But there is grass."

"Hartwell will be angry if I soil my gown," Miranda told her.

"Because of her advanced age, Hartwell cannot recall what fun is," Blythe said. "Besides, I am now in charge and give you permission to sit on the grass."

"But who is in charge when we go inside?" the child persisted.

"I am." Blythe gave the girl a "thumbs up" gesture.

"What does this mean?" Miranda asked, imitating the gesture.

"*Thumbs up* means victory or excellent," Blythe explained. Then she warned, "You must remember never to bite your thumb at anyone, because that gesture is a naughty insult."

"I promise." Miranda gave her a "thumbs up" and plopped down on the grass beneath the weeping-willow tree.

"Can you feel He's strength?" Blythe asked, sitting beside her and leaning against the willow's solid trunk.

"I do," Miranda answered. "Lady Blight, why are you in charge of me, instead of Hartwell?"

"I became your stepmother when I married your father," Blythe explained. "Therefore my wishes take precedence over Hartwell's."

"What's a stepmother?"

"A stepmother is the mother who never gave birth to you."

Miranda gave her a shy smile and said in a small voice, "All the children in Winchester call their mothers *Mama*. I know because I heard them when Hartwell took me into the village one day. May I call you *Mama*?"

Anxiety and hope warred on the girl's face, and Blythe felt an insistent tugging on her heartstrings. Had the child never called Darnel *Mama*? How sad to think this sweet girl had been virtually motherless since the day of her birth. Granted, she'd had her father's unconditional love, but there were many times when only a mother's nurturing would do.

"You may call me anything you wish, including Mama," Blythe said with a smile meant to encourage.

"Mama Blight," Miranda said, placing her smaller hand in Blythe's.

Blythe giggled and gave the girl's hand a gentle squeeze. "I do believe *Mama Blight* has a pleasantly unique sound to it."

"Mama Blight, where did Lady Darnel go?"

"The great adventure," Blythe answered without thinking, referring to the Druidic hereafter.

"What's that?"

"Lady Darnel died and went to heaven," Blythe said baldly.

"I don't think Lady Darnel went to heaven," Miranda said, shaking her head to emphasize her conviction. "Lady Darnel always yelled at Daddy and me. I didn't like her."

Blythe perked up at that bit of unsolicited information. "About what did Lady Darnel and your father argue?" she asked.

"Everything," the girl answered. "Tell me about the fairies."

"Fairies, elves, elementals, and nature spirits live all around us," Blythe said. "Every flower has a resident fairy. Sometimes we can see them, but usually we can only sense their presence."

"If we can't see them, how do we know they're here?" Miranda asked.

"Whenever you sniff a flower's sweet scent the fairy is greeting you," Blythe answered. "When you admire a flower's pretty color, the fairy has caught your attention. Trees have powerful spirits who love us humans. He, the spirit of this willow, can even speak to us; but we must open our hearts if we want to understand his words."

"Make He speak to us, Mama Blight."

"His voice is louder at night when day noises cease," Blythe told her. "The elemental spirits are earth, air, fire, and water. The wind is the frisky child of the air and a particular favorite of mine. Would you like to meet the wind?"

Miranda looked up, gazed at the tree's motionless branches, and announced, "There is no wind today."

"Well, silly, I'll call him to us."

Miranda giggled and clapped her hands together.

"Relax against He and close your eyes," Blythe instructed. "No peeking, or the wind will refuse to visit."

Miranda snapped her eyes shut. Leaning against the willow's trunk, she breathed deeply in instant relaxation.

Blythe smiled at the resemblance between her beloved and his daughter and then closed her own eyes. Moving her lips in a silent prayer, she placed her right index finger to her heart and then her lips. She opened her eyes and pointed her index finger in the direction of the girl's face.

"I felt it, Mama Blight," Miranda cried. "The wind tickled my nose."

"The elusive wind spirit is here, there, and everywhere," Blythe said. "It never stays in one place for long."

"Are you an angel?" Miranda asked abruptly.

"Well, what do you think?" Blythe asked, surprised by her question.

"You don't look like an angel," Miranda answered, staring at her. "But you do behave like one."

Blythe smiled. "And how do angels behave?"

"Angels make miracles. Like calling the wind to tickle my nose."

"Miracles happen every day," Blythe told her. "Flowers bloom, trees grow, and your father smiles."

"Daddy smiles all the time," Miranda informed her. "That's no miracle."

"I have six younger sisters and one brother who live down the Strand," Blythe said, changing the subject. "We could visit them and play together. Would you like to do that sometime?"

"Let's go now."

Blythe laughed. " 'Tis too late in the day for visiting. Perhaps tomorrow."

Miranda gazed at the sky's oceanic horizon. After several silent moments she asked, "Mama Blight, does a shooting star mean an angel has died?"

"Who told you that?"

"Hartwell."

"Sweetheart, angels never die," Blythe said. "Shooting stars are actually the angels racing across the heavens."

"I'm glad," the little girl said. "Thinking angels died made me feel sad."

"I bet you don't know how to grow gold," Blythe said.

Miranda's blue eyes widened. "Do you?"

Being Druid means knowing, Blythe thought, recalling her mother's oft-spoken words.

"Lord Perpendicular, the Earl of Corners, accumulates gold pieces in the corner of your bedchamber," Blythe told her. "Plant a single gold piece in the corner of your bedchamber. When you inspect it in the morning, the coin shall have begun to grow into a gold stalk. Each night the stalk grows taller."

"I don't own any gold," Miranda said.

"I own tons of gold and love to share it," Blythe replied. "Shall we plant a gold stalk in your chamber tonight?"

The little girl's eyes gleamed with excitement. "Yes, but where did you get all of your gold?"

"Have you ever heard of the 'Queen's Midas'?"

Miranda shook her head.

"Midas was a legendary king whose touch turned everything to gold," Blythe told her. "Richard Devereux, the 'Queen's

Midas,' turns a profit on everything he touches. And he is *my* daddy."

"You have a daddy too?" Miranda cried in delighted surprise.

Blythe nodded and smiled, enchanted by the child's innocence. "Many years ago the Queen's Midas married a beautiful woman who was descended from ancient Welsh princes," Blythe added. "That woman is my mother."

"Your mother is a princess?"

Blythe nodded.

"I like you, Mama Blight." Unexpectedly, Miranda planted a kiss on the back of her hand and said, "You are a butterfly-angel."

"Why did you call me that?"

"You are prettier than a butterfly and make miracles happen," Miranda said, and then yawned. "Do you know other stories?"

Blythe put her arm around the girl's shoulder and drew her against the side of her body. "Lean on me, my weary one," she said.

"Mmmm, you smell like roses."

" 'Tis the scent of my soap," Blythe told her. "Now, would you like to hear the story about the eagle and the butterfly or the enchanted frog?"

"Both."

" 'Tis late," Blythe said, glancing at the late-afternoon sky. "I'll tell you one now and the other at bedtime."

"I want the eagle and the butterfly now."

"Once upon a time," Blythe began, "all the winged creatures of the earth, both bird and insect, gathered together for a great assembly. . . ."

God's bread, but she'd actually kept her promise to his daughter.

Standing at the window in his study, Roger watched Blythe and Miranda walking toward the willow tree in his garden. Hand in hand, the woman and the girl appeared deep in conversation.

Roger knew from the tilt of his daughter's head that whatever Blythe was saying held her in thrall. How sad that merely making a promised appearance could fill his daughter's heart with adoration. How depressingly ironic that his only child should hunger for a mother's love as he had once hungered for his own father's loving regard. How frustrating that all of the wealth he'd managed to accumulate could never purchase what his daughter needed most: a mother's love.

Reaching into his pocket, Roger withdrew the blue lapis lazuli ring and stared at it. He intended never to wear the ring, yet for some reason he couldn't toss it aside. Blythe was the only woman who'd ever given him a gift. She wanted something, but he didn't know exactly what yet.

Roger lifted his gaze from the ring and saw Blythe and Miranda sit down beneath the willow. They were barely visible beneath the tree's sweeping branches.

Seeing a noblewoman who obviously loved children was almost a miracle. His sweet butterfly would make a remarkably wonderful mother. Too bad he hadn't waited for her to grow into womanhood. Ah, but it was too late for them now.

"My lord?"

At the sound of his majordomo's voice, Roger turned away from the window. "Yes, Bottoms?"

"The Earl of Basildon requests an interview," the man announced, his voice appropriately haughty.

Richard Devereux brushed past the majordomo and flicked an amused glance at the man, saying, "Thank you, Bottoms."

The earl shook Roger's hand and said, "Obviously, Bottoms is a man who loves his job." He sat down in the chair in front of the desk, stretched his long legs out, and asked, "So, how goes the married life?"

"Perhaps you should ask Blythe," Roger replied, passing his father-in-law a dram of whiskey.

"I'm asking you," Richard said, cocking a copper brow at him.

"Are you here to verify I haven't strangled your daughter?"

"Would I have married her to you if I'd thought a bit of female provocation could send you into a murderous rage?"

Roger grinned. "I always thought Blythe was a sweet child, but I'm learning that she can be a mite irritating at times."

"Then I shall assume the marriage is progressing normally," the earl said, raising his glass of whiskey in salute. "Do you remember Lancaster, the adventurer I financed?"

Roger nodded.

"He has broken the Portuguese trade monopoly in India, and I'm planning to form the Anglo-Indian Trading Company," Earl Richard told him. "One hundred thousand pounds will get it started, but I'll need to promise Elizabeth fifty percent of the profits in order to obtain a royal charter. Are you interested in investing?"

"You know I am," Roger answered, mentally rubbing his hands together at the prospect of the gold to be made by trading with India. "I'll invest fifty thousand, and we'll be full partners."

Richard shook his head. "I can only offer you a twenty-five percent share."

"Who else is investing?"

"Blythe would never speak to me again if I didn't invite her to join us," Richard said, a rueful tone in his voice. "However, once Blythe becomes a mother, her attention will lie elsewhere. Eventually, you will control her shares."

Roger made no reply to that. Instead, he stared at the dark-amber liquid in his glass and hoped his father-in-law would not pursue the topic of parenthood. How could he gently break the news to a trusted friend that he had no intention of consummating the marriage to his daughter?

"Are you still interested?" the earl asked.

"I'll instruct my bankers to transfer the funds first thing in the morning," Roger answered, raising his own glass in salute. "Now, what's the news from court?"

"My spies inform me that London's populace is quiet concerning your release from the Tower," Richard told him. "At court, Oxford and his ilk have been complaining that you've gotten away with murder. Most disturbing is the rumor that one of your own kin is grumbling the loudest, albeit out of the queen's presence."

"Geoffrey." That one word slipped from Roger's lips with all the contempt he felt for his youngest brother.

"Do not leap to any conclusions," Richard advised him.

" 'Tis logical that the real murderer would be grumbling the loudest concerning my alleged guilt," Roger replied.

"Do you have proof that Geoffrey is guilty of murder?" Richard asked.

"He's an incorrigible rake, and I'm almost positive he made love to Darnel," Roger told him.

"At times your moral rigidity reminds me of Burghley." Richard grinned. "Too much integrity can be unhealthy."

"What do you mean by that?"

"Promiscuity is no crime," Richard explained. "A man who savors women, as Geoffrey does, probably would never do physical harm to one. Besides that, what could have been his motive? Rakes care little for their reputations. He had no reason to dispatch Darnel."

Roger cast him a skeptical look, but said nothing.

"At least consider my words. Appearances can be deceptive," the earl continued. "Fixing Geoffrey in your thoughts as guilty could prove foolish because it closes your mind to other possibilities."

"I see the sense in what you say."

"Burghley sends word that you'll soon be invited to return to court," Richard told him. "Elizabeth has been making noises that she misses her 'soaring eagle.' "

"I eagerly await the opportunity to investigate Darnel's murder," Roger replied.

His father-in-law nodded. "Now, I'd like to speak with Blythe."

"She's in the garden with Miranda," Roger said, rising from his chair.

The two men left the study. Stepping outside into the garden, they walked in the direction of the willow tree.

Even from this distance Roger saw his daughter's expression of rapt attention as she listened to whatever Blythe was saying. And then her words drifted through the air to him. ". . . And so the majestic eagle and his clever butterfly could be seen gliding across the horizon forever after."

Miranda responded by clapping her hands together.

Roger smiled at the sight of his daughter so happy. Blythe Devereux had given her what he couldn't: a young woman's nurturing attention.

Blythe looked up as if sensing their presence. Her incredibly disarming violet gaze caught his, and then she smiled, its brilliance and unconditional acceptance dazzling him.

"Look, Miranda," Blythe said, standing and helping the child rise. "Here are your daddy and *my* daddy."

" 'Tis Midas?" Miranda asked, staring with apparent fascination at the tall, copper-haired man dressed completely in black.

The earl smiled at her. "Hello, poppet."

"I heard you married a princess," Miranda said.

"Aye, 'tis the gospel truth."

"My daddy married your daughter," Miranda told him, grasping her stepmother's hand. "She's a butterfly angel."

Blythe blushed when the child's outrageous remark drew her husband's stare. Roger didn't appear too thrilled that she'd befriended his daughter. Couldn't he see that the girl hungered for a mother's attention? Perhaps he thought if Miranda disliked her, he could toss that on top of the mountain of reasons he was building for an annulment.

"Lancaster has opened a trading opportunity with India," her father said without preamble. "Are you interested in investing?"

"I'll invest fifty percent of what's needed," Blythe said without hesitation. "We'll be full partners."

"You sound exactly like your husband," Richard remarked, an amused smile appearing on his face.

"Roger is investing?" Blythe asked in surprise, flicking a glance at him. "Why don't we keep this a family company?"

"As of three days ago I *am* family," Roger interjected, giving her a wry smile.

How convenient for her husband to suddenly remember their marriage vows. Would he suffer a memory lapse if she walked through the connecting door into his chamber that night and slipped into his bed?

"How much do you want?" Blythe asked her father.

"Twenty-five thousand pounds," he answered. "You realize that Elizabeth will skim fifty percent off the top of whatever we make. Fifty percent of what's left belongs to me. Roger and you will split the remainder."

" 'Tis a deal," she agreed.

Her father nodded and then pulled a parchment from inside his doublet. "Will you check these figures?" he asked.

Blythe lifted the paper out of his hand and quickly scanned the columns of numbers. "Your total is correct," she said, passing him the parchment.

"How did you do that without using your fingers?" Miranda asked.

" 'Tis a tiny miracle," Blythe answered. "Now, shall we go inside to wash and change our gowns before supper?"

"No, thank you. I don't care to wash," Miranda said, shaking her head.

"Well, I wish to wash and change," Blythe told her. "Would you consider accompanying me?"

The little girl nodded, obviously reluctant to part with her newfound friend.

"Miranda and I will soon be visiting Devereux House," Blythe informed her father. "We want to play with the other children."

"Your sisters and brother are always eager for new playmates," he replied.

"My banker will transfer the necessary monies to you first

thing in the morning," she said, leaning close to plant a kiss on his cheek. "I'll see you soon, Papa."

Miranda rounded on her own father and gestured for him to crouch down. When he did, she planted a kiss on his cheek in a perfect imitation of her stepmother and said, "I'll see you soon, Daddy."

Roger smiled. "And will *your* banker be transferring money to me?" he asked.

"I have no gold," Miranda answered, and then winked at Blythe. "But I will in the morning. Won't I, Mama Blight?"

"Mama?" Roger echoed in obvious surprise.

"Blight?" the earl said, an amused smile appearing on his face.

Blythe cast them a sunny smile. Taking the girl's hand in hers, she led her across the grounds toward the mansion.

Blythe and Miranda went down to supper together that evening. *Both* had washed their faces and changed their gowns.

"How did you manage to accomplish that?" Roger asked, shifting his gaze from his bride to his daughter's freshly scrubbed face.

"I never divulge strategy," Blythe answered, casting him a flirtatious smile. " 'Tis what makes me an excellent business-woman."

"Daddy, we played the washing game," Miranda told him. " 'Twas ever so much fun."

"I am glad you enjoyed it," Roger said, and then lifted his gaze to his bride's.

"Believe me, you don't want to know the details," Blythe said in a rueful voice, making him smile.

During supper Blythe and Roger sat on either side of Miranda at the high table, and Blythe couldn't help thinking that they were a real family. She knew Miranda felt the same way, because the girl ate little and talked much. The child seemed to have taken a turn for the better since that morning in the study, when her smile had been shy.

I'll bring sunshine into their lives, Blythe vowed. Though her eagle had somehow been injured by his marriage to Darnel Howard, Roger was a full-grown man. Most heartbreaking was the damage done to Miranda by her own selfish mother. They needed the sunshine that Blythe knew she possessed in abundance.

Bottoms served them seasonal fare for supper. There were split-pea soup with beans and onions, roasted chicken, bread with butter, and baked apples with pistachios.

"Eat more and talk less," Roger ordered his daughter, pointing at her bowl. "Why are you picking the beans out of your soup? Beans are good for you."

Blythe watched in amusement as the little girl gave her father a long look. "Hartwell says proper ladies never make vulgar noises or foul odors," Miranda announced. "Each time I eat beans, I make vulgar noises and foul odors."

Blythe burst out laughing. Miranda looked around and gave her a "thumbs up" as if delighted by the fact that she'd entertained her stepmother.

"Tell Mrs. Hartwell"—Roger chuckled—"I give you permission to make vulgar noises and foul odors whenever you eat beans."

"Guess what, Daddy? Mama Blight is going to help me plant a gold seed in my chamber tonight," Miranda said. "In the morning I shall have the beginnings of a gold stalk."

" 'Twould be a miracle," Roger replied, lifting his gaze to Blythe's.

"Miracles happen every day," the five-year-old told her father. "Mama Blight said so."

"Yes, 'tis so," Blythe agreed with the girl.

Roger stared at her for a long moment, and the hint of a smile flirted with the corners of his lips. "Do miracles really happen every day, *Mama Blight*?" he asked, his voice teasing.

Blythe smiled. "My lord, somewhere in this great universe a miracle is happening at this very moment."

"What a staggering thought."

"You, my lord, must guard against being so pessimistic," Blythe returned his teasing.

"Yes, Daddy," Miranda piped up. "Don't be so pisim—don't be pissy."

Roger and Blythe looked at each other and burst out laughing. Their gazes met over the little girl's head and a friendly, almost tender emotion passed between them. It lasted only a fraction of a moment and then was gone.

"Do my eyes deceive me?" Blythe asked as she spied an unlikely couple sitting alone in the far corner of the hall. "Is that Hardwick supping with Daisy?"

Roger gave her a sidelong smile and nodded. "Hardwick's been singing Daisy's praises since she cleaned that mess for him the other day."

"What mess?" Miranda asked.

"Mama Blight's horse fouled the floor over there," Roger told her.

"You rode your horse indoors?" Miranda asked, her expression mirroring her surprise.

"No, I *walked* Achilles through the house to ensure us good luck."

"Daddy, I want to walk my pony through the house," Miranda said, turning to her father.

"Poppet, you own no pony."

"Will you buy me one?" she persisted.

"Perhaps, but only on the condition that you never walk or ride it indoors."

"What's a *condition*?"

"A condition is a solemn promise," Roger explained.

"I promise never to take my pony indoors," Miranda vowed. "Now will you buy me one?"

Before her father could answer, the majordomo approached the high table. "My lord, Andrews and Newell beg an interview," Bottoms announced. "They insist 'tis urgent."

"Escort them to my study," Roger instructed his man. He

turned to his daughter, saying, "If you wait here I'll walk you upstairs when I'm finished."

"I'll deliver her to Mrs. Hartwell," Blythe spoke up.

"Thank you." Roger rose from his chair and said to his daughter, "I'll be along shortly and tell you a story, poppet."

"Shall we go upstairs and plant that gold seed?" Blythe asked as soon as he'd gone.

Hand in hand, Blythe and Miranda climbed the stairs together. The little girl led her to a chamber two doors down from the master bedroom.

"Mrs. Hartwell, I'll put Miranda to bed and wait for his lordship," Blythe told the nursemaid. "Go downstairs and enjoy a mug of mulled wine."

"Well, if you're certain that won't be an inconvenience . . ." Mrs. Hartwell said with a grateful smile and left the chamber.

Blythe helped the five-year-old out of her gown and into her nightshift. When she started to place the nightcap on her, the girl shook her head in refusal.

"No nightcap," Miranda said.

"So be it." Blythe tossed the nightcap over her shoulder onto the floor, making the child giggle.

"Do you think Hartwell will be angry when she sees the nightcap?" Miranda asked in a conspiratorial whisper.

"Who is in charge here, Hartwell or me?"

"You are!"

"In which corner shall we plant this seed?" Blythe asked, lifting a gold piece out of her pocket.

Miranda turned slowly in a circle. Finally, she pointed at the corner located to the right of the door. "That one. 'Tis hidden from view when you open the door."

"A wise choice." Blythe passed the gold piece to Miranda. "You must plant it. Always remember, the stalk will die if you pick it."

"I understand." Reverently holding the gold piece in both hands, Miranda marched to the corner and set it down at the juncture of the two walls. When she turned around, the child wore the most excited expression Blythe had ever seen.

"I did it," she cried, dashing across the chamber.

"So you did," Blythe said. "Climb into bed, and I'll tell you the story of the enchanted frog."

Miranda did as she was told. Blythe sat beside her on the bed, put her arm around the girl's shoulder, and leaned back against the headboard.

"Are you ready?" Blythe asked.

The five-year-old nodded.

"Once upon a time in a faraway land lived a queen and her three princesses," Blythe began. "The queen was very ill and could only be cured if she drank from the magical well of pure water. So she sent her oldest princess to fetch her a mug of this special water.

"When the princess arrived at the well, a hideous frog appeared and said he owned the water. The princess could take a mug of water only if she agreed to marry him. Frightened, the princess shook her head and ran home."

"Did the queen die?" Miranda interrupted, gazing at her through blue eyes wide with wonder.

Blythe smiled and shook her head. "The queen sent her second princess to draw the water, but the very same thing happened.

"Determined to save her mother's life, the youngest princess grabbed the empty mug out of her sister's hand and hurried to the magical well of pure water. 'Frog,' she called. 'Give me a mug of pure water, and I will marry you.' The frog filled her mug with the water, and the princess ran home—as fast as she could without spilling a drop—and gave the water to her mother. The queen instantly recovered from her illness."

"What happened to the frog?" Miranda asked. "Was he angry because he'd been tricked?"

"I'm just coming to that part of the story," Blythe said. "Late that night the voice of the frog called, 'Princess, remember your promise to me.'

"The princess hurried downstairs and let the frog inside. She made him a warm bed near the hearth in her chamber, but still the frog was unhappy.

" 'Princess, I am dying,' the frog croaked. 'Give me one kiss before I expire.' "

"Yuck! Yuck!" Miranda exclaimed.

Blythe smiled at the girl's reaction and then continued, "The princess held the frog in the palm of her hand and said, 'O frog, keeper of the pure water, I gave my solemn promise to wed you, and so I shall if you are still alive in the morning. In case you expire, take this holy kiss with you into the great adventure.' So the princess leaned close and planted a kiss on his lips."

"She really kissed that ugly frog?" Miranda cried.

Blythe nodded. "She'd given him her solemn vow and refused to be forsworn. But something miraculous happened. As soon as she kissed him the frog turned into a handsome prince. In the morning the prince and the princess married and lived happily ever after."

"Oh, what a wonderful story," Miranda exclaimed, clapping her hands together.

"The lesson we must learn from this is to always look beyond appearances," Blythe told her. "Those who are devoted to loved ones eventually reap rich rewards."

Sensing another presence in the chamber, Blythe looked toward the door and saw her husband. Their gazes met. The warm intensity in his eyes made her feel weak and wobbly all over.

"Daddy, Mama Blight told me a story," Miranda called.

"Yes, I heard," Roger said, sauntering toward them. "How will I ever best it?"

Blythe planted a kiss on the five-year-old's cheek and rose from her perch on the bed. "My lord, you need not 'best' anything," she told him. "Miranda will love whatever story you choose because *you* tell it. Good night." Over her shoulder she called to the child, "Tomorrow I'll tell you about a special blackbird."

Blythe crossed the chamber to the door. She bit her bottom lip to keep from laughing when she heard her husband ask his daughter, "No nightcap?"

"Mama Blight gave me permission," Miranda informed her father. "She's in charge now."

"And who do you think is in charge of Mama Blight?" Roger asked. "Will she be willing to sit up all night with you if you catch a cold and cannot sleep?"

"There'll be no need for that," Miranda countered. "I'll drink from the well of pure water. We'll send Hartwell to fetch it. . . ."

Gaining her own chamber, Blythe changed into her nightshift and then stood at the window to gaze out at the night sky while she brushed her hair. The day had been the happiest of her entire married life. Granted, Roger and she had been wed for only three days, but Miranda made her feel needed. She truly belonged with them at Debrett House.

Blythe heard the faint tinkling of her love bell. Her husband was everything she'd ever hoped for in a man. Now, if she could manage to entice him into her bed—

The door swung open, and Blythe whirled around to see Roger crossing the chamber toward her. A tender emotion lit his eyes. He dropped his gaze to her scantily clad body and leisurely perused her.

"No nightcap?" Roger asked with a teasing smile when he lifted his gaze to hers.

"I always hated my own nightcap," Blythe said, returning his smile. "Bliss and I tormented poor Mrs. Ashemole with our rebellion."

"Thank you for being kind to my daughter," he said without preamble. "The one thing she's lacked in her young life is a mother's nurturing."

"Miranda is a charming child," she replied. "Keeping her entertained was no difficult task."

Blythe watched in amused fascination as her husband set the kind "thank you'" aside in his mind and his placid expression changed to irritation. In three short days he'd become so relaxed with her presence in his home that he forgot to banish all emotion from his face.

"You've undercut my prices again," Roger said, his voice accusing.

Blythe raised her brows at him and, with laughter lurking in her voice, replied, "Men who waste time sniffing gardenias are destined to fail in their business ventures."

"Are you determined to pauper us?" he asked, ignoring her comment.

Us. Blythe liked the sound of that word and what it implied.

"My lord, 'tis nothing personal," she answered. "Admit defeat gracefully."

"Never."

"Neither shall I."

"Then I'll share some insider information with you," Roger said, flashing her a devastatingly wicked smile. "Undoubtedly, Rodale and Hibbert will be visiting you tomorrow."

"You know my agents's identity?" Blythe asked, surprised.

"Rodale and Hibbert will rush to Debrett House to inform you I've lowered my prices again," Roger said. His smile grew into a grin when he added, "Unfortunately, you won't be here to receive them."

"And where will I be?"

"I'm planning to go to Smithfield Horse Market and"—Roger hesitated—"I wondered if you would accompany Miranda and me. We could make a day of it."

Blythe felt like whooping with joy. His invitation was almost a miracle and solid proof that she'd begun to tear his emotional barriers down. Lord, but she felt strong enough to scale the bulwarks that shielded his heart.

Never be too available, Blythe heard her grandmother caution. Playing coy couldn't hurt.

"Let me think," she hedged, placing her index finger across her lips as if trying to recall how busy a schedule she had for the next day. "I suppose I—"

"You needn't cancel your appointments for me," Roger interrupted.

"I would never do that," Blythe told him. "But Miranda—"

"Miranda will accompany me whether you go or stay," he interrupted her again.

"And who will supervise her?"

"Mrs. Hartwell."

"Have a little compassion for Hartwell's bruised posterior," Blythe said. " 'Twould be unnecessarily cruel to force her onto a horse."

"Then you'll accompany us?"

Blythe nodded.

"Good night." Turning away, Roger crossed the chamber and disappeared through the connecting door.

"Good night, my eagle," she whispered.

Instead of seeking her bed, Blythe sat at the table that served as her desk. She lit the candle and then wrote Rodale and Hibbert instructions concerning the Debrett Trading Company's latest price cut. While she was enjoying her outing, Daisy would deliver the missives to Devereux House and her father would forward them to her agents. No one at Debrett House would suspect a thing.

How considerate Roger was to reveal his business plans. Otherwise, she would have lost almost two days' worth of profits.

Blythe smiled. She really ought to thank him for his insider information. Tomorrow evening would suit. The supper hour would be too late for him to recoup his losses for the day.

Chapter 7

During those hushed, magical moments before the world awakened, Blythe stood at her bedchamber window and studied the eastern horizon. The perfection of the approaching dawn promised a day with clear blue skies and an abundance of sunshine, an ideal autumnal setting for their excursion to Smithfield Market.

"Saint Swithin, shroud Roger and me within your winds of love," Blythe prayed. "Great Mother Goddess, let this be the day my husband and I become one."

Slashes of orange and mauve light washed the eastern sky. The rising sun, always glorious on the autumnal equinox, appeared especially inspiring this day.

And thee I chuse.

Blythe touched the jeweled cross of Wotan, and the hint of a smile touched her lips. Yea, her mother's prophecy was coming true. She'd already noticed the signs of her husband's softening attitude. Roger had become accustomed to her presence in less than a week; and as the days passed into weeks and months, her beloved would want her closer than the adjoining bedchamber.

Though Devereux House stood only a short distance down the Strand, Blythe felt that a lifetime separated her from her childhood. She fixed her gaze on the mist-shrouded Thames River and, through sheer force of will, banished the momentary twinge of homesickness weighing upon her spirit. A creature of sunlight, Blythe always felt melancholy during this transitional season.

Darkness overtook light during the autumnal equinox, heralding longer nights in advance of the most sacred holiday in the year's cycle, when the thin veil between this world and the beyond separated for exactly three days. The soul awakened at the autumnal equinox in preparation for Samhuinn, the holiest three days in the year.

Blythe knew her mother was especially partial to celebrating the autumnal equinox, for it was on that momentous day nineteen years earlier that she'd gazed for the first time upon the handsome face of her husband. At that very moment the Countess of Basildon would enjoy the freedom to worship in her own special way within the security of the Devereux garden. Thanks to an understanding but skeptical husband.

Blythe smiled to herself. Queen Elizabeth and her courtiers would be shocked if they knew that England's richest earl had married a Druid. On the other hand, discovery was no laughing matter and could prove dangerous. She must remember to be circumspect in all of her actions. Somehow, she didn't think Roger would be quite as understanding of her religious bent as her father.

The delicate tinkling of the love bell caught her attention. The frisky wind, a special friend like the willow tree, was always with her.

Come, Roger, the love bell called. *Surrender your heart of love to Blythe.*

A hushed peace pervaded the morning air. And then the serenity of the moment shattered in a childish shriek.

"Mama Blight!"

Startled by the cry, Blythe whirled around just as Miranda barged into her bedchamber. The five-year-old ran across the room toward her.

"Lord Perpendicular left a gold piece on top of my seed," Miranda exclaimed. "My gold stalk is growing!"

"Well, silly, I told you he would visit," Blythe said, kneeling on one bended knee to accept the child's enthusiastic hug. Hearing footsteps, she looked up and saw a sleep-disheveled Mrs. Hartwell burst into her chamber.

"What the bloody hell is happening?" Roger demanded, entering her chamber through the connecting door. Magnificently bare-chested, he wore only tight black breeches.

Blythe stared at him in surprised pleasure and savored the sight of him so scantily dressed. She didn't need her Druid's instinct to know that her husband was naked beneath those breeches. Lord, but her soaring eagle was a particularly well-formed man.

"My lady, forgive my incompetence," Mrs. Hartwell apologized. "She bolted out the door before I could catch her."

"The gold stalk grew," Miranda repeated, ignoring the sleepy confusion surrounding her.

"Nothing is amiss," Blythe assured her husband. She sent the nursemaid an amused look of sympathy and absolved her of guilt by saying, "Your aching bones are no match for a five-year-old's excitement."

Blythe stood then and escorted the child to her nursemaid. "Return to your chamber with Mrs. Hartwell," she said. "You don't want to be too tired to accompany your father and me to Smithfield *Pony* Market."

"Ponies," Miranda cried, clapping her hands together with childish glee. Willingly, she left the chamber with her nursemaid.

Blythe turned toward Roger. Her gaze fixed on his naked chest with its light matting of brown hair.

"Do you actually believe the idea of purchasing a pony will calm Miranda enough to sleep?" Roger asked, a smile lurking in his voice. He crossed the short distance that separated them. "What excited her so early in the morning?"

"Lord Perpendicular, the Earl of Corners, left a gold piece on top of the seed that Miranda planted," Blythe answered, managing to tear her gaze from his chest.

Her husband's attention was riveted on her breasts, almost

completely visible through the silken nightshift she wore. Without a word, he gently drew her toward him.

Standing so close their bodies touched, Blythe inhaled deeply of his faint scent of bay. She stared into his piercing blue eyes as he lowered his head to capture her mouth with his own.

Uncertain of what to do, Blythe stared at him unwaveringly as his face slowly inched its way to hers. The sight of his oh-so-sensual lips descending to claim hers made her heart flutter with anticipation. And then, as if from a faraway distance, she heard the faint tinkling of her love bell.

Come, Roger. Surrender your heart of love to Blythe.

She closed her eyes at the last possible second, and their lips touched. His mouth felt warm and gently insistent on hers.

"So sweet," Roger murmured, his breath mingling with hers.

Intoxicated by the feel of his mouth and the sound of his husky words, Blythe entwined her arms around his neck. And he responded to her unspoken invitation. She felt the subtle pressure of him drawing her even closer against the hard, masculine planes of his body.

Blythe reveled in these new feelings and returned his kiss in kind. Instinctively, she parted her lips for his tongue and enticed him to explore the sweetness of her mouth.

And then the kiss ended abruptly, as unexpectedly as it had begun.

"I've wanted to do that since the day of our betrothal," Roger admitted in a choked voice, releasing her. After visibly struggling to gain control of himself, he added, "It won't happen again. . . Be ready to leave at eleven. We'll dine at The Angel down on High Street on our way home." Without another word he turned away and marched back through the connecting door to his own chamber.

Judge a man by what he does, not what he says. . . . Pleased with her unexpected progress, Blythe smiled as the door clicked shut behind him.

At ten minutes before eleven, Blythe stood in front of the mirror in her chamber and studied her reflection for flaws. She wanted to look perfect for her first family outing with her husband and her stepdaughter. She wore a violet gown, which exactly matched the color of her eyes, and black leather riding boots. Instead of the violet cloak that complemented her gown, she grabbed a simple black woolen cloak.

Appearing too rich invited trouble. At least, her father had always told her that. Blending with one's surroundings was the wisest course of action. Englishmen from every station in life—cutpurse, merchant, and nobleman—mingled together at Smithfield, popularly known by native Londoners as the Devil's Shop and Ruffian's Hall.

"Daisy, deliver these parchments to Devereux House as soon as I leave," Blythe ordered, passing her the missives to her business agents and a note to her father. "Do not let his lordship's servants see you."

" 'Tis as good as done," Daisy said, pocketing the sealed papers and walking with her to the door.

Roger and Miranda awaited Blythe in the foyer. Excited beyond endurance, the five-year-old gamboled around and around in a fair imitation of a pony.

Outside in the courtyard two grooms stood with their horses. Roger helped Blythe mount. After lifting Miranda onto his own horse, he swung up into the saddle behind her.

"The grooms are accompanying us?" Blythe asked, watching the men mount the two remaining horses.

"They'll guard our horses and whatever we purchase," Roger said. "Have you ever gone to Smithfield?"

Blythe shook her head and turned her horse to ride beside his down the private lane leading to the Strand. London's most prominent horse dealers had usually brought their quality merchandise to Devereux House for her father's perusal.

"At Smithfield 'tis possible to 'lose' property and then purchase it back ten minutes later," Roger told her.

"That is disgraceful," Blythe exclaimed.

"Not everyone in England is so fortunate as to claim the Queen's Midas for a father," Roger replied.

"Misfortune is no excuse for thievery," Blythe said primly.

"Thievery is a relative thing," Roger said with a wry smile. "You, for example, are stealing my corn and wool profits."

"Criminality has naught to do with that," Blythe told him. " 'Tis merely the nature of business." At that she fixed her gaze on the road ahead of them.

The first day of autumn appeared auspicious for their first family outing. Clear blue skies kissed the distant horizon, and brilliant sunshine mirrored her mood. A gentle, crisp breeze had blown the early-morning mists away and heralded autumn's rapid approach. Gold tinged the lush green foliage, and a sea of goldenrod garnished with purple asters covered the open fields.

The Debrett entourage rode north on the Strand until they reached Charing Cross. There they veered to the right. Along the way Roger pointed out various landmarks such as York House and Somerset House. He explained to his daughter the significance of the places to which he directed her attention.

"What is your horse's name?" Miranda asked Blythe during a lull in the conversation.

"Achilles."

"That sounds like a boy."

"Quite right, but my horse is a girl." Blythe looked at Roger and asked, "What do you call your horse, my lord?"

"Hector."

Blythe giggled.

"What is so funny?" Miranda asked.

"According to legend, Achilles and Hector were the two fiercest warriors in the whole world and the bitterest of enemies," Blythe told her. "During the Trojan War they fought on opposite sides and ultimately confronted each other in mortal combat."

"Who won?"

"Achilles slew Hector," Blythe answered, casting her husband a jaunty smile.

Roger gave her an unamused look.

"What should I name *my* pony?" the five-year-old asked.

"Oh, that is impossible to know until you see it," Blythe told her. "When you recognize the pony meant only for you and no other, the naming will be incredibly easy."

Near the outskirts of London proper, the Strand became Fleet Street. They turned left onto The Bailey, which would bring them directly into Smithfield.

"Are we almost there?" Miranda asked, her excitement growing in direct proportion to the increased number of people they passed.

"Stop fidgeting," Roger ordered. "You are making Hector nervous."

"No matter the provocation, Achilles always remains calm," Blythe teased him.

"Females are more docile by nature," Roger countered.

"Unless provoked into unpredictability," Blythe qualified.

"What do you mean by that?" he asked.

"Simply this: A woman can predict quite accurately what a man will do in any given situation," she answered. "Unfortunately, a man can never be certain what course of action a woman will take."

"Very clever," Roger said. "You've inherited your father's quick wit."

"And you admire that quality?"

"No, 'tis an exceedingly annoying trait for a woman to possess."

"How do you prefer a woman's wits?" Blythe asked, irritated. "Scattered?"

"Better scattered than scathing," Roger answered with a wicked smile.

"Mama Blight, what story will you tell me tonight?" Miranda interrupted their verbal duel.

"Tonight your father will do the honors," Blythe told her. "Tomorrow I'll tell you how some of the flowers got their names."

"Oh, I can hardly wait," Miranda cried. Then, after a silent moment, "Daddy, what's the story you have for me?"

"If I told you that," Roger said, smiling down at the crown of her head, "I'd have no story to tell you later."

Surrounded in the west and the north by woodland, Smithfield Market was a grassy meadow located outside London's city walls. As they neared it, Blythe gazed at the surrounding woodland and recognized the telltale signs of summer's passing. Though still shaded by much green foliage, the woodland was giving way to gold, and the sweet scent of fallen leaves on earth wafted through the air.

Lively and noisy and dangerous, Smithfield Market teemed with hundreds of men and women from every station of life. Makeshift stalls ringed the inside periphery of the market, where vendors sold a variety of products such as Stratford bread, Hackney turnips, Holloway cheese cakes, and Pimlico pudding pies. Orange sellers, oyster sellers, and herb sellers mingled easily with hawkers of cures. Most of the horses for sale grazed in roped pens; but the most expensive and valuable horseflesh stood in their own area of pens along the eastern edge of the meadow nearest to London's walls.

"Ah, another day at the Devil's Shop," Roger said, dismounting. He lifted his daughter off the saddle and then helped Blythe dismount. After passing their horses' reins to one of his grooms, he warned his daughter, "As you can see, poppet, many hundreds of people are here. You must promise to hold Lady Blythe's hand at all times. Can you do that for Daddy?"

Miranda nodded and asked, "Where are the ponies?"

"Would you like something to eat first?" Roger asked. "Perhaps an orange or a pudding pie?"

"No, I want to find my pony," the girl answered.

"Lady Blythe might be hungry," he said.

"Oh, I couldn't swallow a bite until after Miranda finds her pony," Blythe said when the little girl looked at her pleadingly. She smiled at the relieved expression that appeared on Miranda's face.

Hand in hand, the three of them walked into the crowded meadow. One of their grooms followed behind in order to secure their purchases. They saw every imaginable kind of horse: milk white, dapple gray, black, or brown, with pretty markings.

Blythe glanced up at the sky as they walked in the direction of the pony dealers. The horizon was a clear blue lake with nary a cloud to mar the radiant perfection of the sun. And yet . . .

A wave of apprehension surged through her. Blythe felt unaccountably disturbed, as if a shadow had swept across the earth. Scanning the area, she detected nothing amiss, but her nerves still tingled riotously in the instinctive alarm for danger.

"Is something wrong?" Roger asked.

"No, I'm merely unused to all of this activity," Blythe answered, managing a smile for him.

When they reached the fairway reserved for ponies, Blythe gave Miranda's hand a gentle squeeze and instructed her, "We'll walk up one side and down the other so you can inspect the ponies. Stop when your heart tells you which pony is meant only for you. Do you understand?"

Miranda nodded.

With Roger and his groom following behind them, Blythe and Miranda walked slowly up the right side of the fairway. Blythe heard people greeting her husband; she felt proud that he was so highly esteemed by London's commoners. Thankfully, no one noticed Miranda and her.

Miranda led Blythe down the length of the pony aisle. The five-year-old paused several times to take a closer look at a pony, but then shook her head. When they reached the end of the fairway, they crossed to the opposite side.

Halfway down the fairway, Miranda stopped short and stared at two ponies in one of the roped pens. A smile spread across her face.

"Here, Mama Blight," Miranda said, pointing at the ponies. "My heart tells me to stop here."

"You're certain?"

The five-year-old nodded.

"Sir, we wish to inspect your ponies," Blythe told the dealer. "May we enter the pen?"

" 'Tis aboot time someone noticed the quality of my ponies," the man said, dropping the cord of rope for them.

"I detect a northern accent," Blythe said, stepping into the pen. "My uncle is a Scotsman."

"From where does he hail, my lady?" the man asked pleasantly.

"Argyll," Blythe answered. "My uncle is the Earl of Dunridge. Do you know him?"

"I know *of* him, but an earl is too important a man for me to know personally," the man replied. Then, "Why, ye must be related to the English queen's Midas?"

"I am the Earl of Basildon's daughter," Blythe said. She gestured behind her and added, "This is my husband, the Earl of Eden."

"Pleased to make yer acquaintance, my lord," the Scotsman said. "I hope ye'll find my ponies to yer likin'."

An excited murmur raced faster than a thoroughbred through the crowd. The Earl of Eden had brought his Devereux bride to Smithfield Market. In mere seconds a crowd gathered outside the pen to glimpse the famous newlyweds.

Unaccustomed to so many people, Blythe wished they'd brought more grooms along for protection. She wanted nothing to mar her stepdaughter's outing.

The Scotsman had only two ponies for sale. One was white with chestnut-red patches, a white mane and tail, chestnut-red ears, and blue eyes. The other was coal-black with a pure-white star on its forehead and black eyes.

"Which one is it?" Blythe asked.

"I don't know," Miranda whispered, holding her hand out to the coal-black pony. The animal sniffed her offered hand and then nuzzled it wetly.

Miranda giggled.

Blythe opened her mouth to ask Roger to inspect the pony, but an unusual thing happened. The black nudged its mate's neck. The other pony bent its head forward, sniffed the girl, and then licked the side of her face.

Miranda giggled with delight, and the pony lifted its head and neighed. The crowd of spectators outside the pen laughed.

Smiling, Roger stepped forward to inspect the black pony first. "He seems healthy," he announced. "How much do you want?"

"My price is twenty-five guineas for each pony," the Scotsman told him.

"Your price is too high," Roger replied. "Besides, I need only one pony."

"I'm verra sorry, my lord," the man said, casting a sidelong glance at the child. "These ponies must be kept together as a set. Both would die of loneliness if separated. They're magical ponies, ye see."

"Magical, my arse," Roger countered. "I'll give you fifteen guineas for the black."

With exaggerated regret, the Scotsman shook his head. "I canna do business with ye, my lord."

Blythe noted Miranda's disappointed expression. "My lord, please inspect the other pony," she said.

Roger slid his gaze to her. "I will not be persuaded to buy two ponies."

"I haven't asked you to buy two ponies," Blythe replied, meeting his dubious look with her sunniest smile. "I am considering purchasing the second pony so that my sisters and my brother will have a pony to ride when they visit Debrett House. One pony in residence could cause an infinite number of squabbles."

Wearing a reluctant expression, Roger walked slowly around the chestnut-and-white pony. When he stood in front of it again, he checked its teeth and then its eyes.

"God's bread," Roger exclaimed, turning to the pony dealer. "This female is blind and not worth a pence, never mind twenty-five guineas."

"She sees with her heart," the Scotsman countered, "and the

black guides her around dangerous objects. One would be lost without the other."

"She's blind?" Blythe echoed, stepping closer. She gazed into the pony's unseeing blue eyes. Suddenly, the black nudged his mate's neck; the chestnut-and-white pony lifted her head and neighed.

Blythe smiled at their charming byplay. "The Scotsman is honest," she told her husband.

"*Honest?*" Roger rounded on her, eliciting more than a few chuckles from their audience of commoners. "The Scotsman is a swindler who wants to sell you a useless, blind pony for twenty-five guineas."

"My lord, no creature is useless," Blythe countered, unruffled by his outburst. "The man told us truthfully that the ponies cannot be separated."

"Why not?"

" 'Twould be unnecessarily cruel to separate two creatures who love each other," Blythe answered.

"Animals are incapable of feeling love or any other emotion," Roger shot back. "I refuse to purchase defective merchandise. There are hundreds of ponies at Smithfield. Miranda will choose another."

"That's it, your lordship," said a man in the crowd of on-lookers. "Put your foot down."

"Aye, show the wife who's boss," another called his encouragement.

Blythe gave their mostly masculine audience an unamused look. Without saying a word, she let them know how much their behavior displeased her.

"Has Hector ever been frightened?" Blythe asked, rounding on Roger.

"Yes, of course."

"Fright is an emotion."

Roger leveled a cold stare on her.

"Has Hector ever been annoyed by a groom?"

"Yes."

"That's also an emotion."

Roger glared at her, and his right cheek suddenly developed a twitch.

"On the way here today did you order Miranda to sit still because Hector was becoming nervous?"

No reply.

Blythe lifted her chin a notch and said in a haughty voice, "That's an emotion too."

The twitch in Roger's right cheek traveled to his left cheek.

"If an animal can be frightened, annoyed, and nervous," Blythe announced, "he or she can also love. . . . Since Miranda prefers these ponies, I shall purchase the female." She smiled brightly at her husband's surprised expression and turned to the dealer, asking, "Is forty-five guineas for the two ponies acceptable?"

"Aye, 'tis a done deal," the man agreed. "And I never lied to ye, my lady. These two *are* magical ponies."

"I believe you, sir."

"You're mad," Roger said.

"Ah, but I have a method to my madness," Blythe replied, gesturing their groom to take the ponies' reins in hand before the dealer could change his mind. "Blindness does not impede fertility. I've a mind to breed ponies and squeeze the Shet-landers out of the market."

"She's Midas's daughter all right," someone in the crowd said in a loud voice.

Ignoring their audience and her husband's disapproving frown, Blythe turned to Miranda and said, "We must give the ponies their names now, because bringing a nameless creature into our home is bad luck."

"I've heard all the silliness I can endure," Roger muttered.

"Ignore your father," Blythe whispered. "What names shall we give these creatures?"

Miranda looked at each pony for a long moment and then asked, "Mama Blight, will you help me?"

Pleased by the request, Blythe inclined her head. At least one Debrett appreciated her intelligence and valued her opinion.

She placed her right index finger across her lips and studied each pony.

"The black is Pericles," Blythe announced finally. "His mate is Aspasia."

"Peri and Aspa?" Miranda echoed in obvious bewilderment.

"Pericles and Aspasia," Blythe repeated, smiling at the girl. "In ancient Greece, Pericles ruled a great city called Athens. Aspasia, his mistress, ruled Athenian society *and Pericles*." She glanced at her husband and added, "Aspasia was exceedingly beautiful and intelligent, and Pericles showed wisdom in valuing her judgment."

Only a deaf man could have missed her meaning. Roger rolled his eyes in pained irritation.

"Take Pericles and Aspasia to our horses," Blythe instructed the Debrett groom. She watched the man lead the ponies away and then turned to her husband, saying, "I neglected to bring any coins with me. You'll need to loan me the money for Aspasia."

The watching crowd roared with laughter at the earl's expression of angry surprise. Even the Scots pony dealer hooted disrespectfully.

"Twenty-five guineas, is it?" Roger said, giving her a devastatingly wicked smile. "Plus an extra five guineas because I would never have paid more than fifteen for the black."

Blythe nodded in agreement. Let him enjoy his moment of glory in front of their audience. She would make more than thirty guineas from besting him in the wool and corn trades that day. Besides, thirty guineas was a small price to pay for the girl's happiness.

"So, you desire a loan of thirty guineas for approximately four hours?" Roger asked her.

"Yes, my lord." Blythe inclined her head, but wondered where this was leading.

"Are you willing to pay five guineas interest per hour?" he asked, making their audience laugh.

"Sacred Saint Swithin, no one charges five guineas interest per hour," she cried.

"I do." Roger gave her a broad grin.

Blythe leveled a frosty glare at him. "I agree to your terms," she said, knowing she had no choice. "Pay the man, and I'll settle with you later."

The crowd of onlookers erupted into appreciative applause. Slowly, they began to drift away to continue with their own business.

"I want to look at a few horses on the other side of the meadow," Roger said after paying the Scotsman. "We'll dine afterward."

"Mama Blight?" Miranda crooked her finger at her.

Blythe leaned down so the girl could whisper in her ear. "My lord, Miranda wishes to pluck a rose," she told her husband, the hint of smile tugging at the corners of her lips.

Roger rounded on his daughter, asking, "Didn't I tell you to go before we left the house?"

Miranda gave him an apologetic shrug. "Daddy, I have to go *now*."

Roger sighed audibly.

His expression told Blythe that he found dealing with women and children a tad frustrating. "We'll be perfectly safe," she assured him.

"Take her into the woods on the other side of the market," Roger said. "I'll be near enough to hear you shout if you need me."

Walking toward the eastern edge of the meadow, Blythe gazed at the surrounding woodland behind the last of the horse pens. The maple trees had gone to gold and soon would be orange and red; the rowan trees were fading to yellow, as were the birch and the oak. Amid the woodland's changing color, the evergreens—holly, pine, yew, and fir—distinguished themselves with their constancy.

"I'll be here," Roger said when they reached the last horse dealer. "Scream if you need me."

Blythe smiled. "I doubt 'twill be necessary."

After experiencing the noisy crush of the market, the woodlands seemed unusually quiet, and an eerie hush pervaded the atmosphere. Blythe felt the first stirrings of unease as soon as she'd left the meadow behind. Glancing over her shoulder, she detected no one nearby.

Thankfully, Miranda needed only a moment of privacy. Blythe could hardly wait to return to the meadow and feel the comforting rays of the sun on her shoulders.

"Look," Miranda cried when they emerged from the shaded woods.

Blythe snapped her head around to look at the five-year-old. Then she lifted her gaze to what the girl was watching overhead.

Materializing from nowhere, a dense cloud with a vertical extent nearly masked the sun's rays; the anvil-shaped upper portion allowed sunlight to glow halolike around it. Amazingly, the sky's horizon remained blue. No other clouds accompanied this one on its flight.

"I never saw such a dark sun," Miranda exclaimed.

Beware the dark sun.

Blythe froze in dawning horror as her mother's prophecy slammed into her consciousness. Frantic with fear, she saw her beloved standing where she'd left him.

"Roger, 'tis the dark sun!" Blythe screamed, grabbing the girl's hand and running toward him.

Whirling around at the sound of her cry, Roger stepped toward them. At that precise moment, an arrow whizzed through the spot where he'd just stood and hit a tree on the edge of the woodland.

"What the bloody hell?" Roger swore, hearing the horse dealer's shout of surprised alarm. After verifying that Blythe and Miranda were uninjured, he returned to the horse dealer and asked, "Are you hurt?"

"No, my lord, merely startled," the man answered. "Thank a merciful God, none of the horses was injured."

"Who would shoot an arrow at you?" Roger asked.

"I have no enemies," the horse dealer answered. "Who would want *you* dead?"

Roger said nothing. His lips tightened into a grim white line as he looked from the horse dealer to Blythe.

Watching him, Blythe recognized anger and fear warring upon his features. She could almost see him thinking as he stared at her. Her husband did not worry for his own safety. He'd just realized Miranda and she might have been killed if they hadn't gone to pluck a rose.

"Aren't you going to inspect that arrow?" the horse dealer asked.

" 'Tisn't likely an assassin would sign his name to the murder weapon," Roger answered.

"I want to go home now," Blythe said in a quavering voice. She kept Miranda in front of her, using her own body to shield the child from view lest the villain still be lingering about.

Roger nodded and turned to the horse dealer. "I'm sorry you and your horses have been frightened by an arrow meant for me," he said, erasing all emotion from his expression. "I'll buy the whole lot of horses."

"All fifteen of them?"

"Deliver them to Debrett House this afternoon." Roger took his daughter's hand in his, saying, "Let's go."

Within minutes they'd mounted their horses and started down The Bailey toward Fleet Street. One groom rode in front of them while the other, with the two ponies in tow, took up the rear. At Charing Cross, they veered to the left and started down the Strand.

"The danger has passed," Blythe announced.

Roger arched a brow at her in silent question.

Blythe pointed toward the sky. The forbidding cloud had disappeared, and the sun shone again in all of its original radiance.

"Who would want to dispatch you?" she asked.

Roger smiled wryly. "Do you have several hours to waste while I list all my enemies?"

"An assassination attempt is no joking matter, my lord. 'Tis a miracle you weren't hurt."

"Do you think a disgruntled wool or corn chandler has decided to end our price war?" he teased.

Blythe did smile then. She knew he was trying to banish her worry.

"*My* associates are suffering no loss of profits," she told him.

"Nor are mine."

"I want to ride my ponies," Miranda announced when they halted their horses in the front courtyard of Debrett House.

"Pericles and Aspasia have had an exciting day and need to become accustomed to their new home," Blythe told the girl. "Why don't we let them have dinner and rest awhile? Later we'll treat them to carrots."

Miranda nodded in agreement as the grooms led the horses and ponies away.

With the five-year-old between them, Roger and Blythe walked toward the house. Entering the foyer, they heard voices raised in anger coming from the great hall.

"What do you mean?" a man demanded.

"I mean what I just said," a woman answered. "I have no idea when they'll return."

Blythe recognized Daisy Lloyd's voice and flicked her husband a worried glance as they crossed the foyer to the great hall.

"You're lying," a second man accused. "Tell us where we can find the earl."

"Bottoms, thank God you're here," the first man cried.

" 'Tis urgent we speak with his lordship," the second man said. "Every minute we delay means money is lost."

Her husband's business agents. Blythe slowed her step. Letting Roger enter the hall ahead of her, she paused in the foyer to help Miranda remove her cloak.

"Go inside the hall, and we'll have a mug of cider," Blythe instructed the child. She doffed her own cloak and walked toward the hall like a woman going to the gallows. She already knew why her husband's agents were here.

"What is the problem?" Blythe heard her husband ask as she stepped into the great hall.

Mr. Newell and Mr. Andrews, her husband's wool and corn agents, snapped their gazes to her when she appeared. " 'Tis your wife," Newell said in a scathing voice, pointing his finger at her.

"With all due respect, my lord, you've married an underhanded viper," Andrews cried.

"She must have been eavesdropping on our meeting yesterday," Newell added. "No sooner had we lowered our prices than Rodale and Hibbert lowered hers."

Blythe looked at Roger and gulped nervously. His complexion had mottled with barely suppressed rage as he stared in seeming disbelief at his agents. She only hoped he wouldn't turn on her in front of them. And then he spoke, his words surprising her.

"Business rival or not, Lady Blythe is the Countess of Eden," Roger told the two men in a clipped voice. "If you ever speak disparagingly of my wife again, your positions will be forfeit. Do you understand?"

"Forgive us, my lord," Newell spoke up hastily.

"We meant no real disrespect," Andrews added.

Joy surged through Blythe. In spite of their differences, her husband had defended her. A good sign, to be sure.

"Return early tomorrow morning," Roger was saying to the men. "I cannot think clearly at the moment."

Both men nodded deferentially and started to leave the hall. Passing Blythe on their way, they gave her frigid glares.

With a smile lighting her whole expression, Blythe started toward Roger. She knew she ought to apologize to him for using that insider information. After all, he had just finished defending her.

Blythe stopped short when her husband met her smile with a cold stare. He looked as if he'd like to throttle her.

"You bloody, treacherous bitch," Roger exploded with anger.

"Please lower your voice. Your shouting will frighten Miranda," Blythe warned, sounding calmer than she actually felt.

"Miranda is *my* daughter, not yours," Roger shot back.

The contempt etched across his face forced Blythe to defend herself. "You *willingly* gave me that information," she reminded him. "Should I have ignored it?"

"Did you hire an assassin to dispatch me?" Roger asked through clenched teeth.

Blythe couldn't credit what she was hearing. In spite of her careful upbringing and her mother's gentle teachings, a boiling fury erupted within her.

"What utter stupidity is this?" Blythe shouted. "If not for me, you would be rotting in the Tower. I did you a favor by marrying you. Remember?"

Roger gave her a final scathing look and turned on his heels. With Blythe close behind him, he marched out of the hall and headed for the front door.

"Where are you going?" she demanded, watching him from the great hall's entrance.

"To sniff gardenias," Roger called over his shoulder, and then disappeared out the door.

"Son of a bitch," Blythe swore, sagging against the wall as all the fight went out of her.

Never had Blythe succumbed to such a negative emotion. Depleted of energy, she closed her eyes and tried to gain control of herself. Suddenly, she became aware of the unusual silence surrounding her, as if every Debrett retainer stood statue-still and listened to the battle that raged between the lord and his lady.

Using her husband's insider information had been unethical. Blythe realized that now. If she hadn't been his wife, Roger would never have shared his plans to lower his prices.

Now her husband believed her to be untrustworthy, and their relationship was in worse condition than before their marriage. But why had Roger shared his plans? Had he been gloating? Or had he begun to trust her and viewed their price war as a chess game between two worthy opponents?

No matter his purpose. She should never have used that information in so timely a fashion; losing a day's profits would not have bankrupted her. Keeping her personal and her business lives separate was becoming more difficult with each passing day.

And then a more horrifying possibility slammed into her consciousness. Somewhere out there an assassin awaited her husband. Oh, where in the great universe had Roger gone? How could she live with herself if the worst happened, especially since his anger at her had incited him to storm out of Debrett House?

Blythe pushed away from the wall and walked slowly into the great hall. And then she heard the heart-wrenching sound of a weeping child. *Miranda!*

The five-year-old sat in one of the chairs in front of the hearth and wept as if she'd just lost her best friend in the whole world. Bottoms and Daisy stood frozen nearby, uncertain how to comfort the little girl.

"What's wrong, poppet?" Blythe asked, crouching down to eye-level with the girl.

"F-fighting and s-shouting," Miranda sobbed, looking up at her through bleary blue eyes. "'T-tis just like Lady Darnel."

"'Tis nothing like that," Blythe assured her in a soothing voice. "Your father and I were not fighting and shouting."

"What were you doing?" she asked, giving her a doubtful look.

Blythe smiled. "Sit upon my lap and I'll explain."

Miranda rose from the chair so that Blythe could sit. Then she climbed up on her lap.

First Blythe brushed the tears off the girl's cheeks and then pulled her reassuringly close. "Now then, your father and I were not fighting," she said. "We were disagreeing."

"Isn't that the same thing?"

"Definitely not," Blythe answered, shaking her head. "People who dislike each other fight, but people who love each other sometimes disagree."

"Do you love Daddy?" Miranda asked.

"I have loved your daddy forever," Blythe answered.

"Does Daddy love you?"

"Yes, but he doesn't know it." Blythe smiled at her. "Always remember this: No matter how much your daddy loves me, he will always love you more."

"What about the shouting?" the five-year-old asked.

"Oh, that," Blythe hedged, gesturing with her hand as if the shouting was of no importance, searching her mind for a plausible answer. "Your father and I were not shouting. Our excitement made us raise our voices. 'Twas entirely my fault. You see, surprise made your father raise his voice. I mistakenly assumed that if I also raised my voice he would understand my words. The problem was a lack of *listening*, not hearing."

"I think I understand," Miranda said.

"When your father returns home, he will still be angry with me," Blythe added. "I made the mistake of following my head when I should have followed my heart. . . . Now, shall we visit Pericles and Aspasia?"

"Can we bring them a treat?"

Blythe looked at Daisy and her husband's majordomo. For some unfathomable reason, both were grinning at her like a couple of blinking idiots.

"Bottoms, please fetch us a few carrots from Cook," she instructed the man.

"With pleasure, my lady."

"And a few tasty apples too?" Daisy asked.

"That would be wonderful," Blythe answered. "Bottoms, bring some apples with the carrots. Daisy, fetch me parchment, ink, and quill. I must send another message to my agents."

Daisy arched a brow at her as if to warn her against foolish action.

Blythe inclined her head in answer to the unspoken warning and said, "I must rectify a mistake."

Daisy nodded and followed the majordomo out of the hall.

Miranda entwined her arms around Blythe's neck and planted a kiss on her cheek. "I love you, Mama Blight," she vowed.

Holding her protectively close, Blythe said, "And I love you, poppet, and promise never to raise my voice to your daddy again."

Chapter 8

Twilight's last slashes of mauve light had already slid beneath the western horizon, and an eerie hush pervaded the air as Roger rode up the private lane leading from the Strand to the Debrett stables. His visit to London's Royal Rooster Tavern, where he had several well-placed friends who could help him identify the assassin, had been frustratingly futile.

Discovering the would-be assassin's employer was a matter of his own life and death. A simple problem with a simple solution. Either he identified his enemy or he died.

Without a doubt, Roger now knew that the person who wanted him dead was also his late wife's murderer. The villain had failed in his indirect attempt to get rid of him—by way of an execution for murder—and so had tried a more direct approach.

How difficult could it be to learn the bastard's identity? Roger smiled wryly. Finding the guilty man from hundreds of courtiers and thousands of London's commoners was no more difficult than finding a needle in a stack of hay.

Dismounting outside the Debrett stables, Roger drew Hector inside. In an instant a groom materialized from nowhere to take charge of his lord's horse.

Roger nodded at the man and started to leave, but the ponies caught his attention. Aspasia, the female, stood with her head resting on the back of the male's neck, a most unusual position for a horse. Pericles stood absolutely still, allowing her to do so.

"Did you put them together?" Roger called over his shoulder to the groom.

"No, my lord. I put them in different stalls, but they wouldn't settle down," the man told him. "Then the countess stopped by to feed them carrots and insisted they be housed together. The ponies quieted as soon as I put them in the same stall."

... *Magical ponies,* Roger recalled the Scotsman's words. *Both would die of loneliness if separated.*

Reaching out with two hands, Roger stroked both ponies at the same time. Pericles looked at him through eyes darker than a moonless midnight, but Aspasia troubled him. She stared at him through sightless blue eyes, yet he felt as though she could see to the very depths of his tarnished soul.

"In love, huh?" Roger muttered to them.

"Did you say something, my lord?" the groom asked, hearing his master's voice.

"I was just talking to myself," Roger answered, turning away from the stall.

There is no emotion called love, Roger told himself as he walked toward the mansion. His father and his late wife had cured him of that foolish notion. Yet, dealing with his father's cold contempt and his wife's despicable wantonness seemed easier at the moment than dealing with his bride.

Blythe Devereux was a beautiful enigma. On the one hand, she'd proven herself to be a calculating businesswoman with a "take no prisoners" attitude. On the other hand, she appeared to harbor the most illogical, thoroughly female philosophy of life he'd ever seen. And she appeared to be a kinder and more nurturing mother to Miranda than Darnel had ever been.

The great hall was deserted. At this hour his daughter would already be in her bedchamber. Instead of walking upstairs to say goodnight, Roger went directly to his study.

After pouring himself a glass of whiskey, Roger sat down behind his desk and sipped the amber liquid. Its strong, burning sensation slid slowly from his lips to his stomach, helping him to relax.

A smile touched Roger's lips, and he raised his glass in salute to his bride. Blythe had used his insider information against him; she'd done exactly as he would have. Though directed at her, his anger had actually been with himself for underestimating her business acumen. When it came to business, his bride apparently thought like a man.

Roger knew one thing for certain. He would not lower his wool and corn prices again. If prices dropped any lower, he'd be giving his commodities away.

Let her win this skirmish, Roger decided. Ultimately, he would win the war. One did not operate at a loss and still make a profit. If he kept his prices fixed, she would soon raise hers to meet his or succumb to financial disaster.

Roger closed his eyes and conjured her hauntingly lovely face. How surprised Blythe would be when she learned that he hadn't lowered his prices. He only wished he could be in the room to witness it; he adored those disarming violet eyes of hers and the way her inviting lips formed a perfect *O* whenever she was surprised.

Setting the glass of whiskey down, Roger lifted his booted feet to rest on top of the desk and closed his eyes. The day's disturbing events had taken their toll on him. Before five minutes had passed, he'd fallen into a deep, dreamless sleep.

Roger awakened disoriented. He opened his eyes, focused on the chamber, and realized he'd fallen asleep in his study. He knew from the dim light filtering in through the windows behind him that the hour was early, too early even for the servants to be about.

Rising from the chair, Roger yawned and stretched. He wandered to the windows to gauge the time but stared in surprise at what he saw. In the distance a figure cloaked in white seemed to float ghostlike across the expanse of lawns toward the willow tree.

For one sickening moment, Roger thought he was seeing things that weren't there. He snapped his eyes shut, but when he opened them again, the white-cloaked figure was still gliding toward the willow. The slight figure paused at the tree, looked around as if verifying that no one watched, and then ducked beneath the willow's sweeping branches.

What the bloody hell was happening in his garden? Roger turned on his heels and marched toward the door.

Roger slowly and stealthily crossed the grounds. He did not wish to alert the intruder to his presence. Ten feet from the willow tree, he heard a voice in prayer and paused to listen.

"Great Mother Goddess, I thank you for keeping my eagle safe from harm and do implore you to continue to deliver us from evil. . . ."

Great Mother Goddess? Roger thought, stunned when he recognized his bride's voice. She actually believed God was a woman? And who in bloody hell was her eagle?

"I dismiss you, Ngu, Lord of the Four Directions and Winds. I dismiss you, Paralda, Lord of the East, and Eurus, the east wind. . . ."

Lord of the East and the east wind? Roger thought, frozen in surprise. What religion was this? And then he knew: His bride was practicing witchcraft.

Roger folded his arms across his chest and waited for her to emerge from beneath the sweeping branches of the willow tree.

". . . I dismiss you, Ghom, Lord of the North, and Boreas, the north wind."

Silence reigned for a long, long moment. And then the willow's branches parted.

"What, in the holy name of God, do you think you're doing?" Roger demanded.

At the sight of him, Blythe widened her disarming violet eyes, and surprise parted her oh-so-inviting lips. Roger wasn't at all enchanted by her adorable features and expressions at this moment.

"I am waiting for an answer," Roger said, blocking her escape route when he noted her gaze slide over his shoulder as if she contemplated making a run for the house.

Inexplicably, Blythe smiled at him, and a relieved expression appeared on her face. She reached out as if to touch his arm, but he quickly stepped back a pace.

Blythe lost her smile. "Are you afraid or angry?" she asked.

"I'll ask the questions," Roger said. "Who is your 'eagle'?"

"You are."

"Are you practicing witchcraft in my garden?" he asked.

Blythe stared at him for a moment and then said, "I hardly think this is the proper place to discuss—"

With a muttered curse, Roger scooped her into his arms and marched back to the house. Even the seductive scent of roses that clung to her could not penetrate his anger. He carried her past sleepy-eyed servants, who were just rising to stoke the morning fires, and up the stairs to her bedchamber.

Roger kicked the door shut with his booted foot and then set her down on the floor. "I'm still waiting for an answer," he said. "Are you trying to practice witchcraft on my property?"

"Surely you do not hold with such absurd notions," she replied, turning her back on him. She started to walk away, but his hand on her shoulder prevented that.

"You still haven't answered my question," Roger reminded her. "Are you a witch?"

Blythe turned around and met his gaze unwaveringly. "No," she answered honestly.

"What were you doing outside?" Roger asked, relaxing a bit. "And what exactly are you?"

"I went outside to worship." Blythe gifted him with a smile filled with sunshine. "I am as my mother and her mother before her."

"Which is?" Roger demanded, narrowing his gaze on her.

Blythe looked him straight in the eye. She uttered one word, a single word that nearly felled him with its implications.

"Druid."

"God's bread, I'm harboring a pagan." And then another thought occurred to him. "The countess is . . ."

Blythe nodded. "My mother is also a Druid."

"What the bloody hell is the difference between witchcraft and . . . and *that*?" he demanded, lowering his voice.

"Do you have several hours to waste whilst I discuss the finer points of theology that separate the two?" she asked. "Suffice it to say, being Druid is the only path to universal truth."

"I forbid you to do *that* anymore," Roger ordered in a loud voice, fear for her safety rising within him. " 'Tis dangerous in the extreme."

"Mama Blight!" Miranda cried, bursting into her chamber before Blythe could reply. "Lord Perpendicular left me more gold!" The five-year-old stopped short and looked at Roger.

"Your father is raising his voice because he's excited," Blythe told the girl, crouching down to give her a sideways hug. "But I promise to remain calm and not raise my voice. Return to your bed, and all will be well."

Miranda padded on bare feet across the chamber to the door, but paused before leaving and said, "Daddy, you should know by now that you love Mama Blight." She left without another word.

Roger was as stunned by his daughter's words as he was by his bride's startling admission. "What was that about?" he asked, rounding on his wife.

"My lord, your shouting yesterday upset her," Blythe told him. "Miranda is overly sensitive, and you must guard your tongue whenever she's within hearing distance. I told her that we were disagreeing, not fighting. Witnessing whatever happened between Darnel and you has marred her, and she cannot bear to hear you or anyone else shouting."

"Your kindness to my daughter does not excuse what you were doing in my garden, and—"

"Worshiping."

Roger narrowed his gaze on her. "I beg your pardon?"

"I was worshiping in our garden," Blythe said with a jaunty smile.

"*My garden.* My agents will be here at nine o'clock," Roger said, ignoring her remark. "Be ready to leave at ten."

"Where are we going?"

"Devereux House."

"Shall I pack my belongings?"

Her question surprised him. "For what?"

"Are you returning me to my parents?"

Roger stared hard at her. He had half a mind to let her dangle with doubt, but couldn't bring himself to treat her so.

"No," he said finally.

Without further explanation, Roger turned and walked through the connecting door to his own chamber. He could almost visualize the consternation that assuredly appeared on her face, and that brought a smile to his lips.

Why was he smiling? Harboring a pagan was no laughing matter. His bride endangered not only herself but his whole household.

And Lady Keely? He would never have thought her capable of such a thing. Roger fully intended to set his father-in-law straight about what had been transpiring beneath his nose for nineteen years.

Together, Earl Richard and he would end this dangerous folly.

Dismounting in the courtyard of Devereux House, Blythe inhaled deeply of early autumn's crisply clean scent. The warming sun had evaporated the morning mists; but Blythe knew that, sheltered within the Thames River's shaded nooks, the mist would linger until afternoon. Though the transitional times of the year—summer into autumn and winter into spring—always cast a melancholy humor over her, Blythe felt her life's blood quickening as Samhuinn drew ever nearer.

"Indeed, these are magical ponies," Miranda announced. " 'Twas the smoothest ride I ever did have. It was like gliding upon a cloud."

Blythe turned at the sound of the five-year-old speaking to Roger. The scowl that appeared on his face at his daughter's use of the word *magical* incited Blythe to giggle, but she managed to control herself. There was no telling what he'd do if she dared laugh at him. She only hoped that her parents would control themselves when Roger began ranting and raving.

To make the situation worse, Miranda had insisted on riding Pericles to Devereux House *and* had stubbornly demanded that Aspasia be reined and tied to Pericles's saddle. As the five-year-old had told her father, "These magical ponies cannot be separated."

Naturally, Roger had balked at his daughter's demands and threatened to leave her home.

Miranda rebelled and threatened to walk the distance alone. Then the five-year-old committed the unforgivable. She bit her thumb at him.

Blythe had managed to suppress the laughter rising in her throat. Still, the child's rebellion had earned her a censorious glare from her husband. Apparently, he believed she was a bad influence on his daughter.

"Are you ready to meet new friends?" Blythe asked, offering her hand to the girl.

Miranda gave her a confident "thumbs up" and then accepted the offered hand. Together, they walked toward Devereux House.

"Mama Blight, see all the children," Miranda cried when they stood in the great hall's entrance.

"They are my sisters and my brother," Blythe told her as the group near the hearth turned around in unison. "And here comes my mother."

Hand in hand, Blythe and Miranda walked across the hall. At the same moment Lady Keely started toward them, and her children followed behind her.

Blythe kissed her mother's cheek and said, "Meet Miranda, my stepdaughter."

"Hello, Miranda," the countess greeted the little girl. "What pretty blue eyes you have, and I do believe you resemble your father."

Lingering insecurity kept Miranda attached to Blythe's hand, but she gushed with obvious excitement, "I heard you were a princess from the mountains."

"Yes, dearest," Lady Keely replied with a smile. "I am descended from ancient Welsh princes, but do not ever mention that fact to Queen Elizabeth or she'll—" With one finger the countess made a slashing gesture across her own throat.

"Your secret is safe with me," Miranda whispered, her expression mirroring her horrified surprise. Then she made a gesture as if buttoning her lips.

Lady Keely nodded her approval and gave her attention to Roger. When she moved to give him a welcoming hug, he stepped back a pace out of her reach. Bewildered surprise registered on her face, but she banished it in an instant.

Blythe flicked an annoyed glance at her husband. Her mother possessed the gentlest soul in all the universe and deserved better treatment. Nobody hurt her mother's feelings and walked away unscathed. Roger would pay for his cruel gesture; Blythe would make certain of it.

" 'Tis a pleasure seeing you again," Lady Keely greeted him, assuming a coolly polite attitude.

"My lady, I desire conversation with the earl and you," Roger said without preamble.

"Jennings, please inform my husband that we have guests," Lady Keely called to the majordomo.

The man nodded and left the hall.

A strained silence descended on the three adults. Escaping it, Blythe glanced at her stepdaughter, who was staring in awe at the Devereux children.

"Mama Blight, there's only six," Miranda whispered.

"Bliss is away at court," Blythe replied, drawing her forward.

"Let me introduce you. . . . Meet Aurora, who is fourteen; Summer and Autumn are eleven, Hope is eight, Adam is four, and Blaze is two years old."

"Summer and Autumn are twins, and Blaze has red hair," Miranda observed as if the Devereux children couldn't hear her. "Adam is the only boy."

Four-year-old Adam marched toward her and leaned so close his nose almost touched hers. In a loud voice he announced, "I like you."

"You do?" Miranda exclaimed, a smile of pure joy lighting her whole expression.

Blythe felt a constricting tightness around her heart at the sight of her stepdaughter's happiness. Had she never enjoyed the company of other children?

"Do you want to play?" Adam asked.

Miranda nodded and then told him, "My daddy bought me a pony yesterday, and Mama Blight bought his blind mate so you can ride whenever you visit me. We can ride them right now, because I brought them with me. Won't that be fun?"

"I *really* like you," Adam said.

"The pony is blind?" eight-year-old Hope echoed. "Oh, she can see clearly beyond the horizon."

Blythe flicked a sidelong glance at her husband. He was staring at Hope with an expression announcing that circumstances were worse than he'd originally expected.

"Mrs. Ashemole," Blythe called to the aging Devereux nurse-maid before her sister could say anything else. "Please take the children to play in the garden. Tell one of the grooms to bring the ponies around."

Miranda looked at her father for permission. When he nodded, she gave Blythe a "thumbs up." Accepting Adam's outstretched hand, Miranda left the hall with the Devereux children.

The earl passed the children as they left the hall. Smiling, he kissed his daughter's cheek and then extended his hand to Roger, saying, "Let's sit in front of the hearth."

Roger shook his head. "I desire private conversation where the servants cannot overhear us."

Richard gave him a puzzled look. "Will my office do?"

"Yes."

Inside the study Lady Keely and Blythe sat down in the chairs in front of the desk. Roger stood as far away from them as he could without being overtly rude. Richard poured a shot of whisky and passed it to his son-in-law.

"Better make yours a double," Roger warned. "And then sit down while I tell you my startling discovery."

"This sounds ominous," Lady Keely remarked. She looked at Blythe, who merely cast her an ambiguous smile.

The earl sat down, gulped a shot, and then poured himself another. He grinned at the younger man, who was pacing back and forth, and teased, "Do your worst, Roger. I'm ready for anything."

Blythe giggled. One glance at her husband's face abruptly ended her merriment.

Roger stopped pacing and faced her father. "My lord, something nefarious at Devereux House has tainted my wife, possibly all of your children."

"And what would that be?" the earl asked, his expression carefully devoid of emotion.

Roger glanced at the countess and hesitated, obviously torn by what he intended to divulge. " 'Tis exceedingly difficult to—"

"Spill it, Roger," Richard interrupted.

"Lady Keely is a pagan," Roger announced baldly. "I do believe she has raised your—"

Richard threw back his head and shouted with laughter. Blythe covered her mouth with one hand in an effort to hold back the giggles. Her mother merely smiled at the younger man's astonished expression.

"My lord?" Roger asked, confused by their responses.

Earl Richard grinned at him. "I know what my own wife and children believe."

"You . . . you allow this?" Roger sputtered. "Why, 'tis shameful blasphemy."

" 'Tis a matter of faith," Richard corrected him. "I knew what Keely was before I married her."

"Well, that's more than I can say for myself," Roger shot back, his anger unabated by the earl's nonchalance.

Losing his smile, Richard cocked a copper brow at him. "Would you have preferred the Tower?"

Roger made no reply.

"Haven't I always given you sound advice?" Richard argued. "Simply ignore my daughter's beliefs; insist that she be circumspect in her actions."

"Is cavorting around a tree in my garden circumspect?" Roger asked.

At that moment Blythe could cheerfully have choked her husband. She felt her parents' disapproving gazes upon her and squirmed in her chair.

" 'Twas an emergency," Blythe defended herself. "I needed to thank the Goddess for protecting Roger. Someone tried to assassinate him yesterday at—"

"What?" the earl exclaimed, sitting up straight in his chair.

"No one was injured?" her mother cried.

Roger gave Blythe an irritated look and then said, "I'll get to that in a moment. My lord, thousands of people—including the queen—believe in and fear the supernatural. Blythe will surely be arrested and executed if anyone suspects she is different."

"Do you fear for my daughter's safety or your own reputation?" the countess asked.

"Darnel's untimely death killed my good reputation," Roger said, his bitterness apparent in his voice. "I fear for Blythe's and Miranda's safety." He looked at the earl and asked, "Do you share their beliefs?"

"Hardly. 'Tis hogslop at best," Earl Richard answered. He sent his wife a contrite look and said, "Sorry, dearest."

"Your tolerance has earned you a special place in heaven," the countess replied. She turned to Roger, saying, "Blythe promised to be as circumspect as I have been all these years." The countess stood then and started to reach out to touch him, but caught herself in time. "Gentle Roger—"

Roger grasped the countess's hand and raised it to his lips, saying, "Forgive my earlier rudeness, my lady. You have always been one of my most steadfast friends."

Blythe breathed a sigh of relief. Her husband had redeemed himself for his cruel treatment of her mother.

Pleased by his apology, Lady Keely smiled and asked, "Do you recall when Blythe was an infant and you were a boy of twelve? A group of us went into the garden one midnight. You formed a circle around the earl, myself, and the babe."

Roger nodded.

"You were participating in a Druidic ceremony," the countess told him. "Was there anything nefarious about what we did that night?"

"As I recall, we merely said a few prayers."

"Exactly."

Richard spoke up then. "The important question is this: Are you capable and willing of protecting my daughter?"

"Yes, I'm capable. Do you doubt my ability?"

"And willing?" the countess asked.

Roger cast Blythe a pained expression. "Aye, that too."

"Excellent," Richard said, dismissing the matter. "Now tell me about the assassination attempt."

Roger opened his mouth to speak, but a knock sounded on the door.

"Enter," the earl called.

Jennings opened the door and stepped inside. 'I apologize for interrupting, my lord," the majordomo said. "Misters Rodale and Hibbert beg an interview."

"My agents?" Blythe gasped.

"Send them in," Roger answered for his father-in-law.

Jennings looked at the earl, who nodded approval.

A moment later Rodale and Hibbert marched into the study. Both men stopped short when they spied their employer.

"Well, what do you wish to tell my father?" Blythe challenged them.

"My lady, we do apologize, but cannot allow you to ruin your corn and wool trades," Rodale said.

"I have confidence in my daughter's judgment," her father told them.

"With all due respect, marriage has impaired her judgment," Hibbert spoke up.

"Aye, my lord." Rodale nodded in agreement. "Lady Blythe and Lord Roger have been embroiled in a price war."

"Papa, I swear I am the only one suffering a loss," Blythe said. "Never would I cheat my suppliers or agents."

Earl Richard turned to the two men. "If nobody except my daughter is losing money, what difference does it make?"

"My lord, you misunderstand," Hibbert said. "Lady Blythe was winning this price war."

"Yesterday she suddenly raised her prices," Rodale added. "She's charging double what Lord Roger is."

Roger rounded on her. "You raised your prices?"

" 'Twas unfair of me to use that insider information," Blythe explained, giving him a smile filled with sunshine. "I decided to make amends by raising my prices."

"So you are *letting* me win?" Roger asked, his anger apparent in his voice. "Is that it?"

His words and his expression surprised Blythe. Without considering the consequences, she asked, "You aren't grateful?"

It was the wrong thing to say to a proud, arrogant eagle. She realized that as soon as the words slipped from her lips.

Instead of answering her, Roger rounded on the two agents and ordered, "Get out."

Rodale and Hibbert didn't even bother to look at Blythe. The forbidding expression etched across the Earl of Eden's face chased them out of the study.

"I do not need you or anyone else to let me win," Roger said in a clipped voice. "I would eventually have won anyway."

"I think not, my lord," Blythe shot back, glaring at him. She would have thought the pigheaded lout would be glad she'd called a truce.

"She's *your* daughter," Blythe heard her mother say to her father. "Why don't they *fix* prices and live in harmony?"

Earl Richard hooted with laughter. "Dearest, all these years I assumed you had no head for business," he replied. "I cannot believe how wrong I was." He looked at his daughter and son-in-law, saying, "My wife is correct. Just fix the damned prices."

"No," Roger replied.

"Never," Blythe said. In a sarcastic voice she added, "At least we agree on one thing, my lord."

"Put your differences aside for the moment," the earl ordered. "Tell me about the assassination attempt."

"Someone shot an arrow at me while we were visiting Smithfield Market," Roger told him.

"Could it have been accidental?" Lady Keely asked.

"A cloud racing across the sky darkened the sun," Blythe answered.

Her mother nodded in understanding.

"Whoever murdered Darnel wants me dead," Roger said.

"What measures are you taking to discover his identity?" the earl asked.

"I visited the Royal Rooster Tavern," Roger answered. "Bucko Jacques and his wife promised to keep their ears open and let me know what they hear."

Richard nodded sagely. "Bucko is a good man with many contacts."

Blythe smiled at her husband. Her beloved eagle hadn't been sniffing gardenias at all. He'd merely gone to investigate the unfortunate incident at Smithfield Market. Perhaps he did harbor a fondness for her in spite of the fact that she was better at business strategy than he.

An hour later the three Debretts made the short trip home. Though Roger remained brooding and silent, Blythe and Miranda were exuberant. For different reasons, of course.

"Did you have fun?" Blythe asked as they rode up the private lane that led to Debrett House.

Miranda nodded and then glanced over at her father. "Is Daddy still excited?" she asked.

Blythe chuckled. She peeked at her beloved and told her step-daughter, "I do believe the worst has passed."

Taking the girl's hand in hers, Blythe walked toward the mansion. Roger followed behind them.

Blythe recognized the metallic sound of kissing swords as soon as she entered the foyer. Pushing Miranda behind her, she hurried toward the hall. A man slid across the floor and sprawled at her feet just as she reached the hall's entrance.

"You're dead," said a deep voice from inside the hall.

"Sacred Saint Swithin," Blythe cried in alarm. What was happening in her husband's hall?

The man sprawled at her feet looked up at her and, with laughter lurking in his voice, begged, "Beauteous lady, pity a dead man. Purchase an indulgence for the repose of my blackened soul."

Blythe giggled.

"Get up, Geoffrey," Roger ordered, his voice filled with cold contempt.

Her husband's family had returned from court.

Chapter 9

"I said *get up*," Roger snapped.

Twenty-five-year-old Geoffrey Debrett sent his oldest brother a puzzled look and in one swift movement leaped to his feet. Turning to Blythe, he gave her an affable smile and winked at her.

"Do not let our black-sheep baby brother confound you," cautioned a deep voice.

"Geoffrey was born a likable fool," added a woman.

"Blythe, you do remember my family from the wedding?" Roger asked.

"Yes, vaguely." Blythe fixed a bright smile on her face as a naughty imp entered her soul and urged her to add, "I suppose I could remember them better if they'd attended our wedding dinner."

The reaction from the Debrett family was instant and varied. Roger merely smirked, but his brother, Cedric stared solemnly at her, with interest flickering in his dark gaze. Sybilla gave her a frosty glare. Geoffrey caught her attention with his hoot of laughter and inclined his head in her direction.

"Touché, dear sister-in-law," he said.

"Elizabeth has gone hunting at Nonsuch Palace until the first day of October," Cedric announced. "We'll be staying at Debrett House until the court moves to Windsor Castle."

Blythe did the quick calculation in her head and breathed an inward sigh of relief. Seducing her husband into her bed would be difficult with the distraction of his family in residence. Her in-laws would be staying at Debrett House for only a week, possibly two if they chose to linger.

"Let us sit down to dinner," Roger said, walking with his brother to the high table. "When does Elizabeth plan to move to Hampton Court?"

"I'd guess around the middle of November," Cedric answered.

"Have you learned anything new regarding Darnel?" Roger asked, lowering his voice.

Cedric shook his head. "I've questioned dozens and dozens of people but, unfortunately, have nothing to report. Be assured, I intend to continue my investigation as soon as I return to court."

Roger and Blythe sat in the center chairs always reserved for the lord and the lady of the house unless royalty visited. Sybilla and Cedric sat on Roger's right while Miranda and Geoffrey sat on Blythe's left.

A salad of damson, purslane, and cucumber arrived first, followed by chestnut soup. The main course consisted of roasted chickens, stewed peas, and rissoles of artichokes.

"*Chicken?* Cannot the wealthy Earl of Eden afford a more expensive staple than this paltry poultry?" Sybilla complained.

"I approved this menu," Blythe said, looking down the table at her sister-in-law. "Eating chicken in autumn relieves the season's melancholy humors."

"Be certain to eat a second helping," Geoffrey advised, and then chuckled at his own wit. When Blythe looked at him, he dropped his gaze to the five-year-old and asked, "How has my favorite niece been faring since last I saw you?"

"Uncle Geoffrey, I am your *only* niece," Miranda informed him.

"Oh, so you are," Geoffrey replied, feigning surprise. "Well, how has my *only* niece been faring?"

Miranda gave Geoffrey a "thumbs up" gesture, which made him smile, and said, "Daddy bought me a pony at Smithfield Market, and Mama Blight bought me its mate."

"Two ponies?" Geoffrey echoed in feigned amazement. "Your daddy must love you very much."

Miranda nodded. "Yes, he does."

"A waste of good coin if you ask me," Sybilla grumbled.

"Mama Blight loves me too," Miranda told her uncle, pointedly ignoring her aunt. "She knows so many bedtime stories. Isn't my new mama wonderful?"

"Indeed, Mama Blight sounds heaven-sent," Geoffrey agreed.

"She's *not* your mother," Sybilla said loudly.

"Sybilla," Cedric drawled, a censorious tone in his voice.

Anger surged through Blythe at the heart-wrenching sight of her stepdaughter's stricken expression. What kind of unnatural woman purposely hurt a child?

"Lady Sybilla, you are mistaken," Blythe said, fixing a cold stare on her sister-in-law. "I am Miranda's stepmother and do love her as much as if she were my own flesh and blood."

Wondering what her husband's reaction to that would be, Blythe shifted her gaze from Sybilla to Roger. A smile flirted with his lips, which encouraged her to continue.

"A mother is the woman who raises a child, not necessarily the one who gives birth to her," Blythe went on.

Noting the angry blotches that now marred her sister-in-law's complexion, Blythe decided a verbal retreat would be discreet. She winked at he majordomo, who was just placing a fresh goblet of cider beside her plate.

"My lady expresses my sentiments exactly," Bottoms muttered in a low voice.

"Servants should know their places," Sybilla remarked, loud enough for all to hear.

"As should poor relations," Blythe drawled.

"What's a poor relation?" Miranda asked.

Geoffrey burst out laughing. "Uncle Cedric, Aunt Sybilla, and I are the Debrett poor relations," he told the five-year-old.

Blythe smiled at their conversation but didn't bother to turn around. Instead, she shifted her gaze to Cedric to judge his reaction to her insult. What she saw wiped the smile off her face.

Cedric was staring at Roger through slightly hooded eyes. The unmasked hatred leaping at her husband from her brother-in-law's eyes shocked her.

"Cedric, what is the news from court?" Blythe asked, trying to divert that evil look from her husband. "Have you chanced to meet my sister, Bliss?"

"Is she one of the queen's maids of honor?" Sybilla asked. Blythe nodded.

"I've met her," Sybilla said. "Bliss is a pleasant young lady." The tone in her sister-in-law's voice implied that Blythe wasn't quite as pleasant as Bliss. "My sister does have the gift of making everyone around her happy," Blythe replied.

"I hope you approve of my redecorating efforts," Sybilla said. "I made a few changes in the countess's bedchamber while Roger was"—she hesitated as though searching for an appropriate word—"*away* last spring."

"Roger wasn't away, Sibby," Geoffrey spoke up. "He was locked in the Tower."

"Whatever," Sybilla shot back. "You know I detest nicknames. Call me Sybilla."

Geoffrey smiled at her. "Anything you want, Sibby—ooops, I forgot."

"Concerning the redecorating," Roger began, his lips twitching with the obvious urge to laugh. "Blythe had asked—"

Beneath the table Blythe kicked her husband's leg, and he clamped his lips shut. He could not be intending to tell Sybilla how much she disliked her redecorating.

"What were you about to say?" Sybilla asked.

In the end Bottoms saved the day for Roger but managed to make the situation more embarrassing. "My lady, the swatches of fabric you ordered for your bedchamber have arrived," the majordomo announced as he refilled her goblet of cider. "I left them in his lordship's study."

"Since I've already redecorated, why do it again?" Sybilla asked.

"What you have chosen is lovely, but I prefer lighter colors,"

Blythe told her. That particular bedchamber was reserved exclusively for the mistress of the house, the Countess of Eden. Why would a woman decorate a chamber she could never use? Had her sister-in-law been preparing for Roger's execution?

"I do apologize," Sybilla was saying to Roger, as if she'd read Blythe's thoughts. "Considering the horrible circumstances, I thought you would prefer all traces of unhappy memories out of sight."

Roger nodded, absolving her of her boldness in redecorating without his permission.

Blythe slid her gaze from Sybilla to Cedric. Gone was his expression of cold hatred, replaced by an intensely interested look riveted on her own bosom. She couldn't credit this brother-in-law's audacity and must remember never to be alone in a room with him. Why, in God's name, did Roger harbor such a dislike of Geoffrey when this brother seemed more disturbing?

"Mama Blight, we never saw such a dark sun as we did yesterday, did we?" Miranda asked, apparently unhappy with her inattention. In a loud voice she added for everyone's edification, " 'Twas when the bad man shot that arrow at Daddy."

"What?" Cedric and Geoffrey exclaimed in unison.

Ignoring his youngest brother, Roger turned to Cedric and said, "Someone tried to assassinate me at Smithfield Market."

"Do you have any idea who would want you dead?" Cedric asked.

"Yes, I do." Roger cast Geoffrey a sidelong glance and then told Cedric, "The same person who murdered Darnel."

Again, Blythe kicked him beneath the table. Too late.

"Did the bad man hurt Lady Darnel?" Miranda asked, her voice mirroring her fear.

"Nobody hurt Lady Darnel," Blythe lied, putting a comforting arm around the five-year-old. "Lady Darnel became ill, and God decided to call her home to heaven."

"Mama Blight, I told you before, Lady Darnel did *not* go to heaven," Miranda said. "She's . . . she's someplace else."

When her youngest brother-in-law chuckled, Blythe sent him

a warning look and then turned her head to stare across the hall at the portraits of the previous Earl and Countess of Eden. She searched her mind for a topic that would not upset her step-daughter.

"Cedric does resemble your father," Blythe remarked to her husband. "Geoffrey and you have the look of your mother."

"Our father had skin as dark as the Spanish don's," Geoffrey said. "Cedric resembles him."

"Roger was always the light in our mother's eyes," Cedric spoke up.

"Yes, but you were Father's favorite," Roger said. "He passed more hours with you than with Geoffrey and me put together."

"What about you, Uncle Geoffrey?" Miranda asked. "Whose favorite were you?"

Geoffrey winked at her. "I believe Hartwell loved me best."

Miranda giggled. "No, Uncle. Hartwell loves me."

"Oh, yes. 'Twas Bottoms who loved me best," Geoffrey corrected himself.

Miranda giggled again and called to the majordomo, "Bottoms, was Uncle Geoffrey your favorite little boy?"

"I loved him dearly," Bottoms answered in a deep, dry tone of voice.

Everyone but Sybilla laughed.

"Are we now required to have a dinner conversation with servants?" the blonde complained.

Blythe opened her mouth to reply, but her husband's tongue was faster.

"Bottoms is more than a servant in my household," Roger rebuked her. "He happens to be a trusted and valued friend."

An awkward silence descended upon the diners. Roger's trusted and valued majordomo cut through the tense atmosphere.

"I hope that means I'm mentioned in your will," Bottoms said from where he stood near the sideboard.

Blythe and Geoffrey burst out laughing, which incited Miranda to laughter. Roger and even Cedric smiled. Only Sybilla remained sour.

When dinner ended, Blythe turned to Miranda and asked, "Shall we go find Hartwell? I believe 'tis time for your afternoon nap."

"No nap," came the girl's reply.

"No nap it is," Blythe agreed. Then she asked, "Would you consider helping me upstairs to find Daisy so that *I* can take a nap?"

Miranda narrowed her blue gaze on her.

Blythe feigned a loud yawn. "Oh, I'm *sooo* tired. I hope I can make it upstairs without falling asleep."

"I'll help you, Mama Blight."

Miranda stood and assisted Blythe out of her chair. Holding her stepmother's hand, she led her slowly but surely toward the hall's entrance.

"What a wonderful daughter I have," Blythe said, fixing an appropriately weary expression onto her face. As she passed her husband, she gave him a wink.

Roger and Cedric chuckled at her ploy.

"Do *not* dare to laugh at poor Mama Blight," Miranda scolded them. "She's very, very tired."

At the top of the stairs Blythe and Miranda met Mrs. Hartwell, who was on her way to fetch the five-year-old for her nap. Playing along, the nursemaid also helped Blythe to her chamber.

"Daisy, we need you," Miranda shouted.

"What's the problem?" Daisy asked, crossing the chamber to assist them.

"Mama Blight is very, very tired and needs her nap," the five-year-old said.

Lying down on the bed, Blythe grasped the girl's hand and said, "Thank you so much. Could you possibly do me another, tiny favor?"

Miranda nodded, eager to help.

"Will you rest quietly in your chamber and then awaken me in two hours?" Blythe asked.

Miranda nodded. "I can do that."

"Give me a kiss before you go."

Miranda kissed her cheek and gave her a hug. Then she left with Mrs. Hartwell.

Blythe leaped off the bed as soon as the door clicked shut behind her stepdaughter. "Have you met my in-laws?" she asked.

"Aye, and a sorrier lot I've never seen," Daisy answered. "Lord Geoffrey is handsome in the extreme, but household gossip says that he's a womanizing wastrel."

"Cedric seems untrustworthy, and I cannot like my sister-in-law either," Blythe said. "I suppose the Goddess makes them and mates them."

"Speaking of your sister-in-law, Lady Sybilla barged in here while you were out," Daisy informed her. "My presence surprised her, of course. The lady said she'd lost something and wanted to look for it."

"What did Sybilla lose?"

Daisy shrugged. "The lady wanted me to leave while she searched your chamber. Her request—make that an order—sounded suspicious to me."

"And?" Blythe asked, cocking an ebony brow at her.

Daisy gave her a contagious grin. "I refused to leave, she became angry, and I told her to *kiss my feet*."

Blythe giggled and gave her a hug, saying, "I do love you, cousin."

Daisy returned her smile. "Doesn't everyone?"

"I doubt Lady Sybilla harbors any fondness for you."

"So what gown will you be wearing to supper?" Daisy asked. "I suggest something that puts your sister-in-law to shame."

"You choose one for me."

Blythe crossed the chamber to gaze out the window. Her smile vanished as soon as her cousin left the room. Blythe considered Daisy's words and wondered what Sybilla could have been searching for. She certainly couldn't ask Sybilla directly. The tension in this family was unlike anything Blythe had ever known.

Blythe decided she would seek the Goddess's wisdom at first

opportunity. Too many dark, unseen forces were at work in the Debrett household. She needed to know where danger lurked in order to protect her new family.

"Well, how do I look?"

"Pretty."

Blythe smiled at the five-year-old and walked around the privacy screen to stand in front of the looking glass. She turned this way and that way to judge for herself exactly how she appeared.

Wearing a violet and gold brocaded gown, Blythe had never looked more beautiful. The gown featured a squared neckline and long, tight-fitting sleeves that ended in a point at her wrists. She wore her cross of Wotan above the low-cut bodice.

Blythe worried her bottom lip with her teeth and wondered if Roger would think her neckline too revealing.

The better to seduce him into your bed, Grandmama Chessy would say.

So be it, Blythe agreed.

Hand in hand, Blythe and Miranda walked down the stairs to the foyer. Entering the great hall, they saw that the family had already gathered in front of the hearth. In unison her Debrett in-laws turned to stare at her, but it was her husband's expression on which she fixed her gaze. Roger watched her through blue eyes that gleamed with approval and possession.

Ever the courtier, Geoffrey stepped forward first. He grasped her hand and bowed low over it, murmuring, "Your beauty does shame the sweetest flower in field or garden."

His outrageous compliment made Blythe smile. "Sir, you haven't commented upon my companion's appearance," she said.

"How frightfully remiss of me," Geoffrey replied. He bowed low over his niece's hand and said, "Mistress Miranda, you are a promising bud about to bloom into a perfect flower."

Miranda giggled.

"Do you think he says such pretty words to all the ladies?" Blythe asked her stepdaughter.

"Of course he does," Roger answered.

Blythe looked at her husband, who was staring coldly at his youngest brother's back, and then glanced at Cedric, who stared boldly at her cleavage.

"What a beautiful and unusual pendant," Cedric remarked.

Blythe knew he hadn't been perusing her necklace, but chose to play along. " 'Twas Roger's gift to me on my thirteenth birthday," she told him.

"My brother has impeccable taste," Cedric said, again dropping his gaze to her body.

"I do believe supper is ready," Roger said, offering her his arm.

Blythe gave him her brightest smile. Without relinquishing her stepdaughter's hand, she reached for his arm but stopped when a commotion near the hall's entrance drew her attention.

"Don't bother to announce me, Bottoms," said a female's voice. *A sultry female voice.*

Blythe stared at the voluptuous woman with flaming red hair who appeared in the entrance and hurried across the hall toward them.

"I sneaked away from Reggie as soon as he fell asleep," the woman purred, throwing herself into Roger's arms. "I simply could not wait another moment to welcome you home from the Tower."

A bolt of jealousy shot through Blythe. Apparently, this was one of the mistresses to whom Lady Tessie had referred.

Soon-to-be ex-mistress, Blythe promised herself.

When she heard Geoffrey chuckling, Blythe realized her expression mirrored her thought. She turned her face into an expressionless mask and cleared her throat.

"Rhoda, I present my wife," Roger said, disentangling himself from the redhead's arms. "Blythe, this is Lady Rhoda Bellows, a family friend."

"Oh, the little Devereux girl," Lady Rhoda said, inspecting her from the top of her ebony head to the tips of her brocaded slippers.

Blythe stepped closer to the redhead, lifted her head in the air, and crinkled her nose like a doe trying to catch the scent of danger. Satisfied, she stepped back several paces.

"What are you doing?" Roger asked, a bemused smile on his face.

"Sniffing for gardenias," Blythe answered.

"Why are you doing that, Mama Blight?" Miranda asked.

"Oh, how utterly sweet," Lady Rhoda gushed. "Your daughter called her *Mama*."

"We were about to sup," Roger said. "Will you join us?"

"No, I really must get home to Reggie," Lady Rhoda refused, flicking a sidelong glance at Blythe. She turned the full force of her charm on Roger and drawled, "I do hope I'll be hearing from you soon. The Yule festivities at court this year promise to be especially grand."

Roger smiled politely but promised nothing.

Lady Rhoda touched her lips with her index finger and then pressed the finger to his lips. "Until then, darling," she whispered in a husky voice. Ignoring Blythe, Lady Rhoda whirled away and left the hall as quickly and unexpectedly as she had appeared.

An awkward silence followed the lady's departure. Finally, Roger cleared his throat and said, "Lady Bellows is certainly given to theatrics." He turned to Blythe and offered his arm again, saying, "Shall we?"

Ignoring him, Blythe took Miranda's hand in hers and said, "Come, poppet. Supper is ready. That is, if you still have an appetite after that performance."

Again, Bottoms supervised the serving of the meal. There were split-pea soup with beans and onions, bread with butter, a variety of cheeses, and baked apples with pistachios.

"Look, Mama Blight." Miranda pointed at the bowl of soup.

"What's wrong, poppet?" Blythe asked.

"Hartwell will be very unhappy with me tonight," the five-year-old said.

"Why?"

"I see beans in this soup."

Roger and Blythe looked at each other and burst out laughing.

"What's the joke?" asked Geoffrey.

"Hartwell insists that ladies should never make vulgar noises or foul odors," Blythe explained.

"Whenever I eat beans, I make vulgar noises and foul odors," Miranda confessed.

Geoffrey threw back his head and shouted with laughter. Even Cedric cracked a smile.

" 'Tis a disgusting and unsuitable topic for the table," Sybilla said. "Why, one of England's most eminent earls—"

Another flurry of activity near the hall's entrance abruptly cut off whatever Sybilla intended to say. A striking blonde in her late thirties crossed the hall toward the high table. The woman was impeccably dressed in a dark-blue riding outfit, complete with matching feathered hat and dark-blue leather boots.

"Darling Roger, I apologize for intruding upon your supper," the blonde said, halting in front of the high table. "I simply had to rush over and welcome you home from the Tower as soon as I returned to the Strand."

"Lady Bellows said the very same thing," Sybilla remarked loudly. "You just missed her."

"That bitch?" the blonde exclaimed. "I mean—"

Roger chuckled. "Sarah, I present my wife, Blythe Devereux. Blythe, this is Lady Sarah Sitwell."

"I'm pleased to make your acquaintance," Blythe lied, managing a polite smile for the older woman.

Lady Sarah flicked a measuring look at her and then gave Roger her full attention again, saying, "I heard you'd wed the bastard's daughter."

"I beg your pardon?" Blythe said, unable to credit what she'd heard.

Lady Sarah looked at her and drawled, "I said—"

"I heard what you said," Blythe cried. "Though I have been bred to respect my *elders*, I will not countenance disparaging remarks about my father."

Lady Sarah stiffened at the word *elder*. That she was sensitive about her age was apparent to all.

"I harbor the tenderest regard for your father, *child*, and would never say a bad word against him," Lady Sarah told her. "The word *bastard* refers to your mother, of course."

Shocked speechless, Blythe could only stare at the older woman.

"Sarah, mind your manners," Roger cautioned the blonde.

"The child is obviously unaware of her less-than-respectable beginnings," Lady Sarah replied. She looked at Blythe and informed her, "Nineteen years ago your father and I loved each other very much and planned on announcing our betrothal. Then your mother arrived from the mountains of Wales. Keely Glendower, Ludlow's bastard by a Welsh whore, engineered herself into a compromising situation, which forced my darling Richard to marry her."

"That's a lie!" Blythe cried in a fury, moving to rise from her chair.

"Relax," Roger ordered, placing his hand on her arm, forcing her to remain seated.

"Child, I was there and should know what transpired." Dismissing her, Lady Sarah gave Roger an inviting smile. "Darling, you must sup with me soon. What would be—"

Blythe narrowed her violet gaze on the woman. With her right index finger she touched her heart and her lips, then she pointed the finger outward at the other woman.

A sudden, strong whirlwind of a draft swept through the hall. The force of it knocked the blonde's hat right off her head.

"What is happening?" Lady Sarah cried, trying to catch the hairpins that were falling from her hair.

"God's bread!" Roger started to rise from his chair to assist her.

The draft ceased as abruptly as it had begun.

"How strange," Blythe said, fixing an innocent expression on her face. Feeling an insistent tugging on her skirt, she looked to the left.

Miranda winked at her.

"As charming as our guests have been, I've endured enough for one evening," Blythe announced, standing. She turned to Miranda and asked, "Poppet, would you like to join me upstairs? I'll tell you how the flowers got their names."

Miranda grinned and nodded.

"She hasn't finished her supper yet," Roger said.

Ignoring him, Blythe rounded on the majordomo and asked, "Bottoms, do we have marchpane in the house?"

"Yes, my lady."

"Send a tray of marchpane and cider to Miranda's chamber."

"Very good, my lady."

At that the woman and the girl walked across the hall to leave. Blythe felt the others watching her, but she refused to look back.

Upstairs, Blythe had just finished helping her stepdaughter change into her nightshift and get into bed when the door swung open. Daisy walked in and set the tray of treats on the bedside table.

"I heard what happened," Daisy said. "Lord Roger has the most gawd-awful taste in women."

Blythe cocked an ebony brow at her.

"I meant excepting you."

" 'Tis of no importance," Blythe said. "Lady Sarah is an embittered old hag trying to cause problems between my husband and me. Go have your own supper, and tell Mrs. Hartwell to take her time."

Daisy nodded and left the chamber.

"Would you care for a mug of cider?" Blythe asked the little girl.

Miranda shook her head.

"How about a piece of marchpane?"

Miranda nodded her head vigorously, making her stepmother smile.

Blythe passed one piece of the almond confection to the child and selected one for herself. "Now, lean back," she instructed the child, placing her arm around her. "I'm going to tell you the story about how the bellflower, also know Venus's looking-glass, got its name."

"What's a *Venus*?" Miranda asked.

"Venus is the ancient Roman goddess of love," Blythe told her. "She was Aphrodite in ancient Greece, but the Romans stole the idea and changed her name. The Romans always did lack originality. Anyway, Venus had a magical mirror that reflected beauty to whoever peered in it. One day Venus misplaced her mirror. A shepherd boy found it and became so fascinated by his own image that he refused to give it back."

"Finders keepers, losers weepers," Miranda reminded her.

"That usually is true, but not when a mere mortal is dealing with a headstrong goddess," Blythe replied. "Venus sent her son, Cupid, to retrieve the mirror. When he tried to snatch the mirror out of the boy's hand, it fell and shattered into millions of pieces. Wherever the shards of glass dropped, this pretty violet bellflower grew."

"What a wonderful story," Miranda exclaimed, and then yawned. "Tell me another one."

"Daffodils are those yellow flowers that dance across the lawns," Blythe began. She looked down and saw that the little girl had fallen asleep.

Blythe leaned over and planted a light kiss on Miranda's cheek. She pulled a gold piece from her pocket and, before leaving the chamber, set it down on the growing stalk of gold for her stepdaughter to find in the morning.

Wearied by the day's events, Blythe decided to retire instead of returning downstairs. She opened her bedchamber door and stepped inside. What she saw made her stop short in surprise.

"What are you doing here?" Blythe asked the intruder.

Lady Sybilla, standing near the desk, whirled around at the sound of her voice. She remained silent but wore a decidedly guilty look on her face.

"What are you doing here?" Blythe demanded again.

"I-I lost an earring while I was redecorating," Sybilla answered.

Blythe knew Sybilla was lying but couldn't figure out why. "If I find it, I'll return it to you," she said. "Please leave now, and from this moment onward respect my privacy."

"I-I do apologize," Sybilla said, brushing past her in a rush to be away.

Blythe didn't believe one bloody word her sister-in-law had spoken.

She needed to send for a locksmith.

No, she needed to hire a guard.

And then Blythe knew what she really needed was Daisy's assistance in finding whatever Sybilla wanted in this chamber.

Chapter 10

Sybilla Debrett, Rhoda Bellows, and Sarah Sitwell had shattered her peace of mind as surely as Cupid and the shepherd boy had shattered Venus's magic mirror.

Now Blythe knew the reason her mother shunned the Tudor court and its courtiers. If the three women she'd met today were any indication, Queen Elizabeth surrounded herself with shallow, immoral people. And the men were probably even worse than their women.

How fortunate she had been to marry Roger. Their union had kept her from living as a maid of honor at the Tudor court. She could hardly bear to think what Bliss was experiencing.

Blythe walked down the length of the second-floor corridor and stopped before the last door on the left. She knocked on her tirewoman's chamber door.

No answer.

"Daisy?" she called.

Still no answer.

Turning away, Blythe retraced her steps down the long corridor. Apparently, Daisy was lingering with the other retainers over supper. She was glad her kinswoman had settled in with the Debrett retainers.

Blythe paused at the top of the stairs and stared at her butterfly betrothal ring with its rubies, emeralds, sapphires, and diamonds. Then she touched her jeweled cross of Wotan.

And thee I chuse.

Her beloved had already chosen his path in life. Those two bold jades, Rhoda Bellows and Sarah Sitwell, would soon learn that *this* wife would accept no infidelity. Yes, Roger had been hooked neater than any fish; now what she needed to do was reel him into her bed. Once that happened, there could be no turning back for him. If only he would wear her wedding gift to him. The power of her love embodied in that ring would surely protect him from the lurking dangers she sensed in the house's atmosphere. On the other hand, a necklace—that symbol of eternity—would afford him even more protection, but she didn't think she could contrive to get him to wear one.

Blythe descended the stairs to the foyer. Passing the great hall's entrance, she spied the three Debrett brothers in front of the hearth. Her sister-in-law was probably hiding in her own chamber, worried that Blythe would tell Roger she'd caught her snooping.

On her way to the kitchen, Blythe passed her husband's study. She halted abruptly when she realized the door was slightly ajar. In the week they'd been married, that particular door had always been closed, and she'd assumed it was her husband's habit.

Blythe retraced her steps to the study and reached out to close the door. Then she heard a noise from within that sounded like rustling papers.

Noiselessly, Blythe pushed the door open and stepped inside. Her sister-in-law stood behind the desk and searched through a pile of papers.

"What are you doing?" Blythe demanded, her voice sounding overly loud in the silent chamber.

The blonde jumped and looked up. "Are you following me?" Sybilla demanded in return.

"Tell me what you are doing, or I'll call Roger," Blythe threatened, advancing on her.

"Call Roger if you wish," Sybilla replied, waving a piece of parchment in the air. "I simply wanted to write a letter but had no paper."

Blythe narrowed her gaze on the blonde. She knew the lady was lying.

"Do you have Roger's permission to be here?" Blythe asked.

"Do I need permission to wander my own home?" Sybilla countered.

" 'Tis my husband's home."

"Exactly, dear sister-in-law," Sybilla replied. " 'Tis your husband's home, *not yours*. Roger has always accorded me the freedom to wander where I will."

Sybilla walked around the desk to leave. Passing Blythe, she said, "If I were you, child, I'd be pondering how to keep my husband faithful instead of following me around. Both Rhoda and Sarah are quite attractive and, I warrant, know how to please a man." At that, the blonde left the study.

Blythe stared after her. Whatever Sybilla wanted must be very important, she concluded, even more determined to discover what it was.

After closing the study door tightly behind her, Blythe paused and looked down the length of the corridor that led to the great hall. Sybilla stood in the hall's entrance, shook her head vigorously, and then disappeared inside. Blythe had little experience with intrigue, but she knew enough to recognize Sybilla's inept attempts at subterfuge and now her not-so-covert signaling. The only things that remained a mystery were to whom Sybilla had signaled and what all her snooping was about.

Blythe continued on her way in the opposite direction toward the kitchen, where most of the Debrett retainers would be gathered at this hour. She heard their voices raised in animated conversations and a chuckle or two of laughter.

She smiled in remembrance. When she was a young girl, the kitchen was one of her favorite places. Her sisters and she would congregate in that warm, deliciously scented room and listen to the easy banter between the Devereux servants.

Blythe pushed the door open and stepped inside. In an instant the people in the kitchen quieted, and all faces turned toward her. Apparently, the lady of the house wasn't as welcome in the kitchen as the children of the house.

A tentative smile touched her lips as she quickly scanned the room for Daisy. Her gaze slid past Bottoms and continued its search for her tirewoman.

"My lady, may I be of service?" the majordomo asked.

"I wondered where Daisy had disappeared," she answered.

A few retainers smiled at that, and a couple even snickered. Their laughter stopped abruptly as soon as she shifted her gaze to them.

"I believe Mr. Hardwick will know where she is," Bottoms told her.

"Hardwick?" Blythe echoed. "Why, Daisy doesn't even like him."

Oddly enough, that statement caused an outbreak of muffled chuckles.

"Where will I find Hardwick?" she asked.

Bottoms gave her a broad smile. He reminded her of a cat who'd just caught a mouse.

"Hardwick usually takes a glass of mulled wine in his chamber at this hour of the evening," the majordomo answered.

"Thank you, Bottoms."

Blythe left the kitchen. No sooner had the door closed behind her than boisterous laughter erupted from within. She paused, stared in bewilderment at the closed door, and wondered what was so funny.

Blythe retraced her steps down the corridor to the foyer. She peeked into the great hall as she passed it and breathed a sigh of relief that her sister-in-law sat in front of the hearth with the others. At least she needn't worry that Sybilla was still snooping around the house.

Reaching the second floor, Blythe again walked the long length of the corridor to Hardwick's chamber. She raised her hand to knock, but then heard a low moaning sound from within.

"Hardwick, are you ill?" Blythe cried, barging into the chamber.

She stopped short as the man reared up in his bed. Beneath him lay Daisy, and both were obviously naked.

"Sacred Saint Swithin!" Blythe screamed as if she were being murdered.

"No, my lady!" Hardwick shouted in a panic, starting to rise from the bed.

Daisy yanked him back down, saying, "Dickie, you're buck naked."

That statement made Blythe scream even louder. Within mere seconds Roger and his brothers burst into the chamber. The three of them stared in surprise at the unlikely couple, caught in the act, cowering beneath the coverlet.

"This is outrageous," Blythe cried. "Daisy was an innocent until she met that . . . that villain."

"M-my l-lord, I c-can explain," the villain sputtered.

Geoffrey Debrett howled with laughter. Blythe stomped on his foot to silence him.

"Come the morning," Blythe said, rounding on her husband, "you will send for a minister to marry them."

"Marriage?" Hardwick squeaked.

"And what the bloody hell is wrong with that, Dickie?" Daisy asked.

Roger spoke up then, saying, "Blythe, I cannot force—"

"Either Hardwick marries Daisy or I will send for her father," Blythe threatened him.

"Odo Lloyd?" Roger sent his man a long, pitying look and shivered with exaggeration. " 'Tis a wedding or a funeral for you, Hardwick. The choice is yours."

"The banns must be posted for three weeks," Hardwick argued.

"My father can have them waived," Blythe told him. "Prepare yourself to go to Devereux House in the morning. I'm positive Odo Lloyd will want to give his *favorite* daughter away in marriage."

Blythe left the chamber and hurried to Miranda's to be sure the child hadn't been frightened by the raised voices. Satisfied that her stepdaughter was sound asleep, she went directly to her own bedchamber and stood at the window to gaze out at the night sky.

She'd been married for a week, and the only one to lose her virginity had been Daisy. How disheartening.

Hearing her chamber door open and then click shut, Blythe turned around to face Roger. Her beloved was smiling at her.

"Hardwick will be ready to leave for Devereux House at ten o'clock in the morning," Roger said, crossing the chamber to her. "I've sent your father a message asking him to get a minister willing to waive the banns."

Blythe nodded. "Thank you, my lord."

"I do apologize for Rhoda and Sarah," he continued. "I have not . . . passed any evenings with either of them since before Darnel—"

"And thank you for telling me that," Blythe said, renewed hope surging within her heart. The shadow of a frown crossed her finely etched features when she asked, "Roger, is there any truth to what Lady Sarah said about my family?"

"How could I possibly know that?" he asked.

"You were at court when my father and my mother married."

"I was a twelve-year-old page and certainly not privy to court gossip."

Blythe raised her brows at him, making him smile.

"As I recall, your father pursued your mother," Roger told her. "Besides, your father would never have had a relationship with Sarah, who was a maiden at the time. As a bachelor, your father consorted only with married—"

Blythe blushed. She'd never considered her father or her mother as having other lives before she was born, and to hear that her father had been a rake shocked her.

"As for the matter concerning your grandfather"—Roger shrugged—"you will need to ask him."

Blythe felt relieved. What he said about her parents coincided with what her Grandmama Chessy had said.

"We must discuss another matter of some importance," Blythe told him. "I found Sybilla searching my chamber tonight. She said she'd lost an earring in here while redecorating, but I do not believe her."

"Losing an earring sounds reasonable to me," Roger remarked.

"I also caught her riffling through the papers on your desk."

Roger snapped his brows together. "How did she explain herself?"

"She said she needed a piece of parchment to write a letter."

His expression cleared. "That also sounds reasonable."

"I'm certain she's lying," Blythe said. "We'll need locks on our doors or guards posted about."

Roger refused. "Locks and guards will cause problems in the family." He reached out and with one finger tilted her chin up. "Thank you for being concerned. . . . Have I told you tonight how lovely you look?"

Blythe smiled. "I thought you'd never notice."

"I noticed the moment you walked into the hall," he told her. "You do remind me of an exotic butterfly."

"And you do remind me of a soaring eagle," Blythe returned, making him smile again. "My lord, I think . . ." Too embarrassed to continue, she dropped her gaze to the floor.

"What is it, little butterfly?"

Blythe lifted her gaze and told his chest, "I think he was hurting her."

Roger tilted her chin up and waited until she summoned the courage to meet his gaze. "Who was hurting whom?"

"Hardwick was hurting Daisy."

"Why do you believe that?" he asked, giving her a puzzled look.

"When I stood outside his door I . . . I heard moans and—" Blythe broke off.

Roger closed his eyes for a long moment. His expression registered amusement mingled with disbelief.

"You are more innocent than a newborn," he said, opening

his eyes as a soft smile flirted with the corners of his lips. "Trust me, little butterfly. Hardwick was not hurting Daisy."

"But the moaning—"

"Moans of carnal pleasure, sweetheart."

Blythe crimsoned. "Nobody moans with pleasure," she argued. "People moan only from pain."

Roger smiled and his face inched closer. Blythe knew he was going to kiss her. She stared at him unwaveringly, and anticipation made her heart beat faster.

At the very last moment Blythe closed her eyes. Their lips met in a slow, soul-stealing kiss that seemed to go on forever.

His strong arms encircled her and drew her against the solid planes of his masculine body, and Blythe entwined her arms around his neck. She reveled in the wonderful feeling of his warm, insistent lips covering hers.

The feel of his sweetly demanding kiss and the faint scent of bay conspired to intoxicate her senses. She returned his kiss in kind. And then some.

"A man could lose himself in the mysterious depths of your violet eyes," Roger whispered in a husky voice. He planted another kiss on her lips and added, "You make me forget myself."

"My lord, Daisy is occupied elsewhere. Could you—" Blythe pointed to the back of her gown.

Roger inclined his head and gestured for her to turn around. When she showed him her back, he quickly completed the task.

Blythe felt his warm lips against her neck, and a delicious shiver rippled down her spine. " 'Tis done, little butterfly," she heard him whisper.

"Thank you, my lord," she said, turning around to face him.

Yearning and regret warred upon her beloved's chiseled features.

"Why are you sad?" she asked.

"How do you know that?" he countered with his own question.

"I see regret in your eyes."

"Have you no regrets, little butterfly?"

"None."

Roger glided the tips of his fingers across the silken skin of her cheek and then drew her against his body, holding her as if he would never let her go. "If only I could once more be as young and innocent as you," he said in a voice that mirrored his pain.

"I'd hardly classify you as elderly," she said, tilting her head back to look up at him.

"I am old here," Roger replied, touching his heart. "That's where it counts the most."

"You said you had no heart," Blythe teased him gently.

"Perhaps I lied." Roger stepped back two paces as if he didn't trust himself to be so close to her. "Sweet dreams," he said, and then vanished through the connecting door to his own chamber.

Blythe stared at that door for a long, long moment and then crossed the chamber to the window. Thousands of stars winked at her from their bed of black velvet. And then she heard the faint chiming of her love bell.

Come, Roger, it seemed to beckon. *Surrender your heart of love to Blythe.*

Blythe sighed, breathing deeply of the refreshingly cool night air. She knew with her Druid's instinct that her time was nearing. Soon the eagle and his butterfly would unite to soar across the horizon together. Forever.

"Well, Hardwick, admit you're glad you married her," Roger teased his valet as they rode down the Strand toward Debrett House.

"Quite so," Hardwick agreed. "I wouldn't wish to trifle with Odo Lloyd."

"I would never have known you were happy from that pinched expression of yours," Daisy spoke up. "Are you certain your codpiece isn't pulled too tight?"

Looking down his nose at her, Hardwick cast his bride a reproving look.

Roger and Blythe glanced at each other and smiled.

The September sun had reached its highest point in the sky and had begun its westward descent, casting lengthening shadows across the road. Blythe judged the hour to be just after two o'clock as their entourage of five rode up the private lane to Debrett House.

"How old must I be before I marry?" Miranda asked.

Roger chuckled. "Why, poppet? Whom were you thinking of marrying?"

"You, Daddy."

"Little girls cannot marry their daddies," Blythe informed her. "Besides, I'm already married to your father."

"Then who will I marry, Mama Blight?" the five-year-old asked.

"Someone just as wonderful as your father," Blythe answered, glancing at her beloved.

"Who will that be?"

Blythe gave her an ambiguous smile. "The man of your dreams."

"Is Daddy the man of *your* dreams?"

Blythe blushed with embarrassment as the three adults turned in unison to stare at her. "Your daddy is a wonderful man. . . . Do these questions mean you enjoyed Daisy's and Hardwick's wedding party?"

Miranda nodded. "Let's marry Bottoms to Hartwell, and then we can have another party."

The four adults laughed at her suggestion.

"Laugh if you wish," Hardwick drawled, "but the child's idea does have merit."

Reaching the courtyard, the two men dismounted. Then they turned to assist their ladies. The five of them walked into the foyer and paused a moment before going their separate ways.

"Lady Blythe and I will care for ourselves today," Roger said,

rounding on his valet. "You and your bride take the remainder
of the day and the evening to celebrate your marriage."

"Thank you, my lord," Hardwick said, already ushering Daisy
up the stairs.

"I thought they celebrated their marriage last night," Blythe
quipped.

Roger shrugged and gave her a little smile. "Now then, Lady
Debrett, aren't you glad we refrained from sending for a locksmith or guards? If we'd done that, Cedric and Geoffrey would
have been waiting to pounce on us as soon as we walked
through the door."

Lady Debrett. Blythe liked the sound of that. His casually
spoken words warmed her heart considerably.

"Actually, I ordered Mrs. Hartwell to sit inside my chamber
while we were gone, and Bottoms busied himself in your
study," Blythe replied. "Caution is never wasted, my lord."

"How did I manage to survive the last thirty years of my life
without you watching over me?" Roger teased her.

"Beginner's luck, I suppose." Blythe winked at him and then
noticed Bottoms waiting to greet them.

"Lord Roger, this arrived from court while you were out,"
Bottoms said, handing him a sealed parchment. The majordomo
turned to Blythe and told her, "Rodale and Hibbert are waiting
for you in his lordship's study."

"You should have left them in the hall," Blythe said, certain
her husband would be displeased by her agents' presence in his
private domain.

"I couldn't," Bottoms replied. "Lady Sybilla is entertaining a
guest and refused to let them wait there."

"Go along," Roger said. "I'll sit with Miranda in the hall until
you're finished."

"Good news?" she asked, dropping her gaze to the missive
from court.

"The best," he answered. "I will be welcomed into the royal
fold again when the queen moves to Hampton Court for the
Yule holidays."

"Congratulations, my lord." Blythe walked down the corridor to her husband's study. Did his use of the word *I* have special significance? Did he intend to leave her at Debrett House and return to court and his previous life? The matter was nonnegotiable. She went wherever he went.

"Good day to you," Blythe called, breezing into the study.

Rodale and Hibbert shot to their feet.

"Good day, my lady," Rodale greeted her.

"We want to apologize," Hibbert said in a whining voice that sounded like a hungry dog. "Our speaking to Earl Richard without your permission was wrong."

Blythe decided to let them dangle for a few minutes. Letting one's employees know who was in charge was a good business practice.

"So you are apologizing for sneaking behind my back," she qualified.

"Exactly," Rodale said, his face reddening with her backhanded rebuke.

"We had the best intentions," Hibbert whined.

Blythe gave the man a condescending smile. "As the saying goes, 'The road to hell is paved with good intentions.'"

Both men bobbed their heads in unison. They were ready to agree to almost anything.

Fix prices and live in harmony. Blythe heard her mother's words.

"From this moment on I want my prices set according to my husband's prices. If he raises his, we raise ours, and vice versa," Blythe instructed them. "Nobody wins and nobody loses."

"A wise decision," Rodale agreed.

"There is another matter," Hibbert said, and then hesitated as if reluctant to broach the subject with her.

Blythe fixed her violet gaze on the man.

"'Tis your father," Hibbert began, and then looked at his colleague for support.

"I'll handle this," Rodale told him. "My lady, rumor says that

Earl Richard wants to teach your husband and you a lesson in sound business procedures."

"Devereux Wool and Corn Company has lowered its prices," Hibbert blurted out.

"No matter. Do exactly as I've instructed you," Blythe said. "My father will moderate his own prices once he sees that our price war has ended."

"I never believed that the earl would hurt his own daughter," Rodale said.

"I'll see you next week for a report on our progress?" Blythe asked, implying that she did not want to see them before then.

Both men nodded and left the study. The door clicked shut behind them.

Blythe let out a sigh of relief. At least she'd taken the first step toward setting matters straight with her husband, which probably was the first step toward getting him into her bed. Her eagle was such a proud man. Besting him in business had been supreme folly.

Instead of leaving the study immediately, Blythe wandered across the room to gaze at the autumn landscape within her husband's garden and wondered how Roger would react to her price fixing. Losing gold for the sake of one's pride was folly in the extreme. Certainly he would understand and agree with her about that.

Blythe spied Cedric with his rapier in hand on the far side of the garden. The man dueled with an invisible opponent. Rapier play seemed to be the only thing her brother-in-law excelled at.

And then Blythe saw him slash his weapon across her beloved willow's sweeping branches. She could almost feel the willow's pain. That did it!

Blythe yanked the window open and shouted as loud as she could, "Hey! Stop that!"

Cedric paused in midswing and looked around but was unable to detect from where the voice had come. He resumed his sword-play and again slashed the willow.

Using her right index finger, Blythe touched her heart and her lips. Then she pointed the finger outward at him. A sudden wind swept through the garden, and the willow's sweeping branches wrapped themselves around him.

Blythe smiled with satisfaction when she heard her brother-in-law curse.

"I'm in the study," she called.

Disentangling himself from the branches, Cedric turned around and gazed toward the study window. Then he sauntered across the garden toward her. His dark eyes gleamed with interest as they touched her face and slid to her chest.

"So, how was the wedding of the decade?" he asked.

"Very nice, indeed." Blythe said. "I want you to cease attacking the trees with your rapier, especially that willow, who happens to be a particular friend of mine." She froze, realizing what she'd just revealed about herself.

"Friend?" Cedric echoed.

Blythe blushed. "I meant favorite."

"I think the willow got the better of me," he said dryly, then teased, "How well do you know that oak tree over there?"

"Oh, don't hurt the oak," she cried. "You must not challenge any tree, shrub, plant, flower, or animal."

Cedric could only stare at her.

"Where is the sport in dueling with a creature who cannot fight back?" Blythe argued.

"With whom shall I duel?"

"If you must have a partner, *I'll* duel with you."

"I think not, my lady," Cedric said with a smile, his gaze on her heating at her innocently spoken but highly suggestive words. "The only rapier with which I'd challenge you is made of flesh and blood, not steel."

Blythe stared at him blankly. "What the blazes are you talking about?" she asked.

Cedric chuckled, which only confused her more. He opened his mouth to reply, but the door behind her swung open.

"I saw Rodale and Hibbert leave," Roger said, walking into the room. "What are you doing over there?"

"Speaking with Cedric," she called over her shoulder.

Roger crossed the chamber to stand beside her.

"Your wife has just ordered me to stop slashing trees and decapitating flowers," Cedric told him. "Care to join me outside, brother?"

Roger shook his head. "I have several hours of work ahead of me."

Cedric raised his rapier in salute to them. "Then I shall be forced to challenge my own shadow."

Roger closed the window.

"His constant sword practice is unsettling," Blythe said, rounding on her husband. "What exactly does he do that is productive?"

"He lives off his brother's fortune and probably hopes I'll die without an heir," Roger replied.

"That thought is even more unsettling."

"I was joking," he said. "I left Miranda waiting for you in front of the hearth."

Blythe inclined her head and left the study. Irritation surged through her as soon as she stepped into the hall. Miranda sat alone in the chair in front of the hearth while Sybilla sat with Sarah Sitwell at the high table and ignored the girl's presence.

Instead of crossing to the girl, Blythe advanced on the high table. She absolutely refused to host her husband's former paramours in her home, nor would she countenance rudeness to her stepdaughter. From now on, anyone who hurt her stepdaughter's feelings would answer to her.

"I want you out of my house," Blythe told Lady Sarah when she reached the high table. "Do not return without an invitation."

"I invited her," Sybilla said.

Blythe turned a cold violet gaze on her sister-in-law. "If you want to entertain guests, then I suggest you purchase your own home. Debrett House belongs to my husband *and me*."

Sybilla's face mottled with rage. "Now, listen—"

"No, you will listen to me." Blythe cut off her words. "No one who speaks disparagingly of my mother is welcome here, nor do

I intend to entertain my husband's *former* paramours. If those rules are not to your liking, you may leave Debrett House at any time. I will not force you to stay."

"We'll see about that," Sybilla snapped. She turned to her guest and said, "I apologize for this unseemly behavior. Let me walk you to the door."

"Base breeding does tell," Lady Sarah remarked, rising from her chair. She looked at Blythe and added, "I am not *former* yet."

Blythe made no reply. She watched them leave and then crossed to the chair where her stepdaughter sat. She probably should have held her temper in the child's presence.

Miranda grinned at her.

Blythe sat down in the second chair and gestured for her to sit on her lap. Miranda needed no second invitation.

"Aunt Sybilla won't be going to heaven either," the girl said, her blue gaze sparkling with mischief. "Mama Blight, what's a paramour?"

"Never mind about that," Blythe said. "Do you want to hear another story?"

Miranda nodded.

"My lady?"

Blythe looked up to see Bottoms standing there.

"Lord Roger wishes to speak with you in his study," the majordomo informed her.

"Please deliver Miranda to Hartwell," Blythe said, lifting the girl off her lap and rising from the chair. " 'Twill be good practice for you."

"Practice, my lady?"

"Since you are the reason Hardwick and Daisy married," she said, with a conspiratorial wink, "they'll probably name you godfather of their firstborn. Nice work, Bottoms."

"Thank you, my lady," the majordomo replied in his deep baritone voice. " 'Twas almost too easy."

Blythe paused before her husband's closed study door but decided against knocking. Fixing a brilliant smile on her face, she breezed into the study and gestured for him to remain sitting.

"Hello again," Blythe said, sitting in the chair in front of his desk.

Her husband wore a pained expression on his handsome face. Apparently, her sister-in-law had snitched on her.

"Sybilla was just here," Roger said.

"I meant every word I said to her," Blythe announced without bothering to ask him what tales her sister-in-law had carried to him.

Roger gave her a devastating smile and asked her, "Would you like to go to court with me when I return there?"

"I was planning on it."

"If you want to be a success at court, you must refrain from insulting others," he advised her. "Now you will have two enemies at court."

"You mean three. You've forgotten about Lady Rhoda."

Roger inclined his head. "I was counting on your help in eavesdropping on the women's gossip. Some inadvertent remark could help me discover Darnel's murderer."

"Of course, I'll help you."

"Will you do me another favor?"

"Anything," Blythe answered without hesitation, leaning forward in her chair.

"Have patience with my family," Roger said. "They will surely be gone in a few days."

Chapter 11

His family lingered at Debrett House for five long weeks.

With a sprightly step that reflected her relief at her in-laws' departure, Blythe walked across the wide expanse of lawn toward the quay where her husband stood with his brothers. The mist-shrouded morning had melted into a golden noontide, and the sky's heavenly blue blanket promised an evening that would surely be moonlit and clearer than crystal. Autumn's blaze of color had ripened past its prime, and now dying October's winds shook the leaves from her friends, the trees.

The crisp scent of Samhuinn pervaded the air, and Blythe's lifeblood sang the song of her ancestors. Samhuinn would begin that evening at sundown. Then the veil between the seen and the unseen worlds would part for her mother and her.

Thank the Goddess and Saint Swithin, her in-laws planned to return to court before the holiday began. Their presence was almost unendurable. In fact, Blythe had so little reserve of patience after five weeks that she'd instructed Cook to hold dinner back until later in the day so she needn't share another meal with them.

Awaiting Sybilla, the three Debrett brothers stood near the quay where two of Roger's barges were docked. Traveling upriver to Windsor Castle was easier by barge than horseback.

One barge was laden with her in-laws' baggage and horses, while the canopied barge would carry them in comfort to court.

Reaching the men, Blythe handed Cedric the lunch basket she'd asked Cook to prepare for them. " 'Tis a fair enough day for a journey upriver," she said brightly.

"You wound me, my lady," Geoffrey said, bowing over her hand in courtly manner. "The least you could do is assume a counterfeit sadness for our departure."

"I'm certain we will soon meet again," Blythe replied, blushing at being so easily read. She glanced at her frowning husband and then slid her gaze to Cedric, saying, "You haven't forgotten your arsenal of rapiers, I hope. Whatever would you do without them?"

"I have forgotten nothing," her brother-in-law replied. "I will think of you whenever I practice."

"How flattering," Blythe said dryly. "Here comes Lady Sybilla now."

Cedric leaped onto the barge first and then turned to assist his wife. Geoffrey boarded after her, and the boatsman prepared to shove off.

"Wait!" Miranda raced across the lawns in the direction of the quay. "I have a farewell gift for Aunt Sybilla."

Roger took the package out of his daughter's hands and passed it to his brother. Cedric, in turn, handed it to his wife.

"Open it now, Aunt," Miranda said.

Sybilla unfastened the pretty pink ribbon and lifted the top of the box. In the next instant she startled everyone with a blood-chilling scream.

An imprisoned frog leaped from his confinement inside the box onto her lap. When she screamed again, the frog leaped off her lap into the river.

The three Debrett brothers chuckled. Blythe giggled and winked at her stepdaughter.

"You little wretch," Sybilla shrieked. "You deserve a good paddling."

" 'Tis a Halloween prank," Miranda explained, still laughing at her aunt's frightened reaction.

"Blythe told her to do this," Sybilla complained. "She's a bad influence on the child."

Roger made no reply to that but gestured to the boatsman, and the barge began its journey upriver. He rounded on his daughter and said, "Well done, poppet."

The three of them walked across the lawns to the house. Roger went directly to his study to work on accounts before dinner. Blythe took Miranda upstairs to prepare her disguise for the celebration that night.

"Does my lord have any old clothing from when he was a boy?" Blythe asked, passing the majordomo in the foyer.

Bottoms gave her a puzzled look.

"We need disguises for this evening," she explained.

"His lordship's clothing is boxed and set back in the deepest corner of his dressing room."

"Thank you," Blythe said.

"Thank you," Miranda echoed her stepmother.

"Wait here," Blythe ordered when they stepped inside her bedchamber. "I'll bring you something suitable for tonight."

Blythe walked through the door that connected her bedchamber with her husband's. She hadn't stepped foot inside his room since that painful scene on their wedding night. The chamber was simply furnished and decorated; apparently, her husband was a man who had more important things to do than luxuriate in his riches.

Blythe headed straight for the closed door on the opposite side of the chamber. Entering the dressing closet, she sniffed the faint scent of bay that wafted through the air. Blythe touched her husband's garments as she passed them on her way to the rear of the closet. Sure enough, her beloved had stored more than a dozen boxes there.

Opening the first, Blythe lifted a pair of breeches that were much too big for Miranda and probably worn when Roger was an adolescent. The second box contained clothing only a tad smaller. Apparently, her husband had arranged the boxes of clothing from largest to smallest.

From the bottom box Blythe withdrew a pair of breeches that he had worn as a young boy. With the help of a belt, they would fit Miranda. Now she needed a dark shirt, a jerkin for warmth, and a cap. She found the shirt and the jerkin easily, but dug deeply to the bottom of the box before finding a cap.

Blythe replaced the boxes in the order she had found them and left the dressing closet. Reluctant to leave her beloved's chamber, she paused a moment with the borrowed clothing in her hands. The knit cap felt unusually heavy.

Reaching inside, Blythe pulled out a book. She crossed the chamber to the window, stared at the book for a moment, and then opened it to the inscription page. The journal belonged to Roger's mother.

What wonderful reading this would be, Blythe thought. It could give her some new insight into her husband's childhood. Roger had probably long forgotten its existence and would never know if she borrowed it for a few days.

Taking the journal with her, Blythe retraced her steps to her own chamber. She placed the journal in the top drawer of her desk and then turned to wink at Miranda.

Excited beyond endurance, the five-year-old fairly skipped around and around the bedchamber. In short order the little girl was transformed into a little boy.

Blythe changed into a black skirt with large pockets, a white linen blouse with scooped neck, and a black woolen shawl. "We always dress in dark colors on Samhuinn so that spirits won't follow us home," she told the little girl.

"What about the cork?" Miranda asked, apparently anxious to blacken her face.

"We'll smudge our faces after we eat dinner."

"Mama Blight, are Daddy and you going to give me brothers and sisters like you have at Devereux House?" Miranda asked abruptly.

"I am willing, but your father has the final say in that matter," Blythe said.

"Then I'll ask him for some."

"If you want to persuade a man to give you something, you need to use strategy," Blythe told her.

"What's that?"

"Strategy is the plan you follow to get whatever you want."

"Tell me what to do."

"My Grandmama Chessy says you must bat your eyelashes at a man like this," Blythe said, demonstrating with great exaggeration. "Next you must pucker your lips into an inviting pout. Like this . . ." Again, she demonstrated what she meant. "The man will offer you a gift, but you must refuse it with a shy, innocent smile. Men absolutely adore shy and innocent. He'll offer you a second gift and a third, but each time you must refuse it."

"Why?" Miranda asked. "I never refuse gifts."

"After being rejected three times, the man will become frantic with frustration," Blythe explained. "Then he will offer you what you really want. This time you may accept his gift and say, 'Well, I don't wish to hurt your feelings.' "

"Does this always work?" Miranda asked.

"Grandmama Chessy swears by it," Blythe answered. "She's an expert on men, you know."

"No, I didn't know that."

Blythe smiled at her reply and asked, "Shall we go to dinner now?"

Hand in hand, Blythe and Miranda walked downstairs. They sat down at the high table to await dinner.

"Who is this little boy?" Roger asked, sitting down with them a few minutes later.

Miranda giggled. "I'm your daughter, Daddy."

The servants arrived then with their dinner of roasted chicken with pine nuts, onion-and-leek soup, bread, butter, wine, and apple cider.

"For you, my lord," Bottoms announced, setting a covered plate down in front of him.

Roger lifted the cover off the plate. Two white doves flew up, startling him.

" 'Tis your Halloween prank," Miranda cried, clapping her hands together.

Roger looked over his daughter's head at his bride and muttered, "Those birds will foul the whole house."

Bottoms set a covered plate down in front of Miranda, who flinched in fear. Then he lifted the cover to reveal a box.

"I would never startle you, poppet," Blythe assured her, putting an arm around the child's shoulder. " 'Tis a gift."

Miranda gave her a suspicious glance. "What is it?"

"Open it and find out."

"Sacred Saint Swithin," Miranda exclaimed in a perfect imitation of her stepmother when she lifted the top off the box.

Attached to a gold chain was a jeweled pendant. The center stone was black onyx, surrounded by an emerald, an aventurine, a ruby, an amethyst, and four star sapphires.

" 'Tis a necklace designed to adorn and to protect," Blythe said, lifting it out of the box and setting it over the girl's head. "The necklace is a symbol of eternity and powerful protection. This black stone is onyx and a powerful protector. See, Hercules is engraved on it. Ancient Romans wore this symbol when they went into battle."

"Who is Hercules?" Miranda asked.

"The strongest, most invincible man in the world." Blythe looked at her husband and asked, "Do you remember him?"

Roger rolled his eyes. "Yes, and his twelve labors."

"The emerald represents the north," Blythe instructed her stepdaughter. "The aventurine represents the east, the ruby symbolizes the south, and the amethyst stands for the west. So you are protected from all directions."

"What's the blue?" Miranda asked.

"Blythe, don't you think this gift is inappropriate for a five-year-old?" Roger spoke up.

"No, I don't." Blythe turned back to the girl and continued,

"The blue stones are star sapphires, and a powerful guardian dwells within each."

"Like an angel?"

"Exactly. The blue matches your pretty eyes, too."

Miranda threw her arms around Blythe's neck and exclaimed, "I love you, Mama Blight."

"And I love you, sweetheart."

Miranda rounded on her father and batted her eyelashes at him, asking, "Daddy, can we get a baby brother or sister?"

Roger's expression mirrored his surprise. "No."

"Why?"

"I just bought you two ponies," Roger answered.

Miranda pouted provocatively, making her stepmother smile. "What's wrong with your lips?" Roger asked.

"Nothing," the five-year-old answered glumly.

"How about a new dolly?" Roger offered.

"No, thank you," Miranda answered, shaking her head with exaggerated sadness. She held one finger up to Blythe, implying that the dolly was his first gift offering.

"I might get you a puppy for your New Year's gift," Roger coaxed.

Miranda held a second finger up to Blythe and then turned sad eyes upon her father, saying, "Thank you for thinking of me, Daddy, but I'll wait for a brother or a sister. I am content until then."

Roger lifted his gaze to Blythe. Reading the question in his eyes, Blythe shook her head and shrugged.

Samhuinn dusk shrouded the world of men by the time Roger, Blythe, and Miranda crossed the Devereux dowager house gardens on their way to Devereux House for the Halloween festivities. Blythe inhaled deeply of October's crisp twilight and felt anticipation surging through her body.

The night had been created for magic, and an eerie splendor pervaded the atmosphere. A rising tide of potent energy charged the hushed air with expectancy, while the muted, darkening colors of dusk slashed across the sky's horizon from east to west.

Blythe could hardly contain her stepdaughter, who was drawn by the bonfire flames in the night and the sounds of laughter emanating from her parents' garden. Emerging from between the rows of shrubbery, they saw the revelers and hurried across the lawns toward them.

"Who is this little sooty-faced boy?" Lady Keely asked by way of a greeting.

The five-year-old giggled. " 'Tis Miranda."

"I would never have guessed that was you," Earl Richard exclaimed, feigning surprise.

Interrupting them, a small girl approached and handed the five-year-old a sprig of yew. She looked at the earl and complained, "Papa, I don't like being a girl."

Blythe giggled, and Roger threw back his head and shouted with laughter. The little girl was actually four-year-old Adam Devereux.

"Adam, humor your mother for one night," the earl told his son. "Your sisters are having fun being boys."

Blythe turned around. Disguised as boys like Miranda, her sisters were holding hands and dancing around the Samhuinn bonfire.

"Come on, boy," Adam said to Miranda. "Let's dance."

Miranda looked at Blythe, who nodded at her, and then ran off with Adam to join the others.

"You missed the apple-bobbing contest," Lady Keely said, "but we'll be roasting chestnuts and telling stories later."

"Roasted chestnuts," Blythe exclaimed, clapping her hands together like a young girl. "I can hardly wait."

Her husband smiled at her girlish behavior.

"Shall we adjourn to my study?" Richard asked Roger. "I've received several preliminary reports on our latest business venture."

Roger nodded and started toward the house, but paused when his father-in-law did.

"You own a quarter of the shares," the earl called to Blythe. "You are welcome to join us."

"Mama Blight, dance with us," Miranda called.

"Celebrate, sister," Adam added to the invitation.

Torn between business and celebration, Blythe stood in indecision. She looked from the children to her father and her husband and then back at the children.

"If you'd rather stay here," Roger said, "I'll share the news with you later."

"Thank you, my lord," Blythe said, casting him a brilliant smile.

Earl Richard and Roger walked toward the mansion and then disappeared inside.

"Why does Papa always appear at our Samhuinn bonfire and then disappear into his study until we go inside to roast chestnuts?" Blythe asked her mother.

"Your father is a skeptic and as sensitive to the unseen as a brick," Lady Keely told her. "I do believe Roger is cut from the same cloth."

Blythe nodded. "Mama, let's join the fun."

"Dearest, I would speak with you first," the countess said, placing a restraining hand on her arm.

"Very well."

"When I commune with the dead tonight, I will seek Grandmother Megan's counsel about the dark sun," Lady Keely said.

"But I'll be here with you."

"Slipping away from Debrett House may prove difficult," her mother said.

"I've set a ladder beneath my bedchamber window," Blythe told her. "Roger will never know I've gone out."

"You are my firstborn, the nectar of my love for your father," Lady Keely said, placing the palm of her hand against her daughter's cheek. "Whatever happens tonight, believe that Roger would never hurt you."

"I don't understand," Blythe said, confused.

"Understanding my words is unnecessary," Lady Keely replied, smiling mysteriously. "Only remember and believe them."

"Mama, do you worry for my safety? You cannot believe that Roger hurt Darnel—"

"Nothing like that," her mother interrupted. "Trust Roger. He loves you dearly but doesn't know it yet."

"I do trust him," Blythe told her. "I even raised my prices to meet his."

Lady Keely laughed. "Daughter, I see too much of your father in you."

"Come, Mama," Blythe said, grabbing her hand. "Let's celebrate with the children."

One hour after midnight, the beginning of Samhuinn's darkest moments, Blythe sat on the edge of her bed and listened to the heavy silence within Debrett House. Nothing stirred.

Blythe appeared serene, but wild anticipation quickened her heartbeat. Soon her mother and she would cast the magic circle, and the thin veil between the here and now and the beyond would part for them.

Once more Megan Glendower, her mother's mother, would speak to them from beyond the horizon. She would know what the dark sun represented and how to vanquish it.

Blythe harbored no fears about the dead. Death was akin to birth in her Druid philosophy. Life was a never-ending circle of birth, growth, death, rebirth. The communion between the tangible world and the unseen filled her with almost unendurable excitement, and her lifeblood sang the song of her ancestors.

The hour to sneak out of Debrett House had arrived. Even now her mother would be gathering the necessary stones to cast the enchanted circle.

Upon returning home earlier that evening, Blythe had changed into her gauzy nightshift, lest her husband need to visit her chamber for some unforeseen reason. Now, with precious moments ticking away, she decided to forgo donning her skirt and blouse. Instead, she grabbed her black woolen cloak and wrapped it around herself. She left her feet bare lest she make any unnecessary noise.

Blythe crossed to the door connecting her chamber to her husband's and pressed her ear to it. All remained quiet on the other side. Roger would never know that she'd sneaked out of the house during the night.

Whirling away from the door, Blythe silently crossed the chamber to the window. She opened one shutter, but then froze in fear when the other side squeaked, protesting the movement.

Blythe stood statue-still for a long moment but heard no sound of her husband awakening. Gathering her cloak around her, she lifted one leg over the windowsill and felt blindly for the ladder's top rung.

Finally finding it, Blythe lifted her left leg over the sill until she stood on the ladder's top rung. Then she started down the ladder and refused to stop until both of her feet stood on solid earth.

Blythe sent up a silent prayer of thanks to the Goddess and took a deep, calming breath. Falling would have meant discovery, and she feared that more than breaking a leg.

Suddenly, strong hands grabbed her from behind. When she opened her mouth to scream, a hand covered it.

"You little fool," said a harsh voice beside her ear. The voice belonged to her husband.

Roger whirled her around to face him.

Blythe looked up and thought absurdly that she hadn't realized how tall her husband really was until now, when he towered menacingly above her.

"What are you doing out here?" she demanded.

"Waiting for you, of course."

"How did you—"

"Your father mentioned guarding Lady Keely in the middle of the night because she worshiped on Samhuinn Eve," Roger told her. "I noticed the ladder beneath your window when we returned home tonight."

Blythe lost her bluster. "And you decided to protect me?"

"*Prevent* would be a more appropriate word."

" 'Tis imperative I worship with my mother tonight," she said, turning away.

Roger reached out and easily pulled her back when she started to walk away. Caught off balance, Blythe fell against him and her cloak slipped off her shoulders.

"You're almost naked," he exclaimed in a harsh whisper.

"Be at peace, husband," Blythe said in a soft voice, placing the palm of her hand against his cheek. "I must seek the Goddess's wisdom in order to protect you from the dark sun that endangers your life."

"You are doing this for me?" Roger asked, surprised. "Why?"

"I love you," Blythe answered, her voice a silken caress. "I have loved you since the beginning of time."

Her declaration of love shocked Roger even more than his late wife's indiscretions. The only women who'd ever uttered those words to him had lied. Those devious creatures had wanted to bind his heart to them for their own financial gain. The only woman who had truly loved him had been his mother.

Now here was this woman, younger than springtide, declaring her love for him. How could she possibly profit by it? Her father was the richest man in England, and she was a successful businesswoman in her own right. And yet his bride had risked life and limb to climb down a ladder in the dark in order to pray for him.

No one had ever prayed for him before.

Roger had half a mind to let her go, but then she shivered with the night's chill. He stared at her body through eyes that gleamed with unrequited desire; his breath caught raggedly in his throat when he fixed his gaze on the ivory flesh of her breasts, visible through her ridiculously sheer nightshift.

Blythe had become an irresistibly beautiful woman. And she belonged to him. He ached to bury himself deep within her, possess her body and her soul.

With a defeated groan, Roger scooped her into his arms and walked toward the house. Wrapping her arms around his neck,

Blythe uttered no word of protest but stared at him as if in a trance.

Upstairs, Roger carried her into his bedchamber and closed the door with his booted foot. He carried her across the chamber to the bed but set her down on her feet on the floor beside it.

Roger stepped back a pace and said in a husky voice, "Escape to your chamber now if you want."

"I am your wife," Blythe answered. She closed the short distance between them, entwined her arms around his neck, and pressed her body against his.

"I want you," she breathed against the base of his throat. "As much as you want me."

Before he could embrace her, Blythe stepped back a pace. For one awful moment Roger thought she was going to desert him.

And then she moved.

Reaching up, Blythe slipped the straps of her nightshift off her shoulders. The gown fluttered to the floor to form a pool of silk. She stood naked before him, a proud beauty who belonged only to him.

Roger worshiped her with his eyes. He dropped his scorching gaze from her exquisitely lovely face to her pink-tipped breasts and then traveled down to her tiny waist, her curvaceous hips, her daintily formed feet.

Holding her gaze captive to his, Roger pulled his shirt over his head and tossed it on the floor, where it mingled with her silken nightshift even as they were about to mingle with their bodies. His boots and his breeches followed his shirt, until he stood naked.

Unfortunately, his bride refused to drop her gaze below his neck. In that instant Roger remembered that the lush, inviting woman who stood so wantonly naked in front of him was actually an uninitiated virgin. He knew he must go slowly with her lest she flee in fright, yet he wanted her badly. His task was almost as impossible as catching a pretty butterfly.

"Let me feel your gaze upon my body," Roger said in a husky voice, inching closer. He reached out to caress her flushed cheek and then glided his hand down her slender neck to her breasts. Flicking his thumb across her nipple, he heard her sharp intake of breath.

"Are you afraid, little butterfly?" he asked.

"Yes."

Roger smiled at her honesty. "But you desire this?"

"Yes."

He held his hand out to her in invitation and asked, "My lady, will you lay upon my bed with me?"

Blythe gave him a smile filled with sunshine and without hesitation placed her hand in his. He drew her close against his body for a long moment, savoring the sensation of her incredible softness, before lifting her into his arms and placing her down on the bed.

Roger stared at her for a brief moment and then lay down beside her. Without giving her time to think, he gathered her into his arms; his mouth covered hers in a slow, soul-stealing kiss that lasted for almost an eternity.

"Are you still afraid?" he asked.

"Yes," she breathed against his lips.

Roger drew back to plant a playful kiss on the tip of her nose. "What are the earthly pleasures you like to feel, little butterfly?" he asked.

She thought a moment before answering with a smile. "A gentle breeze upon my back, the sun warming my shoulders, the willow's branches tickling my face, the morning dew beneath my feet."

"Making love feels like all that and so much more," he told her. "Will you trust me?"

"I have always trusted you, my eagle."

Roger kissed her again, and Blythe returned his kiss in kind. He flicked his tongue across the crease of her lips, and when she parted them for him, he slipped his tongue inside to explore her sweetness.

Lifting his lips from hers, Roger sprinkled dozens of feathery-light kisses across her eyelids, temples, nose, and throat. He captured her lips again and kissed her passionately, while his hand caressed her from her throat to her sensitive breasts to the secret place between her legs.

"The dew lies here between your thighs," he whispered.

Blythe moaned throatily. She pressed her lithe body against the hand that stroked her moist womanhood.

Roger captured one of her pink nipples between his lips and suckled gently upon it. Feeling her tremble with blossoming desire, he suckled harder and inserted one long finger inside her.

"Spread your legs for me," he ordered.

Dazed with desire, Blythe heard his command and obeyed.

Roger knelt between her thighs. His erection teased the dewy pearl of her womanhood.

"One moment of pain," he told her. "Forgive me."

With one powerful thrust, Roger buried himself deep inside her. She cried out in pained surprise when he broke through her virgin's barrier, but he covered her mouth and kissed her thoroughly until the first shock had passed. For several long moments he lay still and let her become accustomed to his fullness.

And then Roger began to move, enticing her to move with him.

Blythe wrapped her legs around his waist as innocence vanished and instinct surfaced. Catching his rhythm, she moved her hips and enticed him deeper and deeper inside her body. Moaning her need, she met each of his powerful thrusts with her own.

"Soar with me, little butterfly," Roger whispered against her ear.

Suddenly, a thousand suns exploded inside Blythe and carried her to paradise and beyond. Only then, when he felt her complete surrender, did Roger release his own need. He groaned and shuddered and poured his seed deep within her.

They lay perfectly still for long moments, their labored breathing the only sound in the chamber. Finally, Roger rolled to one side, pulling her with him, and planted a kiss on the crown of her head.

He looked down and saw those enormous violet eyes of hers staring up at him. "Close your eyes and sleep."

And she did.

He loved her. That startling realization hit Roger with the impact of an avalanche, nearly felling him with its implications.

Roger stared down at his wife's hauntingly lovely face. Though an annulment was now out of the question, Blythe must never learn the extent of his feelings for her. Professing his love would mean living in misery; somehow she would use that knowledge against him, as Darnel had done. He refused to risk being hurt again.

Though it hurt him to do so, he would lock his bedchamber door against her. He would keep her out of his bed—and out of his heart.

Chapter 12

His sevens and eights were fornicating again.

Roger flung his quill down on the desk. Disgusted with his lack of discipline, he bolted out of the chair and stood at the window while he tried to compose himself.

A powdery blanket of snow, the first of the season, covered the lawns. Sparkling sunbeams danced like fairies across the white fluff, and sprays of wild roseberries added a festive touch to the hedgerow.

In the six weeks since he'd sworn never to touch his wife again, sweet memories of her lush body and passionate kisses consumed him.

Blythe had pointedly ignored him for the first two weeks following his announcement that he intended never to sleep with her again. He had expected her to lower her corn and wool prices, but she'd purposely shamed him by fixing her prices to meet his. During the third and fourth week after his rejection, she had assumed a coolly polite attitude, while he'd behaved like a baited bear ready to attack anyone unfortunate enough to cross his path.

And then last week Blythe had announced that she didn't want to attend court with him. He'd vetoed that idea, of course. The Earl of Oxford, his personal nemesis, would accuse him of murdering another wife if his new bride failed to appear by his side.

His bride. Once again Roger saw her lying naked upon the bed, felt her silken skin caressing his, savored the sensation of invading her heated folds.

He pressed his forehead against the window, felt its coolness, and tried to compose himself. How would he survive the weeks of sharing a chamber with her at court?

The barges were already loaded, and the grooms were bringing their horses up from the stables. In less than an hour his bride and he would journey upriver to Hampton Court. Then he could begin investigating Darnel's murder and clear his name of all suspicion.

Roger returned to his desk and began to pack his ledgers. There was no telling how long they would be at court, and he fully intended to continue working while there. His most able competition—namely, his wife—planned to do the same, and he refused to let her get the upper hand in anything.

Roger left the study and walked down the corridor leading to the foyer. Spying Miranda and Blythe clinging to each other, he paused in the shadows and listened to their conversation.

"Mama Blight, don't leave me," Miranda whined, flinging her arms around the kneeling woman.

"Your daddy needs me to attend court with him," Blythe said, hugging the girl tightly, her voice a gentle caress. "He needs my advice concerning some very important matters, but I'll be returning on New Year's Day with a gift for you. And perhaps I can sneak back to Debrett House on Christmas."

"I'll miss you," Miranda said, resting her head against her stepmother's shoulder.

"I'll miss you more," Blythe insisted, and then planted a kiss on the child's temple. "Hartwell will bring you to Devereux House every day so that Adam and you can play together. Won't that be fun?"

"Yes, I'll like that," the five-year-old answered.

"Bottoms promised to escort you to the stables every day," Blythe went on. "You will bring Pericles and Aspasia carrots, won't you?"

Miranda nodded. "Who will tell me my bedtime story?"

"Hartwell will do that," Blythe answered. "When I return I will have so many court stories to share with you . . . Lord Perpendicular will still be visiting you each night. Do you promise not to pinch the gold while I'm gone?"

Miranda nodded.

Of course the Earl of Corners would be visiting his daughter each night, Roger thought as he stood hidden in the shadows. His wife had given Bottoms and Hartwell a pouch of gold each to plant in her absence.

That Blythe sincerely harbored a fondness for his daughter was all too evident. She would have made an excellent mother for his children, the kind of mother he'd mistakenly believed Darnel would be.

Clearing his throat, Roger stepped into the light and started toward them. Blythe kissed the little girl's cheek and then told her to bid her father farewell.

Miranda dashed toward him. Laughing, Roger scooped her into his arms and held her close.

"Daddy, don't go," Miranda cried.

"I'm sorry, poppet, but I have important business at court," he said. "When I come home, I'll bring you a gift."

"I don't want a gift," she said, wrapping her arms around his neck. "I want *you*, Daddy."

Roger's heart ached at his daughter's words. He didn't deserve this child's unconditional love. He wanted never to leave her, but he knew he had no choice. Uncovering Darnel's murderer was the only way to restore his good name and reputation.

" 'Tis a warm enough day for December," Bottoms announced, walking into the foyer from the courtyard. "That touch of snow will be gone before noon. The barges await your pleasure, my lord."

"Give Daddy a kiss," Roger said.

Miranda hugged and kissed him, and then gifted her stepmother with another kiss.

Blythe glanced over her shoulder as they started out the door.

Bottoms and Miranda were holding hands and watching them. Blythe gave them a bright smile, and the little girl waved in return.

Blythe cast one final sweeping glance at the garden she'd grown to love. She called a silent farewell to her friend, the willow, and in answer the tips of its branches twitched in the gentle breeze.

Roger climbed on board first and then turned to assist her. She settled on a cushioned seat and looked over her shoulder for one last glimpse of Debrett House. Only the Goddess knew what unexpected dangers awaited them at court.

The full-bodied bluster of winter was still weeks away, yet the advancing season teased the discerning eye. Frozen droplets of moisture clung like pussy willows to the barren branches of trees.

Though she cast an appreciative gaze over the passing scenery, Blythe was intensely aware of her husband's presence by her side. They hadn't been this close and alone since Samhuinn Eve when they consummated their vows.

Blythe swallowed a smile when she thought of her husband's impending downfall at her hands. Forced by circumstances to share a chamber and a bed with her, Roger would be hard-pressed to keep from touching her.

True, Blythe had no longer wanted to accompany him to court, mostly because she'd been concerned for the babe she knew she was carrying. Her lips twitched with merriment. Blissful in his ignorance, her eagle had no knowledge that he was about to gain a second nestling.

Blythe refused to share her impending motherhood with him. She wanted to win his love without using the babe as leverage. She needed him to want her for herself, not the child she carried.

Aristotle Debrett, Blythe decided as she began humming a sprightly tune. Naming her son in honor of the distinguished philosopher and tutor of Alexander the Great would assure him of wisdom. On the other hand, naming him Alexander in honor of the world's greatest warrior might be even better. After all, Alexander had subdued the whole world and so, too, would her son subdue his world.

"And why are you so happy?" Roger asked, drawing her attention. "I thought you didn't want to accompany me to court."

"I changed my mind," Blythe replied. " 'Tis a remarkable day for a ride on the river."

"Capricious, aren't you?"

Blythe gave him a smile. He seemed to be glad that they were once again on speaking terms. She dropped her gaze to the documents he'd been reading and said, "If you'd put those papers away, you could revel in this glorious scenery."

"I fear I lack your mathematical genius," Roger told her.

"Are you having trouble with your numbers?"

"My sevens and eights are misbehaving," he said with a rueful smile.

"Perhaps I can help," she offered.

Roger smiled at her words. "I'm positive you could, but I prefer to work alone."

"Then suffer, dear husband."

For some unfathomable reason her reply made him laugh. "You'll never know how much I am suffering, little butterfly."

Little butterfly. His term of endearment gave her renewed hope.

And then Blythe caught her first glimpse of their destination.

Situated twelve miles southwest of London, Hampton Court sparkled in the sunlight beneath its coating of powdery snow like the most exquisite jewel in England's royal crown. On what seemed like hundreds of acres the palace stood with its endless roofline of turrets, pinnacles, and chimney stacks. Trees, hedges, and shrubs grew as far as the eye could see.

"Sacred Saint Swithin!" Blythe exclaimed softly. "How many people live here?"

"A thousand when the queen is in residence."

"And all of them need wool in winter and corn to eat," Blythe said to herself.

"I do believe your father holds a monopoly on supplying corn and wool to the queen," Roger remarked.

"Perhaps I can deliver it cheaper," she said, giving him a jaunty smile.

At the landing stage, Roger leaped out first and then assisted her. He gestured at Hardwick to take care of their baggage.

"Hampton Court is comprised of ten different courts, myriad gardens, hundreds of chambers, dozens of kitchens, stables, a tiltyard, and tennis courts," Roger told her conversationally, escorting her toward the main building.

"How will I ever find my way around without getting lost?" Blythe asked.

"Order a page to escort you wherever you wish to go," Roger answered.

A city unto itself, Hampton Court was a hive of dizzying activity. Horses clattered continuously through the courtyards on the way to the stables. Tradesmen with carts of foodstuffs crowded the common areas, along with purveyors of finery and jewelry and noblemen with their families.

Tightly grasping her husband's arm, Blythe gazed in wide-eyed wonder at the perpetual movement that swirled around her. When he stopped short suddenly, she nearly tripped and then focused on the man blocking their path.

A tall, middle-aged nobleman stood before them. He wore a crimson velvet doublet and breeches, a matching hat with a plume of feathers, garters with silver ends, and Spanish leather shoes.

Staring at him, Blythe thought of a peacock. A human peacock.

The man stared coldly at Roger. Her husband barely nodded his head in acknowledgment.

"Have you returned then?" the man asked.

"No, Oxford," Roger replied, a hard edge to his voice. "You're standing here alone, speaking to yourself."

Edward deVere, the seventeenth Earl of Oxford, Blythe concluded. She'd heard the rumors about his troublesome nature, especially that he'd taken immense pleasure in arresting her beloved and locking him in the Tower.

"I see imprisonment hasn't cured you of that abominable sense of humor," deVere remarked. He glanced at Blythe and added, "So, is Devereux's daughter your intended next victim?"

Roger reached for his rapier, hanging at his side. Blythe touched his hand in warning.

"Lord deVere, the journey upriver has wearied me," Blythe said with a forced smile. "If you would step aside and let us pass, I wish to find our chamber and rest awhile."

Oxford inclined his head, saying, "Lady Debrett, you must step aside for me."

What an arrogant, contemptible man, Blythe thought. Acres of open space surrounded them, yet here they stood arguing about who would step aside. Oxford had deliberately put himself in front of them to cause trouble.

"Do you mean to step aside for him?" Blythe asked, glancing sidelong at her husband.

"Not bloody likely."

"We shan't be moving, my lord earl." Blythe released her husband's arm and casually placed her right hand over her heart. She turned to her husband again, remarking, "I do believe the weather is changing." Saying that, she placed her right index finger across her lips as if pondering the next move for both parties.

A sudden gust of wind swept across the grounds and flipped the earl's hat off his head. With a muttered curse, the seventeenth Earl of Oxford chased his scarlet plumed hat across the lawns in the direction of the river.

With that problem solved, Blythe smiled sweetly at her husband's perplexed expression and asked, "Shall we find our chamber or should we look for Bliss first?"

"Did you do that?"

"Do what?"

"Never mind," Roger said, shaking his head. "We'll go to our chamber. Bliss and your grandparents will soon hear of our arrival and come to us."

Entering the palace proper, Roger escorted her through a maze of corridors and long galleries. Servants dressed in blue livery carried trays of food. A small army of grooms, their arms laden with firewood, hurried to deliver their loads to the yeomen who would lay fires in the hearths.

Highborn courtiers and their ladies called out greetings to her husband and paused to peruse his Devereux bride. Fascinated by their outlandish garb, Blythe returned their stares. Her father always wore black, as did her husband, and she was unaccustomed to the unusual sight of preening males.

Blythe wondered how she would ever get along at court. These fellow countrymen of hers seemed so foreign. She had nothing in common with them. How miserable Bliss must be.

Apparently, Roger was in favor again: The chamber reserved for the prodigal courtier returned to his monarch's bosom was fairly spacious. The room contained a four-poster bed with heavy draperies to ward off winter's chill. On one side of the chamber stood the hearth, with two chairs positioned in front of it. There was also a writing table placed near the window, from which one could take a spectacular view of the Thames.

A room with a view, Blythe thought. Elizabeth had missed her husband's presence at court.

" 'Tis lovely," she said.

"I'm glad you like it."

Hardwick and Daisy walked into the room and were followed by a parade of grooms, who carried the baggage and left after Roger rewarded each with a coin. A yeoman arrived last and lit the fire in the hearth. He, too, received a coin from her husband.

Watching this, Blythe realized that she had better bring a purse with her wherever she went. Coins were required for services rendered. She'd bet the profits on her corn trade that the bigger the coin, the better the service one received.

"My lord, shall we begin unpacking?" Hardwick asked. "Or would her ladyship care to rest a—"

The door flew open, drawing their attention. Bliss Devereux dashed into the chamber, calling, "Sister!"

Blythe met Bliss in the middle of the chamber, and the two sisters embraced. "I missed you," Blythe said.

Seeing her grandparents standing just inside the doorway, Blythe released her sister and made a dash for her grandfather. She hugged him first and then her grandmother.

"Elizabeth has been asking if you've arrived yet," Duke Robert told Roger. "She's anxious to see her 'soaring eagle.' "

Roger smiled, obviously pleased to be summoned into her presence so soon. He turned to his man, saying, "Take Daisy and settle yourself. While my wife visits with her sister, I shall attend the queen and then stop at the stables to check on Achilles and Hector."

"Will you accompany me?" he asked his grandfather-in-law.

Duke Robert nodded and opened the door to leave.

"I'll see you tonight, darling," Grandmama Chessy said, planting a kiss on Blythe's cheek. "Be certain to rest. You appear a bit under the eaves."

Blythe nodded.

"What are you wearing tonight?" the duchess asked as she crossed the chamber to leave with her husband. "First impressions are so important, you know. Wear something spectacular."

Everyone filed out, and the door clicked shut behind them.

Blythe sat down on the edge of the bed and patted the spot beside her in invitation. Having her sister with her would help smooth her way at court, and she felt grateful.

"How do you find your way without getting lost?" Blythe asked.

"You'll learn," Bliss told her, plopping down on the bed.

"What is she *really* like?"

"The queen?" Bliss smiled. "She's everything we ever imagined and more, but she does possess a frightfully bad temper."

"Has she ever turned her anger upon you?" Blythe asked.

Bliss shook her head and then winked at her sister. "You know the effect I have on people. 'Tis my gift from the Goddess. . . . But Grandpapa refuses to let any of the eligible men near me," she complained. "Gawd, he's stricter than Papa. Enough about me. How goes the married life?"

Blythe looked into her sister's violet eyes, so much like her own, and the strain of the previous two months welled up painfully within her. She burst into tears.

"That good, huh?" Bliss said, putting a comforting arm around her. "Don't weep, sister. You'll make it rain."

"Is your touch making me feel better?" Blythe asked, managing a wobbly smile for her.

"Of course," Bliss answered. "Now, share your problems with me, and the load will be lighter."

"My husband's family irritates me," Blythe began. "Except for Miranda, whom I love dearly."

"And?"

"My husband's mistresses paid us a social call one evening," Blythe said in a small voice.

"Former mistresses, I warrant," Bliss replied. "Who are they?"

"Sarah Sitwell and Rhoda Bellows."

"You mean, Lady Rodent?"

Blythe giggled. "She does possess a ratty expression."

"The only thing missing is a long, skinny tail," Bliss agreed. "What else is on your mind?"

"Roger doesn't love me," Blythe admitted, her bottom lip trembling with the effort not to cry. "He had planned to annul me, but passing one night in my bed put an end to that. Since then he's locked me out of his bedchamber."

"Holy Hippocrates, what a bastard," Bliss muttered.

"There is more," Blythe said.

Bliss tilted her head to one side and waited for her to continue.

"I-I carry his child, but haven't told him yet."

"I'm only a shade above sixteen and entirely too young to be someone's aunt," Bliss drawled in a perfect imitation of their grandmother.

Blythe burst out laughing, and Bliss joined her.

Bliss sobered first. "Seriously, sister, Roger is no innocent boy and must suspect that this could happen."

"Since we passed only one night together, I doubt he's considered the possibility of siring a child upon me," Blythe said.

"Sister, the Goddess moves in mysterious ways," Bliss replied, putting an arm around her shoulder. "Once was all she needed to ensure that the eagle remains with his butterfly."

"I do love you," Blythe said, resting her head upon her sister's shoulder.

"Make that double for me," Bliss replied. "When will you tell Roger the good news?"

"Perhaps when we return to Debrett House."

"Make it sooner rather than later," Bliss advised. "Else you'll go gray with the worry."

Blythe sighed. "I cannot seem to summon the necessary courage."

"I must leave to attend the queen, but I'll see you tonight in the hall," Bliss said. "We'll speak of this later. Oh, I've discovered something quite interesting and will show you tomorrow morning, if you can slip away."

"Roger would never deny me your company," Blythe said. "What is it?"

"I cannot tell you," Bliss answered, kissing Blythe's cheek and then rising from the bed. "You must experience this for yourself."

And then she was gone.

Blythe rose from her perch on the bed and gazed out the window at the Thames. She could hardly believe she was in her chamber at Hampton Court. Tonight she would meet the Queen of England. How could she nap knowing that? She was too excited to work on her ledgers and wished she had remembered to bring her late mother-in-law's journal. Unfortunately, the diary lay where she'd put it the day she found it, inside the top drawer of her desk.

Several hours later Blythe stood in front of the looking glass in her chamber and studied her image. She appeared elegant in a black velvet gown with a squared, low-cut bodice. The only splashes of color adorning her were the jeweled cross of Wotan, the butterfly betrothal ring, and her violet eyes. The simple, dark gown accentuated her natural beauty.

"You should be wearing a gown that screams for attention," Daisy said, standing beside her. "Don't you want to dazzle those courtiers?"

"For my husband's sake, I seek only to impress the queen," Blythe told her.

"That gown won't impress her," Daisy replied. "Let me help you change into the red one."

Blythe shook her head. "On the contrary, Elizabeth will appreciate my wisdom."

"How do you know that?"

"Elizabeth has already seen sixty-one years and harbors no desire to meet a vividly dressed eighteen-year-old," Blythe answered. "The queen deserves all attention riveted upon her person, not mine."

"Well, kiss my feet," Daisy said with a smile. "I think I understand. The queen will be jealous if you dazzle all of her courtiers."

"Something like that."

"However did you get so wise?"

"I'm not wise," Blythe admitted. "My mother advised me which gowns would be appropriate."

"But the duchess dresses vividly," Daisy remarked.

"Yes, but Grandmama Chessy has seen almost as many years as the queen," Blythe answered. "And do not tell her I said so."

Daisy would have spoken, but they heard the sound of the door opening.

"Are you ready yet?" Roger called.

The two women walked around the privacy screen. Daisy left the chamber while Blythe stood motionless and watched her husband cast an admiring eye over her. He seemed to appreciate the cut of her gown, as his gaze lingered on the swell of flawless ivory flesh above its low-cut bodice.

"Black was a wise choice," Roger said, walking toward her. "The conservative color accentuates your youthful loveliness."

"Thank you, my lord," Blythe replied, "but I wasn't trying to accentuate my youth. Appearing drab will make the queen like me more."

Roger smiled. "And who imparted those words of wisdom? Not your grandmother, I warrant."

"No, 'twas my mother."

The faint sounds of music mingling with voices and laughter reached her ears and grew louder with each step forward. And then they stood together in the entrance to the queen's Presence Chamber, filled to capacity with hundreds of colorfully garbed courtiers dancing or milling about.

England's finest musicians stood on the left side of the rectangular chamber and played their various instruments. On the long wall opposite the chamber's entrance, Queen Elizabeth sat in a chair upon a raised dais and surveyed the activity of her courtiers. The middle of the chamber was reserved for dancing.

Everywhere Blythe looked was a sea of vivid, eye-catching color. Accessories of gold and precious gems sparkled in the torchlight.

Blythe cast Roger a look filled with apprehension. She felt conspicuously out of place in her black gown. In fact, her husband and she appeared like drab wrens when compared to the preening peacocks strutting to and fro.

Glancing toward the dais, Blythe saw Bliss speaking to the queen, who turned her gaze toward the hall's entrance. Standing near the dais were her grandparents, apparently awaiting her arrival.

"Are you prepared to meet the queen, little butterfly?" Roger asked, giving her hand an encouraging squeeze.

"I've been practicing my throne-room curtsies all afternoon, my lord," Blythe answered. "I'm as ready as I'll ever be."

Keeping a firm grasp on her hand, Roger stepped forward into the crowd. Though he nodded at several courtiers who called greetings to him, her husband never stopped walking but led her directly toward the dais.

For her part, Blythe kept her gaze fixed on the queen. She felt the stares of the watching courtiers and knew they must be curious about this other Devereux daughter.

"We'll stand nearby and await her acknowledgment," Roger whispered. "To do otherwise would be a breach of protocol."

Blythe gave him a smile of understanding. The prospect of meeting the queen made her too nervous to speak.

Standing beside her husband, Blythe concluded that her sister's assessment had been correct. The queen was all that they had ever imagined and then some. Though she was approaching old age, Elizabeth still possessed the legendary presence for which she was famous, the same quality that had bound her subjects to her loyally for thirty-six years.

Elizabeth wore a white and gold brocaded gown that bore a fortune in diamonds and other precious gems. Around her royal neck were strands and strands of diamonds, emeralds, and rubies. Pearls laced her red-gold hair, and she wore a jeweled ring on every finger.

The royal brilliance nearly blinded Blythe. She felt she was looking at a goddess.

Roger grasped Blythe's hand and drew her forward when the queen nodded at him. He bowed low from the waist, while Blythe dropped a deep, graceful curtsy.

"Arise," Elizabeth bade them. She turned her attention on Blythe immediately, saying, " 'Twas artfully done, Lady Debrett."

Blythe blushed, unable to tell if the queen was insulting or complimenting her. She inclined her head and smiled while the queen perused her from her upswept, uncovered ebony hair to her black satin slippers.

Blythe sensed that the queen was pleased by her choice of apparel. She sent a silent thank-you to her mother for offering such sound advice.

"Again, Roger, welcome home to my court," Elizabeth said. She flicked another glance at Blythe and added, "You have the look of your mother."

"Thank you, Your Majesty."

"How do you know 'twas said as a compliment?" Elizabeth asked.

Blythe was momentarily taken aback by her question. "I do resemble my grandfather who is standing over there," she answered, recovering herself. "I'm positive you would never insult your favorite duke in front of others."

Elizabeth inclined her head, indicating she liked the answer, but she wasn't about to let Blythe off the proverbial hook so easily. "Why would you believe that Ludlow is my favorite duke?"

"Grandpapa told me so," Blythe answered without hesitation. "He spoke truthfully about your brilliance, so I must assume he spoke truthfully about being your favorite."

That earned her a royal smile, heady stuff for an eighteen-year-old innocent. Changing the subject, Elizabeth asked, "So, Lady Debrett, how goes the married life?"

A trick. Blythe knew she was caught in a bind between insulting the queen or her own husband.

"With all due respect," Blythe answered, "I wouldn't wish to answer in front of all of these people."

Blythe felt her husband's grasp on her hand tighten. She sensed the listening courtiers lean forward as if hoping to become privy to a new scandal.

" 'Tis entirely too late to retract the question," Elizabeth said. "Answer it."

It was a royal order, not a request.

"Though I am content in my marriage, I do regret having been unable to perform my duties as your maid of honor," Blythe answered smoothly. "I consider my sister the most fortunate of young ladies."

The queen arched a graying brow at her. "You resemble your mother but sound exactly like your father."

"I shall take that as a compliment too," Blythe said with a smile.

That remark earned her a royal chuckle. "Do you possess any other accomplishments besides your wit, child?"

"Accomplishments?"

"I was already fluent in five languages when I was your age," Elizabeth boasted.

"I am partial to Greek," Blythe answered, and then felt her husband give her hand a warning squeeze. "And I do adore numbers."

"You adore numbers," the queen echoed in surprise, leaning forward in her chair. "Explain yourself."

"I adore numbers that represent profits on my businesses," Blythe told her.

"Businesses?"

Blythe nodded. "I own five ships and several businesses."

"Astonishing. My dearest Bliss owns no profit-making business," the queen remarked.

"My sister's talents lie elsewhere," Blythe replied. "However, she is wise to invest her coins with me as well as our father."

Elizabeth burst out laughing. "I see my dear Midas has managed to sire wonderfully intelligent daughters." She cast a jaundiced eye upon her courtiers, saying, "Most females at court are highly fed and lowly taught. 'Tis rather disheartening."

Blythe remained silent. She had no idea of how to respond to that.

"You must accompany Bliss to my sitting chamber tomorrow," the queen invited her. "We can finish this conversation in private."

"Your Majesty honors me," Blythe said.

"Yes, I know." Elizabeth slid her gaze to Roger and told him, "My soaring eagle, you are the most fortunate of men to have married such a sensible young woman." In a louder voice she added, "Would that all of my courtiers could produce such fine children for England." She looked again at Blythe, and with a gesture of dismissal said, "Dance, mingle, enjoy yourself."

Blythe curtsied and Roger bowed. Together they backed away from the royal presence.

"Well done, little butterfly," he whispered.

Blythe cast him a smile filled with sunshine. She'd made it through the worst of the evening and had earned his praise for her splendid performance. Perhaps there was hope for them after all.

The Duke and Duchess of Ludlow met then across the chamber. Blythe hugged her grandfather and then her grandmother.

"Grandmama, you look especially lovely tonight," Blythe said. "Oops, I forgot to call you Aunty Dawn."

"Never mind about that. Everyone knows Ludlow is your grandfather and I am his wife," the duchess said. "Darling, why did you wear such a drab color?"

" 'Twas my mother's opinion that I should appear suitably subdued the first time I met the queen," Blythe told her.

"Darling, if you were any more subdued we'd be burying you," her grandmother replied.

The musicians began playing again, this time a stately pavane. Roger turned to her, asking, "Would you care to dance?"

" 'Twould be politic of you to dance with the queen first," Blythe answered.

Roger inclined his head. Turning away, he walked back across the chamber in the direction of the dais.

For a moment Blythe admired her husband and then looped her arm through her grandfather's. "I have a question for you," she told him. " 'Tis of a delicate nature though."

"Do you require privacy?" Duke Robert asked. "If so 'twill need to wait for morning."

Blythe shook her head and said, "Lady Sarah Sitwell visited Debrett House one evening and—"

"Sarah Sitwell is no lady," her grandmother spoke up.

"Chessy, let the child finish before you start maligning people."

"Me? Malign people?" the duchess echoed. "I never did such a thing."

"Sarah told me that Mama is a bastard by birth and coerced Papa into marrying her," Blythe said, dropping her voice so none but her grandparents could hear.

Her grandmother burst out laughing. "Child, Sarah Sitwell wanted your father for her own," the duchess told her. "As far as that coercion goes, nothing could be farther from the truth."

"What is the truth?" Blythe asked.

"Your father wanted your mother, but she was reluctant," the duchess told her. "*I* concocted a scheme with him that placed your mother in a compromising position. And the rest is history."

"I never knew that," Duke Robert said. " 'Twas well done of you, Chessy."

"Thank you, Tally."

"And the other part?" Blythe asked her grandfather.

Duke Robert put his arm around her and said, "Trust me, child. Your mother is legitimate issue."

"I do trust you, Grandpapa," Blythe said, her expression clearing. "Thank you for your honesty."

Blythe glanced toward the center of the chamber and saw Roger dancing with the queen. And then the Earl of Oxford stood before her, blocking her view.

"My lady, may I have this dance?" he invited her.

"My lord, I do regret I am promised to my brothers-in-law first," Blythe refused. There was no way she would even consider dancing with this insufferable lout.

"I shall seek out your company later," Oxford said, and walked away.

"I do not like him," Blythe whispered to her grandparents. "Grandpapa, signal Cedric over there, else I shall look like a liar."

Summoned by the ducal gesture, Cedric approached and bowed over Blythe's hand. "How fares my lovely sister-in-law?"

"Well, thank you," Blythe answered. "Will you dance with me?"

"With pleasure, my lady," Cedric replied, his dark eyes warming considerably on her.

He led her onto the dance floor, and they began the courtly steps of the pavane.

"Where is Lady Sybilla?"

"Do you really care?"

His question surprised her. "I care a great deal about Sybilla," Blythe answered. "After all, she is my sister by marriage."

"You are a terrible liar," Cedric told her.

Blythe giggled. "And where is your rapier, my lord? I almost didn't recognize you without it."

"I do not engage in sword practice twenty-four hours a day," Cedric said. "I enjoy other pursuits as well."

"I do suppose a man must eat and sleep sometimes," she replied.

Cedric chuckled.

"Give over," ordered a voice beside them. " 'Tis my turn to partner this beautiful woman."

Blythe snapped her gaze to the left and saw Geoffrey. She laughed as Cedric placed her hand in his brother's.

"And how fares my favorite sister-in-law?" Geoffrey asked.

"Very well," Blythe answered. Swinging to the right, she saw her husband near the dais and missed a step. Roger was frowning at her. He couldn't be angry because she was dancing with his brothers, could he?

Roger turned his back and walked in the opposite direction. Blythe followed him with her gaze and missed another step when she saw him escort Lady Rhoda onto the dance floor. Her stomach lurched sickeningly at the sight of her beloved partnering the voluptuous redhead.

"Please escort me to my sister," Blythe said, stopping mid-dance.

"Are you ill?" Geoffrey asked.

Blythe managed a wan smile and lied, "I'm overtired from the long day."

"Perhaps I should fetch Roger."

"No, my sister will suffice."

Reaching the side of the dais where Bliss stood, Blythe grabbed her hand. For the first time in her life, her sister's touch didn't make her feel better.

"Can you show me how to get back to my chamber?" she asked, her desperate urgency mirrored in her voice.

"Do not let that sight bother you," Bliss said, looking past her at Roger and Rhoda. "Besides, no one leaves without the queen's permission."

"The babe makes me queasy," Blythe told her. "I fear embarrassing myself."

Bliss nodded. "Let me give the queen your regrets. She wouldn't want to keep you here if you are ill."

Blythe watched her sister approach the queen and at the royal acknowledgment step close to whisper in Elizabeth's ear. The queen snapped her gaze to Blythe and then scanned the hall to locate Roger.

What had her sister whispered in the queen's ear? She hoped Elizabeth would refrain from creating a scene, as Blythe knew from rumor she was quite capable of doing upon occasion.

The musicians suddenly stopped playing. All of the courtiers turned toward the dais in surprise.

Blythe froze in a near panic. Had Bliss told Elizabeth that she was with child? She slid her gaze to her sister, who winked at her.

"Eden, step forward with your wife," Elizabeth ordered.

Wearing a puzzled expression, Roger advanced on Blythe and then escorted her to the front of the dais. Blythe dreaded what she knew was coming next.

"Congratulations, my soaring eagle," Elizabeth said.

Obviously confused, Roger opened his mouth, but the queen was already speaking.

"Congratulations are in order for the Countess of Eden," Elizabeth announced. "She is carrying Eden's heir."

The courtiers applauded politely.

Blythe flicked a sidelong glance at her husband. To his credit, Roger quickly banished his stunned expression.

"You shouldn't keep such joyous news from me," the queen chided him.

Roger proved himself a skilled courtier. He lifted Blythe's hand to his lips and then lied, "I would never withhold joyous tidings, Your Majesty. 'Tis early yet, and we wished to be certain before making the announcement."

"Oh, my sweet darling," Grandmama Chessy gushed, rushing toward them. The duchess hugged both Blythe and Roger, then turned to her husband, wailing, "Oh, Tally. I'm much too young to be someone's *great*-grandmother."

Everyone in the hall, including the queen, chuckled at the Duchess of Ludlow. Except Blythe and Roger.

"Chessy, many things are possible if one lives long enough," Elizabeth said. She turned to Roger. "The babe makes your wife ill. Escort her to your chamber, and when she is comfortable return to Us here."

"Thank you, Your Majesty."

With all the gentleness of a man in love, Roger took Blythe's hand in his and led her toward the chamber's entrance. The sea of courtiers parted for them, and several even called out their best wishes.

Though she tried to keep her expression placid, Blythe suspected the butterflies in her stomach were more from her unease over Roger's reaction than from the baby. She didn't believe that her husband would be quite as calm once they quit the chamber. She could feel the tension in his grasp.

Once out of sight of the Presence Chamber, Roger dropped her hand. Blythe was too frightened to peek at him.

He quickened his long-legged stride, forcing her to walk faster in order to keep up with him. She was sickeningly dizzy by the time they reached their chamber.

Roger opened the door and let her enter first. Blythe heard the door slam behind them and closed her eyes in misery. It was worse than she would have expected.

Silence reigned for long moments.

Finally, Blythe summoned her courage and turned around slowly. When she lifted her gaze to his, the expression of contempt on his face nearly felled her.

"Damn Burghley and your father for the meddlers they are," Roger swore, his voice rising in direct proportion to his swelling fury. "A good hanging would have saved me from this bad marriage."

Chapter 13

"Amen to that," Blythe said, rounding on him in anger. "A good hanging would have saved *me* much."

Surprised by her outburst, Roger fixed his gaze on her but failed to heed the fury etched across her features. "You did this apurpose," he accused, pointing a finger at her. "You tricked me into this trap."

"Let me recount the ways I have abused you," Blythe snapped. "I hid in the shadows beneath your window, and when you appeared, I scooped you into my arms. Keeping you captive within my embrace, I carried you to bed and plucked your virginity."

"Your sarcasm is unbecoming," Roger said, turning to leave. He reached for the doorknob, but her words stopped him.

"Nor does cruelty become you," Blythe said in a quavering voice, her pain apparent.

"I apologize," Roger said with a heaving sigh. Slowly, he turned around to face her. "You are correct; I trapped myself. Blaming you for my inability to resist the siren's call of your beauty is wrong of me."

Only a blind woman would have missed the torment stamped across his features.

"Roger—" Blythe stepped toward him, intending to offer comfort.

"The queen expects me to return posthaste to the Presence Chamber," Roger said, holding his hand up in a gesture for her to stay where she was. "Bar the door behind me, and do not allow anyone entrance except your sister or your grandparents."

"Why?"

"A murderer walks among us at court," he reminded her.

"Oh, I had forgotten."

"Forgetting can be unhealthy, my lady."

"You will be careful?" Blythe asked in a worried voice. Whoever had murdered Darnel had been trying to get rid of her beloved. This time the villain might try a more direct approach, as he had at Smithfield Market.

"You need harbor no worry on my account," Roger said, his blue gaze softening on her.

"Remember, a wise man trusts no one but himself."

"I'll consider your advice," Roger said, turning to leave. "Now bar the door."

Blythe did as she was told. Alone again, she fought the tears that welled up in her eyes and then changed into her nightshift and robe. Instead of retiring, she stoked the fire and sat in one of the chairs in front of the hearth.

In the warmth and safety of her chamber, Blythe let her concern for Roger finally surface. The closer he came to discovering the real murderer's identity, the more dangerous the situation would become, and that frightened her.

Her sister and she would worship together at the first opportunity; perhaps they would be able to summon enough power to keep the dark sun at bay and maybe even discover its identity. The thought of Baby Aristotle growing up without his father was too painful even to consider.

Blythe fixed her gaze on the hypnotic flames. The fire warmed her into contentment. The Goddess had chosen to reunite Roger and her in this lifetime. The eagle and the butterfly would soar together across the horizon for all of eternity. All would be well in the end.

* * *

A man singing off-key awakened her. As the singing grew
louder she recognized her husband's voice. How provoking. Her
beloved never sang. And then his slurred words reached her ears.

> "There once lived a virgin on the Strand.
> Ebony hair, violet eyes, and what a soft hand.
> One night she opened her shutter.
> So I climbed inside to futter.
> Her name was Blythe,
> I took her to wife,
> And the doing ruined my life. Hey ho!"

Bang! Bang! Bang!

"Let me in, sweet wife," Roger called, pounding on the door.

Blythe unbarred the door and yanked it open.

Roger gifted her with a boyishly devastating grin and stepped
inside the chamber.

Indicating her displeasure, Blythe cocked an ebony brow at
him. Her nose twitched as he passed by her. Her husband reeked
from the quantity of wine he'd consumed.

After barring the door again, Blythe turned around and
watched him. He plopped down on the edge of the bed and
began to struggle with his boots.

"My boots are misbehaving," Roger said needlessly, looking up
at her. "Would you possibly consider giving me your assistance?"

Blythe nodded and crossed the chamber to remove his boots.

"How talented you are," he told her with a pleased smile.
"Listen: An Irishman, a Scotsman, and a Spaniard were
repairing the roof at Saint Paul's. Suddenly, a strong gust of
wind blew them right off. Do you know what happened to
them?"

Blythe said nothing. Disgusted by his drunkenness, she merely
stared down at him.

"Who cares?" Roger said, shrugging his shoulders and grinning at her.

" 'Tis uncharitable to voice such thoughts," Blythe scolded, narrowing her gaze on him. "I have Irish and Scots relatives, you know."

"Oh, I beg your pardon." Roger looked truly contrite. He gave her a lopsided grin and said, "Listen: A Spaniard, an Italian, and a Frenchman were repairing the roof at—"

"I don't care," she interrupted.

"You've heard this story somewhere before," he said, an expression of disappointment appearing on his face. "Why didn't you tell me?"

Blythe rolled her eyes. Her husband was behaving like a fool. She had no experience with drunken men.

"Come here, wench," Roger ordered, patting the bed beside him. "Give me a kiss."

"The morning will soon be here," she said in refusal. "Go to sleep, my lord."

"I want a kiss." Roger gave her a wickedly charming grin and added, "I want more than that, but I'll start with a kiss."

"Kiss my feet," Blythe said, borrowing her tirewoman's favorite expression.

"One kiss, my lady. 'Twill help my sevens and eights."

"About what are you talking, Lord Pebblebrain?" she asked, her hands on her hips.

"My sevens and eights keep futtering," Roger said in a loud voice. "Those two naughty numbers are keeping my accounts in a lusty disarray."

Blythe was unable to suppress the horrified giggle that bubbled up in her throat. "Numbers do not do . . . *that*."

"Come, love. Since you already carry my seed, I may as well have the pleasure of lying in the bed I've made," Roger said, giving her an exaggerated wink. He flopped back on the bed and cupped his groin, saying, "Come, Lady Butterfly. Land on this."

"Am I an easy glove to slip into at pleasure?" Blythe asked, annoyed.

"In a word, yes."

"You wretched blotch of nature."

"Does that mean *no*?" Roger asked in a disappointed voice. "Who will I futter if not you?"

"Fiddle the devil," she snapped, turning her back on him.

"Wench, your lord and master has need of those pretty titties of yours," Roger said, assuming a stern tone of voice. "I want to bump you— *Hey ho!*"

Roger reached out to grab her hand. Whirling around, Blythe clenched her fist and slugged him. Caught off balance, he fell back on the bed, murmured something unintelligible, and then began snoring.

Blythe sighed. Men could be such children. Grandmama Chessy and her own mother had never mentioned that little fact. Perhaps they'd feared she would refuse to wed.

Grabbing a woolen cloak, Blythe carefully covered her husband with it. She stoked the fire in the hearth, wrapped herself in her fur-lined cloak, and sat down in the chair again.

Brilliant sunshine streamed into the chamber through the window when Blythe awakened a few hours later. She realized the hour was later than she usually slept. And then she heard the loud snoring.

Rising from the chair, Blythe stretched and then stoked the fire in the hearth. Quietly, trying not to awaken her husband, she washed and changed into a gown. Her sister would soon be tapping at her door to take her to see whatever it was that she considered so important.

Blythe heard the bed creak with movement and then a low moan. She hurried across the chamber and whispered in a soothing voice, "Lie quietly, Roger. Do not open your eyes."

"Why?" Roger opened his eyes and tried to sit up. He groaned as if in excruciating pain when the sun struck his face. Falling back on the bed, he pulled the cloak over his head.

"I told you to keep your eyes closed," Blythe said, laughter lurking in her voice.

"Must you sound so happy?" Roger asked, his voice muffled beneath the cloak. "Do something."

Blythe stifled a giggle. Her gaze touched his body, and she stepped back in surprise at the sight of his groin bulging like a boulder. He couldn't still be in the mood for *that*, could he? How could a man suffer the ill effects of too much wine and still desire bedsport?

"Help me," Roger growled, sounding like a petulant boy.

"I will pray for you," she told him.

"Shit," he swore. "Do something productive."

Blythe opened her mouth to tell him she didn't know how to cure what ailed him, but a light tap on the door drew her attention. "That will be Bliss," she said. "I must go."

"Don't leave me like this," he moaned.

"I'll return shortly," Blythe called over her shoulder as she headed for the door. The last sound she heard before stepping into the corridor was his groan of profound protest.

Blythe closed the door quietly and smiled at her sister.

"Is Roger ill?" Bliss asked.

"He's suffering from too much wine."

"Shall I help him?"

"Did he dance with Rhoda or Sarah after I retired for the evening?" Blythe asked.

"No."

"Did he dance with any other lady?"

"No."

"Then you may help him when we return," Blythe told her. "As the Greeks always said, 'Through suffering we gain wisdom,' and my eagle needs a lesson about the perils of too much wine."

"Sister, you lack the necessary empathy to be a healer," Bliss remarked. "By the way, you aren't angry with me because of last night, are you?"

"I could never be angry with you," Blythe said. "My condition would eventually have become public knowledge anyway.

You merely saved me the trouble of summoning my meager courage."

Bliss led her through the dimly lit, deserted corridors. They did spy an occasional servant, but their masters were sleeping late after a night of revels.

"Where are you taking me?" Blythe asked.

"The queen's Long Gallery," Bliss answered. "The gallery leads to the Chapel Royal and the queen's private apartments."

The two sisters walked another ten minutes before reaching their destination. At the gallery's entrance, Bliss gestured that this was the place and stepped inside.

"What do you want to show me?" Blythe asked.

"Walk with me to the far end of the gallery," Bliss answered.

Blythe gave her sister a puzzled smile and stepped forward. She hadn't taken more than five paces when she felt a prickly sensation tickling the nape of her neck.

"'Tis drafty in here," she remarked.

Bliss made no reply but pointed to the side of the deserted gallery.

Blythe glanced at the rows of long, tapered candles on either side of the gallery. Their flames flickered not one whit. No draft in the world could tease a person's neck without playing havoc with a candle's flame.

Grasping her sister's hand, Blythe walked deeper into the gallery. An oppressive bleakness settled upon her, and she glanced nervously at her sister, who was watching her reaction. The Long Gallery seemed to stretch endlessly before her.

Uneasiness made Blythe slow her pace, and panic swelled within her chest. Her heartbeat quickened. Without warning, Blythe broke free of her sister and whirled away. She bolted out of the gallery the way they'd come. She heard her sister calling her name but ignored her in the rush to escape that unholy bleakness.

Closing her eyes, Blythe leaned against the corridor wall outside the gallery. She welcomed the coolness that seeped into her trembling body.

"Did you feel something?"

"Apparently, I did," Blythe said dryly, gazing up at her sister. "What horror dwells within that gallery?"

"Catherine Howard," Bliss answered matter-of-factly.

"Cat Howard?" Her answer shocked Blythe. "She's been dead for over fifty years."

Bliss nodded. "When the unfortunate queen was arrested, she ran wildly through that gallery in a futile attempt to reach the king and beg for his mercy."

"Her soul has been trapped inside that gallery for over fifty years," Blythe said, shuddering as she glanced toward the gallery's entrance. "We must help her pass to the other side."

"I knew you'd be willing to help," Bliss said.

"Why didn't you do something before?"

"I was uneasy about being in there alone."

"I understand," Blythe said. "When shall we help her?"

"Master Shakespeare will be presenting his latest play, *Romeo and Juliet*, to the queen on the twenty-first day of December," Bliss said, looping her arm through Blythe's and leading her back down the corridor. "While everyone is being entertained in the hall, we will slip away and rendezvous here."

Blythe nodded in agreement. "Will you help my husband recover now?"

"Of course."

Reaching her chamber, Blythe opened the door silently. Snoring again and with the cloak still pulled over his head, Roger lay on the bed where she'd left him. The two sisters advanced on the bed.

Lest he awaken, Blythe gingerly drew the cloak away from his face. Bliss placed her fingertips on his temples and then closed her eyes in concentration. She moved her lips in a silent chant.

Several moments later Bliss opened her eyes and nodded at her sister. Blythe carefully covered her husband's face with the cloak.

"Will he be well?" Blythe whispered, escorting her sister to the door.

"Yes, but 'tis always darkest before the sun shines," Bliss answered, and then winked at her.

Blythe knew what her sister meant. She swallowed a giggle and closed the door, then pressed her forehead against it while she rested for a moment. Lord, but she felt a tad queasy herself.

"What was your sister doing to me?"

Blythe whirled around at the sound of his voice. She'd thought he was sleeping.

"I'd know *your* touch anywhere," he said, giving her a wan smile. "And you'd never let anyone except your family chant over me. So—"

Roger abruptly stopped talking. His eyes widened in surprise, and he clutched his belly. Leaping off the bed, he bolted past her out of the chamber.

Blythe heard the sound of him retching in the corridor and hoped she wasn't required to clean it. She covered her mouth as a sweat broke out over her upper lip. Lord, he was making her sick too.

"I told you those incantations don't work," Roger said, walking into the chamber a few minutes later. In spite of his words, a healthy color had returned to his complexion.

"Bliss prayed for you to puke out the poison," Blythe told him.

"I do feel better," he admitted. "You look a bit pale."

"If I could lie down . . ."

Roger put his arm around her and helped her to the bed. "Daisy should be here soon," he said. "I'll send her to fetch us breakfast. I'm so hungry I could eat the whole cow."

"Do not mention food," Blythe moaned, earning herself an amused chuckle.

"Those who score must pay the price," Roger said with a wry smile. "You, little butterfly, will be paying for the next eight months."

"Roger, were you drowning your sorrows last night?" Blythe asked, fearing the answer she would get.

"To which sorrow do you refer?"

"The sorrow of siring another child."

Standing beside the bed, Roger caressed her pale cheek. "Sweetheart, I drank too much wine because I was *celebrating* the imminent arrival of a second-born."

"Thank you for that." Blythe gifted him with a smile.

Before he could reply, a knock on the door drew their attention. The door swung open, admitting Hardwick and Daisy.

"Oh, you are already dressed," Hardwick said. "I apologize for our tardiness."

"The countess feels queasy this morning," Roger said. "Take Daisy to the kitchens and fetch a mug of clear broth and a hunk of bread. No butter."

"What can we bring for you, my lord?" Hardwick asked.

"Anything hot and heavy," Roger answered. He glanced at his wife and added, "Serve it in the hall. I'll meet you there when Daisy returns."

When Hardwick and Daisy had gone, Roger turned his back on Blythe and crossed the chamber to the table where they kept the water basin. He removed his shirt and began washing his face.

"Eating a hunk of bread before you rise each morning will ease the queasiness," he called over his shoulder. "Stay away from greasy foods; they'll nauseate you."

"How do you know?" she asked, surprised by his knowledge.

His face dripping water, Roger turned around and gave her an amused look. "I've been through this before, remember?"

Blythe nodded and proceeded to watch him prepare for the day. A warm feeling grew in the pit of her belly as she watched him shave and then change into fresh clothing.

This was the way marriage was supposed to be. A man and a woman living together, sharing their lives. The man would care for the woman who carried his seed within her and gave birth to his child.

And then Roger ruined the moment for her. He crossed the chamber and sat on the edge of the bed.

"Enjoy your stay at court, for 'twill be your only visit with me," he told her. "Once we leave for Debrett House in a few weeks, you will be permanently retired from court life."

His announcement puzzled her. "What do you mean?"

"You won't be returning to court."

"My lord, I understand your words but not your reasoning."

"I refuse to make the same mistake twice," Roger said.

"What mistake is that?"

"Never mind."

"I would like to know what crime I've committed in your eyes," Blythe persisted.

"You haven't done anything *yet*," Roger replied. "I shan't give you the opportunity to play the wanton with Elizabeth's courtiers."

"Play the wanton? How dare you suggest such a thing!" she cried. "If you will recall, I preferred to remain with Miranda, but *you* insisted I accompany you to court."

Without bothering to reply, Roger rose from the bed and stared down at her. "The babe you carry will be your only child."

The door swung open and Daisy hurried across the chamber to set the breakfast tray on the bedside table. Blythe leaned against the headboard and reached for the mug of broth.

Roger turned to Blythe, saying, "Eat your bread and then sleep; 'twill make you feel better. Do *not* forget your interview with the queen." At that, he quit the chamber.

"Wake me in two hours," Blythe instructed her tirewoman after he'd gone. "I'll want a bath before I attend the queen. See that it's ready for me when I awaken."

Daisy nodded and drew the bed curtains closed.

Blythe felt weary because of the restless night she'd passed in the chair in front of the hearth, but her troubled thoughts kept her from sleeping. Her husband's strange behavior and accusations confused her, and again she wondered what had happened in his marriage to Darnel that would so change her beloved from a young man with an easy and generous smile to the angry and hurt man Blythe knew now.

* * *

Several hours later Blythe stood in front of the mirror and put the finishing touches on her appearance. Excited and nervous, she wondered what she would say to the queen. That Bliss would be with her eased her worry. If she was lucky Grandmama Chessy would be there too. Her grandmother possessed the remarkable talent of keeping conversation flowing.

Someone knocked on the door. Blythe walked around the privacy screen and nodded at Daisy to open it. Dressed in blue livery, a twelve-year-old page stood there.

"Mistress Bliss sent me to escort Lady Debrett to the Sitting Chamber," the boy said.

Blythe smiled at the incredibly handsome boy who, surprisingly, sported two blackened eyes that matched his thick black hair. His piercing blue eyes shamed the color of his livery.

"What is your name?" she asked as they started down the corridor.

"Brandon Montgomery," he answered without looking at her. The boy escorted her through the confusing maze of corridors as if the palace were his own estate.

"Where did you get those blackened eyes?" Blythe asked.

"Near the stables."

She cast him a sidelong smile. "I meant 'how.' "

"My enemies united against me," he said.

"Who are your enemies?"

"Grimsby, Spennymoor, and Cockermouth."

"Three against one doesn't sound like a fair fight to me," Blythe remarked.

The boy slowed his pace. "As you can see, it wasn't," he said with an affable grin. "However, each of them sports a black eye, so I suppose I'm ahead of the game."

"Violence is unnecessary," Blythe chided him softly. "There are other ways to settle your differences, you know."

"Tell that to Grimsby, Spennymoor, and Cockermouth."

"About what did you argue?"

He seemed to hesitate. "My deceased family."

"What about your family?"

Brandon Montgomery stopped walking abruptly and faced her. "I am the heir to Stratford."

Blythe stared at him blankly. He appeared to be waiting for some sort of reaction from her. "And?"

"Don't you know?" he asked in surprise. "My grandfather, the Earl of Stratford, was executed for being a traitor."

"Since you are her page, the queen must harbor no ill will toward you," Blythe said.

"I am an orphan. My father left custody of me to the queen," Brandon said flatly. "I cannot remain a page forever, but no one seems willing to foster me in his household."

"Because of your grandfather?" she asked, surprised. "What happened to your parents?"

Brandon fixed his piercing blue gaze on her. "My father strangled my mother and then drowned himself in the River Avon," he answered baldly.

"I'm so sorry," Blythe said, touching his shoulder. The proud expression on his face and his incredible blue eyes reminded her of Roger. "Do you know my husband?"

"Everyone knows the Queen's Eagle."

"Do you like him?"

"I admire him greatly," the boy said with a winning smile.

Blythe nodded at the compliment to her beloved. "You may foster at Debrett House. We will educate you as befits an earl's grandson."

"With all due respect, Lady Debrett, you should speak with your husband before making such an offer."

"Do not concern yourself about that." Blythe waved her hand in a gesture of dismissal. "I will speak with the queen myself."

Blythe hesitated when they reached the Long Gallery. She'd forgotten about having to walk through there to reach the queen.

Brandon flicked her a questioning look, but then Bliss appeared. She practically flew out of the gallery door.

"There you are," Bliss said, breathless from her dash through the gallery. "I'll escort you from here."

Blythe drew a gold piece from her pocket and offered it to the boy.

Brandon shook his head. "Escorting you was my pleasure, Lady Debrett."

"You need pocket money."

He smiled. "Aye, but not yours."

"I will invest this gold piece for you," she said.

Brandon inclined his head. "Lady Debrett, I hope I can be of service to you again." Turning on his heels, the boy walked in the direction from which they'd just come.

"Montgomery is a sad case," Bliss remarked, grasping Blythe's hand. "How fares Roger?"

"Much better."

Hand in hand, Blythe and Bliss stepped into the Long Gallery. The two sisters looked at each other and nodded. Lifting their skirts, they sprinted the length of the gallery and did not stop until they'd reached the opposite side and scooted out the door.

Blythe leaned against the wall and tried to catch her breath. Suitably calmed after a few minutes, she nodded at her sister, who led her a short distance down another corridor.

"These are the royal apartments," Bliss said, walking into an antechamber crowded with the queen's ladies.

Blythe followed her sister past the ladies and then entered the inner chamber.

Dim and stuffy, the Privy Chamber contained only one window. Adornment smothered the astonishingly small room.

The sisters instantly dropped a curtsy to the seated queen. Grandmother Chessy and her longtime crony, Lady Tessie Pines, sat with the queen.

"Welcome, Lady Debrett," Elizabeth greeted her. "Be seated."

"I am honored, Your Majesty," Blythe said in a voice barely louder than a whisper.

"How fare your parents?" the queen asked.

"Both enjoy perfect health."

"Good." Elizabeth turned to the older women. "Finish your story, Tessie."

"I told Pines to pay the vendor the five hundred pounds I owed the man," Lady Tessie began.

Grandmama Chessy chuckled throatily. "What did Pines say to that?"

"Pines said, 'For what?' " Lady Tessie answered. "To which I replied, 'You cannot possibly want an argument two weeks before Christmas.' "

"So what happened?" Elizabeth asked.

"Pines left the room and returned a short time later," Tessie continued. "When I asked if he'd paid the vendor, Pines said that all had been taken care of and he had no wish to discuss the matter again. However, I should consider that Christmas had arrived early."

Elizabeth and Grandmama Chessy smiled at that.

"So that brooch will be your gift?" Chessy asked.

"Not if Pines wants to nest between my legs anytime during the next year," Lady Tessie answered.

Everyone laughed. Blythe blushed at their topic of conversation. She never would have imagined that the queen would speak about such vulgar trivialities.

"Well, Cheshire and Pines, I thank you for your company," Elizabeth said, dismissing them. "Now I wish a private conversation with my dearest Bliss and her sister."

The two older women rose from their chairs and curtsied. "I'll see you later, my darlings," Chessy called over her shoulder.

Once the door clicked shut behind them, Elizabeth gave her full attention to her newest courtier. Blythe squirmed mentally in her chair.

"I hope you are well today," the queen remarked.

"I feel much better, Your Majesty."

"I see you've brought no embroidery with you."

"I dislike sewing."

"My dearest Bliss has no fondness for it either," Elizabeth

remarked. "So, tell me about your businesses. Do they turn a profit for you?"

"Lately, my sister has been embroiled in a price war with her husband," Bliss interjected.

The queen smiled. "Who is winning?"

"I was," Blythe answered. "Then we called a truce."

Elizabeth laughed. "Oh, how pleased I am with my dear Midas's daughters. . . . Did you know your husband once boosted your mother over the wall of my Privy Garden?"

Blythe and Bliss looked at each other and giggled.

"While a page, Roger was always involved in one prank or another," Elizabeth continued. "He once charged the other pages a gold piece each to see a nonexistent ghost in my Long Gallery."

Blythe cast her sister a meaningful glance.

"Your mother had told him a ghost haunted my Long Gallery, and Roger thought to start a touring business," the queen added. "Of course, the ghost never appeared."

"Speaking of pages, Your Majesty," Blythe ventured, "would it be possible to take Brandon Montgomery to Debrett House and foster him with us?"

"Why would you want to do that?" Elizabeth asked, obviously surprised.

"I like him."

"The Montgomery boy has no inheritance and nothing to recommend him," the queen said.

"I am rich beyond avarice and need no money," Blythe replied. "The boy appears to possess several qualities I admire."

Elizabeth fixed her gray gaze on Blythe and asked, "Such as?"

"Courage, pride, and a gentle heart."

"You met him for only ten minutes," Bliss interjected.

"Courage and pride are qualities difficult to hide," Blythe said.

"I have no problem with the boy fostering at Debrett House," Elizabeth told her. "That is, if Roger is agreeable."

"My husband will be agreeable," Blythe said confidently.

"And if he isn't?" the queen asked.

"I'll pauper him before Easter."

"Lady Blythe, I applaud your spirit," Elizabeth said with a smile. "Now, I must ready myself to meet with several ambassadors. Send my ladies to me when you leave."

The sisters curtsied and backed out of the chamber. Gaining the antechamber, Bliss flicked a hand toward the Privy Chamber, and the women scurried to assist their queen.

Instead of going their separate ways, Blythe and Bliss decided to walk outside and catch a breath of fresh air. The sisters strolled the grounds for a time, and then came upon Cedric Debrett and Edward deVere practicing with their rapiers.

"Good day to you, Cedric," Blythe called when he noticed them. She wondered why Cedric would be consorting with his brother's sworn enemy.

Pausing in their swordplay, the two men sauntered toward them. Cedric kissed her hand in courtly fashion, and deVere nodded at her.

"Have you met my sister?" Blythe asked her brother-in-law.

Cedric turned to Bliss and said, "You are as lovely as your sister."

"Thank you, my lord."

"Have you met your husband's mistresses yet?" Oxford asked baldly.

Blythe felt as if she'd been struck. The earl's crassness stunned her speechless.

"Look over your right shoulder," Oxford told her. "You'll see him with one of them now."

Unable to resist, Blythe whirled around. Sure enough, Roger and Rhoda Bellows walked together in the distance. Only a blind woman would miss Lady Rodent's flaming hair.

Feeling the curious gazes of the men upon her, Blythe took a deep breath and managed to keep tight control of her composure. A public stroll across the gardens hardly qualified as an affair.

"Perhaps we should return inside," Blythe said to her sister.

She looked up at the sky; gray clouds were gathering quickly. "I fear the weather is about to change."

Bliss nodded and grasped Blythe's hand, escorting her across the grounds. "Is my touch making you feel better?" she asked.

"Not much."

"Do not let Oxford upset you," Bliss said when they reached Blythe's chamber. "Shall I come inside and sit with you?"

Blythe shook her head. Gaining the privacy of her chamber, she wandered to the window but was unable to see Roger and Rhoda.

What she needed to raise her spirits was a hot bath, but she'd already bathed that day. The queen's servants might think her odd if she insisted on two baths when many people never even took one bath in a year.

Air was just as wonderful an element as water.

Blythe dragged a chair across the chamber to the window and opened the shutters. Next she pulled the coverlet off the bed and padded the chair with it. She undressed until she stood naked. Then she sat down to let the fresh air glide over her body. She loved the air, first cousin to her old friend the wind.

Closing her eyes, Blythe conjured in her mind's eye a stairway. Slowly but purposefully, she walked up those stairs and a door opened for her. Stepping inside, she stood in a garden equal in beauty to Eden, a paradise filled with willow trees and roses and butterflies. The angelic sound of giggling children made her smile. . . .

The door crashed open, startling her out of her meditation.

Blythe glanced over her shoulder. Appearing like a wet dog, her husband marched into the room.

Roger muttered something about uncertain weather, looked in her direction, and stopped short. He dropped his mouth open in surprise. And then she read lust in his gaze.

"God's bread, you're naked!" Roger exclaimed. "Cover yourself!"

"What's a little bared flesh between husband and wife?" Blythe asked.

Grabbing a cloak, Roger threw it over her to cover her nakedness. He turned his back on her and crossed to the opposite side of the chamber to change his clothing.

"Save yourself the time and energy," he advised her. "Your scheming won't work on me."

"What scheme?"

"Your scheme to seduce me," he answered, donning his bedrobe. "I have long experience with seduction and know when a woman seeks to influence me by using her body. I cannot be seduced."

Blythe knew he expected her to become angry. Instead, she smiled sweetly and replied, "Are you trying to convince me or *yourself*?"

Roger scowled at her. He poured himself a dram of whiskey and sat in the chair in front of the hearth.

Blythe watched him for a long moment and then stood to drag her chair back across the room to sit beside him. "I have business to discuss with you, my lord," she said without preamble.

"Corn or wool?"

"I want to foster Brandon Montgomery with us at Debrett House."

That certainly gained his attention. He snapped his head around to look at her and asked, "Why?"

"The boy must be fostered somewhere," she answered.

"Blythe, men agree to foster boys in their households in order to make money from the arrangement."

"So?"

"Brandon Montgomery hasn't a halfpenny to his misbegotten name," Roger said.

"Misbegotten name?" she echoed.

"His grandfather was executed for rebellion," Roger told her. "His father strangled his mother and then drowned himself. There's bad blood running through the boy's veins."

"How wrong you are," Blythe cried. "Brandon possesses more pride, courage, and dignity than any ten of your shallow courtiers."

"First we purchase blind ponies; next we are to foster a social pariah," Roger snapped. "How many other strays do you intend to adopt?"

Blythe narrowed her violet gaze on him and then cocked an ebony brow, always a bad sign. "You are wrong, my lord. First, I took pity on *your* need, and then came Miranda. The blind pony was third. . . . Roger, Brandon Montgomery will be accepted into society if he fosters with us."

"Does it matter to you what I desire?" he asked, sounding defeated.

"I'm sorry for my cruel words. Of course, your wishes matter. You will be his foster father and see to his education." In a soft voice she added, "The boy is so alone. Wouldn't you want some kindly couple to care for Miranda if she were alone in the world?"

Roger sighed heavily and stared into the hearth's flames. "Very well, we'll take the boy with us when we leave."

"Thank you." Blythe reached out to touch his arm. "You will be rewarded for this in another life. . . . What were you doing with Lady Rhoda today?"

Roger turned his head slowly to look at her and asked, "Are you spying on me?"

"Spying?" Blythe cocked a brow at him again.

"You are my wife, nothing more and nothing less," Roger told her. "What I do with Rhoda Bellows, Sarah Sitwell, or any other lady is no business of yours."

"What kind of illogical thinking is that?" Blythe asked, her voice rising. "You owe your fidelity to me."

"Fidelity?" Roger shot back. "What an unusual word to hear slip from a woman's lips. Remember, I didn't choose you for my wife; circumstances forced our marriage."

Blythe flinched as if she'd been struck. "Well, I see you have evened the score between us," she said. "First I hurt you, and then you hurt me."

A heavy silence descended upon them. The gulf that separated them seemed too wide to bridge.

"Shall I send for Daisy?" Roger asked, breaking the silence.

"I won't be celebrating tonight," she answered, refusing to look at him.

"Your presence is expected," he said.

"I don't give a fig what is expected," Blythe said. She made a sweeping gesture with her hand and added, "Go on and dance with your whores, my lord. Be warned. If you return here drunk, I won't open the door."

"Perhaps I'll sleep elsewhere."

"And perhaps this will be your last night on this earth."

Chapter 14

Returning early and sober to their chamber, Roger lived to see another sunrise. Sleeping in the same bed with him did not solve Blythe's marital problems, however. For five long days Roger ignored her presence in his life.

Roger arose each morning, ate the breakfast his man delivered, and then left their chamber. Late each afternoon he returned to dress for the evening's social events.

Though he insisted he was investigating Darnel's murder, Blythe could feel the gulf between them widening into an ocean of distrust. Her husband and she were little more than intimate strangers.

Blythe busied herself with visiting her sister and her grandmother, but she failed to appear in the Presence Chamber each evening. She insisted her pregnancy wearied her, but the truth was she had no wish to witness her husband partnering his paramours on the dance floor. The thought of Edward deVere telling her tales of her husband's love life deterred her from presenting herself at the court's evening entertainments.

A creature of sunlight, Blythe knew that once she had celebrated the sacred rites of the Winter Solstice, her confidence and sunny disposition would return to her. The longest night of the year would mark an end to her insecurities; sunlight would come into the world and grow stronger each day thereafter. Perhaps then she would understand what the "dark sun" meant.

Blythe rose from the chair in front of the hearth where she'd been sitting and wandered across the chamber to the window. Though the morning was rapidly aging, she still wore her nightshift and bedrobe.

Gazing toward the Thames River, Blythe watched barges docking at the quay and unloading their cargoes of actors for that evening's presentation of Master Shakespeare's latest play. She'd never attended the theater and could hardly wait for the night to arrive. Her only regret was that she wouldn't be able to see the production through to its end. While the others were being entertained, Bliss and she planned to slip away and send that unfortunate soul in the Long Gallery into the great adventure.

Blythe sighed. There would be other times in her life to see a play; the most important thing was to help that lost soul.

Someone knocking on the door drew her attention. Blythe wondered idly who it could be. She'd given Daisy the morning off, and her sister wasn't due to arrive for another hour.

"Who's there?" she called, remembering her husband's warning to her.

"Brandon Montgomery."

Blythe opened the door and gave the boy a sunny smile. In return, the boy gazed at her through piercing blue eyes that mirrored his adoration of her. Lord, but he reminded her of her eagle. Perhaps because they both possessed such a startling blue gaze.

Brandon Montgomery bowed from the waist and gifted her with an easy smile. "I've been waiting to speak to you for the past five days," he said. "I want to thank you for suggesting to the queen that I foster at Debrett House."

"So my husband has spoken to you about that?"

"Yes, my lady."

"Never forget, Brandon, that miracles happen every day," Blythe told him. "Would you care to come inside while I await my sister?"

"I'd like that very much."

Blythe stepped aside to allow him entrance and then closed the door behind him. Leading the way, she crossed the chamber to sit in one of the chairs in front of the hearth, but looked up in surprise when the boy knelt before her on one bended knee.

"Lady Debrett, I am forever indebted to you," Brandon announced fervently. "I pledge you my unwavering loyalty and shall willingly lay down my life to protect you and yours."

"I do humbly accept your pledge but doubt that risking your life will be necessary," Blythe replied with equal solemnity. She had the urge to giggle but knew the boy was serious and would be highly insulted by any levity. Like a queen of yore, she added, "Arise, my gallant young lord, and sit in that chair."

Brandon did as she told him.

"Call me Lady Blythe," she said.

The boy gave her a shy smile, dropped his gaze to the floor in front of him, and said, "Very well, Lady Blythe."

"Always look people in the eye when you talk to them," she instructed.

Brandon lifted his piercing blue gaze to meet hers and grinned.

"Though your reputation is your most valuable asset, responding to critics is a waste of time," Blythe told him. "Ignore the taunts of fools like Grimsby, Spennymoor, and Cockermouth."

"With all due respect, Lady Blythe, my honor demands I pick up the gauntlet and defend it whenever 'tis challenged," Brandon replied.

The boy sounded like her infuriating husband, Blythe thought. From eight to eighty, men behaved like pebblebrains when it came to their honor.

"I meant you should choose your fights carefully," she amended with a smile that belied her thoughts. "Now, would you care to know how much your money has grown?"

The boy cast her a puzzled smile. "What money?"

"The gold piece I invested for you."

Brandon nodded.

Blythe rose from her chair, crossed the chamber to the table, and then returned with one of her ledgers. "Ah, yes, here it is," she said after flipping through the pages. "Your gold piece has grown into five."

"Five gold pieces?" Brandon echoed in obvious surprise.

" 'Tis what I said. Would you care to spend or reinvest it?"

The boy wet his lips with his tongue while he pondered what to do. "What would you do, Lady Blythe?"

Blythe read in his expression that he'd like nothing more than to take the five gold pieces, bolt out the door, and act the part of the rich nobleman in front of Grimsby, Spennymoor, and Cockermouth. However, the boy needed to learn the value of turning a profit and spending wisely.

"I'd take one gold piece with me to spend and reinvest the other four," Blythe answered his question.

"Is there any chance I'll lose them?"

"None."

"Then I'll take the one and reinvest the other four."

"A wise choice." Blythe set the ledger aside and rose from the chair to fetch her purse from the table. Handing him the gold piece, she asked, "Brandon, have you ever heard of a 'dark sun'?"

"No, my lady. Why?"

"Never mind," she said. "Come, I'll escort you to the door."

Blythe crossed the chamber with the boy. She opened the door a crack but then paused, asking, "If I needed your assistance, could I trust you to secrecy?"

"I've just sworn my oath of allegiance to you," the boy answered. "My word is my honor."

"Good. This is what I want you to do for me," Blythe said with a conspiratorial smile. "While the others are watching Master Shakespeare's play tonight, I must slip away and meet my sister in the queen's Long Gallery. Can I count on you to lead me there and keep silent about it?"

"Of course, but why do you need to go to the Long Gallery?" Brandon asked.

"I cannot share that with you now, but—"

Disappointment and hurt were etched across his features. Those two emotions seemed like old friends to the boy, and Blythe would not add to his long list of betrayals. What he needed more than anything else was someone to place her trust in him.

Blythe inclined her head and said, "A ghost haunts the Long Gallery and—"

"A ghost?" he exclaimed.

"Bliss and I will attempt to persuade that poor, lost soul to journey to the other side," she told him.

"What other side?"

"Paradise." Blythe narrowed her violet gaze on him and asked, "Are you willing to show me the way to the Long Gallery?"

"I will protect you with my life," Brandon vowed.

"That will be unnecessary," she replied. "I will be in no danger, and you may not accompany me inside the Long Gallery. Are you still willing?"

Brandon nodded.

Blythe read the excitement in his expression and knew he judged this to be even better than downing his three young enemies.

"I'll see you in the Presence Chamber tonight," Blythe said, opening the door for him to leave. She dropped her mouth open in surprise when she spied her sister-in-law standing there. "Sybilla, what are you doing here?"

"Cedric and I haven't seen you for five days," she answered. "I came to see how you were feeling."

"Go along, Brandon," Blythe said. After the boy disappeared down the corridor, she turned back to her sister-in-law and said, "I am well but need to rest if I want to attend Master Shakespeare's play tonight."

"Then I shan't stay," Sybilla replied. "Cedric and I worried for your health. Several of the courtiers have been wondering if you'd gone the way of Darnel. You know how these people are."

"I will calm everyone's peace of mind by appearing in the Presence Chamber tonight," Blythe said. "Excuse me."

Blythe closed and barred the door. Leaning back against it, she wondered if the other courtiers were actually speculating about whether Roger had killed her or not. *Her poor beloved.* She wished he could discover the real murderer's identity. Only then would his reputation be restored.

Blythe was halfway across the chamber when she heard another knock on the door. Muttering under her breath, she retraced her steps and called, "Who's there?"

"Bliss."

"How now, sister?" Blythe said by way of a greeting, opening the door.

"Are you ready?" Bliss asked, holding the white candle up as she entered the chamber.

Blythe nodded and closed the door. She hurried across the chamber to fetch her stiletto and pouch of magic stones.

"Ladies Rhoda and Sarah are annoyed," Bliss said as she donned her white ceremonial robe. "Apparently, Roger has been ignoring them."

That bit of information filled Blythe's heart with joy. Perhaps she needn't be concerned about what her husband had been doing each evening.

"Thank you for sharing that with me," Blythe said, donning her own white ceremonial robe. "The festival of light marks the sun vanquishing the world's darkness. Perhaps the light will burn brightly in *my* world after today."

While her sister watched, Blythe began forming the enchanted circle in the middle of the chamber. She hadn't worshiped properly since her marriage to Roger, and now her lifeblood hummed the song of her ancestors.

Starting in the north, Blythe set the emerald down. Then she placed the aventurine in the east and the ruby in the south. Leaving the western periphery open, she gestured to her sister, who entered the circle first.

"All disturbing thoughts remain outside," Blythe said, and closed the circle in the west with the amethyst.

Blythe set the amber down in the center, the soul of the circle, beside the black obsidian her sister had placed there in order to repel dark magic. Next she drew her jeweled stiletto and fused the circle's invisible periphery shut. Returning to the center of the circle, her sister and she faced the east and dropped to their knees.

"The Old Ones are here, watching and waiting." Blythe began the prayers their mother had taught them.

"Stars speak through stones, and light shines through the thickest oak," Bliss continued.

"One realm is heaven and earth," Blythe said.

"Hail, Great Mother Goddess," Bliss called, lighting the Yule candle and holding it high. "Bringer of light out of darkness and rebirth out of death."

"I beg a favor," Blythe said. "Guard the child I carry within my body and deliver my beloved from unseen evil—the dark sun of your prophecy."

Suddenly, unexpectedly, a strong draft swept through the chamber and snuffed the candle's light. The two sisters screamed in surprise and then heard the door slam.

"By God's holy bread, what the bloody hell are you doing?"

"Shit," Blythe muttered.

"Make that a double," Bliss whispered.

The sisters turned around slowly. Roger Debrett was advancing on them like a hostile general invading an enemy's camp.

"No," Bliss exclaimed.

"Breaking the circle is forbidden," Blythe cried.

Ignoring their warning protests, Roger marched through the invisible periphery of the enchanted circle and yanked his wife to her feet. Then he turned his angry gaze on his young sister-in-law and ordered, "Get out."

Bliss needed no second invitation to leave. She removed her ceremonial robe as she hurried across the chamber toward the door. After pausing for one brief second to give her older sister a sympathetic look, the sixteen-year-old escaped out the door.

Blythe looked at her husband. Roger appeared ready to explode. In a futile attempt to deflect his anger, she purposefully turned her back on him and retrieved her magic stones from the floor. Only the Goddess knew what would happen to them now that Roger had interrupted her worshiping.

Intending to put her stones and stiletto away, Blythe stepped toward the table, but her husband's hand on her arm stopped her. She dropped her gaze to his hand and then lifted it to his face.

"You promised to be circumspect," Roger said, his voice accusing.

"I *am* circumspect," Blythe replied. "Usually, the Yule is celebrated outside."

"What if someone had barged in here?" Roger demanded as if she'd never spoken. "Why didn't you bar the door? Do you want Darnel's murderer to get you? Or do you wish to be hanged for being a witch and take our child to the grave with you?"

"I wish for none of these things," she answered. "For whom do you fear—the child or me?"

"Both, you little fool."

Roger yanked her into his arms and crushed her against him. When she looked up in surprise, his mouth captured hers in a long, slow, soul-stealing kiss. Surrendering to his passion, Blythe entwined her arms around his neck.

"Come to bed with me," Blythe whispered against his lips, yearning to feel their bodies joined as one.

Her words had the opposite effect on him than she'd intended. The love spell circling them lifted.

Roger broke the kiss and stepped back a pace as if realizing what he'd been doing. He gave her a scathing look and growled, "Bar the door behind me." Without another word, he whirled away and left the chamber.

Several hours later Blythe primped in front of the glass while she waited for her husband to return to their chamber. Appearing simple yet elegant, she wore a black and gold brocaded gown with a squared, low-cut neckline and tight-fitting bodice. She'd pulled her ebony hair back severely and woven it into a knot at the nape of her neck.

Blythe heard the soft rap on the door but paused another second to steal one last peek at herself. She hoped she'd dressed appropriately for the evening. She wanted to look perfect for her beloved.

"Damn it, Blythe," Roger called, banging loudly. "Open this bloody door."

Blythe hurried across the chamber and unbarred the door. She stepped back when he entered.

"I hope you're ready," Roger said, marching into the chamber without looking at her.

"You ordered me to bar the door," Blythe reminded him, narrowing her violet gaze on his back. "Did you also expect me to sit beside it in the event you wanted immediate entrance?"

At her words, Roger whirled around and stared at her as if really seeing her for the first time in five days. A smile lit his whole expression as he slowly perused her.

"Forgive my rudeness," Roger said, crossing the distance between them to raise her hand to his lips. "You are the loveliest flower I've seen in many a day."

"You appear quite handsome yourself, my lord," Blythe returned the compliment, gifting him with a smile. "All the other couples will turn green with envy when they see our beauty."

"Shall we, my lady?" he asked, inclining his head.

"I'm so excited," she said, walking out the door ahead of him. "I've never seen a play produced."

"If you like it," Roger told her, "I'll take you to the theater whenever you wish."

Blythe cast him a sidelong glance. "I'm positive Miranda would enjoy it too."

"Then Miranda will accompany us whenever we go," Roger promised.

The Great Hall was the site of the play's production. Cedric and Geoffrey Debrett were the first people they met when they entered the crowded chamber.

"Ah, sweet sister-in-law, your uncommon beauty shames these wilting Tudor roses," Geoffrey complimented her, bowing over her hand in courtly fashion.

"I never realized what an impertinent flatterer you are," Blythe said with a pleased smile. She glanced at her husband, who appeared none too happy with his brother's attention to her. Deflecting whatever harsh words might arise, she turned to Cedric and smiled in greeting.

"How are you, my lady sister-in-law?" Cedric asked politely, bowing over her hand.

"I am well," she replied. "I see you are *sans* wife and rapier."

"Sybilla is a bit under the eaves this evening," Cedric said. "She'll be along if she recovers."

"Nothing serious, I hope."

"I'm certain she is merely tired from remaining at court so long."

"Sibby is always the center of gaiety here at court," Geoffrey said dryly. "Whatever shall we do without her charming presence tonight?"

"I see my grandparents across the chamber," Blythe told her husband. "I'd like to greet them before the queen arrives."

"I'll escort you there," Roger said.

Together they headed across the chamber. Her grandparents, apparently in favor with Elizabeth, sat near the dais.

"I saw Cedric practicing his rapier with Edward deVere the other day," Blythe whispered to her husband.

Roger shrugged. "My brother would practice with a slug if no one else was available."

"Good evening, Grandpapa," Blythe greeted the Duke of Ludlow and kissed his cheek. She turned to hug the duchess, saying, "Grandmama."

"Seeing you up and about is heartening," Duke Robert said.

"Sit here, darling," her grandmother invited her.

Blythe sat in the vacant chair beside her grandmother. She

noted that Brandon Montgomery had positioned himself against the wall near her grandparents' chairs.

Smart boy, Blythe thought, nodding at him. Brandon inclined his head in her direction.

"Excuse me for a moment," Roger said abruptly. "I must speak with Burghley before the queen arrives."

Blythe watched her husband walk away. She would have spoken to her grandmother then, but the queen and her entourage walked into the hall. Everyone rose from their chairs and bowed in deference to her. When Elizabeth sat in her chair upon the raised dais, everyone else in the hall sat too.

The Lord Chamberlain's Men, Master Shakespeare's acting troupe, immediately went into action. The chorus entered and, after bowing to the queen, began their recitation together:

> "Two households, both alike in dignity,
> In Fair Verona, where we lay our scene,
> From ancient grudge break to new mutiny,
> Where civil blood makes civil hands unclean.
> From forth the fatal loins of these two foes
> A pair of star-crossed lovers take their life . . ."

Blythe glanced toward her sister, who was staring hard at her. Bliss nodded at her to set their plan in motion.

After inclining her head at Bliss to let her know she understood, Blythe leaned close to her grandmother and whispered, "Excuse me for a moment. My condition, you know. Yon Brandon Montgomery will escort me."

"I'll tell Roger when he returns," her grandmother replied, patting her hand.

Blythe rose from her chair and circled the periphery of the noble crowd. Brandon Montgomery fell into step beside her. At the same moment, Bliss rose from her chair and headed in the other direction to use a different exit lest someone note their leave-taking.

Blythe sent up a silent prayer that her husband would not

intercept her before she escaped the hall. If that happened, he could very well decide to escort her to the privy himself and thereby ruin their plans.

Nearing the hall's entrance, Blythe glanced over her shoulder to ascertain where he was. She nearly tripped over her own feet when she spied him. Roger stood with Sarah Sitwell, his head bent close to the blonde's to hear whatever she was saying.

Blythe felt her stomach lurch sickeningly at the sight of her husband's defection. Perhaps her husband's former paramours were not so former after all. Insidious insecurity coiled itself around her heart.

Outside the hall, Blythe marched with grim determination down the corridor. She wouldn't allow her husband's philandering ways to bother her; worrying could mar their babe.

"Lady Blythe?"

She turned around. "Yes?"

"I don't mean to criticize," Brandon said, "but you're going the wrong way."

Blythe nodded distractedly and retraced her steps. Together they walked in the opposite direction.

"Is aught wrong?" the boy asked. "You appear unwell."

" 'Tis merely my condition," Blythe lied.

Brandon blushed at her words, but continued to lead her through the confusing maze of corridors. Finally, they reached the corridor where the entrance to the Long Gallery was located.

Blythe stopped at the end of the long corridor. "You will wait here, no matter what you hear transpire from within that chamber," she ordered the boy.

"I understand."

Blythe walked the distance to the Long Gallery and stepped inside without hesitating. She knew she couldn't wait for her sister. If she paused at the entrance, the thought of the bleak hopelessness within the gallery would make her sick, and she'd never summon her courage to enter it.

Cast in darkness, the Long Gallery possessed an unnaturally eerie hush. Blythe couldn't see the farthest end of the chamber, though she did see a dim light from a torch shining from the corridor beyond the gallery. Only one long, tapered candle glowed near the center of the gallery.

Blythe wondered why only one candle would be lit at this hour. When she'd walked through this chamber with her sister the other afternoon, a long row of candles had been lit on both sides of the gallery. Had her sister been through here on her way to the Great Hall and snuffed the candles in preparation? Seeing beyond the horizon was always easier if a person's earthly vision was obscured.

After taking a deep fortifying breath, Blythe stepped further into the gallery. Again she felt bleak oppressiveness settling upon her shoulders as if all of the world's weary hopelessness existed within this gallery. Again she felt the fine hairs on the nape of her neck prickling with sensation. Again she glanced toward that solitary candle flickering not one whit.

A loud creak sounded from the darkened end of the gallery. And Blythe knew she was not alone.

"Cat Howard?" she called in a quavering voice. "Your Majesty?"

No answer. Nothing stirred.

"My name is Blythe Debrett," she called, certain that rambling would bolster her courage. "I've come to help you pass into the great adventure. Your Majesty, I'm afraid you are quite dead—"

Suddenly, a cord from behind caught her neck, cutting off her breath. Someone pulled it tightly.

Blythe tried to scream and reached for the cord. She fought wildly, kicking backward as best as she could. In a panic she thought that the deceased queen was trying to kill her. And a split second later she knew that the person behind her was made of flesh and blood—*Darnel's murderer!*

Flailing frantically, Blythe tried to put a finger between the cord and her throat. She felt herself losing strength. *God, no!* Her baby would die, and Roger would go to the gallows for killing them.

"Blythe!" Her sister's voice sounded as if from a great distance away.

And the cord loosened.

Gasping for breath, Blythe dropped to the floor but heard the sounds of booted feet running away. Someone lit a candle, and then she heard her sister scream.

"Brandon!" Bliss shouted, dropping to her knees to cradle her sister's head in her lap. "Oh, sister. I'm sorry I took so long to get here. Cedric Debrett stopped me on the way out of the hall."

"Not too late," Blythe gasped, opening her eyes. "Right on time."

"Bloody hell, look at her neck," Brandon Montgomery cried, staring down at her.

"Get Roger," Blythe rasped.

"Help! Murder!" the twelve-year-old shouted, bolting out of the gallery.

"Everyone will come running now," Blythe moaned in a hoarse voice.

And so they did.

Within minutes, Blythe stared up at a sea of concerned faces. Among them were her grandparents and her two brothers-in-law. Looking more worried than she'd ever seen him, Roger knelt beside her and held her within his protective embrace.

"Someone tried to strangle her," Bliss said needlessly.

"Oh, my poor darling," her grandmother cried. "Hold me, Tally. I feel faint at what we nearly lost."

"Give her room to breathe," Roger ordered the growing crowd of courtiers. He looked down at her and asked, "Did you see your attacker? Can you tell me anything about him?"

Blythe shook her head. Now that she was safe in his arms, tears of fright and relief welled up in her eyes.

"Did either of you see my wife's attacker?" Roger asked, glancing up at Bliss and Brandon.

Both shook their heads.

"You were missing from the hall when Montgomery called for help," said a familiar voice. "Where were you, Debrett?"

Blythe recognized Edward deVere's voice. The Earl of Oxford was implying that her own husband had tried to strangle her.

Roger glanced at her, hesitated, and then glared at the Earl of Oxford. He made no reply to the charge.

"Help me up," Blythe said, diverting attention from her husband.

Roger helped her rise but kept a steadying hand around her. She looked up at him and managed a wan smile.

"Well, Debrett, we are waiting for your answer," the Earl of Oxford sneered.

"The hands on my neck belonged to a woman," Blythe lied, making everyone gasp.

"Roger, this certainly clears your name," Duke Robert spoke up.

"I heartily agree with you," Lord Burghley announced as others in the crowd nodded at the duke's logic.

"Those bruises on your neck don't seem to be caused by naked hands," Edward deVere observed, leaning close. " 'Tis one straight line, as if a cord of some kind had been used. Are you lying for him?"

"Oxford, you really are more stupid than a horse's arse," Blythe said, making everyone laugh. "Why would I protect a man who'd tried to kill me?"

" 'Tis certainly a troubling question to be considered," deVere replied, his face reddening with angry embarrassment. "Tell me what Debrett has to hide. Why can't he account for his whereabouts?"

"Roger was with me," Sarah Sitwell announced.

"Blythe, this isn't what you think," Roger said.

"I want to return to our chamber now," she replied, giving him a cold look.

A look of supreme regret crossed her husband's face. Roger lifted her into his arms and carried her out of the gallery, trailed by a line of friends and relatives. When Daisy opened the door for them, he turned toward the crowd before stepping inside.

"I will be caring for my wife," Roger told them. "You may

visit her in the morning." He turned to Hardwick and Daisy, ordering, "Leave us."

Crossing the chamber, Roger placed her gently down on the bed and then retraced his steps to bar the door. He turned around, stared at her for a long moment, and then advanced on her.

"Sit up while I get you out of that gown," Roger said, perching on the edge of the bed.

"I can undress myself," she told him.

"Please let me help you," he said, a pleading note to his voice.

Blythe realized he was trying to atone for being with Lady Sarah instead of protecting her. She had half a mind to let him dangle, but she couldn't do it. The expression of aching regret etched across his features was too much for her to bear. She finally nodded, but rising emotion prevented speech.

Roger undressed her and helped her into her nightshift and bedrobe. She leaned against the headboard and watched him in silence.

When he offered her a dram of whiskey Blythe shook her head and said in refusal, "I don't drink spirits."

"Drinking spirits is easier than communicating with them," Roger coaxed, a wry smile touching his lips.

Blythe smiled and accepted the glass. She took a tiny sip and then grimaced as the amber liquid burned a path to her stomach.

Roger lifted the glass out of her hands and set it down on the table. Then he tilted her chin up to examine her badly bruised throat.

"I'm sorry I failed you," he said in a broken whisper. "I should have been there to protect you."

Blythe said nothing. She actually liked him repentant, which he wouldn't be if he knew what she'd been doing.

"I wasn't with Sarah because of any illicit affair," Roger said without preamble. "She asked me to walk outside the hall with her because she needed my advice concerning a business investment."

"I believe you," Blythe told him, reaching out to touch his hand. Relief etched itself across his chiseled features, making him appear younger. "What were you doing in the Long Gallery?" he asked. "You shouldn't have wandered that far from the hall."

"I had an appointment to meet Bliss there."

"Why?"

"Bliss and I decided to help Cat Howard cross over," Blythe answered honestly. He'd been honest with her. Could she be any less with him?

"About what are you talking?" Roger demanded.

"Cat Howard haunts the Long Gallery and—"

"You little idiot, ghosts do *not* exist, except in idle brains," Roger snapped. "Didn't you realize the danger? There is a murderer loose at court who will stop at nothing to get to me."

"Except for the bruises, I am perfectly fine," she insisted.

"You are perfectly *lucky*, not fine," he corrected her. "I forbid you to mumble those infernal incantations again. Do you understand?"

"You'd be better off ordering the sun to stop shining," Blythe told him. "You'll get the same results."

"Thank you for letting me know," Roger said in a clipped voice. "You will be returning to Debrett House in the morning."

"I won't go."

"You swore before God to obey me."

"Not in this." Blythe placed the palm of her hand against his cheek. "I can help you search for Darnel's murderer."

"If I am protecting you, I cannot investigate the murder," Roger argued.

"Brandon Montgomery will escort me everywhere. . . . Roger, can we argue about this in the morning?" she asked in a tired voice. "I need you to hold me now. Please don't leave me again tonight."

Roger nodded. He gathered her into the circle of his embrace and planted a chaste kiss on the ebony crown of her head.

"I was frightened," Blythe admitted, resting her head against his chest.

"Believe me, love," Roger said in a voice barely louder than a hoarse whisper. "Seeing you lying there frightened me too."

Chapter 15

He loved her. He had loved her forever.

Early the next morning Roger stood beside the bed and stared at his sleeping wife. She appeared so fragile in their enormous bed, too delicate to bear his child. Her skin was flawlessly pale, and her ebony tresses fanned out against the stark whiteness of the pillow.

Roger dropped his gaze to the dark purple marks circling her throat. Renewed panic swelled within his chest, making breathing difficult. He'd nearly lost her to an assassin. Only God knew what he would have done if that bastard had stolen the sunlight from his life, for Blythe was the sunshine in his existence.

Turning away from the bed, Roger crossed the chamber to the door. He needed to find a servant to fetch Daisy. Someone had to stay with her until he returned.

Roger stepped into the hallway and nearly tripped over a small body sitting in front of his chamber.

Brandon Montgomery. The boy leaped to his feet and faced him. Piercing blue eyes met piercing blue eyes.

"What the bloody hell are you doing?" Roger demanded.

"Protecting Lady Blythe."

"Have you no faith in my ability?"

"I knew you'd be up and about early in order to discover the bastard who dared to touch her," the boy answered.

"I do believe we are going to get along famously," Roger

said, smiling at him. "Go inside and bar the door. Let no one except Daisy Lloyd enter, and above all do not awaken the countess."

"You can depend upon me, my lord," Brandon said, looking him straight in the eye. "I won't fail you."

Roger waited until he heard the bolt being thrown. He headed down the deserted corridors cast in early-morning shadows until he reached another building, one closer to the queen's apartments. Here were the chambers reserved for Elizabeth's closest friends, longtime favorites who'd exhibited unwavering loyalty to her since before Roger was born. One of the queen's most noble qualities was her loyalty to those who'd remained steadfast to her.

Roger stopped in front of one particular door but paused a moment to listen, hoping the occupants were already up. He tapped softly, almost politely on the door.

No answer.

He knocked again, this time louder.

Still no answer.

Roger banged loudly on the door. He had half a mind to shout the chamber's occupants awake, but he couldn't bring himself to show such disrespect. Yet, how could they sleep when Blythe was endangered by a madman?

Roger raised his fist to pound on the door but heard a voice from within.

"Who goes there?"

"Roger Debrett."

Roger heard the bolt being thrown, and then the door opened. The sixty-two-year-old Duke of Ludlow stood there in a scarlet silk bedrobe.

Roger couldn't help but stare.

"What the bloody blazes do you want?" Duke Robert growled, his complexion reddening. "Or have you come to admire my bedrobe?"

Roger lifted his gaze to the older man's. "I need advice."

"At this hour?" the duke asked, one ebony brow cocked at him, reminding him of his wife.

"No hour is too early when my wife's life is endangered," Roger told him.

"Especially when your wife happens to be my grand-daughter," Duke Robert said, his gaze softening on him. "You didn't leave her alone to come here, did you?"

Roger shook his head.

"Come," the duke said, opening the door wider and stepping back to allow him entrance. "Sit in the chair in front of the hearth."

They crossed the chamber together. Roger sat down while Duke Robert stoked the fire. Finally, the duke turned around, but caught Roger staring again at the ridiculous scarlet robe.

"Is there a problem of which I'm unaware?" Duke Robert asked.

"I . . . I never imagined you wearing scarlet, Your Grace," Roger said, struggling against a smile. "Though I do admire your impeccable taste in intimate attire."

" 'Tis Chessy's latest gift to me," Duke Robert said, rolling his eyes.

Roger nodded in understanding.

"Can I get you a dram of whiskey?" the duke said.

"No, my wife swears to let me suffer if I ever return to our chamber with spirits on my breath."

A throaty chuckle from behind the bedcurtains drew his attention, and then he heard the duchess saying, "That's *my* granddaughter."

"Chessy, Roger has come for advice," Duke Robert called. "About what he hasn't said. Perhaps you can help."

The bedcurtains parted. The Duchess of Ludlow rose from the bed. She, too, was clad in a scarlet bedrobe.

"Tally and I match," she said needlessly. "Isn't that sweet?"

"Very sweet, indeed, Your Grace," Roger replied.

The duchess sat down in one of the chairs while the duke stood in front of the hearth. Both looked at him expectantly.

"Blythe refuses to return to Debrett House," Roger told them. "I fear for her safety if she remains at court."

"'Tis simple. Just order the girl to leave," the duke said, earning himself a frown from his wife. "Force her onto your barge if you must. I know I'd sleep sounder if she were there instead of here."

"Really, Tally, your foolishness surprises me," the duchess chided her husband.

Duke Robert rounded on her. "Whatever do you mean?"

"If you force Blythe onto your barge, she will return to court posthaste," the duchess said, turning to Roger, ignoring her husband's question. "Unless you care to waste an inordinate amount of time at the quay."

"Blythe is a biddable child," Duke Robert interjected. "Just order her to go and to stay at Debrett House."

"*To go and to stay?* Is Blythe a dog?" The Duchess of Ludlow burst out laughing. "I am truly amazed that you men can strategize the downfall of nations but lack enough common sense to deal with an intelligent young woman."

Roger snapped his head back and forth to look at them while they bickered about his wife. Growing frustration made him want to scream.

"What am I to do?" Roger asked finally, his voice mirroring his irritation.

The Duchess of Ludlow turned her head slowly and gave him a displeased look. "First of all, show respect for your elders."

Roger had the good grace to flush. "I apologize. Worry makes my temper short."

"That's better, darling," the duchess drawled. "Now, tell me the reason you want to send Blythe home."

"What kind of a question is that?" Duke Robert demanded. "'Tis obvious the man fears for his wife's life."

Ignoring her husband, the duchess fixed her gaze on Roger and asked, "Getting Blythe out of the way has naught to do with your paramours?"

"I have no paramours," Roger said in a clipped voice, his blue gaze never wavering from hers.

"Excellent." The Duchess of Ludlow smiled, apparently satisfied with his answer. "Now, are you willing to travel occasionally between Debrett House and court?"

"If 'twill keep Blythe safe."

"Chessy, what do you have in mind?" Duke Robert asked.

"Something subtle, I think. Ah, yes, I have it now," the duchess said, casting Roger a feline smile. "At first opportunity you will flirt outrageously with Sarah, Rhoda, and any other lady who attracts you. Blythe will become jealous. Then inform her that you intend to return to Debrett House because you fear for her safety and value her life more than catching Darnel's murderer. Though she may harbor a few suspicions, my granddaughter will seize the opportunity to get you away from your former paramours."

"How can I discover a murderer at court if I am at Debrett House?" Roger asked.

"I'm just coming to that part," the duchess said, looking down her pert nose at him. "Tally will send you a note saying he has something interesting for you to see at court. You will promise Blythe to be gone for only a couple of days, but you'll remain at court for a week. Then Tally will send you another note saying he thinks he has important information concerning Darnel's murder, and again you will travel to court. As long as you don't mind the jaunt, we can keep this up until Blythe is heavy with your child. Trust me, she won't have any desire to move from Debrett House then."

"Your Grace, I do admire your strategic ability," Roger said with a smile.

"Thank you, darling." The Duchess of Ludlow returned his smile. "By the way, I think you should invite Elizabeth to visit Eden Court when she goes on progress this summer. Come spring, you could persuade Blythe to go down to Winchester in order to prepare for the royal visit. That should effectively keep her out of harm's way."

Roger stood then and kissed her hand. "Until this evening, Your Grace, when we set our scheme into motion."

After shaking his grandfather-in-law's hand, Roger left the ducal bedchamber. His mood had lightened considerably. In fact, as long as Brandon Montgomery stood guard over his wife, he needn't return to their chamber. Instead, he headed in the opposite direction. Cedric should be at the jousting field by now, and Roger had the urge to challenge him to a duel. Perhaps he'd be lucky this time and actually best his brother with the rapier.

"Are my bruises very noticeable?"

"No," Roger answered, glancing over his shoulder.

"You didn't even look," Blythe complained.

"Hurry, will you?" Roger ordered, shrugging into his doublet. "We don't want to arrive after the queen."

Purposefully contrary, Blythe sauntered behind the privacy screen to study her reflection. She sighed at her image. Hideous purple bruises circled her neck. She didn't mind in the least, but she feared that the other courtiers would look with suspicion at her husband. She couldn't bear that kind of speculation concerning her beloved.

And what devil possessed Roger tonight? Her husband had been gentle and kind and loving the previous evening. Since he'd returned to their chamber that afternoon, he'd reverted to his old aloof self.

Humph, she thought, and men had the audacity to criticize women for their moodiness.

"For God's sake, will you hurry?"

"I'm ready," Blythe said, walking around the privacy screen. "You could pretend to be grateful that I've agreed to help you tonight."

Roger's gaze on her seemed to soften, and he walked across the chamber to kiss her hand. "I am exceedingly grateful you've agreed to eavesdrop on conversations," he said, ushering her toward the door. "You never know what can be overheard."

'I feel like a spy," Blythe said as they started down the corridor.

"Once we reach the Presence Chamber, we must separate and mingle," Roger reminded her. "If you must leave for any reason, signal Brandon if I'm unavailable. I've armed the boy with a dagger."

"You needn't worry about me," Blythe replied. "I won't be wandering alone for a long, long time." In a casual voice she asked, "Where were you all day?"

"Practicing my rapier with Cedric."

"Did you win?" she asked.

"No, not once."

"Oh, that explains your foul mood."

And then they stood in the entrance to the Presence Chamber. Blythe hesitated when she gazed at the crush of nobles and their ladies, and her heartbeat quickened as she realized that her would-be assassin walked among those people in the enormous hall.

Though she trembled at the thought of actually speaking with the villain who'd tried to murder her, Blythe managed a wobbly smile for her husband and stepped into the Presence Chamber. She hadn't taken more than five steps when he touched her arm and said, "I'll see you later." Off he went in the direction of the queen.

Blythe felt a moment of panic before she spied her grandparents standing with a group of their friends directly across the hall from the entrance. Taking a deep calming breath, she started toward them but stopped when she heard a voice calling her name.

"Lady Blythe, how are you feeling this evening?" Geoffrey Debrett asked.

Relief surged through her at the welcome sight of her youngest brother-in-law. Here, at least, was no would-be murderer.

"Thank you, I am well," she replied.

"Sweet sister-in-law, would you honor me with this dance?" he invited her.

Blythe shook her head. "I wish to greet my relatives. Perhaps later?"

"I shall clear a path to them for you," Geoffrey said, looping her arm through his.

Together they circled the periphery of the crowded dance floor. Blythe flicked one glance across the hall in search of her husband and spotted him dancing with the queen.

"Thank you, Geoffrey," Blythe said when she reached her grandparents. Her brother-in-law smiled and bowed to her before drifting away.

"Good evening," Blythe greeted her grandparents with a smile.

"Good evening, poppet," her grandfather said.

"Good evening, darling," her grandmother added. "Stand here, close to me."

Thankful for friendly faces, Blythe stood close to her grandmother and watched the dancers. And then she spied Roger dancing with Rhoda Bellows, who was wearing the lowest-cut gown she'd ever seen. Her husband couldn't seem to drag his gaze away from that redhead's ample cleavage.

When the music ended and another song began, Blythe felt a heavy depression settling upon her shoulders. Roger seemed loath to let Lady Rhoda escape his company. And then her husband danced with the redheaded rodent a third, a fourth, and even a fifth time.

"Darling, why don't you dance?" the duchess asked, leaning close to whisper in her ear. "I'm certain I can find a dance partner for you."

Crimson with embarrassment, Blythe shook her head. All she needed to make her misery complete was her grandmother offering to solicit dance partners for her.

"I'm a bit under the eaves," Blythe told her. "I believe I'll retire for the evening."

Without waiting for her grandmother's reply, Blythe signaled Brandon Montgomery, who was at her side in a moment. "Will you escort me to my chamber?" she asked him.

"With pleasure, my lady," the boy replied.

Blythe bade her grandparents a good night and then followed Brandon toward the entrance. She flicked one last peek in her husband's direction. He still danced with the adulterous rodent and seemed not to notice her leave-taking.

Blythe walked in miserable silence beside young Brandon. She managed a smile for him when she reached her chamber and bade him good night.

"I'll be standing guard until the earl returns," Brandon told her.

Blythe nodded at him but didn't trust herself to speak. She burst into tears as soon as the door clicked shut behind her and cried herself to sleep.

Blythe awakened alone the following morning and passed the day in her chamber. When her husband returned late in the afternoon to dress for the evening's activities, she was too miserable to put forth the questions that had tortured her as the day dragged on: Where had he been and with whom had he passed all those long hours?

"Remember to mingle," Roger reminded her as soon as they stepped into the Presence Chamber.

"You mingle enough for both of us," Blythe replied, unable to mask the bitterness she felt.

Without bothering to reply, Roger marched in the direction of the queen. Blythe found her grandparents across the chamber and slowly made her way to stand near them.

Drowning in misery, Blythe kept her gaze riveted on Roger. First he danced with the queen, then he headed straight for Sarah Sitwell.

"I cannot believe my husband treats me thusly," Blythe complained to her grandmother. "No wonder Darnel sought the company of others."

"Darling, two can play at the same game," the duchess whispered, leaning close. "Why not flirt and dance with other men? That should make the rascal come around."

"I refuse to stoop to his level," Blythe said. "I believe I'll retire."

"But you've only been here an hour," her grandmother protested.

"An hour? Those sixty minutes felt more like an eternity to me." At that Blythe signaled Brandon to meet her at the entrance. Together the woman and the boy walked in silence through the myriad corridors to her chamber.

Trying to keep her mind a blank, Blythe donned her nightshift and robe and then sat in one of the chairs in front of the hearth. She refused to cry again.

Two can play at the same game. Why not flirt and dance with other men?

Her grandmother's advice could be correct. After all, men usually wanted what they couldn't have or what everyone else wanted. Apparently, men's and women's relationships were like business dealings—subject to the law of supply and demand.

The first smile in several days touched her lips, and the cloud of misery surrounding her heart evaporated like mist beneath a noonday sun. She knew exactly what she had to do to gain her husband's attention.

Blythe dressed to kill the following evening; the intended victim was her husband's heart. She wore her most provocative gown, created in scarlet and gold brocade with an alluring low-cut neckline, a formfitting bodice, a dropped waist, and flowing sleeves. She'd brushed her ebony mane back and knotted it at the nape of her neck. Around her neck the cross of Wotan gleamed invitingly against her flawless ivory cleavage.

"Are you ready?" Roger called, bursting into their chamber.

Much to her satisfaction, her husband stopped short when he saw her. His blue gaze fixed on the cut of her neckline, but he made no comment.

"I'm ready to eavesdrop the night away," Blythe said, giving him a sunny smile.

Wearing an expression of disapproval, Roger followed her out of the chamber. In silence they passed through the increasingly familiar corridors to the Presence Chamber.

"We'll need to rise early if we want to visit Debrett House tomorrow," Roger remarked at one point.

Blythe said nothing.

Before stepping inside the Presence Chamber, Blythe cast him a jaunty smile and said, "Do not forget to mingle, my lord." Without another word, she left him standing there. She felt his piercing gaze on her back but refused to look at him.

Instead of seeking the security of her grandparents, Blythe strolled about until she spied Walter Raleigh, recently returned to court after being out of favor because of his marriage to the Throckmorton girl.

"Good evening, Lord Raleigh," Blythe greeted him.

"I am no lord, Lady Debrett, merely a sir," Raleigh replied. "Though I do appreciate your promoting me to a more exalted position. Why are you not clinging to your grandmother for protection?"

Blythe blushed. She glanced at her husband, who was dancing with the queen, and answered, "I've decided to follow my husband's example and mingle freely."

Raleigh smiled. "Not too freely, I hope, for Eden's sake."

Blythe's blush deepened to a becoming scarlet, which made the man chuckle again. "Ah, I've forgotten how pretty a sincere blush can be."

"Will you ever be going adventuring again?" Blythe asked, changing the subject.

"I've several possibilities in mind," Raleigh replied.

"If you need an investor," Blythe said, "I might be interested. Call upon me sometime."

Raleigh inclined his head. "Would you care to dance, my lady?"

"Why, sir, I'd love to dance with you."

Raleigh escorted Blythe onto the dance floor. Though she kept up her end of their conversation, she only had eyes for her husband, who still danced with the queen. When the music ended, Blythe and Raleigh stood next to Cedric and Sybilla.

Blythe danced next with Cedric, while Roger partnered

Rhoda Bellows. She did catch her husband watching her at one point, but he quickly turned away.

When Roger danced with Sarah Sitwell, Blythe partnered Geoffrey. Her husband looked none too happy with her choice of partners. She watched him so intently that her brother-in-law asked, "Are you dueling with my brother?"

That got her attention. "Dueling, sir?"

Geoffrey winked at her. "Aye, sister-in-law, your choice of weapons being dance partners."

Blythe smiled at the image but declined the next dance with him, saying, "I really ought to greet my grandparents."

Casually, she strolled around the periphery of the dance floor to where she spied her grandparents. Brandon intercepted her before she reached them.

"My lord believes 'tis time for you to retire, since we must journey to Debrett House early," the boy told her.

"We? Are you visiting Debrett House with us?"

Brandon grinned and nodded. "Lord Roger already has the queen's permission to take me along."

" 'Tis good news then."

"Shall I escort you to your chamber?" he asked.

Blythe glanced over her shoulder. Roger stood with his head bent close to Sarah Sitwell's to listen to whatever she was saying, but his piercing gaze rested upon Blythe.

"Tell my lord that I am not ready to retire yet."

Before the boy could protest, Blythe walked away. She passed the Earl of Oxford on her way to her grandparents and realized how she could best Roger. Retracing her steps, she halted in front of her husband's nemesis.

"Good evening, Lord deVere," Blythe greeted the loathsome earl. "I am ready now."

"Ready for what?"

"To dance with you, of course."

The Earl of Oxford inclined his head and escorted her onto the dance floor. Blythe peeked in her husband's direction. He appeared even more unhappy than when she'd danced with his youngest brother.

"I am heartened to see you are still breathing," Oxford remarked.

"What do you mean?" Blythe asked. She knew very well what he was implying.

"Only that the villain who tried to dispatch you failed in his attempt," Oxford answered in a rare moment of diplomacy. "Oh, there is Raleigh. I wonder that Elizabeth allows such a base commoner to mingle with her true nobility."

"What a coincidence," Blythe said, an imp entering her soul. "Whilst I danced with Sir Raleigh, he spoke of you."

"What did he say?" asked Oxford.

"I blush to repeat it, my lord."

"Tell me," he demanded.

Blythe stopped dancing and leaned close to whisper in his ear, "Raleigh told me you pad your codpiece."

"Excuse my rudeness," Oxford said, his eyes widening in shocked anger. "I cannot allow this insult to pass."

Leaving her there, Oxford marched off the dance floor in the direction of Walter Raleigh. Blythe signaled to Brandon that she was ready to leave.

Meeting the boy at the hall's entrance, Blythe spared a quick glance in Raleigh's direction. The man was laughing uproariously as the Earl of Oxford confronted him.

Blythe smiled at the sight and stepped out of the hall. They hadn't walked more than five paces when the boy spoke.

"I wonder what upset Oxford," Brandon remarked.

"I told him Raleigh said he pads his codpiece," Blythe admitted.

Brandon blushed but laughed. Another's husky chuckle joined the boy's laughter.

Blythe whirled around. Roger walked three paces behind them.

"Retire for the evening," Roger ordered the boy. "Deliver breakfast to our chamber at seven in the morning, and be prepared to leave for Debrett House."

"Yes, my lord," the boy said, unable to mask his excitement. He hurried in the opposite direction.

"You told me to mingle," Blythe defended herself, rounding on him as soon as they walked into their chamber.

"I meant mingle with the ladies of the court," Roger said, his voice stern.

Her beloved was jealous.

"Oh, my mistake," Blythe said, giving him an innocent smile.

Turning her back on him, Blythe started to cross the chamber to the privacy screen but then realized she needed his assistance because she'd given Daisy the evening off. She retraced her steps and, pointing to the back of her gown, said, "Could you please unfasten the buttons for me?"

When he nodded, Blythe showed him her back. She felt his hands on her gown unfastening the tiny buttons with expertise. Unexpectedly, she felt him trace a finger down the column of her exposed back, and a delicious shiver ran down her spine. Had his jealousy incited him to touch her after all these weeks of celibacy?

And then she felt the warmth of his lips caress the nape of her neck. Blythe sucked in her breath as he slid his lips seductively across her flesh.

Slowly, Blythe turned around to face him. She yearned to feel his lips on hers.

"Go to bed," Roger ordered. "We must rise early if we want to make the trip to Debrett House."

Blythe managed to keep her disappointment off her face. Apparently, his jealousy wasn't enough to incite him to bed her. Well, two could play the same teasing game. Without bothering to spare a glance in his direction, she proceeded to undress and slip into her nightshift. Then she went to bed.

Blythe swam up from the depths of unconsciousness and opened her eyes. The bed was empty. The predawn hour still bathed the chamber in darkness, except for the glow from the hearth where she spied her husband stoking the fire.

What had awakened her? And then she heard the soft, almost tentative rapping on the door.

Sitting up, Blythe leaned against the headboard and watched her husband cross the chamber to open the door. She recognized Brandon Montgomery's voice.

"My lord, your breakfast tray," the boy was saying.

"Return to your chamber and pack all of your belongings," Roger ordered, lifting the tray out of the boy's hands. "You won't be returning to court. Meet us at the quay at eight o'clock."

"Yes, my lord," Brandon answered, and then left.

"Eat your breakfast," Roger ordered, crossing the chamber to set the tray on the table. "When we leave here today, you won't be returning to court."

"Then I won't go." Her words fell between them like an ax.

"Do you like court life so much that you would remain here without your husband?" he asked.

Blythe stared at him blankly, uncertain of what he meant.

"Except for an occasional business visit, I am retiring from court life," Roger announced.

"But what about—"

"Darnel's murder is in the past," he interrupted her. "Your safety concerns me now. Besides, there are many at court who would believe me guilty even if the real murderer is discovered. . . . Now, eat your breakfast or I'll ask the queen for a divorce."

Blythe gifted him with a smile filled with sunshine. The eagle and the butterfly were retiring to Debrett House, where they would live happily ever after. No more former paramours to worry about.

"By the way, Elizabeth may be visiting Eden Court this summer while on progress," Roger said, flicking a glance at her.

Blythe nodded, acknowledging his words. Eden Court was her husband's ancestral home in Winchester, the Place of the Winds, where Saint Swithin's shrine was located.

Find happiness with the soaring eagle in the Place of the Winds.

Blythe felt her heart soar. Her mother's prophecy was coming true.

Beware the dark sun.

Only the disturbing thought of the dark sun marred what was fast becoming the happiest day of her married life.

Winchester. The Place of the Winds.

Blythe knew she would be in her element there.

Chapter 16

"Brandon, sit here. Your constant movement makes me queasy."

Blythe gave the boy a smile as he obeyed, plopping down beside her beneath the canopy on their barge. As they glided downriver toward Debrett House, she knew the prospect of becoming part of a real family excited him, and her heart ached at the sight of his expectant expression. Orphaned from the age of eight, the boy had never basked in the warmth of a loving family.

Blythe flicked Roger a sidelong glance. Her husband seemed engrossed in his ledgers.

Blythe admired the perfect winter's day. Christmas had blessed her countrymen with clear blue skies and a powdery blanket of snow that glistened upon the stark branches of the trees. As they neared the Strand, wood smoke from the great houses scented late December's crystalline air.

"Do you ride?" Blythe asked the boy.

"Yes, but I own no horse."

"At first opportunity your foster father will take you to Smithfield Market," Blythe promised. "Won't you, my lord?"

"Yes, of course," Roger answered without looking up, apparently not giving the least attention to what she was saying.

"You will purchase a black horse and name him Ajax," she added.

"The hero of the Trojan War?" Brandon asked, smiling at her.

"Ah, I knew I'd seen you somewhere before," Blythe said without thinking. "You also lived with us in Greece."

"I beg your pardon?" the boy asked in confusion.

"Blythe." Roger's voice held a warning note, but she didn't bother to look at him.

"Where is your ancestral home?" Blythe asked, diplomatically changing the subject.

"Montgomery House lies near Arden, but I'm certain 'tis fallen into disrepair and the land grown wild," Brandon answered. "For all I know, the Crown may have confiscated it."

"Lord Roger and I will make the necessary repairs while you foster with us," Blythe told him. "If need be, we'll buy the house and the land back from Elizabeth. After all, the Earl of Stratford cannot be a man without a home. Isn't that correct, my lord?"

"About what are you talking?" Roger asked, looking up from his ledger.

"I said we'll repair Montgomery House and develop its land while Brandon is with us," she repeated.

"Are you mad?" Roger asked, obviously surprised by her overly generous suggestion.

Blythe fixed a reproving look onto her face and replied, "My lord, do not address me like that in front of our foster son. If need be, I'll pay."

"You're damned right about that," Roger shot back, and then gave his ledgers his attention again.

"The wonderful thing about having money is what you can do with it to make other people happy," Blythe told the boy. "Now, tell me Stratford's major businesses."

"Malting and gloving," Brandon answered.

"Oh, good. You won't be in competition with me," Blythe said. "I'll put up the capital to establish you in both businesses and tutor you in turning a profit. Always remember, the malters and the glovers who sign with you must never be made to suffer, even if you must suffer a loss yourself. Be farsighted in your dealings, because shortsightedness reaps no profits in the long run."

"Lady Blythe," Brandon said, his expression solemn. "Why are you doing this?"

"I recognize your noble qualities," Blythe answered matter-of-factly. "Besides, you do remind me of my husband."

"What do you mean?" Roger asked, his head snapping up.

Blythe gave her beloved a bright smile. "My lord, Brandon has your eyes. If I didn't know better I'd say he was your son or your nephew or some other relation."

"Blue is blue," Roger told her, shaking his head at her absurd notions.

And then Debrett House came into view. Since they weren't expected until New Year's Day, no servants waited to assist them at the quay, but the Debrett footmen and groomsmen began gathering as their barges glided closer and closer.

"Daddy!" Miranda cried, dashing across the great hall toward them when they entered. "Mama Blight!"

The five-year-old threw herself into her father's waiting arms and hugged him as if she'd never let him go. Then she lavished the same attention on her stepmother.

"Lord Perpendicular visited me every night," she exclaimed.

"I knew he would," Blythe said with a smile. "I have two surprises for you."

"I love surprises," Miranda cried, clapping her hands together.

"Meet Brandon Montgomery, the Earl of Stratford, your foster brother," Blythe introduced them.

"What's a foster brother?" Miranda asked.

"A foster brother is a kind of cousin," Brandon told her. "I've always wanted a little sister, and now I have one."

Blythe cast her husband a sidelong glance and added, "Your daddy has finally agreed to give you a baby brother or sister next summer."

Again Miranda clapped her hands. "Which will it be, Daddy?" she asked.

"I don't know," Roger answered. "Let's sit at the table and refresh ourselves."

Blythe felt her heart soar when the four of them sat down at the high table. They were officially a *real* family. She looked at Brandon, and his expression told her that this was the first time in memory that he'd ever sat down to dinner as part of a loving family.

"Mama Blight, where is the baby now?" Miranda asked.

" 'Tis growing inside me," she answered.

"How did it get there?"

"Your daddy planted it like he plants the flowers in his garden."

"Oh." That seemed to satisfy her for the moment, then, "Well, how will it get out?"

Blythe blushed when she heard her husband's chuckle. She glanced at Brandon, who was also blushing.

"Don't you think your foster brother would like to meet Pericles and Aspasia?" Blythe asked the five-year-old.

"Who are they?" Brandon asked, apparently glad for the change in conversation.

"My ponies," the little girl answered. "Do you want to feed them carrots?"

"I can't think of anything I'd rather do," Brandon answered. The boy rose from his chair and asked, "Which way?"

"Big brothers always hold their little sister's hand," Miranda informed him as she also rose from her seat.

"Oh, I beg your pardon," Brandon said, offering her his hand.

Miranda accepted it, and they left the hall.

Blythe watched them until they disappeared from sight and then looked at her husband to gauge his reaction.

"Several hours of work await me in my study," Roger said, rising to leave. "I'll see you at supper."

Though disappointed by his desertion, Blythe managed a smile and nodded. They had the next forty years or so to be together. A few hours of waiting to be alone with him mattered little.

Blythe placed the palm of her hand across her belly and
recalled the first evening at Debrett House when she'd sat alone
at this same table. So many things had changed in such a
short time.

Do not worry, Baby Aristotle, she thought, all will be well
with your father now that we've come home for good.

And then Blythe spied the majordomo crossing the hall. In his
hands, the man carried a silver tray laden with letters. Perhaps
some were from her agents.

"Bottoms, come here," she called.

"Yes, my lady."

"What do you have there?"

"Missives that arrived while his lordship was at court," Bottoms answered.

"I'll deliver them," Blythe said, her nose twitching from the
heavy gardenia scent that taunted her with its presence in her
home. "Why don't you supervise the preparation of Brandon's
chamber?"

"Yes, my lady." Bottoms set the silver tray on the table in
front of her and left the hall.

Blythe worried her bottom lip with her teeth as she stared at
the tray. She knew what she was about to do was wrong but
couldn't stop herself. No gardenia-scented harlot was going to
ruin her homecoming with Roger.

Reaching out, Blythe sifted through the ten missives that lay
so innocuously on the silver tray. All reeked of gardenias, and
all were addressed to her husband in the same flourishing script.

Blythe rose from her chair and lifted the missives off the
silver tray. A woman with a purpose, she marched across the
hall to the great hearth and tossed the missives into the flames.

May the Goddess forgive me, Blythe thought, guilt instantly
swelling within her breast.

Turning away, Blythe sat in one of the chairs in front of the
hearth to ponder her sin of deception. Grandmama Chessy would
have applauded her action, but her own mother would have
looked disapprovingly on her perfidy. What else could she have

done? At best her marriage was built on a shaky foundation; she needed no rivals for her husband's affection and attention.

Entering her chamber that evening, Blythe spied the night-shift and bedrobe that Daisy had set across the bed. She changed into her nightclothes and then carried her gown into the dressing closet. Her poor little love bell hung limply in front of the closed window.

Blythe smiled to herself. After sniffing those gardenia-scented missives, she had the need to hear her love bell chiming. But when she opened the window, the bell remained still. No wind registered in her mind.

Disappointed, Blythe walked back into her chamber but left the door open a crack lest a night breeze catch the bell. She wandered across her chamber to the window and gazed outside. That solitary star that she'd seen before twinkled at her from the black velvet sky. How lonely the star seemed; it reminded her of her husband.

The journal. Thinking of her beloved made her remember his mother's journal.

Blythe hurried across the chamber to her desk and lit a candle. She opened the drawer, lifted the journal out, and opened it to the first page, dated the first day of May in the year 1563, eight months before her beloved was born.

Blythe smiled. Her mother-in-law had written this while her beloved eagle grew inside her.

"Are you coming to bed?"

Startled, Blythe snapped the journal shut and looked over her shoulder. Clad in his midnight-blue dressing robe, her husband stood inside the doorway that connected their chambers.

Coming to bed, not going.

"I'm coming," she called, returning the journal to its drawer.

Blythe snuffed the candle and rose from her chair. Her husband closed the door behind him and met her at the bed.

"Are you planning to sleep here with me?" she asked.

" 'Tis winter," he answered without looking at her. " 'Twill be warmer if we are together."

"Quite right." Blythe removed her bedrobe, tossed it aside, and climbed into bed.

Roger did the same, and Blythe's breath caught in her throat at the sight of his virile body. He climbed in beside her and drew the coverlet up.

Why hadn't he invited her to share his bed? That was the usual procedure when husband and wife retained separate chambers.

"Your bed is larger than mine," Blythe ventured. "Do you think we would be more comfortable there?"

"I like the smell in here," Roger answered.

That surprised her. "My chamber smells?"

"Like you."

"I smell too?"

Roger smiled. "Like roses."

"Oh." Blythe returned his smile.

Abruptly, Roger turned his back and said, "Good night."

"Good night."

Wasn't he planning to touch her? Apparently not. And then she heard it: the faint tinkling of the love bell.

Come, Roger, it seemed to call. *Surrender your heart of love to Blythe.*

Blythe relaxed and closed her eyes. She knew the Goddess and her friend the wind were sending her a message through that little bell.

"What the blazes is that?" Roger asked, sitting up.

Blythe looked at him. She couldn't very well inform the object of her affection that the bell was part of a love spell.

" 'Tis my chiming bell," she answered without elaborating.

"Your what?"

"I've hung a bell above the window in my dressing closet," Blythe answered. "When the wind blows, the bell tinkles soothingly."

"What kind of blockhead leaves the windows open in the middle of winter?" Roger muttered, climbing out of the bed and marching toward the dressing closet.

He disappeared inside. Within seconds the chiming of the bell ceased.

Roger returned to bed, pulled the coverlet up, and rolled onto his side with his back to her. "Good night, again," he said gruffly.

Blythe inched closer to his warm body and whispered against his back, "Good night, my lord. Sweet dreams . . ."

The following three days proved an emotional battleground for Blythe. Though heartened by her husband sleeping beside her, she suffered greatly thinking of his paramours and feeling guilty for having burned their letters.

Blythe awakened alone the next morning. That didn't surprise her, because she'd slept later than usual. Hurriedly, she washed and dressed and then left her chamber; she wanted to discuss tutors for Brandon with her husband.

Reaching the foyer, Blythe spotted Bottoms. The majordomo was closing the door behind someone.

"What do you have there?" Blythe asked, seeing the missive.

"A message for my lord."

"I'll deliver it," she said, lifting the parchment out of his hand. "Is his lordship in his study?"

"Yes, my lady."

Blythe raised the sealed parchment to peruse the handwriting, and the overpowering scent of gardenias hit her with the impact of a slap. She crinkled her nose in distaste and then looked at the majordomo, saying, "That will be all, Bottoms."

"Yes, my lady."

Lady Gardenia was certainly persistent. Instead of walking down the corridor to her husband's study, she marched into the great hall and tossed the missive into the hearth.

Mentally wiping her hands together for a foul job well done, Blythe turned around to go in search of Miranda and Brandon. With a curious little smile playing across his lips, her husband's majordomo stood not six inches from her.

Caught in the act, Blythe could only stare at the man. Then the majordomo spoke, putting her mind at ease.

"Well done, my lady," Bottoms drawled. "Cook has warmed you a mug of her special cider. Would you care to break your fast now?"

"Bottoms, I'd love a mug of Cook's special cider."

Again Blythe slept beside her husband that night but awakened alone in the morning. When she finally reached the foyer, Bottoms was once more closing the door on a courier. The man turned around, saw her standing there, and dropped his gaze to her outstretched hand.

" 'Tis unscented," Bottoms said, passing her the missive.

Blythe stared at the sealed parchment for a long moment. Obviously, the message wasn't from Lady Gardenia. Should she deliver it to her husband or not?

"From where had the courier come?" Blythe asked, lifting her gaze to his.

"Hampton Court."

Blythe dropped her gaze to the parchment. Indecision gripped her. Roger would be furious if she tossed an important message into the hearth.

" 'Tis from Lady Sitwell," the majordomo told her, drawing her attention.

"How do you know?"

"I asked."

"Thank you, Bottoms."

Blythe marched into the great hall and tossed the parchment into the flames. She breathed a sigh of relief. Apparently, the more crimes one committed, the less guilt one felt.

The same thing happened on the third morning.

Bottoms closed the door behind a courier, turned around, and saw her standing there. "Lady Bellows," he said, automatically passing her the missive.

"You mean Lady Rodent," she corrected him.

"My sentiments exactly." The majordomo walked away.

Again Blythe tossed the missive into the hearth in the great hall. Disheartened by the number of women chasing her husband, she retreated to her bedchamber to ponder what she

should do. She couldn't very well pass the rest of her life intercepting couriers at the front door. Eventually, her husband
would discover what she'd been doing, and she wasn't particularly looking forward to that day.

And then Blythe heard the faint tinkling of her love bell. Its
chiming seemed to taunt rather than encourage her.

Lingering in her chamber on the fourth morning, Blythe sat in
the chair in front of the hearth. Destroying her husband's messages was wrong; yet she couldn't summon the inner strength to
let them reach him.

"Enter," she called, hearing a knock on the door.

Blythe glanced over her shoulder to see the majordomo
advancing on her. In one hand, he held a sealed parchment.

"Lady Gardenia," Bottoms informed her, passing her the
missive.

"Persistent, isn't she?"

"Read it."

"That would be wrong."

"Forgive me, my lady," Bottoms drawled. "I do not know
what possessed me to suggest that. Reading it would be almost
as wrong as tossing it into the hearth."

Blythe smirked at his wit, but before she could reply, she
heard a voice behind them.

"Toss what into the hearth?" Roger asked, walking into the
chamber.

Blythe whirled around in her chair. Sacred Saint Swithin,
she'd been caught! Bottoms dropped the parchment onto her lap
and then froze, rooted the floor where he stood.

"Nothing of importance," she lied, finding her voice.

Blythe squirmed in her chair when her husband stood before
her. He dropped his gaze from her face to the parchment on
her lap.

"Bottoms, leave," Roger ordered in a clipped voice without
bothering to look at his man.

The majordomo needed no second invitation. Deserting her,
he hastily retreated out the door.

"Are you manipulating the corn and wool trades again?" Roger asked.

"No." Blythe wished it were that simple.

"Give me the missive," Roger ordered.

" 'Twas delivered to me," she lied. " 'Tis from my agents."

The expression on his face told her that he didn't believe a word she'd said.

"Give me that missive," he repeated, holding his hand out.

Reluctantly, Blythe passed it to him. She knew he recognized the flourishing scrawl and gardenia scent.

"I cannot believe you stooped to intercepting a message meant for me," Roger said, reading the parchment. He fixed his piercing blue gaze on her and asked, "Why did you try to hide this from me?"

His quietly spoken words made Blythe feel like the lowest creature on earth. She knew she was wrong but hadn't been able to control herself. Should she admit to her jealous insecurity?

Not bloody likely. Her Devereux pride prevented her from sharing those feelings.

Blythe managed to tear her gaze away from his and stared at her lap. She shrugged her shoulders and mumbled, "I suffered a simple impulse."

"An impulse?" Roger echoed, his incredulity all too apparent in his tone of voice. "How many impulses have you suffered since we've been home?"

"Not many."

"How many?"

"Counting this one, fourteen impulses."

Blythe steeled herself for his ranting and raving. She deserved to be on the receiving end of his righteous anger. If he'd done to her what she'd done to him . . . she refused to even consider the violent weather conditions London would suffer because of her turbulent emotions.

Roger stood there in silence and stared at her for a long, long moment. Finally, he dropped the open missive onto her lap.

"If you'd bothered to read it, you would have known that

Madame Dunwich is an investor of mine," he said in a quiet voice. "Lucille keeps me informed of London's gossip, and I allow her to invest in a few of my more secure ventures. She scents all of her correspondence to everyone."

Blythe felt the hot, embarrassed blush rising upon her cheeks.

Without another word, Roger started for the door. Unable to control one last impulse, Blythe spoke up and halted him in his tracks.

"And what about Ladies Sarah and Rhoda?" she called in an accusing voice.

Roger stopped short and turned around slowly. His blue gaze fixed unwaveringly on hers.

"I told you those two were in my past and meant nothing to me," he said.

"Both sent you messages that you cannot explain away as business," she countered.

"I can only control my own behavior," Roger said in a clipped voice. "Apparently, my word of honor isn't good enough for you."

Blythe dropped her gaze to her lap. He was correct, of course. She should have accepted what he said as truth.

The door clicked shut behind him.

Now she'd done it. How could she have been so stupid? Her beloved would resume sleeping alone, and their relationship would be as if they'd never gone to court. Except for Baby Aristotle.

Roger surprised her though. Blythe heard the connecting door open as she lay in her lonely bed that night. Fearing another argument, she snapped her eyes shut in feigned sleep. The bed creaked as he climbed in beside her and pulled the coverlet up.

Blythe sensed him leaning closer.

"Good night, little butterfly," Roger whispered, planting a chaste kiss on her cheek. He turned his back to her and seemed to fall asleep immediately.

Blythe felt her heart soar with his endearment. Perhaps all was not lost. Sublime relief rushed through her body, and she fell into a deep, dreamless sleep.

When she awakened alone the next morning, Blythe lingered in her bed, savoring the thought of Roger sharing it with her, and then ate a leisurely breakfast in her chamber. Morning had aged into a feeble old man by the time she washed and dressed and descended the stairs to the foyer below.

The first thing she saw was Bottoms closing the door behind a courier. Another one, she thought in dismay.

Bottoms turned around and saw her standing there. " 'Tis from your grandfather, the Duke of Ludlow," he announced, handing her the missive.

Blythe glanced at the ducal seal, then smiled and said, "I'll deliver it to my lord." Clutching the sealed parchment as if it were the Magna Charta, she walked into her husband's study and advanced on his desk.

Roger looked up and then bolted to his feet.

"This arrived by courier from Hampton Court," Blythe announced, passing him the missive.

Roger gave her a long, measuring look and then asked, "What does it say?"

"I would never read a letter addressed to you," she replied.

"What a pleasant surprise." Roger looked at the missive and noted the ducal seal. " 'Tis from your grandfather. You might as well sit down; he may have greetings for you."

"Well, if you insist." Blythe sat in the chair in front of his desk.

Roger sat when she sat and then broke the seal. After reading the missive, he passed it across the desk to her. "I'm sorry, Blythe. I must return to court immediately, but I'll be gone for only a few days."

At his words, Blythe felt her heart sink to her stomach. She read the missive and then looked up at him. "I'll go too," she said, unable to mask her disappointment.

"No, stay here with Miranda and Brandon," Roger replied. "I'll be returning in two or three days."

"But you'll be gone for New Year's."

"We have a lifetime of New Year's Days to pass together," he old her. "If this new information helps me discover Darnel's murderer, then—"

"You said Darnel's murder was in the past," she protested.

"I consider the attempt on your life in the present," Roger shot back.

"Returning to court could be dangerous."

"I'm perfectly capable of taking care of myself."

Blythe sighed in growing frustration. Logic wasn't getting her anywhere. If she couldn't physically accompany him to court, the love that dwelled within the ring she'd given him would offer some protection.

"Will you do me a favor?" she asked.

"What?"

"Wear the wedding gift I gave you."

Roger looked away and stared at the wall of books across the study, feigning a poor memory. "Uh, what was it again?"

Blyth's spirit plummeted. Not only did her husband not wear her ring, but he couldn't even recall what it was.

"The lapis lazuli ring with the inscription *Love conquers all,*" she said in an aching whisper.

"Humph! I couldn't possibly wear a ring inscribed with a sentiment I don't believe," Roger replied without looking at her. "But thank you for thinking of me. Will you excuse me now? I'd like to finish this ledger before I leave."

Blythe managed a nod but didn't trust herself to say another word. In misery, she rose from the chair and left the room.

Retreating to her chamber, Blythe gazed out at the winter's day. Frost feathered her old friend the willow and etched itself around the windowpanes.

For hours Blythe tried to bolster her sagging spirit. All she managed to do was give herself a headache to match the ache in her heart. Her husband refused to wear the ring because he didn't love her, had never loved her, would never love her.

Immersed in her own pain, Blythe never heard anyone enter the chamber until she heard the voice.

"I'm leaving now," Roger said.

Blythe squared her shoulders and pasted an expressionless mask onto her face. Slowly, she turned around and dropped her gaze to his hand. *No ring.*

"I wish you a safe journey upriver," she said, raising her gaze to his. Her voice, colder than the winter's day, prevented him from crossing the chamber to her.

"I'm sorry for ruining your holiday," Roger apologized. "I'll be back in a couple of days."

"I hope you find what you're looking for."

Roger seemed to hesitate, then inclined his head. "Thank you." And he was gone.

Tears welled up in her eyes as Blythe gazed out the window again. She watched him hurry across the gardens to the quay. The Debrett barge slipped its mooring and began the journey to Hampton Court.

Too bad the Thames hadn't yet frozen, she thought. The trip on horseback would have been longer and colder. And then the bluster went out of her.

Blythe felt a painful lump of emotion lodge in her throat as she struggled against the tears. She'd married a man incapable of love, and now she carried his child. How many times over the next forty years or so would he leave her on a moment's notice and flaunt his immorality with the harlots at court?

Then her Devereux pride surfaced. If that was the kind of marriage Roger Debrett desired, she'd seek a divorce. Money could purchase a great many things. Divorce included.

What her husband needed was a lesson about losing valuables through inattention. She knew precisely where to go until he realized the error of his philandering ways. Roger would come looking for her when he desired a true marriage.

Blythe smiled. Of course, she would insist he go down on bended knee before she even considered a reconciliation.

Chapter 17

 "Roger!"

At the sound of his name, Roger stopped on his way across Hampton Court's snow-carpeted expanse of lawn. He turned in the direction of the voice and saw his youngest brother sauntering toward him. A mask of disapproval etched itself across Roger's face at the unwelcome sight of his brother.

Deceitful bastard, Roger thought. His brother's oh-so-sincere smile didn't fool him for one minute.

"Welcome back to court," Geoffrey greeted him. "Where's Blythe?"

"My wife is at Debrett House, where she should be," Roger replied in a voice colder than the day.

Geoffrey's smile drooped at Roger's tone of voice. "What brings you back to Hampton Court so soon?"

Roger gave him a long look and then answered, "I'm still investigating Darnel's murder as well as the assault on Blythe."

"I could help you," Geoffrey offered, perking up.

His baby brother's offer startled Roger for a moment, but then he realized the ploy. "No, thank you," he refused. "Will you excuse me?"

Intending to brush past his brother, Roger took one step toward the palace. Geoffrey reached out and grabbed his forearm.

"Remove your hand or you'll regret it," Roger threatened.

Geoffrey paled and dropped his hand. "Brother—"

"Do not call me that," Roger interrupted him.

"Why do you hate me?" Geoffrey asked, confusion etched across his face.

Roger stared at him coldly. He had no intention of telling his brother what was common knowledge. Geoffrey was a traitorous womanizer who thought nothing of severing the bonds of brotherhood when blood ties clashed with his own physical need. Without bothering to reply, Roger took another step in the palace's direction but stopped at the heart-wrenching sound in his brother's voice.

"Please, Roger, I don't understand," Geoffrey said, his voice pleading. "Since boyhood we've always been the best of friends, and I admire you for the honorable man that you are. What has changed your opinion of me? Yes, I do admit I take life less seriously than you, but—"

"You bedded Darnel," Roger snapped, unable to control himself another moment.

"I never touched her," Geoffrey insisted, appearing stunned by the suggestion. "What kind of monster would bed his own brother's wife?"

Roger struggled against the love he once harbored for his youngest brother and the memories they shared. Both of them had suffered beneath their father's cold contempt; only Cedric had basked in the warmth of their father's love. United in their loneliness, the oldest and the youngest Debrett sons had been particularly close.

"Debrett!"

Roger and Geoffrey whirled around at the sound of someone calling them. The Duke of Ludlow was crossing the grounds toward them.

"I have important business with my grandfather-in-law," Roger said. Without another word, he turned his back on his brother and walked away.

"Welcome to Hampton Court," Duke Robert greeted him. "You wasted no time in getting here."

"Have you discovered anything new?" Roger asked without preamble.

"Really, Debrett, you ought to acquire a few social graces," the duke chided him, earning himself a frown for his trouble. He chuckled at the younger man's response and added, "To answer your question, no. How fares my granddaughter?"

"Blythe is well," Roger answered as they walked across the lawns toward the palace. He gave his grandfather-in-law a lopsided grin and added, "She's a tad unhappy with me at the moment."

Duke Robert smiled at that. "I've kept your chamber reserved."

"Thank you, Your Grace." Roger withdrew two sealed parchments from inside his doublet and passed them to the duke. "At the risk of being impertinent, could you have one of your servants deliver these?"

Duke Robert glanced at the names written on the missives and then arched an ebony brow at him, saying, "Ladies Sarah and Rhoda?"

"Nicely worded dismissal papers," Roger explained. "Their constant barrage of letters is upsetting my wife, and I have no intention of continuing my affairs with them. Unfortunately, neither lady seems to understand the word *no*."

"I'll see that these get delivered," Duke Robert replied, slapping Roger's shoulder in easy camaraderie.

"And where is your lovely bride, Debrett?" a voice nearby asked. "Have you strangled her yet?"

Roger and Duke Robert stopped short and turned toward the voice. Edward deVere, the Earl of Oxford, stood with a group of his cronies not ten feet away.

"Your Grace, will you excuse me for one moment?" Roger asked his grandfather-in-law.

"Certainly," the duke replied.

Roger walked toward the group of gaudily dressed courtiers and halted six inches from his nemesis. "What did you say?" he asked in a deceptively quiet voice.

"I asked if you'd buried the lady yet," deVere repeated, making his friends laugh.

Clenching his right hand into a fist, Roger slugged the seventeenth Earl of Oxford and sent him crashing to the ground. Blood gushed like a red river from the felled earl's nose.

"If you ever again dare to speak one word *to* me or *about* me, I will take the greatest pleasure in making your son the eighteenth Earl of Oxford," Roger threatened him. He smiled at their audience and said, "I apologize for the interruption. Good day to you."

"I've been wanting to do that for years," Duke Robert said as they walked away.

"If I had known that," Roger quipped, "I would have struck him twice. Once for me, and once for you."

The Duke of Ludlow chuckled and then left Roger just inside the building's foyer, saying, "Chessy is waiting to play cards. I'll speak to you later. Happy hunting."

Roger walked to his chamber and barred the door. He turned around and gazed at the room. There was the same four-poster bed with its heavy draperies, and there was the same hearth with the two chairs positioned in front of it.

Crossing the chamber, Roger stood at the window and looked outside. And there was the same view of the Thames.

Turning around again, Roger carefully surveyed his chamber. Everything was the same, yet something was different.

Blythe was missing.

When had he become accustomed to having her near?

Roger winced inwardly. How disappointed she'd looked when he told her he would be returning to court. How hurt she'd been.

Roger focused on the empty chamber and sighed. He didn't want to be here; he wanted to be home. Without Blythe, the sunshine had disappeared from his life. On the other hand, he couldn't return to Debrett House on the same day he'd left. His wife would assume that he'd missed her, and then she'd believe that he loved her, which would create more problems.

Tomorrow. First thing in the morning he would send for the barge and go home. They would still have part of the holiday together.

And how the hell was he to pass the hours until dawn? *Cedric*. He could waste a few hours practicing his swordplay with his brother.

Ten minutes later Roger stood outside his brother's chamber. He lifted his hand to knock but paused when he heard his sister-in-law's voice raised in anger.

"How dare those two interfere with my plans," Sybilla was saying.

"I suggest you be more careful," Cedric replied.

"Do *not* speak to me about being careful," Sybilla countered. "If it weren't for me, you would be content to live as we do."

"What is wrong with the way we live?" his brother asked.

"We possess no real power or position at court," Sybilla shot back. "We live as we do because of your brother's generosity."

"I regret the day I bared my soul to you," Cedric remarked.

"Fortune favors no cowards," Sybilla snapped.

What the bloody hell were they discussing? Roger wondered, staring at the door in confusion. He'd never heard his brother and sister-in-law argue, but he supposed every married couple had their differences.

Roger raised his fist and knocked on the door. A moment later it swung open to reveal his brother.

"What are you doing here?" Cedric asked in obvious surprise.

Roger grinned and held his rapier up. "I've come for a little swordplay."

"All the way from Debrett House?"

"I needed to do an errand at court," he answered. "I'll be returning to Debrett House in the morning."

"And how fares my dear sister-in-law?" Sybilla asked, coming into view to hand her husband his rapier. "Has Blythe accompanied you?"

"She remained at Debrett House." Roger couldn't credit the

abrupt change in his sister-in-law's demeanor. Only a moment ago she'd been snapping and snarling at his brother.

"I'll see you later," Cedric said to his wife before he stepped outside, closing the door behind him.

A short time later Roger and Cedric stood in the center of the deserted, snow-covered lawns near the Clock Tower. Armed with their tipped rapiers, both positioned their bodies in the same fighting stance: right feet forward, knees slightly bent, weight resting upon their left legs. They inclined their heads and crossed rapiers.

Faster than a flash of lightning, Cedric flicked his wrist to the right. Roger's rapier flew out of his hand and dropped on the lawn several feet away.

"Care to play again?" Cedric asked dryly, cocking a dark brow at him.

Roger burst out laughing and shook his head, saying, "Brother, I always want you on my side in a battle." Then he added, "I need your help."

"You know I'd do anything for you," Cedric replied, interest flickering in his dark gaze.

"I want you to return to Debrett House on the first day of Lent," Roger said. "I'll persuade Blythe to accompany Sybilla and you to Winchester in order to prepare for the queen's visit this summer. That way I can return to court and be assured of her safety. Besides, I want my heir born at Eden Court, as I was."

"You needn't worry for your wife's safety when she's under my protection," Cedric replied.

"Thank you, brother." Without another word, Roger started in the direction of the palace to collect his belongings and leave.

"Where are you going?" Cedric called. "Don't you want to practice?"

"No, I'm going home to my wife."

"At this hour? 'Twill be midnight by the time you arrive."

"There's nothing for me here," Roger replied. "Tell Ludlow where I've gone."

Hours later the Debrett barge rounded the bend in the Thames River and the long view of Debrett House came into sight. *Home.* What had once been merely a house was now a home because of Blythe Devereux and the sunshine she'd brought into his life.

Midnight on New Year's Eve. Roger gazed up at the night sky. A thousand glittering stars winked at him from their bed of black velvet. The old year, filled with unspeakable grief, was finally dying; the new year, filled with hope, was about to be born.

Roger frowned at those gleaming stars. Something in the lovely night sky bothered him.

And then he knew. For some unfathomable reason Blythe's emotions usually matched the weather conditions. Or vice versa. The midnight sky was placid; then so, too, would his wife's mood be untroubled. If that were true, she'd recovered quickly from his desertion—much too quickly.

Roger smiled at the foolish thought and gave himself a mental shake. Believing his wife's emotions affected the weather was beyond absurd, simply too ridiculous even to consider.

In a hurry to see his wife, Roger leaped onto the quay before his barge was securely moored. He entered the mansion through the garden door and cut through the kitchen, where a handful of servants leaped to their feet at the unexpected sight of their lord.

Roger ignored their presence and dashed up the servants' staircase. Reaching the second floor, he slowed his pace and finally stood outside his wife's bedchamber.

Roger paused there for a long moment and listened. All was quiet within the chamber. Apparently, Blythe was sleeping.

Noiselessly, Roger opened the door and stepped inside. The bed drapes had been closed against winter's chill, but he intended to warm her that night as no bed drapes or coverlet could. Should he undress and climb into bed beside her? No, he wanted to gaze upon her hauntingly lovely face first.

Roger approached the bed and drew the drapes aside. He frowned when he saw the unused bed.

She'd gone to sleep in his bed, Roger thought, relaxing. Blythe had wanted to be close to him, so she'd decided to sleep in his chamber.

Without bothering to be quiet now, Roger yanked the connecting door open. Even from this distance, he knew the bed was empty. God's bread, where was she?

"Bottoms!" Roger shouted, rushing down the stairs.

Marching into the great hall, Roger spied his majordomo and his valet standing near the chairs in front of the hearth. Each man held a crystal goblet filled with whiskey.

Damn them! His wife was hiding, and his two most trusted servants were enjoying a leisurely nightcap. From the way they were swaying on their feet, Hardwick and Bottoms were apparently bent on drinking themselves into a stupor.

"My lord, you aren't dressed for evening," Hardwick exclaimed, staring in horror at his travel-weary clothing.

Roger ignored him. "Well?" he asked, giving his majordomo his full attention.

"We didn't expect you home so soon," Bottoms said.

"Damn it, where is she?"

"Gone, my lord," Bottoms answered in a sad voice.

"Where?"

"I can't say," the majordomo answered.

"Can't say or won't say?" Roger asked in a clipped voice.

Bottoms looked down his long nose at him and answered, "Both."

"I'll deal with your impertinence later." Roger turned his attention on his valet, always easier to intimidate than his majordomo, and asked, "Where has Lady Blythe gone?"

Hardwick appeared decidedly uncomfortable. He shrugged his shoulders and answered, "I honestly don't know, my lord."

Roger fixed an incredulous glare on the man. "Do you actually expect me to believe that my wife packed her belongings and left our home, and you didn't see or hear anything?"

"My lord, I swear 'tis the truth," Hardwick cried. "Lady

Blythe sent me into Londontown to do an errand. She'd already gone by the time I returned."

"Call Daisy," Roger ordered. "She'll know."

"Daisy left with her ladyship," Bottoms offered, drawing his attention.

"Knowing my wife has protection certainly eases my mind," Roger said sardonically. The nursemaid, he thought, and turned to leave the hall.

"Where are you going?" Bottoms asked.

The man's impertinence stopped Roger dead in his tracks. How dare the servant question the master! Slowly, Roger turned around and ordered, "Fetch Hartwell here."

Roger noted the uneasy glances the two servants exchanged. There was something they hadn't told him yet.

"Lady Blythe insisted there were certain things from which she couldn't bear to be parted," Bottoms began, and then looked at the valet for help.

A mixture of confusion and dread shot through Roger.

Hardwick cleared his throat. "Lady Blythe has taken Miranda, Hartwell, and young Brandon Montgomery with her."

"She's abducted my daughter?"

"Miranda belongs to her ladyship too," Bottoms defended his mistress.

Roger didn't bother to reply. He knew his wife would never endanger Miranda and now he knew exactly where to find them. Blythe had packed her belongings, including his daughter, and moved into Devereux House. She was an impulsive creature, but she was no scatterbrain.

Roger fixed contemptuous looks on both servants and then turned away to leave the hall. He would deal with their incompetence later. At the moment he intended to fetch his wife and family home.

"She isn't there," Bottoms called.

Halfway across the hall, Roger halted and whirled around. "Isn't where?"

"Lady Blythe asked me to tell you that searching for her at

Devereux House would be futile and would needlessly alarm her parents," Bottoms informed him.

Roger felt his right cheek beginning to twitch with annoyance. He sauntered back to his man and asked, "What destination did she have in mind?"

"She didn't say."

"Let me get this straight," Roger said in a voice choked with anger, feeling his left cheek beginning to twitch, fighting the urge to strangle his majordomo. "My pregnant wife packed her belongings, including my daughter, and then left for who-knows-where. *And you let her go?*"

"I wouldn't use those exact words," Bottoms replied in a small voice.

Roger fixed his piercing gaze on the middle-aged man and asked, "What words would you use?"

Bottoms slid his gaze away and shrugged his shoulders.

After a long moment Roger lifted the goblet of whiskey out of his majordomo's hand and downed its contents in one long gulp. He grimaced and shivered as the amber liquid burned a path to his stomach. Then he tossed the goblet on the floor, where it shattered into a hundred tiny pieces.

What was he to do now? Roger wondered. He couldn't very well march into Devereux House and tell Earl Richard that he'd misplaced his daughter.

And then it came to him. His runaway bride had only two places where she could hide: Basildon Castle in Essex, her father's ancestral home, or Ludlow Castle in Shropshire, her grandfather's ancestral home.

Roger took the goblet of whiskey from his valet's hand. After downing its contents, he handed the goblet back to his man and then ordered, "Hardwick, rouse eight of my groomsmen. Tell four to ride to Basildon Castle and the other four to ride to Ludlow Castle."

"Yes, my lord." Hardwick grinned and started to walk toward the entrance.

"What shall I do, my lord?" Bottoms asked.

"Pack your belongings," Roger answered.

"What?" Bottoms exclaimed.

"You're fired," Roger informed him. "I want you out of my house in ten minutes."

Hardwick started back across the hall toward them, protesting, "But, my lord—"

Bottoms shook his head at his newfound ally and gestured for silence from the valet. With his head held proudly high, the majordomo slowly crossed the hall to leave.

"Bottoms."

The majordomo whirled around, a hopeful expression etched across his face. "Yes, my lord?"

"Before you leave, clean this mess off the floor," Roger ordered.

Bottoms dropped his gaze to the shattered crystal and then looked up again. "I am no longer in your employ," the majordomo informed him. "Clean it yourself."

One miserable week passed. The second week was even worse than the first.

On the fifteenth afternoon following his wife's disappearance, Roger sat behind the desk in his study. Unshaven and unkempt, he lifted the goblet of whiskey to his lips and then set it back down on his desk. God's bread, but he'd drunk a substantial quantity of whiskey during the past two weeks.

Roger slid his gaze to the door when it swung open, admitting Hardwick. The valet crossed the chamber and set a tray laden with food on the desk in front of him.

"Take it away," Roger ordered.

"You need the nourishment," Hardwick said, eyeing the goblet of whiskey.

"Are you my nursemaid?"

"I'm merely assuming Bottoms's duties."

Roger sighed and leaned back in his chair. "Any word about

the old man's whereabouts?" he asked, remorse shooting through him at the mention of his former majordomo's name.

"No, my lord."

"Where can the old bugger have gone?" Roger asked. "He should have known I'd regret what I said within an hour."

"Perhaps *thinking* before you speak would be a good idea, my lord," Hardwick drawled, sounding exactly like the former majordomo.

Roger ignored the man's impertinence. "You don't suppose anything has happened to him?"

Hardwick shrugged noncommittally. "The groomsmen have returned from Essex and Shropshire."

"Why didn't you say so?" Roger asked in irritation.

"I saw no need to send them in," the valet answered. "They had no luck finding her ladyship."

"That will be all," Roger said in dismissal. He watched the valet leave and then sagged in his chair.

Where the bloody hell had Blythe taken herself and his daughter? He'd never forgive himself if something happened to them. All Blythe had ever wanted was his love. Well, she had it, but past experience had kept him from professing his feelings. Even now he knew he would be unable to utter those three little words she longed to hear—*I love you.*

Roger rose from his chair and left the study. Wearily, he climbed the stairs and walked down the corridor to his wife's bedchamber. He felt closer to her there. Her sweet essence clung to the room.

Roger wandered across the chamber and gazed out at the winter's day. Sunlight glittered off the icicles that hung from the hackberry tree, where several starlings had gathered to feast on the few remaining berries. Nature rested somewhere beneath that cold blanket of snow, even as his child rested within his wife's womb.

Watching the stark branches of the trees swaying in the wind, Roger remembered his wife's chiming bell. He marched across the chamber and walked into her dressing closet. The sad little bell hung limply in front of the window.

Roger opened the shutters. Instantly, the bell sprung to life, its sweet song making him feel closer to his wife. *Come, Roger. Surrender your heart of love to Blythe.*

Without thinking, Roger withdrew the blue lapis lazuli ring from his pocket and studied it. *Love conquers all.* An incurable romantic, his wife believed in the power of love. As he once had.

If he wore the ring, would she return to him? It seemed such a silly idea. And yet . . .

Roger slipped the ring onto the third finger of his left hand. Wearing it might not bring her back to him, but it certainly made him feel better.

"My lord? Oh, there you are."

Hardwick stood in the doorway. The valet handed him a sealed parchment and said, " 'Tis from the Earl of Basildon."

With a rising feeling of dread, Roger opened the missive. In his father-in-law's flourishing script was written *Come immediately to Devereux House.*

Roger started for the door and handed the valet the missive as he passed him. He dreaded the scene that was bound to take place at Devereux House. His father-in-law would be none too happy when he learned his daughter was missing.

"My lord, please consider shaving before you see the earl," Hardwick cried, following him out of the dressing closet.

"For what?" Roger asked.

"Forgive me, my lord," Harwick replied. "You do appear unkempt."

Roger stared at his man. "And how would I appear if I showed up at Devereux House looking clean and content and then informed the earl that my wife—*his daughter*—is missing?"

"I see what you mean," the valet agreed.

Ten minutes later Roger stood before the front door of his father-in-law's mansion. Rumpled and unshaven, he looked like the quintessential slob, but his thoughts dwelled not upon his slovenly appearance. He was too busy worrying about how to break the news to the earl.

Steeling himself for the worst, Roger reached for the knocker, but the door swung open first. His mouth dropped open in surprise when he spied the impeccably dressed majordomo.

"Bottoms!"

"How well you are looking, my lord," the man drawled. Over his shoulder, he called, "You take this one."

Roger stepped into the foyer and saw Jennings, then recalled that the two men were cousins. All those days he'd scoured London for his majordomo, and the man had been only two doors down from Debrett House. His concern for the older man's safety had been for nothing.

"What are you doing here?" Roger asked him.

"I work here," Bottoms answered.

"My lord, please follow me," Jennings said. "The others are already gathered inside."

What others? Roger wondered, but followed the man into the hall.

Earl Richard and Lady Keely, as well as the Duke and Duchess of Ludlow, turned in the direction of the hall's entrance when he entered. Lady Keely hurried toward him as soon as she noted his lamentable condition.

"Roger, are you ill?" the countess asked.

"I'm quite well, thank you," he answered.

Richard gave him a broad grin and asked, "Would you care for a drink?"

"I've drunk more in the past two weeks than I care to recall," Roger answered, holding his hand up in a gesture of refusal.

"I thought Blythe insisted that you curb your drinking," the Duchess of Ludlow remarked.

Uncertain of how to reply, Roger froze momentarily and then lied, "My wife has relented somewhat."

The duchess cast him a feline smile.

Suddenly, Roger suffered an uneasy feeling that they knew

something. Bottoms must have told them of Blythe's disappearance. Then why was Earl Richard smiling at him?

"How odd. 'Tis so unlike my granddaughter to relent on any issue," the Duchess of Ludlow remarked. "You know how single-minded she is once she's decided upon a course of action."

Roger ignored that remark. He looked at his father-in-law and his mother-in-law, but then he lost his courage. The Earl and Countess of Basildon had been steadfast friends since his boyhood. He couldn't bring himself to break their hearts by sharing the news that their daughter was missing.

"Dearest, have you recently lost something you treasured?" Lady Keely asked, looping her arm through his.

My wife, Roger thought. "I can't recall misplacing anything," he answered.

"No offense, darlings, but 'tis just like a man to lose a valuable and not even know the object is missing," the Duchess of Ludlow said, and then chuckled throatily. "You men can be so inattentive at times. As a matter of fact, I was just saying the very same thing this morning to Blythe."

Oblivious to the smiling faces around him, Roger stiffened in shock and faced his grandmother-in-law.

"At least, I was trying to impart my vast knowledge of men to her," the duchess continued as if nothing was amiss. "Unfortunately, Miranda chose that moment to ride her pony through my hall; and to make matters worse, the damned pony had the audacity to foul my clean floor. Miranda, sweet child that she is, was bent on bringing good luck to my household."

Without a word Roger turned on his heels and marched across the hall to the entrance. While he'd been drinking himself into a stupor from worry, his wife had been in residence only three doors down from Debrett House. The insensitive, cold-hearted— Oh, he could cheerfully throttle her.

And then the hint of a smile softened the grim set to his jaw. Yes, he had a mind to throttle her, but first he intended to kiss the little minx into oblivion.

"Come back and visit us again soon," a voice drawled.

Roger focused on the servant opening the door for him.

"We shall miss you," Bottoms added.

"Thank you," Roger replied, cocking a brow at his former majordomo. "I do hope you'll serve Lord Richard better than you served me." He burst out laughing when he heard the door slam shut behind him.

Chapter 18

Where in the universe had Roger disappeared?

Sitting in front of the hearth in her grandfather's great hall, Blythe busied herself with knitting a blue blanket for Baby Aristotle and worried over her husband's failure to claim her. Grandmama Chessy had told her just that morning that Roger had left court on the same day he'd arrived. Two weeks had passed since then, and still her eagle flew along.

She couldn't very well pack her belongings and return to Debrett House. Not now. Not after so many days had passed. When she'd worshiped on New Year's Eve, her vision had told her that the coming year would bring harmony, contentment, and peace to her life. What more could any woman want?

Love. She craved her husband's love.

And then Blythe heard her stepdaughter's joyful cry. "Daddy!"

Blythe bolted out of the chair and whirled around. As if her thoughts had conjured the man, Roger stood poised like a grim statue in the hall's entrance.

Anger at his tardiness quickly replaced the hurt rejection she felt. He'd certainly taken his sweet time coming to claim her.

Ready for battle, Blythe started across the hall at the same moment that her husband stepped forward. Then she noticed his slovenly appearance.

"Are you ill?" she asked.

Roger made no reply. Blythe momentarily feared for her safety when he reached for her with both hands.

Grasping her upper arms firmly, Roger yanked her against the hard, unforgiving planes of his body. She tilted her head back to look up at him, but he claimed her lips in a devastating kiss that left her limp and sagging against him. And yearning for more.

"I ought to box your ears for this stunt," Roger whispered harshly.

Blythe swallowed the horrified giggle that threatened to escape her lips. "The children and the servants are watching us," she managed to choke out.

Releasing her, Roger looked at the nursemaid and the tire-woman and ordered, "Take the children upstairs and pack their belongings."

Once they disappeared out the door, Roger scanned the crowd of ducal retainers and snarled, "Get the bloody hell out of this hall!"

The Talbot servants tripped over their own feet in their haste to obey the angry lord. Within mere seconds, the hall had emptied of all but the two of them.

"For two long weeks I've been searching for you," Roger informed her, fixing his piercing blue gaze on her. "If you had bothered to stay put, you would have known that I returned to Debrett House the same day I left because I'd hoped to pass the New Year together. Unfortunately, you'd already abducted my daughter and my unborn child and fled. *Now, get the bloody hell back to Debrett House!*"

Masking the heartache and the anger she felt, Blythe fixed a bland expression onto her face. Yes, her husband had finally arrived to claim her, but his only concern was for Miranda and Baby Aristotle.

"Why should I return to a place where I am unappreciated?" Blythe countered.

"Do I look like a man who doesn't appreciate your presence in my home?" Roger countered with a rueful smile.

He did appear a tad rank, but that was of no importance. His attitude was paramount at the moment, and his words shouted his true feelings for her. Or lack of feelings, she corrected herself.

My home were the operative words. Not *our* home.

"But you don't love me," Blythe said before she could swallow the words.

"Love has nothing to do with marriage," Roger informed her.

That did it. Blythe showed him her back and folded her arms across her chest. If only he'd said "I'm uncertain of my feelings" or "I have difficulty sharing my innermost emotions," she would have been sympathetic and forgiving him. But now . . .

"I spoke the truth when I said my other affairs had ended," Roger said in a quiet voice.

Did he actually expect her to leap with joy because he'd decided to end his tawdry affairs with court jades?

"Blythe," Roger said in an aching whisper, standing so close she felt the heat emanating from his body. "With the exception of your parents and my brother, everyone in my life has deserted or betrayed me for one reason or another. Come home with me. *Please.*"

Blythe knew what that admission had cost her eagle in pride. The fight left her as quickly as it had come.

Slowly, she turned around and gifted him with a smile. And acceptance.

"Yes," she answered, placing her hand in his. "What took you so long to come for me?"

"I never imagined you'd run away only three doors down from Debrett House," Roger admitted, putting his arm around her, drawing her close against him. "I sent my poor groomsmen to Essex and Shropshire."

"My lord, you must learn never to bypass the obvious," Blythe said, casting him a teasing smile.

Lifting her hand to his lips, he pressed a kiss on it and said, "I promise I have learned a hard lesson."

An hour later the Debrett entourage halted their horses in Debrett House's front courtyard. When her beloved lifted her out of the saddle, Blythe gazed into his blue eyes and struggled against the bubble of laughter she'd felt since they'd ridden past Devereux House. It really was too bad that her parents and grandparents had come outside to wave at them as they passed by on their way home. She'd never seen her husband so embarrassed.

"Good afternoon," Blythe greeted the valet when she walked into the mansion's foyer.

"Welcome home, my lady," Hardwick returned with a smile. "I'll be serving refreshment in the hall."

The majordomo's absence surprised Blythe, who'd isolated herself inside the Talbot House for the past two weeks lest her husband discover where she was hiding. She gave the valet a concerned glance and asked, "Is Bottoms ill?"

"Bottoms now resides at Devereux House," Hardwick informed her. "Lord Roger fired him."

"Go to Devereux House and bring him home," Blythe ordered, rounding on her husband.

Roger gave her a look that said he had no intention of going anywhere. Then he marched into the hall and left her standing there with the valet.

Undaunted by his attitude, Blythe followed him into the hall, saying, "You must apologize to Bottoms for your rash behavior."

"I will not." To emphasize his point, Roger plopped down in the chair in front of the hearth.

Blythe cocked an ebony brow at him to indicate her displeasure, but he refused to look at her. Finally, she turned to the valet and instructed him, "Go to Deyereux House and tell Bottoms that Lord Roger wishes to speak with him."

"Yes, my lady." Hardwick hurried away before his lord could stop him.

"Mama Blight, will you sit in the garden with me?" Miranda asked.

"Sweetheart, Brandon will take you outside," Blythe answered, gesturing the twelve-year-old to take his foster sister away. "At the moment I'm busy correcting your daddy's mistakes."

That remark earned her a frown from her beloved. She slid her gaze away from his and watched the boy and girl disappear.

Thankfully, the Debrett servants exhibited the wisdom to clear the hall so their lord and their lady could speak privately.

Blythe walked to the high table, poured cider into two crystal goblets, and returned to the hearth. After handing her husband one of the goblets, she sat in the chair beside his.

"Why were you in such a good mood the night you abandoned me?" Roger asked abruptly.

"I did not abandon you," Blythe defended herself. "I merely granted you the breathing space you seemed to need. Besides, how do you know I was in a good mood that night?"

"The sky was clear."

Blythe smiled at his words. Perhaps he wasn't such a skeptic after all.

"I had a vision quest that night and knew you'd be coming for me," she told him. "I hadn't planned on waiting two weeks."

"Vision quest?" Roger echoed, giving her a puzzled smile. "I don't understand."

"If a person wishes to look into the future, she must sit on a bull's hide at a crossroads on the eve of the New Year," Blythe told him.

Roger lost his smile. "And you did this?"

Blythe nodded. "Yes, I sat on the bull's hide at Charing Cross and saw you coming to claim me." She gazed into the hearth's flames and worried her bottom lip with her teeth, then added, "One thing bothers me though. You didn't appear at my grandfather's hall to claim me. You were standing on top of a grassy cliff that overlooked a river."

"Let me get this straight," Roger said, his disbelief apparent in his voice. "You ventured to Charing Cross at midnight on New Year's Eve and sat on a bull's hide?"

Blythe would have had to be a blind woman not to read the displeasure stamped across his features. She nodded reluctantly and braced herself for the worst.

Roger bolted out of his chair and in the process accidentally dropped his goblet of cider. The crystal shattered into a hundred tiny pieces.

"I'll clean that," Blythe said, rising from her chair, trying to divert him from what she'd done.

"Sit down!"

Blythe did as she was told.

"I cannot believe how deplorably foolish you are," Roger began.

"I brought Brandon with me for protection," Blythe defended her actions.

Roger's laughter made her even more uneasy. The expression on his face told her he didn't approve of her vision quest or her choice of protectors. She had hoped to put him in a better mood by the time their former majordomo arrived. Now she couldn't imagine what he'd say to the poor fellow.

Blythe squirmed mentally when Roger began pacing back and forth in front of the hearth. He paused several times and opened his mouth as if to speak, but then thought better of it and resumed his angry pacing.

"My, what a happy sight," a voice drawled.

Roger turned to stare at his former majordomo. Blythe rose from her chair and gifted the man with a welcoming smile. No one spoke for several long moments.

"My lord, you wished to speak with me?" Bottoms asked.

Roger remained silent.

Filling the void, Blythe said, "His lordship wishes to retain your service again."

"I'm sorry, my lady," the man answered. "I've found other employment."

"Lord Roger is desperate and so sorry to have caused this misunderstanding between you," Blythe told him, refusing to take no for an answer. "Aren't you, my lord?"

"Yes, quite sorry," Roger replied through clenched teeth.

Bottoms stared at Roger for a long moment. "He doesn't *look* sorry."

"Do not press your luck," Roger warned.

Bottoms raised his brows at his former employer and then

urned to leave. Blythe hurriedly stepped forward and touched his forearm to prevent him from disappearing out the door.

"Lord Roger and I need you at Debrett House," Blythe told the man. "Look at his shabby appearance. Why, his lordship has fallen apart without you. . . . Don't we need him, Roger?"

"I would be pleased to have him return to my employ," Roger said stiffly.

Bottoms hesitated, as if wavering between going and staying.

"We'll double your old salary," Blythe promised.

"Done."

"Are you mad?" Roger asked, rounding on her.

"I'll pay the difference," she countered.

"Damned right you will," Roger told her. He looked at his newly hired majordomo and muttered, " 'Tis extortion."

Blythe cast her husband a pleading look.

"Gathering your belongings," Roger relented. "Come home."

" 'Twill be unnecessary," Bottoms informed him with a satisfied smile. "I left my bag in the foyer."

For one awful moment Roger appeared ready to explode. Then he gave the man a broad grin and said, "So, you are ready to begin your duties without delay?"

Bottoms nodded.

"Good." Roger caught the man's gaze and then shifted his own to the shattered goblet on the floor. "Start by cleaning this mess," he ordered, and then walked away. He paused in the hall's entrance and added, "Blythe, I want to speak to you privately. Upstairs. *Now*."

Blythe looked from her husband's retreating back to the grinning majordomo, who bent to gather the pieces of shattered glass.

Shaking her head, Blythe left the hall and walked down the corridor to the kitchen in an effort to postpone the stinging lecture that her husband was planning to deliver. She peeked out the garden door to ascertain that Brandon and Miranda were safe and then slowly retracted her steps through the kitchen to the main foyer.

Reluctantly, Blythe started up the stairs but hesitated outside her husband's door. Steeling herself for his anger, she reached up and knocked on his bedchamber door.

No answer came from within.

She knocked again, this time louder.

Still no answer.

Where was he? Blythe wondered, a feeling of relief surging through her. Even as a child, she'd always hated her father's lectures when she misbehaved; being subjected to it as a full-grown woman was unbearable.

Intending to hide within her chamber until he came looking for her, Blythe hurried down the deserted corridor and flew into her chamber. She closed the door behind her and pressed an ear to it to listen for the telltale sounds of her husband's footsteps.

Blythe heard a noise behind her and whirled around in surprise. Clad in his black silk bedrobe, her husband stood in front of the mirror and shaved.

"Bar the door and then sit down," Roger ordered in a quiet voice.

"Where's Daisy?"

"I sent her away."

Blythe barred the door and sat in the chair in front of the hearth. "I wouldn't speak if I were you," she advised. "You'll get soap in your mouth."

Roger cast an amused look over his shoulder as if he understood her ploy. He said nothing and continued shaving.

Blythe stared at his back. Broad-shouldered and narrow-waisted, her husband appeared magnificently manly in his silken bedrobe. She dropped her gaze and noticed his rumpled clothing and boots carelessly tossed on the floor. She felt the heated blush rising upon her cheeks when she realized her beloved wore nothing beneath that flimsy bedrobe.

"I suggest that Brandon and Miranda take their lessons with my sisters and brother at Devereux House," Blythe said, masking her nervousness. " 'Twill give us more time to search for a good tutor."

"That sounds logical," Roger replied. "Surprisingly so, coming from you."

"Why are you shaving in my chamber?" she asked, steering the conversation away from her illogical thought processes.

Roger reached for a linen and wiped the excess soap from his face. Slowly, he turned around and smiled at her. "I like your chamber."

His pleasant calmness caught her off guard. She'd been expecting a terrible tongue-lashing for worrying him, yet here he was smiling at her. And he had the audacity to call *her* illogical?

"How fare Ladies Sarah and Rhoda?" Blythe asked.

Roger's smile grew into a grin as he sauntered across the chamber toward her. "I never saw them." He halted in front of her. "Ask your grandfather if you don't believe me."

"What did you wish to discuss with me?" Blythe asked, now steering the conversation away from her lack of faith in him.

Roger crouched down on one bended knee in front of her. Reaching out, he drew her hand to his face and slid it across his freshly shaven cheek, asking in a husky whisper, "How does it feel?"

Blythe dropped her gaze from his blue eyes to the hand that held hers. "Roger, you're wearing the ring I gave you," she exclaimed.

"So I am," he said, dropping his own gaze as if to verify the fact. "Let's sit on the bed. 'Twill be more comfortable."

More comfortable for what? Lecturing me?

Roger stood and offered her his hand.

Unable to resist, Blythe accepted it. She sat on the edge of the bed but refused to look at him.

"Never engineer me into an embarrassing situation as you just did in the hall with Bottoms," Roger said in a quiet voice.

" 'Twas for you own good, my lord," Blythe replied, snapping her head around to meet his gaze. "You never would have forgiven yourself if you'd let him walk out the door."

"True, but I dislike being trapped in front of servants," he told her. "In the future please refrain from criticizing me in public. If

you have a grievance against me, tell me in private. As I a
doing with you at the moment."

"I promise," she said, encouraged by his quiet gentleness.

"And refrain from leaving Debrett House without letting m
know your destination."

Blythe nodded. "Anything else?"

"Yes," Roger said, cocking an eyebrow at her in a perfe
imitation of her habit. "Refrain from sitting on bull hides
Charing Cross."

Blythe giggled and turned the full force of her sunny smile o
him. His next words, though, tugged at her heartstring.

"Why did you leave me?"

Because you don't love me. "I felt unappreciated," sh
answered. "My lord, I do desire a true marriage."

"And what is that?"

"A husband and a wife should love, honor, and respect eac
other," Blythe told him. She continued in a rush, "Roger, I d
love you more than words can express."

"I know you do," Roger said. He put an arm around her an
drew her close, saying, "You told me one summer's day in you
father's garden. 'Twas your thirteenth birthday, and I still carr
the reminder of your regard on my cheek."

Blythe felt her heart breaking at his refusal to return he
words of love, but pride demanded she smile as if unaffected
And then she heard a faint chiming from within her dressin
closet.

Come, Roger. Surrender your heart of love to Blythe, the littl
bell called. *Come, Blythe. Accept your husband's beleaguere
heart.*

Her husband could have bedded down with any of the myria
jades that filled the Tudor Court. Instead, he'd returned to her o
the same day he'd left. Though he was recovering from his emo
tional injuries, her eagle still feared soaring with her. He neede
more time. Whether he knew it or not, Roger Debrett was a ma
in love.

"I can offer you honor and respect," he said, his uncertainty mirrored in his voice.

" 'Tis a good beginning." Blythe entwined her arms around his neck and whispered invitingly, "Kiss me."

"Let me worship you with my body," Roger said in a husky voice, drawing her into the circle of his embrace, pressing his lips to hers.

In an unspoken answer, Blythe pressed herself against him and returned his lingering, soul-stealing kiss. And the two of them fell back on the bed.

Roger kissed her again, then, drawing away, caressed her silken cheek with one long finger. Within seconds he'd divested her of her gown and shrugged out of his bedrobe.

Blythe wore only her jeweled cross of Wotan, and her unbound ebony hair cascaded to her waist. She reminded him of a pagan goddess sprung miraculously to life.

Blythe reached out and glided her hand across his muscled chest. She dropped her gaze to his aroused manhood. And then her hand followed her gaze.

Roger moaned with mingling emotion and need but held himself in check. He caressed her from her hauntingly lovely face to her breasts with their dusky nipples, proof that his seed grew within her body. He planted a kiss on her belly, and then slid his tongue down her belly to the sweet juncture between her thighs. Flicking his tongue across her moist womanhood, Roger heard her sharp intake of breath at this unexpected pleasure.

Surrendering to the exquisite sensation, Blythe melted against his tongue. She cried out as throbbing pleasure surged through her.

"Open your eyes," Roger whispered hoarsely, rearing up, positioning himself between her thighs.

And when she did, Roger slid forward slowly and pierced her softness. He withdrew and gently pierced her again, teasing her over and over until he felt her trembling with rekindled need. Holding her steady, Roger thrust deep and rode her hard.

Blythe surrendered herself—body, heart, soul. She accepted her beloved for what he was, a magnificent but mortal man. She accepted what he was able to give her and in return gave herself completely to him.

With mingling cries, Roger and Blythe exploded together and then lay still. He moved to one side, pulling her with him, and cradled her in his arms.

"Sunshine," he whispered, and dropped a kiss on the top of her head.

Two hours later the Earl and Countess of Eden cuddled together beneath the coverlet and dozed in sated sleep. A distant pounding disturbed their peace. Blythe opened her eyes at the same moment her husband did.

"Mama Blight?"

"Don't answer," he whispered.

"She'll only cut through your chamber," Blythe whispered back.

Roger grinned wolfishly at her. "I barred my door before I came in here."

Blythe giggled. Her husband had planned her seduction.

"Mama Blight, are you in there?" Miranda called.

"Yes, sweetheart."

"Come and play with me," the five-year-old invited her.

"I . . . I'm busy at the moment," Blythe refused. "I'll play with you later."

Roger couldn't control his chuckle.

"Is Daddy in there?" Miranda called.

"Yes, I'm helping him with his sevens and eights," Blythe answered the little girl.

"Oh." After a long moment of silence her stepdaughter called, "Can I feed Pericles and Aspasia some apples?"

"Tell Cook I said yes," Blythe answered. "Then ask Brandon to escort you to the stables."

"Thank you."

Roger and Blythe reached for each other but then heard another voice outside their door.

"You should have asked for something more than feeding

pples to a couple of ponies," Brandon said loudly. "You missed
golden opportunity."

"What's that?"

"A golden opportunity is an excellent chance to gain what-
ver you want," the boy explained. "Your parents would have
greed to anything right now."

"Why?"

"Just because."

"I see."

Bang! Bang! Bang!

Blythe winked at her husband and called, "Who's there?"

" 'Tis Miranda. Mama Blight, will you buy me a monkey?"

"Ask your father," Blythe answered with laughter lurking in
er voice.

"Daddy?"

"No monkey!"

"Come along now," they heard Brandon say. "Always
emember: Grab a golden opportunity when it appears because
ou usually don't get a second chance."

The children's voices drifted off down the corridor.

"I do believe Brandon could be a bad influence on Miranda,"
Blythe remarked, turning to her husband.

Roger gently pushed her onto her back and leaned over her.
Nose to nose with her, he said, "No worse an influence than you
are."

Softening his words, he planted a kiss on her lips and ran his
ongue across the crease in them. "Now, where were we?" he
asked.

"Here?" Blythe asked, flicking her tongue across his lips.
"No, that isn't where we were," she corrected herself, and then
dropped her hand to his groin. "Here, I think."

Chapter 19

Ash Wednesday, the first day of Lent, Blythe thought with a mental grimace. The season of fish, fish, and more fish. Goodness, but these Christians loved penance.

Standing at her bedchamber window, Blythe stared out at the late-winter's day, and her optimistic nature surfaced. Lent heralded the springtide, when renewed hope surged through the world as it awakened from the long winter's slumber.

The melancholy days of January had lengthened into February, with gray skies that delivered snow, sleet, and then rain. The swelling buds on the birch, hazel, and maple trees appeared ready to burst as nature yawned and stretched and prepared to awaken to another spring.

The late-February day had dawned clear and mild. Blythe smiled inwardly. Her husband's garden appeared as peaceful as Eden before the fall. Unfortunately, as the vile serpent had slithered into paradise, so, too, had her in-laws slithered into Debrett House a few days earlier.

Blythe didn't mind Geoffrey in the least, but—may the Goddess forgive her—she disliked Cedric and Sybilla. She'd given Daisy orders to guard her chamber whenever she left, and Bottoms kept a watchful eye on her husband's study lest her sister-in-law start snooping around again.

Blythe sighed as she thought of her enigmatic husband. Roger

nd she had passed five weeks in *almost* wedded bliss. Each
ight they slept together, yet he'd been unable to say those three
words that were hiding beyond his lips.

I love you. . . . Blythe knew without a doubt that Roger loved
er. Still, she longed to hear him speak those powerful words.

The chirping of birds in the willow drew her attention. Drop-
ing her gaze, Blythe spied her youngest brother-in-law sitting
lone on the bench beneath the branches of her old friend.

Geoffrey appeared melancholy, and Blythe wondered what
was wrong. The coming of spring was a joyful time, yet her
brother-in-law looked as if he'd lost his last friend in the whole
wide world. As a matter of fact, he'd been unusually quiet since
his arrival at Debrett House.

Turning away from the window, Blythe grabbed her cloak
and walked toward the door. The least she could do was cheer
Geoffrey up, and with Brandon and Miranda taking their lessons
at Devereux House, she wouldn't be disturbed.

Blythe hurried downstairs. Passing the great hall, she saw
Cedric practicing his rapier and Sybilla sitting in front of the
hearth. Further down the corridor she noted her husband's
closed study door and knew he was working inside.

Stepping into the garden, Blythe advanced on her brother-in-
law and called, "Why are you so glum?"

Geoffrey snapped his head up and gestured at her to remain
where she was. "Do not come any closer," he warned. "If Roger
sees us together, he'll believe we are engaged in an illicit affair."

Surprised by his words, Blythe paused for a fraction of an
instant. Then she strolled toward him and sat beside him on the
bench.

"Please go away," Geoffrey said. "I don't relish the thought
of having my own brother challenge me to a duel."

"Have you been drinking?" Blythe teased him.

"Roger doesn't trust me," Geoffrey said.

"That's ridiculous," she scoffed. "What reason could your
own flesh and blood have to distrust you?"

"You didn't see him at Hampton Court," Geoffrey said, his expression solemn. "He accused me of bedding Darnel."

His words shocked her. "Why would he believe such a horrible thing of you?" she asked, recovering herself.

Geoffrey shrugged. "I've never given him any reason to doubt my loyalty."

They sat in silence for a while. For once in her life, Blythe couldn't conjure the appropriate words to soothe another's soul.

"Roger and I were closer than most brothers when we were children," Geoffrey spoke up finally. "We united against our father's contempt."

"I'm positive your father loved each of his sons," Blythe disagreed.

Geoffrey chuckled without humor and shook his head. "You never met Simon Debrett. Cedric was his favorite, but I could never understand why."

" 'Tis reasonable that he'd favor the son who resembled him," Blythe said.

"Is it?" Geoffrey countered. "I would have thought that the Earl of Eden would have favored his heir, but he used his whip on poor Roger whenever he could. I was the lucky one; our father merely ignored me."

"He beat my husband?" Blythe echoed in a voice no louder than a whisper.

"Yes, until Roger became a page at court and your father championed his cause," Geoffrey told her. "As I heard it, your father threatened to pauper my father if he ever raised his hand to Roger again."

Blythe smiled. That was something she could well imagine her father doing.

"Cedric enjoyed father's undivided attention," Geoffrey went on. "Roger basked in our mother's love for five years before she died birthing me. But I never had anyone. *Except Roger.*"

"I'm certain Roger loves you," Blythe said, placing a comforting hand on his arm. "Your mother would have loved you if she hadn't died."

"No, Roger despises me. I saw it in his eyes that day at Hampton Court," Geoffrey replied. "After seeing you with Miranda, I wish I knew something—*anything*—about my own mother."

"All families suffer bad times," she said. "Together Roger and you will solve your problems. Miracles happen every day, you know."

"I know no such thing."

"Trust me in this," Blythe said. "All will be well."

"Perhaps you are correct," Geoffrey replied. "You've made Miranda into a happy five-year-old, and Brandon Montgomery now has a future before him. Miracles seem to follow you."

Blythe smiled at the notion. And then someone calling her name drew her attention.

"My lady!" Bottoms called, crossing the garden toward them. "His lordship wishes to speak with you."

Blythe shifted her gaze to the study window that overlooked the gardens. She could just barely see the dark figure of her husband standing there.

"I'll see you later," she said, rising from her perch on the stone bench.

Blythe went directly to her husband's study. She fixed a sunny smile onto her face and, without bothering to knock, breezed into the room. Her beloved stood behind his desk.

Crossing the chamber, Blythe pretended she didn't notice his irritated expression. She sat down in the chair in front of his desk and asked, "You wanted to speak with me?"

Roger sat when she sat. "What were you doing outside?" he asked bluntly, gesturing toward the window.

"I spied Geoffrey sitting alone beneath the willow," Blythe said, seizing the chance to make peace between the brothers. "He appeared so melancholy that I decided to cheer him up."

"I see," Roger said, dropping his gaze to the papers on his desk.

"No, you don't see. You are as sightless as a blind man."

Roger snapped his head up and stared at her.

"Geoffrey believes you distrust him," she said. "How can you possibly think your own brother would betray you?"

"Cain slew Abel."

"Geoffrey is *not* Cain," Blythe told him. "He idolizes you and cannot understand why you believe him capable of such monstrous behavior."

"Mind your own business," Roger ordered.

"As your wife, your business is my business," she said.

"Let it be, Blythe." Roger took a deep breath and then changed the subject, saying, "We are leaving Debrett House in the morning."

"What do you mean?"

"I want our child born at Eden Court."

"The babe isn't due until mid-July," Blythe said. "What's the rush? You don't actually believe that Geoffrey and—"

"This decision has nothing to do with my brother," he told her. " 'Twill take months for us to prepare for the queen's visit."

"I'll tell Daisy and Hartwell to start packing," she said, rising from her chair.

"I haven't finished."

Blythe sat down again and gave him a puzzled look.

"Cedric and Sybilla will accompany you directly to Winchester, but I'll be stopping at Windsor Castle," Roger announced. "I have business with the queen and will meet you in Winchester no more than two or three days later."

"I'd rather ride with the devil to Winchester," Blythe said, making him smile. "However, we'll do things your way this time."

When she left the study, Blythe went directly upstairs to her chamber. Daisy sat in front of the hearth, guarding the empty room.

"My arse is widening from this constant sitting," Daisy complained, standing when she entered the room.

"Tell Hartwell to start packing the children's belongings," Blythe ordered. "We leave for Winchester in the morning."

When her cousin had gone, Blythe crossed the chamber to

gaze outside. Her brother-in-law still sat beneath the willow. Apparently, Roger hadn't invited him to travel with them. Her heart ached for Geoffrey's pain. She couldn't imagine what life would be like if she hadn't grown up basking in the love of her father and her mother.

And then Blythe knew what to do in order to ease her brother-in-law's pain. Sitting inside her desk drawer was the journal that proved his wonderful mother had loved him. Blythe hadn't read it yet, but certainly the late countess had written about her sons in it. Besides, Geoffrey said he wished he knew something about his mother.

How could she slip it to him without seeming to do so? She didn't think he would appreciate her pity, and she didn't want her husband to discover that she'd gone through his belongings, even though she'd only been innocently searching for Miranda's Samhuinn disguise.

Blythe smiled as an idea formed in her mind. She would leave the journal behind when she left for Winchester the next morning. In order to make this work she would need to send her business agents a message. . . .

Another unseasonably mild winter's day greeted Blythe when she stepped into the courtyard the next morning. She'd purposefully lingered within her chamber until her husband and her in-laws had left the house. Then she'd placed the journal on her desk. On top of it she'd set reports for her agents.

Blythe glanced at their small entourage. Cedric and Sybilla were already mounted, as were a contingent of her husband's groomsmen and outriders. Trying to appear casual, Brandon had mounted Ajax, the horse she'd recently purchased for him, but excitement shone from his blue eyes. Miranda sat in her father's saddle while Geoffrey held Hector steady. Pericles and Aspasia had been tethered to one of the carts, which carried their belongings along with Hartwell and Daisy.

"What kept you?" Roger asked by way of a greeting.

"I was looking for some reports for my agents," Blythe lied. She turned to Geoffrey and asked, "When Rodale and Hibbert arrived on Friday, will you give them the reports on top of my desk?"

"Of course."

"I don't want the servants to see them," she added for good measure. "You must personally fetch them from my desk."

"I understand," Geoffrey said.

"I'm ready," Blythe said, turning to her husband. "Will you help me mount Achilles?"

Roger lifted her into the saddle and then mounted behind Miranda. At his gesture the Debrett entourage started down the private lane that led to the Strand.

" 'Tis a fair enough day for a ride," Sybilla remarked, drawing Blythe's attention.

The sight of her sister-in-law smiling nearly knocked Blythe off her horse. She glanced at Cedric. Her brother-in-law looked unusually happy too.

Alert to the change in their demeanor, Blythe wondered what had put them into such a good mood. She glanced at her husband; he seemed oblivious. A sudden feeling of doom coursed through her, but she managed to force her attention onto the road ahead of them.

"Mama Blight, tell me a story," Miranda called from her perch in front of her father.

Blythe gifted her stepdaughter with a sunny smile. "Have I told you the story about Big Ears, the King of the Fairy Cats?"

Miranda shook her head.

"Once upon a time there lived a Druid named Nuinn . . ."

"*Damn it!* Geoffrey bedded Darnel, as did Oxford and several others," Roger shouted, banging his fist on the table. "She told me so herself."

In growing frustration, Roger rose from his chair and began pacing the Counsel chamber, saying, "I've been at Windsor for two days now but cannot discover enough evidence to prove him or anyone else guilty. How can it be that nobody saw or heard anything the night of Darnel's murder? I think we should arrest all of her lovers and question them vigorously."

After venting his anger, Roger looked at the three men seated at the table and winced inwardly. Their expressions mirrored their dismay at his loss of control over his temper.

Earl Richard shook his head sadly as if he couldn't bear the sight of his years of tutelage gone to waste. Duke Robert averted his eyes as if embarrassed by the outburst. The seventy-five-year-old Lord Burghley raised his brows to indicate his displeasure.

Suitably reprimanded without any exchange of words, Roger had the good grace to flush. He sat down again and then looked at each of his companions.

"I apologize for my lack of composure," he said in a quiet voice.

"What you believe may be true," Lord Burghley replied, "but we cannot falsify evidence."

"I agree," Duke Robert spoke up. "How could we live with our consciences afterward if we did that?"

"Let it go for now," Earl Richard advised.

"Have you forgotten that someone attacked Blythe at Hampton Court?" Roger asked, fixing his gaze on the earl. "The murderer's freedom endangers my wife and children."

"I am as concerned as you," Richard told him. "But what reason would one of Darnel's lovers have for murdering her? A motiveless murder makes no sense."

Roger opened his mouth to argue but heard the sound of someone running and shouting his name. All four of them turned in surprise toward the door.

Disheveled and muddied, Geoffrey Debrett burst through the door and marched across the chamber toward them. He drew an old journal from a leather satchel and placed it on the table in front of his brother.

"What are you doing here?" Roger asked coldly, without bothering to spare a glance at the leather-bound book.

"I've ridden all night to save you from your pigheadedness," Geoffrey announced, making the three watching lords smile. "We must speak privately."

Roger met his brother's gaze and wondered how two brothers could resemble each other so closely yet behave so differently. Thank God, he'd sent Blythe to Winchester.

"I have no wish to speak with you," Roger announced, shifting his gaze to the far wall.

"Please, Roger," Geoffrey pleaded.

Roger heard the pain in his brother's voice but through sheer force of will refused to look at him. They'd been closer than most brothers, united in misery against their father's disdain. Though Roger did struggle valiantly against it, love for his younger brother swelled in his chest. If getting rid of Geoffrey meant listening to him, Roger preferred witnesses to their conversation.

"Whatever must be said will be said in front of Burghley, Talbot, and Devereux," he said finally.

"Have you seen that before?" Geoffrey asked, pointing to the journal.

Roger shifted his gaze to the journal. It seemed somehow familiar, but he couldn't recall where he'd seen it before.

"Mother's journal?" Roger asked, opening the cover and perusing the first page.

"Have you read it?"

"No."

"That journal proves that you are the bastard son of the Earl of Stratford," Geoffrey announced, shocking everyone in the chamber.

"I'll kill you," Roger snarled, bolting out of his chair.

He grabbed his brother's throat and began squeezing the life's breath from his body. Caught off guard, Geoffrey could do nothing to defend himself. Earl Richard and Duke Robert leaped out of their chairs and rescued the younger Debrett.

After regaining his composure, Roger gave his brother one last murderous glare and then brushed past him to the door. He stopped short when he felt the cold, sharp tip of a rapier touch the side of his neck.

"Stay where you are," Roger heard Geoffrey order the watching lords. "Turn around slowly, brother."

Roger did as he was told. Feigning nonchalance, he leaned back against the door and waited for the opportunity to disarm his brother. His baby brother was proving himself capable of violence, if not the actual murder. And, most importantly, Roger had witnesses.

"Are you bent on murdering me too?" Roger asked.

"No, I merely want your ear for five minutes," Geoffrey replied.

"I'm listening."

"Cedric always had father's attention, while you enjoyed mother's love for five years," Geoffrey began, his voice cracking with emotion. "Brother, your love for me was the only bright spot in my boyhood."

"I have no wish to hear this," Roger said, his voice curt.

"You will listen," Geoffrey ordered, caressing the side of his neck with the smooth edge of the blade. "I never bedded Darnel Howard, nor did I murder her. Mother's journal proves it."

"What do you mean?" Roger asked, shifting his gaze to the tattered journal and then back to his brother. How could the words of a long-dead woman prove his brother innocent?

"Mother loved the Earl of Stratford," Geoffrey said. "Unfortunately, Montgomery was already married, but his marital state did not prevent him from siring you. Roger, you are Stratford's natural son. If you don't believe me, read the journal."

"I cannot believe this," Earl Richard muttered.

"Horseshit," Duke Robert agreed.

Only Lord Burghley remained silent and awaited further information.

Roger stared at his brother. If it was true, he would have a logical reason for his father's hatred of him.

"Stratford sired me too," Geoffrey added. " 'Tis written in mother's journal."

Roger snapped his brows together. Thrown off balance by his brother's words, he asked, "You admit to being a bastard?"

Geoffrey nodded.

"Poor Cedric is wound so tightly," Roger remarked, assuming all three brothers shared the same sire. He folded his arms across his chest, relaxed against the door, and added, "This unfortunate discovery will probably kill him. I hope Sybilla isn't too shocked. You know how prim and proper she is." He flicked a glance at his father-in-law and said, "My lord, I do apologize for my parentage. I hope you do not regret giving me your daughter in marriage."

"Some of the world's most honorable men have been bastards," Richard replied. "Do not think less of yourself."

"Cedric is no bastard," Geoffrey said in a quiet voice, lowering his rapier. "He is Simon Debrett's only legitimate son. 'Tis the reason father hated us."

"Then Cedric should possess his rightful title," Roger announced.

"Eden, do not rush into rash action," Burghley spoke up finally. "Simon Debrett failed to repudiate you, which is tantamount to acknowledgment of paternity."

"Simon Debrett was a cruel, pompous arse who undoubtedly refused to admit that his wife loved another," Roger said. "Knowing him as I do, I cannot blame mother for seeking happiness in the arms of another man. I'll explain the situation to Cedric. He's welcome to the earldom if he wants it."

"I believe Cedric and Sybilla know what that journal contains," Geoffrey told them. "Mother recounts how hurt she was when Cedric turned against her and called her a whore; he would have done that only at Father's urgings. . . . Brother, consider the fact that your fortune is self-made, not inherited."

Roger stared at him blankly.

"I think I understand," Earl Richard announced suddenly, rising from his chair. He lifted his rapier off a nearby table.

Duke Robert moved when his son-in-law moved. He also lifted his rapier off the table.

"I'll take care of this," Lord Burghley said, lifting the journal off the table. "I'll issue an arrest warrant, and a contingent of the queen's men will ride with you to Winchester."

Roger looked from his brother to his friends, but his expression remained blank. "You're arresting Cedric for being legitimate?" he asked.

"Sweet Jesus, do you think I'd ride all night to proclaim our bastardy to the world?" Geoffrey asked. "Cedric wants the title and your fortune. 'Tis the reason he murdered Darnel."

Roger shook his head, saying, "I cannot believe my own brother—"

"You believed it of me."

"But Cedric—"

"Cedric has a motive for murder," Geoffrey insisted. "You've entrusted Blythe and Miranda into his care."

"Bloody hell," Roger swore, realizing the truth in his brother's words. He reached the table in three long strides, grabbed his rapier, and dashed for the door.

With the exception of Lord Burghley, the men bolted after him. They hurried down the corridors in the direction of the stables.

"Brother, I apologize for doubting your loyalty," Roger said as they reached the stableyard. "How will I ever make amends?"

"How about paying my gambling debts?" Geoffrey asked with a wicked grin.

"I can do better than that," Roger replied. "I'll find you a rich wife."

The male mind would always confound her, Blythe decided as she peered out her chamber window. In the garden below, Brandon was demonstrating the art of weaponry to an audience of one, Miranda. The dagger Roger had given him excited the boy beyond measure, judging from the inordinate amount of time he spent practicing to skewer the unwary.

Blythe lifted her gaze from the children to the heavenly blue blanket overhead. No cloud marred the sky on the gloriously sunny, mild Sunday, and she felt as if she could see beyond the horizon into the future.

Winchester and her husband's home, Eden Court, were everything she'd ever imagined. In fact, the only thing marring the perfection was her husband's absence, but he would arrive in a day or two.

Blythe slid the palm of her hand across her softly rounded belly. Four months gone and another five to go until Baby Aristotle made his appearance. She could hardly bear the wait. Eden Court would be a wonderful home in which to raise their children.

At the sound of her stepdaughter's clapping, Blythe looked at the children again, and an idea popped into her mind. She intended to give them her own brand of religious instruction, and the best time to do that would be before Roger arrived.

Turning away from the window, Blythe fastened her belt of golden links around her waist. Attached to the belt was her black leather sheath containing the small, jewel-hilted stiletto and her pouch of magic stones. She donned a lightweight woolen cloak and left the chamber.

Blythe was glad she'd released Hardwick, Daisy, and Hartwell from their duties that day. The three tireless retainers certainly deserved a day off, and now she could enjoy the company of her children without an audience. Yes, today was the right time to begin their unorthodox religious training.

Blythe descended the stairs to the foyer and walked down the corridor to the rear of the mansion. Passing her husband's study, she heard her sister-in-law's voice raised in irritation and paused to listen for a moment.

"Coward," Sybilla snapped at someone behind the closed study door.

"Lower your voice or someone will hear you," Cedric warned.

Blythe leaned close to the door. She knew eavesdropping was wrong, but she couldn't resist.

"You never complained about dispatching Darnel before today," Sybilla said.

Their topic was murder. Blythe stood statue-still as shock waves coursed through her body. Every moment she lingered there brought a rising swell of panic to her senses.

"You failed to consult me," Cedric was saying. "Else I would have vetoed the idea."

"Murdering Darnel almost gave you your rightful title," Sybilla replied. "We must finish the job before Roger arrives."

"My father never repudiated Roger's legitimacy," Cedric argued. "Without my mother's journal to prove what we say, 'tis the same as an acknowledgment."

"Simon Debrett was too proud a man to admit publicly that his wife had bedded another," Sybilla countered. "He told you the truth in hope that you—his only son—would rectify the wrong done to him. Fortunately for us, Roger possesses an uncanny knack for making money, which we will inherit once he's dead."

Blythe felt the earth moving beneath her feet. She pressed a hand to the wall to steady herself. Cedric and Sybilla had murdered Darnel and now plotted to murder Roger! They would need to walk over her dead body to get to him. And their next words proved they planned to do exactly that.

"Blythe is a sweet creature," Cedric said. "The thought of sending her to an early grave sickens me."

"She carries your brother's heir. Besides, Roger will go to the gallows for murdering her," Sybilla replied. "Our plan is quite simple. With his own daughter dead, the Earl of Basildon will refuse to come to your brother's rescue as he did the last time."

"Still, I cannot like—"

"Miranda and the boy must die too," Sybilla interrupted him.

"Are we murdering children now?" Cedric sounded shocked by his wife's suggestion. "How can I condone murdering my own niece?"

"Miranda stands next in line for the Debrett fortune," Sybilla reminded him. "We'll dispatch them today while Hartwell and Daisy are away."

"Still, I cannot like—"

"I'll do the deed," Sybilla said, sounding disgusted. "You need only keep your lips shut."

"Very well," Cedric consented after a long moment of silence.

"I knew you'd view things my way. You know, I cannot believe how incredibly stupid Roger is," Sybilla remarked. "'Tis a wonder he never guessed that Simon Debrett sired only you. After all, you are the only dark son."

The dark son . . . Beware the dark sun.

Blythe stared at the door in horror. The prophesied danger wasn't in the sky. It stood inside the study.

Blythe moved quietly and quickly down the corridor. First she intended to hide the children and then lead the killers away from them.

Stepping outside, Blythe hurried across the garden toward Brandon and Miranda. She spared a glance at the sky and noted the threatening clouds darkening the distant horizon. The sun and the glory had gone out of the day.

"Come with me," Blythe ordered the children, grabbing the little girl's hand. Without breaking stride, she marched in the direction of the stables.

"Where are we going, Mama Blight?" Miranda asked.

"We're going to play hide and seek," Blythe said, managing a smile for the girl. "We hide, and Uncle Cedric seeks."

Brandon coughed, drawing her attention, and cast her a questioning look. Blythe dropped her gaze to the little girl and then shook her head at him. The boy nodded in understanding.

Within ten minutes Blythe led the way out of the Debrett stableyard. Miranda sat in front of her on Achilles, and Brandon rode behind them on Ajax.

They entered Winchester fifteen minutes later. The town appeared unusually deserted. Overhead the darkening sky promised a storm of gigantic proportions.

Blythe rode toward the lower section of the town, where Winchester Cathedral and the shrine to Saint Swithin were located within a wide and beautiful walled close. Inconspicuous from a distance, a low central tower rose above the general level of the church's roof.

"Saint Swithin was an Anglo-Saxon bishop who performed miraculous deeds," Blythe said conversationally, trying to put her stepdaughter at ease as they dismounted beside the Lady Chapel on the eastward side of the cathedral. She pointed to the monumental tomb and added, "Swithin lies there because he wished to be exposed to falling drops from heaven for all of eternity."

Blythe grabbed Achilles's reins and led the girl and the horse inside the Lady Chapel. Brandon followed behind with Ajax.

"Are we bringing the horses inside for good luck?" Miranda asked.

"Yes, we are." Blythe led them onto the altar and then ordered, "Saint Swithin will protect you if you remain inside this sanctuary. Do you understand?"

"What about you?" Brandon asked.

"I plan to create a diversion."

"Mama Blight, don't leave me," Miranda cried, wrapping her arms around her.

"Listen to me," Blythe said, kneeling in front of the child. "Uncle Cedric is a bad man who wants to hurt us. Even now your daddy is on his way to rescue us. Will you obey Brandon in all things?"

Miranda nodded.

Blythe stood then and rounded on the twelve-year-old. "Do not let Cedric or Sybilla near you. Use the dagger if necessary."

"Where are you going?" Brandon asked.

"To lead them in another direction."

"I'll do that," the boy offered. "You stay here with Miranda."

"They can't hurt me," Blythe said, giving him a confident smile. "Catching a butterfly is an impossible task."

With those parting words, Blythe turned on her heels and led

Achilles out of the chapel. She paused outside beside the tomb and whispered, "Sacred Saint Swithin, perform another miracle this day. Send me mist and wind and rain to shield my way. Protect my children, both born and unborn. Deliver me from evil. Amen."

Blythe mounted Achilles. Before riding away, she looked up at the forbidding sky, and the first raindrop hit her face.

Drawing the hood of her cloak up to cover her head, Blythe glanced at the tomb of her patron saint one last time and murmured, "Thank you."

Blythe and Achilles galloped out of Winchester. She knew her in-laws would have discovered that they were missing by now and would be searching the area for them.

Planning to catch their attention and lead them away from Winchester and the children, Blythe rode in the direction of Eden Court. She would be safe enough; the surrounding woods abounded with hiding places.

Mist laced the air by the time she neared the vicinity of Eden Court, and the wind had grown in strength. Fat raindrops began to drop from heaven.

In the distance Blythe spied two figures on horseback. She yanked Achilles to an abrupt halt just as a gust of wind blew the hood of her cloak off her head.

"There!" she heard one of them shout and then point in her direction. *Cedric and Sybilla.*

Sharply jerking the reins, Blythe propelled Achilles into the surrounding woods. Here the winds relaxed, but the mist grew thicker.

"Wait!" Cedric shouted.

"Come home!" Sybilla called.

Becoming one with her horse, Blythe careened through the woods at breakneck speed. Bushes reached out to strike her steed, but Achilles never faltered or frightened. Blythe ducked her head to escape the slaps of tree limbs and held on to her horse for dear life.

Uncertain of where she was going, Blythe broke free of the

woods and found herself on a grassy knoll above a chalk cliff overlooking the mist-shrouded Itchen River. Here the angry wind's howling grew louder and stronger.

Blythe realized in a panic that she'd only managed to trap herself on top of a cliff, the same cliff that had appeared in her dream. She whirled in a circle, trying to find an avenue of escape.

There was none.

Perched near the edge of the woods, a willow beckoned her with its comforting, sweeping branches. Blythe decided she would take her stand with the willow at her back. She dismounted and led Achilles toward the tree.

Leaning against the willow, Blythe drew her ceremonial stiletto and waited for her in-laws. She flicked a quick glance at the puny blade and prayed, "Sacred Saint Swithin, help me."

And then Cedric and Sybilla appeared. Husband and wife dismounted, and with their cloaks flapping around their legs from the punishing winds, they advanced on her slowly.

"Stay where you are or die," Blythe threatened, raising her stiletto. Achilles chose that moment to rear up frighteningly as if to emphasize her mistress's order.

Both Cedric and Sybilla stopped short a few yards away. They exchanged nervous glances. Her brother-in-law spoke first, asking, "What is the problem?"

"The babe unbalances your mind," Sybilla said. "This weather is deadly. We only wish to return you to the safety of Eden Court."

"I know all about you," Blythe said. "I overheard you talking about Darnel's murder."

"So the world is lightened of one whore," Sybilla replied. "What does it matter when a title and a fortune are at stake?"

"Every soul in the universe matters," Blythe said. "Even yours."

"I left my dagger at Eden Court," Sybilla said, glancing at her husband. "Draw your sword and be done with it."

"Cedric, Roger and you are half-brothers," Blythe argued. "The babe I carry is your nephew."

Cedric stared hard at her for a long moment and then turned to his wife saying, "I cannot run a woman through with my sword."

"Draw your sword and force her off the cliff," Sybilla snapped. "You can manage that, can't you?"

Slowly, Cedric drew his rapier and started toward her.

"Think for yourself, brother-in-law," Blythe cried. "You never touched Darnel; your only crime has been one of silence. Do not let this she-devil tempt you with the promise of riches."

"Do it," Sybilla ordered. "You'll hang for your silence as assuredly as I'll hang for the deed."

"Would you pass the remainder of your nights sleeping beside a murderess?" Blythe countered. "When will she decide she prefers Roger's fortune for herself?"

"Husband, I have your best interests at heart," Sybilla said in a silken voice. "Do not listen to her lies."

Cedric stood in indecision. Finally, he rounded on his wife and said, "I've always preferred a truly gentle woman. Perhaps I should force *you* off the cliff and marry Blythe myself."

"The lady already has a husband who loves her more than life itself," a voice behind them said. Tall and forbidding, Roger stood poised for battle with his rapier in hand.

Blythe smiled with joy and relief. Her beloved had come to her rescue. *And he loved her.*

"Where are Miranda and Brandon?" Roger asked.

"I've hidden them."

"Smart lady." Roger gave her a sidelong smile and then lifted his rapier to point it at his brother, saying, "Prepare to die, murdering bastard."

"You are the bastard, not I," Cedric replied with a confident smile, lifting his own rapier. "Brandon Montgomery's grandfather sired Geoffrey and you."

Roger made no reply but advanced slowly, deliberately on his brother. The two men began circling each other, each poised for attack, neither willing to make the first offensive move.

From the corner of her eye, Blythe spied Sybilla inching closer to the circling brothers and knew she intended to trip Roger. She darted around the two men and touched the point of her stiletto to her sister-in-law's neck.

"Don't move another inch," Blythe threatened.

Though she longed to watch her husband, Blythe kept her gaze fixed on Sybilla. Her sister-in-law was wise enough not to test her threat.

"Admit it, brother," Roger was saying to his brother. "You murdered Darnel, hired assassins to dispatch me at Smithfield Market, and then tried to strangle Blythe."

"*I* did all of those things," Sybilla announced. "Cedric hasn't the stomach for murder."

Surprised by her admission, Roger snapped his head around to stare at her. Cedric chose that moment to attack, thrusting his rapier forward. Roger recovered in time to save his own life. He leaped back out of the arc of the blade.

"Cedric, toss your rapier away," Blythe called, frightened by her husband's near-miss. "Or I'll skewer your wife like a pig."

Cedric chuckled without humor. "Really, sister-in-law," he drawled without taking his eyes from his brother. "I need no added incentive to fight."

"I'll handle Sybilla," a deep voice beside her said.

Blythe nearly swooned with relief when she spied her grandfather standing there. With his rapier in hand, her father stepped into the clearing. Geoffrey appeared next, and then ten of the queen's own guard.

"Roger, you don't need to fight him," Richard called. "We heard their confessions."

"The grievance and the retribution are mine," Roger answered, shaking his head.

Blythe struggled to prevent herself from pleading with him to let the queen's men take Cedric and Sybilla away. Her husband's honor was at stake. And more. Much, much more. His own brother had betrayed him, and now he deserved to take his brand of retribution. That he would always regret the moment he murdered his brother was a conclusion Roger needed to reach on his own before he struck the final death blow. Or had the final death blow struck at him.

"Prepare to die for your crimes," Roger said, staring coldly at a man he would once have given his life to protect.

"I'm for you, brother," Cedric replied with a smile, as if he knew he could beat him with one tiny flick of the wrist.

Armed with untipped rapiers, the Debrett brothers stood in the middle of the circle formed by the queen's men. Both positioned their bodies for the fight. Roger hunched his shoulders forward like a street brawler. Cedric maintained the classical pose, as if he considered his brother an unworthy opponent, something less than a threat.

More unexpectedly than a sudden gust of wind, Cedric flicked his wrist to the right, but Roger was ready this time. He neatly sidestepped to the left and in one fluid motion thrust the tip of his rapier toward his brother's stomach.

Cedric leaped back just in time to save himself.

And then the fight began in earnest. The two brothers circled each other once. And then twice. Long moments passed as each tried to gauge the other's weakness. Roger held his rapier hand down near his waist, ready to thrust at first opportunity. Cedric held his rapier high in preparation for attack.

Blythe bit her bottom lip to keep from crying out. Her beloved had never beaten his brother in a duel. There had to be a way she could help him!

With her right index finger Blythe touched her heart and pressed her finger across her lips. And then she waited.

For ten long minutes the metallic clanking of kissing steel mingled with the howling wind on top of that cliff. The brothers dueled with thrusts and arched cuts in attack, defense, and counterattack.

Their intensity stretched those moments into an eternity. Neither could gain the advantage.

Suddenly, Cedric thrust his rapier forward. Roger blocked with a parry and moved his body back at the same time. Without pausing he thrust his own rapier upward toward his brother's face.

And Blythe seized her golden opportunity. She pointed her right index finger at her brother-in-law and, closing her eyes, sent up a silent prayer to her old friend the wind.

In a defensive move to escape his brother's rapier, Cedric tried to leap back, but a powerful gust of wind caught him off balance. He fell flat on his back and lost his rapier in the movement.

"You are a dead man," Roger said, pointing his rapier at his brother's face.

"Gentlemen never aim for the face, only the belly." Cedric managed a sickly smile. "Finish the job."

Roger stared hard at him in apparent indecision. Conflicting emotions warred across his features.

"Do it," Cedric taunted him. "Or are you a coward as well as a bastard?"

"I refuse to pass the remainder of my life regretting the moment I slew my own brother," Roger said finally, raising the tip of his rapier. He looked at the queen's men and ordered, "Get him out of my sight before I change my mind."

The queen's men rushed forward and yanked Cedric to his feet. Duke Robert grasped Sybilla's arm and escorted her toward the horses. Earl Richard sheathed his own rapier, nodded at his daughter, and followed the others.

When Roger turned to face her, Blythe sent him a look that said he'd made the correct decision. And then she gifted him with a smile filled with sunshine, love, and acceptance.

The heavy mist evaporated as if by magic, and the wind ceased its howling.

Roger dropped his rapier and opened his arms in invitation, and Blythe rushed forward. He crushed her against his body as if he never wanted to let her go.

Blythe gazed up at him, and his face inched toward hers. Their lips met in a kiss that seemed to last for all of eternity.

Roger poured all of his love for her into that single, stirring kiss, and Blythe returned it in equal measure.

"If you tell me where to find Miranda and Brandon," Geoffrey said with laughter lurking in his voice, "I'll leave you to your pleasure."

"I hid them inside the Lady Chapel at Winchester Cathedral," Blythe answered.

Geoffrey nodded and turned to leave.

"Be careful. Brandon itches to skewer someone with his dagger," she called after him.

Roger grinned at that.

"How did you know where to find me?" Blythe asked him.

"Love told me."

She gave him a puzzled look.

"I love you," Roger told her. "I have loved you forever, my sweet butterfly."

"I knew that," Blythe said with a sunny smile. "I was waiting for you to realize it too."

Roger hesitated, and a shadow crossed his face. "Blythe, I am not the man you think I am. I—"

Blythe placed her finger across his lips, silencing him. "I care not a whit who sired you."

Roger planted another kiss on her lips and whispered, "Love does conquer all."

Overhead the cloud cover parted, and rays of filtered sun shone down on them. Blythe looked up and saw a solitary eagle soaring across the distant horizon. In her heart she knew a pretty butterfly perched upon his outstretched wing.

Epilogue

"I suppose we'll need to choose a new name," Blythe said, looking from her hours-old daughter cradled in her arms to her husband, who perched on the bed beside her. "Aristotle won't suit for a girl."

"You name our daughter," Roger replied, leaning forward to plant a kiss on her cheek. "When the Lord blesses us with a son, I'll name him."

"You mean, when the Goddess blesses us," she corrected him.

"Whoever."

"I'm naming her Willow after an old friend of mine," Blythe announced, gazing with love at her sleeping daughter.

"Willow Debrett," Roger said, letting the words slip off his tongue. "I like the name."

A hushed silence descended on the bedchamber as both father and mother watched one of the most interesting sights they'd ever witnessed: their infant daughter sleeping. They smiled when Willow puckered her lips and moved her mouth as if suckling upon her mother's breast.

" 'Tis the feast of Saint Swithin," Blythe said, glancing toward the window where the summer's sunlight streamed into the chamber. "Whatever weather we have will last for forty days."

"Willow deserves the best of everything, including a lifetime of sunshine," Roger replied. He pressed a finger into the palm of his daughter's hand, and she wrapped her tiny fingers around it.

Blythe felt her heart fill with joy at the sight of her husband's happiness. No man in all of England deserved sunshine and peace more than her beloved.

"I'm relieved the queen canceled her visit to Eden Court," Blythe said. "Now we'll have the whole summer to enjoy our children. I wish we could stay here forever."

"We must attend the queen's birthday celebration in September," Roger told her. "Perhaps we can return to Eden Court before winter arrives."

A knock on the door drew their attention. Roger glanced at her and asked, "Are you ready for company?"

Blythe nodded.

"Enter," Roger called, rising from his perch on the bed.

The door swung open. Miranda, Brandon, and Geoffrey marched inside the chamber and advanced on the bed. All three of them wore expectant expressions.

"Rodale and Hibbert sent these from London," Geoffrey said, setting sealed missives on the bedside table.

Blythe turned to Miranda, asking, "What do you think of your new sister?"

The child grinned and gave her a "thumbs up."

"And what do you think of your cousin?" Blythe asked Brandon.

"She's almost as pretty as you," he answered.

"I do believe you are becoming a flatterer," Blythe said ruefully. "Your Uncle Geoffrey is a bad influence."

Geoffrey chuckled. "And what shall we call the newest member of the Debrett family?"

"Willow," Blythe answered.

Miranda giggled. "Like the tree?"

"Exactly."

Brandon leaned close to Miranda and whispered something in her ear. She nodded and then rounded on her father.

"Daddy, I'm positive Willow will want a monkey," she informed her father.

"We'll discuss the monkey when we return to London in September," Roger said, and then gave his brother a meaningful look.

"Let's go," Geoffrey said, taking his cue. He escorted Miranda and Brandon out of the bedchamber.

"I think I handled Miranda rather effectively," Roger said, perching on the edge of the bed again. "She won't be pestering me for a monkey."

Blythe smiled. "Until we return to London."

"She's so soft," he said, gliding one long finger down the side of the baby's cheek.

"I want to spend every possible moment with Willow," Blythe said, her gaze shifting to the missives on the bedside table. "Would you consider attending to my business affairs for a few weeks?"

"Only if you help me tally those infernal columns of numbers," he answered.

"Are your sevens and eights fornicating again?"

"Not with you waiting in my bed each night."

Blythe glanced at her sleeping daughter. "Put her in the cradle and cuddle me."

Ever so gently, Roger lifted the baby out of her arms and placed her in the cradle. He paused there for a long moment to study her and then leaned close, whispering, "Daddy loves you."

Returning to the bed, Roger leaned back against the headboard, gathered Blythe into his arms, and held her close. He gazed down into her startling violet eyes and asked, "And what gift would you like for giving me my second daughter?"

"My heart's desire," Blythe answered in a voice barely louder than a whisper.

"Which is?"

"The gift of your love."

Roger nuzzled her neck. "You already possess my body, my heart, and my soul."

"No more sniffing gardenias?" she asked, arching an ebony brow at him.

He grinned. "Only roses."

Roger lowered his head, and their lips met in a smoldering kiss. Blythe heard a tiny whimper from Willow but ignored it until it became a healthy cry.

"Willow prefers my arms to her cradle," Blythe said.

"All babies cry," Roger told her, kissing her again. "Willow will be fine for another minute or two."

Willow's cry became a lusty screech.

Breaking the kiss, Blythe turned a worried gaze upon the cradle. And then they heard the unexpected, angry rumble of thunder. Both snapped their gazes to the window. The perfect sunny day had clouded over in an instant, and pelting rain slashed inside the open window.

"God's bread!" Roger leaped off the bed and closed the window. Then he lifted the crying baby out of her cradle, deposited her in her mother's arms, and resumed his place on the bed beside his wife.

Willow stopped crying.

"Sacred Saint Swithin," Blythe gasped, pointing with her free hand toward the window.

Roger followed her finger with his gaze. Reappearing as suddenly as it had vanished, brilliant sunshine streamed through the closed window.

He glanced at his wife and then his daughter. "Do you actually believe . . ."

Blythe nodded. "Willow has the gift."

"That defies belief."

"You once believed you could never love me," Blythe said, cuddling against him.

"No, little butterfly, I feared loving you too much," Roger told her.

Blythe gifted him with a smile filled with sunshine, love, and acceptance. "Kiss me?" she asked.

"With pleasure, my love."